The

Photograph

Photos don't lie but people do...

I0600989

James Fields

Edit and set up by
www.gondorwriterscentre.com

The
Photograph

Photos don't lie but people do...

James Fields

ISBN: 978-0-6453719-8-7

DEDICATION

To Peter Bryce Reid for stirring my
Campbell/MacIntosh blood.

ACKNOWLEGMENTS

Infinite gratitude to those who made it possible for you to enjoy this novel.

Many, many people on the long journey read, listened, criticised, and encouraged, as did Elizabeth, Kate, Meera and Sylvia during a snowy winter week at the Writer's House, Varuna in 2016. A special thanks must go to the Varuna Alumni Association for providing me the opportunity to spend a confidence-boosting month writing, researching, and rejoicing with Ireland's brightest and best writers and other artists at the Tyrone Guthrie Centre, County Monaghan in 2018.

More recently, the ever-encouraging Elaine Ouston of Gondor Writers Centre introduced me to the wide world of graphics, publishing, and distribution.

Bill Gannon, artist extraordinaire and explorer, generously provided cover artwork as merely another of life's challenges, while Iris Viduka, humble to a fault, completed the cover graphics. Ferns Hideaway kindly lent me their fireplace at short notice.

However, those closest and dearest who have been strapped in for the full ride – Rob, Chicken and Rak - my utmost thanks for your unquestioning support, understanding and love.

PROLOGUE

Yeppoon, Queensland – 30th December 1999

Not normally a party animal, Dave Lawson was now excited about tomorrow evening's Millennium Eve bash here at his place with friends and family. Christmas had been quiet, but this was going to be big!

Yet, it was misplaced emotion. His placid, predictable world was about to implode.

'David!' The sudden yell caught him digging out the last of the dirty, chunky rocks. Straightening up, he dropped the shovel and wiped the sweat from his face with his floppy hat. It was steamy.

'Maggie?' he called back up towards the voice, squinting into the sun. She seldom disturbed him when he was away in the garden.

'Come up now! It's important!'

Bugger, what's this about, he wondered. The hectare of scrubby coastal hillside overlooking the southern Barrier Reef had been someone else's unfinished dream when they'd bought it nearly 20 years earlier. With the big party to be held up at the house, he was desperate to complete the garden walls that could be seen from there. But Maggie knew that. He'd better go.

'Okay! Coming!'

Dave turned to their grey-haired terrier now stirring in nearby shade. 'C'mon Mack. Let's see what can't wait until I've finished.'

Minutes later, Dave found Maggie waiting under the faded patio-table umbrella in front of the house, grinning like the entrance to Luna Park. Catching his breath after the steep walk, he glanced out to sea, his body readily absorbing that ever-cooling breeze.

1

From the terrace here, they'd be able to watch the Millennium fireworks down in the town – those over at the island resort too, of course. Yeah, Maggie's party idea was a good one, he concluded.

Relaxing, he flopped his long frame down at the table opposite his wife as Mack headed to his water bowl. 'What's up, Maggs? Catering problems for tomorrow night? People have cancelled?'

Her smirk widened.

'Maggie!'

'Well, sorry to disturb your work, Sweetheart, but I just felt it couldn't wait. No, the party's all sweet, 18 still coming, and Terrible Terri's still arriving later this afternoon. However, we've had the strangest phone call. Well, you have!'

Her face, actions and tone became that of a jubilant game-show host. 'David Lawson, you are listed in the will of a famous British photographer!'

'What?'

Jerky with excitement, Maggie scanned the note in her hand. 'Yep, a Miss Fergusson from Scotland rang – said she was a lawyer executing the will of photographer, Kat Cale, who passed away in Scotland in May. You're in it!'

Kat … Kat … The shock grabbed him, as it would from a sudden snake bite in the garden. He gaped back at Maggie as if her news had been of their impending divorce instead. A hand went up to the long scar on the left side of his face, extenuated by the sweat.

'Kat Ca … Cale? Scotland? Rang … j … just now?'

'Well, the lawyer rang.' Her voice held surprise. 'She seemed relieved to have tracked you down.'

'How … how did she know to ring … ring here?'

'Well, you can ask her yourself, Sweetheart. She was calling from Brisbane. Arrived in Australia yesterday, she said. Didn't want to talk much, except to say she'd be up here on tomorrow's early flight. Sounds the independent type. Do all lawyers work on New Year's Eve?'

He dropped his head – anxiety, fear, and now dread, crowding into his brain.

2

Soon, he felt Maggie move, get up. 'I think you need a beer, Dave.' A pause. 'Odd name. We don't know any famous photographers... any Kat Cale, do we?'

Her steps faded. No, *we* don't, Maggs, he answered in thought. But ... but *I* do ... Well, I did! He lifted his head, searching about, as if to check the sky for threatening rain. 'She can't have just died *now*.' He said it aloud to close the matter. End it. 'It was years and years ago!'

His mind was reeling when Maggie returned with two cold cans. 'Okay, Darling? You seem upset.' Sitting down, she pushed one across to him. 'Here, drink this!' Then, her practical voice. 'I'm thinking the pots with the flowering frangipani for the terrace tomorrow night. Hmm? Now, the lawyer – she should be well finished before ...'

He wasn't listening. He fumbled to open the can and spilled some of the beer as he drank. 'But ... but; I'm not ready for this. I didn't want any of this to happen.'

It was some moments before Maggie spoke again. 'Sorry, David? You just said you didn't *want* this to happen. Did you already know about it – the will?'

Bloody Maggs – always so sharp. After all these years she'd presume to know everything about him. But he'd been careful never to mention his time in Scotland. Before they'd met. Before Darwin. And she didn't know of that letter. Two weeks ago.

'Dave, you haven't answered. Do you, or did you know this, um, Kat Cale?'

Of course I knew her, an inner voice screamed. *I bloody-well killed her!* And like a clamorous cavalry charge those shocking events of 1972 came thundering back into his head.

'Sweetheart, it doesn't have to be a big deal. Just tell me about it.' Maggie's eyes were pleading.

But he couldn't. Couldn't even begin to. They sat there in long silence until Maggie thumped the table. Both cans clattered onto the patio pavers, splashing beer about. 'All right, David, have it your way! I just don't understand the need for secrecy. Terri will be here soon, and she'll also want to know why you're acting like this!'

3

Maggie stood up, glared at him a little longer, then strode back into the house. Little Mac got out from under the table, also hesitated as if to pass judgement, then scampered after her.

The couriered envelope had arrived when Maggie was out – Christmas shopping with her friend Rachel. Puzzled by the UK address, he'd signed for it anyway. Inside was a formal letter which explained the *recent* death of famous British photographer Kat Cale; he was listed as a beneficiary of her will. He'd calmly stuffed it all into the rubbish bin in his work shed, determined to burn it later, and continued with life like it had never arrived. Two weeks ago.

Well, that's what he'd been doing for decades, wasn't it? Carrying on as if none of that terrible, terrible tragedy in Scotland had ever happened. But now, the protective devices that had served him so well and for so long were screaming under the strain of Maggie's questions and the reality of a nosey lawyer's visit.

He didn't want any of this, especially on the eve of their one big party in years! Christ, he groaned inwardly, what … what if they – good friends, family – found out he … *he was a killer*. First that letter, today a phone call, and … and tomorrow a bloody lawyer! Suddenly, he'd lost control of his life. And his past!

PART 1

Scotland – June 1970

1.

Ask her ...

The bright red jumper beckoned from near the dancing, darting crowd. Go on, give it a go. No one knows you in Scotland. He took a deep breath, and like one of those lion cubs on its first hunt he'd seen in *Born Free*, stepped with care through the human scrub towards his quarry.

He stopped in front of the girl and, hoping to look cool, nodded towards the dancers. 'Um ... 'scuse me. Want to ... um, dance?' It crashed out in pieces as he tried to shout over the loud, live music and his own deafening nervousness.

She was pretty in a fragile way, and her nervous eyes, like those of a jittery bird, quickly took him in. They then dulled and found something more interesting just to his left. 'Thank you, no. I'm waiting for someone.' Her body now matched that fluctuation to the left.

He remained there; the bent grin still locked to his face. Until the rejection fully melted his resolve. Then he stumbled to get away, as might the lion cub upon finding its intended victim was too large and dangerous. Head and shoulders dropped as he retreated into the jungle of onlookers around the dance floor.

He eventually found sanctuary where people might not have witnessed his latest failure. Glancing back over the crowd he watched the ritual begin again as another young man approached the girl. Although the interaction suggested he was also a stranger, together they blended into the dancing throng. And soon that familiar backwash of disappointment and shame came swirling into his guts. He needed a drink to flush it out.

At a temporary bar back behind the crowd, he ordered two cans of Harp Lager and gulped down the first. *I'm waiting for someone:* Jesus, was it international? Stupid though to hope it'd be different over here. He thought of Joan, the girlfriend of sorts he'd had on the ship coming to the UK a month earlier. They'd spent some time together and promised to keep in touch. Yeah, yeah. But he knew they'd been just the leftovers once all the others had paired off after the ship had departed Perth. The over-tall spazzo and the plain, lifeless girl – like the damaged stuff in shops that no one ever buys.

Picko, of course, had had a ball, and Wendy, two cabins along, had blokes fighting outside her door. He and Joan had struggled to keep up a conversation; she knew nothing about Janis Joplin or Joe Cocker or even Hendrix, and he'd never heard of the Claremont footy club.

He started the second Harp, his stomach still churning. C'mon, be positive, his grandad would have said. Well, he was into his long-held travel dream, and here in the Scottish Highlands in mid-June, it remained light and mild at 9.40pm. The music was a bit Bob Dylan for dancing, but okay, and that afternoon he'd tried a marijuana smoke and survived. He could still smell it in the crowd. He and Picko had seen the folk festival posters at the youth hostel here, arriving from the Isle of Skye in the Kombi van. After some grub, they'd followed others to the local sports ground, and Picko'd chatted up that blonde Dutch bird on the way. Still somewhere in the crowd with her.

A human roar from the stage drew his attention. The band had been replaced by a fat man with a guitar and a big grin. He was interacting with the avarice audience as if they were all personal friends.

'That's Hamish Imlach up there.' It was the barman who'd served him, now gesturing towards the crowd. 'Aye, most of them have come here to Fort William, just to see him – from Inverness, Aberdeen, even Glasgow. He's quite a character. You a fan too?'

The young customer shook his head and got out more money. 'You've got a terrible thirst, Laddie,' noted the barman. 'Over a bit o'skirt, is it?' His eyes narrowed. 'Usually is.'

6

The crowd gave another howl. 'Och, he's starting on the *Cod Liver Oil.*' Moving with the music, the older man produced another Harp from a crate under the tartan-draped trestle. 'Now, that's your third beer and you've nary said a word. P'raps you're a *Sassenach*, and dinna' wish to be lynched.' He was shouting over the cheering crowd.

'A what?'

'Ah-ha! I've got it to speak!' The ruddy-faced barman stepped back, gesturing to an imaginary audience. 'A Sassenach is an Englishman – south of the Borders, aye.' With a frown, he leaned forward. 'Well?'

The young traveller didn't answer. 'Come on then, Laddie. Where's home? Two wee words ain't givin' much away.' The barman persisted with the frown. 'Hmm, let's see. A well-tanned face, so I'd guess India. Aye, or Jam-ai-ca?' He sang the last word, then paused. 'Well? Am I right?'

The young man swigged at the new can. The barman was teasing him, he knew. 'Australia,' he eventually offered.

'Och, you don't half talk, do yer. Those three words your daily allowance?'

God, this bloke's persistent. Get it over with. 'Um … sorry. Name's … Dave. Um … Dave Lawson.' He paused. 'But … but mates call me Henry – y'know, after … after the famous writer.'

'Who's that then when he's had a wash?'

'Hen … Henry Lawson, of course!'

'No, don't know him. Anyway, I'm Gordon.' The barman stuck out his hand, grinning. 'After the gin.'

They shook hands. 'Following the World Cup? Big game tomorrow: Brazil and Italy. And all in colour now.'

Dave shook his head as Gordon leaned in closer. 'Now, my son Bernie leads a rock band. Ugly young sod, he'd give quids for your blond scruffy hair, clear face, and height.' He threw a hand up. 'You've gotta be more out there, Laddie!

The young Australian had heard that a hundred times before. More. He took another gulp of beer.

7

'Now, do yer want a wee dram to go with that Harp, young Henry Larsen? There's quality here.' Gordon indicated a collection of bottles with exotic labels on the crowded trestle behind him.

'It … it's Lawson. But, no … no thanks.'

The barman pushed a newly opened can towards him. 'Well, have another lager then, Aussie. On the house, now. I'm already nursing a wee dram under here.' Gordon tapped the bar and looked around. Then, the portly barman lifted a large, brimming tumbler from under the bar, threw back his head, drank its contents, and replaced it back out of sight. All in one well-practised move, Dave thought. 'Welcome to Scotland, young Larson.'

***

It was Picko's turn to cook dinner, but he hated cooking, so that meant it was Dave's turn. Again. Touring the UK youth hostels with griping Picko, it had become easier to do it himself.

They'd just arrived in busy Glasgow from Fort William, and a heady mix of culinary smells and sounds now welcomed Dave into the expansive hostel kitchen. Around him, people prepared meals, poked at maps, or read Frommer's *Europe on $10 a Day*. Nearby, some Kiwis discussed Garfield Sobers' belligerent batting in the current Rest of the World Cricket series. Good to hear, as he and Picko would catch some of next week's game in Nottingham before they crossed to the Continent.

'Dave!' He looked around. 'Dave, look who's here. Angie and …' Picko entered the kitchen with two familiar females. They were dressed like other young travellers – flared jeans, loose shirts out, desert boots. One had a jumper tied around her waist. Wasn't she that South African chick they'd met at …?

'Sue, I'm Sue,' the second girl gushed, raising a hand. Canadian? They joined Dave at the cooking bench.

'And it's Antjie, not Angie.' That Afrikaans accent – many South Africans had boarded the ship at Cape Town. Although serious, she was quite attractive.

Picko took over. 'And you'll remember me, I'm Picko. The cook here is Dave. We met you at … at?'

'Inverness.' Wide-faced Sue beamed at them. 'About two weeks ago. A group of us went to that nautical pub. Remember?' She pointed up at Dave's neck. 'Hey! You've got yourself some of those cool Guilamine beads! All the cool travellers wear 'em.'

'Yeah,' Picko answered first. 'The silly bastard swapped half his music tapes for them on Skye, and thought it'd make him cool. Ha, well. But now, what are we gonna listen to driving around Europe?'

Embarrassed, yet pleased at Sue's reaction to his much-treasured Moroccan beads, Dave gestured towards a neighbouring gas ring. 'Start … start cooking with that. Our … our food'll keep hot.' The water around the tinned Frey Bentos pie bubbled loudly in confirmation, and Sue soon had the contents of a Rice-a-Riso packet tinkling into a saucepan.

Soothed by a combination of pie aroma, and Door's songs from a ceiling speaker, the four young people ate without hurry and swapped stories. Picko was the first to finish and offered his Woodbines around. 'So, what's your plans for the summer, girls? We're here for a couple of nights with some ideas of old Spaz, um, Dave's. He's a gardener – wants to see gardens.'

Antjie found some matches. 'Well, we're off to the Continent, man. But, first got to catch my sister in London before she heads back to Jo'burg on Friday's flight. But that night, we'll be boarding the Calais ferry at Dover. Which means France on Saturday, three nights time. Right, Sue?'

Sue beamed, then both girls threw their arms in the air, and twisted their bodies from side to side while chanting, '*Woo-hoo, woo-hoo, woo-hoo-hoo.*' Others in the room looked around at the commotion.

Although visibly embarrassed, Picko was interested. 'So how you gonna travel about Europe, girls, once you get there?'

Sue was still chuckling, 'Um, don't know yet – probably hitching. But we'd prefer to share some transport. Right, Antj?' Her friend nodded.

'Yep, can understand that. Hitching to London then?'

'Yeah.'

'Organised a ride yet?'

Antj answered. 'Hell, no. Why all the questions, you smiling, Aussie bugger?'

Picko grinned across at Dave. 'We're heading to London soon, and then to the Continent, and want to share our petrol bill. Why not with the two prettiest birds in Scotland?'

'Yah, flatterer. But when? Has to be tomorrow. So much to get done in London.' Antjie stubbed out her cigarette with emphasis.

'Well, um, we could leave tomorrow. Yeah, couldn't we, Dave?' Picko's grin widened. 'Right, mate?'

Caught out, Dave over-reacted. 'Hey, hang ... hang on. Can ... can't go yet. Still ... still lots ... things to see here.' *Their plans – bloody Picko had agreed!* 'Ro ... Robby Burns, Cul- ... Culzean Castle. Cricket next ... next week.'

'Dave. We know Antjie and Sue. They want to return to London and cross to France. And so do we. Right, mate?' He paused. 'Now, we'll come back in October and see Robbie bloody thingo then.'

Dave knew that tone – Picko used it at home with his little sister. *The bastard.*

Sue stood up, again beaming. 'Look, we don't want to cause any problems. Antjie and I'll wash our stuff, and perhaps get a hot drink, while you two sort it out. Now really, guys, you don't need to fit in with us. We're happy to take our chances.'

Dave watched the girls collect their plates and disappear into the still-busy kitchen. Then, Picko turned on him, now with a low, loaded voice. 'What in the fuck are you playing at? You know this is a great chance to share the van. You're always banging on about saving money. And with two chicks too! Don't you want to get a root? I thought a spazzo like you would jump at the chance.'

He leaned across the table and gave Dave's shoulder a friendly push. 'Hey, we could screw our way all around Europe! I think Antj has the hots for me, and they say Canadian birds don't sit back and wonder what a dick looks like. Wait'll she sees that extra-long wanger of yours, Davy-boy!'

Dave tried not to blush. 'Pik … Picko, of course I want to share the … the van with chicks, but not … not just yet. There'll be other chances.'

'But,' Picko started again. 'Now look, all it needs is a bit of flexibility. Sure, we agreed about the cricket, but I'd much rather tour Europe with two hot chicks than go to the cricket any bloody day. Wouldn't you? And we'll be back here next season. We just need to be flexible with our plans, that's all, you silly bugger.'

Picko leant in really close, again that low, menacing voice. 'When Sue and Antjie come back, Spazzo, you'd better have the right answer. For all of us!'

2.

Standing on the battlements, Dave Lawson watched the National Trust guide puff out his chest towards the expectant tourists. 'The medieval founders of Culzean Castle estate, here on the Ayrshire Coast, chose this high rocky promontory with defence in mind. Later descendants, however, utilised the Gulf Stream's influence to grow –'

A hand on his arm interrupted Dave's concentration. 'Och, you don't need him and his blather!' It was Jean, the cheery woman from the small gift shop. 'Here's a wee estate map to get yourself to our garden you asked about.'

'Um … thanks.' He accepted the folded map and her encouraging grin.

With this guide, Dave was soon at the castle estate's famously luxuriant walled garden. Alone within its high rough-stone walls, he wandered the historic glass houses, and the many herbaceous borders that bloomed almost unnaturally in the tepid June sun. He took photos of palm trees, ripe-smelling pineapples and other semi-tropical plants that appeared to have strayed as far from their natural homes as he had.

Once satisfied, he moved on to the beige stone castle itself. The outside he found was suitably substantial and grand, and dominated the adjoining coastline. However, inside the castle seemed a mishmash of additions and alterations from different eras, as if the correct style had yet to be decided upon.

Before leaving, Dave bought some post cards in the gift shop, and mentioned to Jean his next destination, Robbie Burns' cottage. She again surprised him, this time with the offer of a lift; if he could wait 40 minutes until she finished work.

Pleased, Dave returned to the battlements for a smoke and some sun, the Island of Arran out to sea. Picko would have found his note by now.

I'm sorry to sneak off early, but I think it's the only way to please everyone. I'll get the train down from Glasgow to London tonight. See you all at Earl's Court hostel first thing tomorrow. France on Saturday with the girls!! Look after my tape player.

Sorry,

Dave.

Picko will be so pissed off; probably still angry when they meet tomorrow. Yet, for once, Dave decided to postpone his concern. On one hand, Picko was right. A cricket match and some castles did sound lame compared to sharing the Kombi with Antj and Sue – and yeah, a possible shag. He liked Sue; she'd remembered him and had thanked him with a touch when he'd finally agreed to share with them. And hopefully she'll also think this new plan of his was pretty cool. Yet, there were no guarantees just how long the girls would stay with them. Picko usually gave people the shits after a while.

Could be all for nothing, but at least this way, he, Dave, would have done his duty by his grandfather, Ric, and his boss, Charlie, and would still catch up with the others tomorrow morning. The garden photos were for old Charlie, who wanted to build a similar walled garden on the Mornington Peninsula, south of Melbourne. Years earlier, the volatile Italian landscaper had been the only person willing to give Dave, a struggling, stuttering 15-year-old, an apprenticeship. *No matter he don't talk proper. I only speak Wog; no one listen to Wog. He big and young, I want big and young for gardening. He start tomorrow!*

So, now feeling unusually satisfied, Dave enjoyed this interval and the intermittent sunshine, even sharing a greeting with other visitors. He'd defied Picko, woken before dawn and found his own way to Culzean Castle on the early bus from Glasgow. Cool. And it was great just being on his own. Not left wondering what Picko or any others wanted to do – or not do. Sure, it'll be a rush getting the train back in Glasgow tonight, but so far so good. He recalled the heavy blur of his teenage years from the blame and shame of his father's death; introversion, depression, and panic attacks, often followed by sedation.

13

So, this newfound independence, being here today as just another tourist enjoying Bonnie Scotland, was big. Anyway, touring the UK and Europe *alone* had been the original plan when he'd booked a ticket on the *Achille Lauro*, months before Picko had suddenly decided, unasked, to join him.

***

Dave found Robbie Burns' thatched cottage to be an anti-climax. Perched on the edge of a busy bitumen road, it was as if the centuries-old dwelling had been erected on the wrong film set. Did Jean sense this, Dave wondered, for she next suggested New Cumnock, an interesting Burns town, and near to her home. Equally, local buses travelled south from there to Dumfries, perched on the busy London to Northern Island train line, where London trains left every four to five hours. A far quicker option than returning to Glasgow, she added. Consulting his map, Dave agreed.

Driving to New Cumnock, Jean gave a running commentary on Robbie Burns, and stopped at Afton Water and other related sites before dropping Dave at the bus station in the quiet town centre. He was in a nearby shop buying more post cards when the 4.35 bus to Dumfries left early. The shop lady said there'd be another in an hour, but with a growing sense of freedom and general satisfaction hardly felt before, Dave decided to start walking.

As the road south linked with the meandering Nith River and its dappled leafy canopy, he thought of Sue and describing to her this first day of real felt freedom – in about 14 hours. Cool! And, as cars passed and the emotional burdens of his young life eased, he began to sing favourite hits like *Tin Soldier, Magic Bus, Piece of my Heart.* Then, more, until he eventually accepted a lift from a mud-faced farmer in a muddy Land Rover, to the next village.

It was around 5.30, and clouds were gathering when a small black Wolseley stopped for him. The next bus was due soon. Should he wait? Nah!

A hail of healthy noise greeted Dave as he opened the back door and squeezed in with his backpack beside a bassinet with a baby, and a small child. Over the clamour, the young parents, Leslie and Derek, described their budget car tour of the Continent four years earlier and suggested places not to miss – Granada, the Hofbräuhaus, Pompeii. Then, Derek, driving, had them laughing with an endless supply of crude versions of Burns' poems. Dave was disappointed when the car eventually stopped near their home, still north of Dumfries.

'We are so envious of you,' Leslie said as he got out.

He stared at her. 'En … envious of me?'

'Aye, of course. You're so independent!' She smiled. 'Good luck, now. And remember, a London train leaves Dumfries quite late – you'll be there in the morning.'

He waved at the disappearing Wolseley, then continued down the A76, still enshrouded in laughter and healthy children's noise. The Nith, within its curtain of trees, now accompanied him on his left, with multi-green farmland reaching away to the right. 'Dumfries tonight, London tomorrow, France on Sat'day – woo-hoo-hoo.' He yelled, twisting his feet on the bitumen. 'Freedom, freedom – woo-hoo-hoo.' He could do anything, go anywhere. So free – so normal – for the first time ever.

Dave looked up as the dimming evening sky gave a deep rumble. Soon, large drops of rain caught him, and increased into a heavy downpour as he ran for the shelter of some birch trees at a road junction. Cold and quite wet, he quickly took off his pack and pulled out a raincoat. Stepping back to put it on, he heard a high revving motor, and sliding, squealing tyres on gravel.

Then *wham*! Deep, sharp pain, somewhere.

Everywhere.

Nowhere.

15

PART 2

Scotland – July 1970

1.

'Hey, Dad! What a surprise!'

He's here in the hospital, tall as a tree, and that big, enough-for-everyone grin. The oiled jelly-roll, the two-handed comb of his hair: left side, right side, comb back in the shirt pocket. Like Elvis.

'G'day, Junior.' Then, Dad quickly pulls my ear as he always does. 'Got ya.' It always stings, but you never complain cos Dad hates a grizzle-guts. And the other dads don't do it. It's so great to see him again.

'I heard you were here in hospital, kiddo, so thought I'd pop in and see what's cookin'. Had your head shaved, eh? Like one of your convict ancestors, ha! So why you in here?'

I run a hand over my head. Jeepers, it is all gone, my long hair's gone! 'Um, not really sure what's wrong yet, Dad. Lots of pain, but I'll be okay. Gee, thanks for comin'. So, what records you bought lately, and what work are you doin' on the car? And, and how's the footy goin'?'

'Hey, slow down, you little bugger. Everything's jake. But, nah, thought I'd give the footy a rest this season. Gotta let the young blokes get a game, eh?' And there's that wink.

'So, how's Scotland, Junior? Plenty of pooftas in kilts, eh? You're growing so tall – Jesus, prob'ly taller than me now – the girls'll go for that suntan.'

'Yeah, the first three week have been just great, Dad. So much to see – castles, pubs, and stuff. But still not much luck with girls. If ... if you hadn't gone ... and ... . It totally floored me, y'know. Floored us all.'

16

'Hey, hang on, Junior. You aren't blaming me for all your crap, are ya?' Dad steps back from the bed with that serious look. 'You told me to dive!'

'I ... I didn't really mean it. Just ... just wanted you to be better than all the other dads. That's all.'

Dad grins like a split watermelon and throws his arms out. 'And I am!'

'But ... but you ... died. Broke your neck in the shallow water, the policeman said.' It's hard to face him now, so I look away.

'Jesus, Junior.' Now Dad's giving me his impatient look. 'Hope you're taking care of my Samurai sword. And the footy trophies. You're meant to have those things.'

'They're all gone, Dad.'

'What?'

'The thing is, Mum chucked out all your stuff after the funeral. Even got a smaller car. A Ford Prefect, I thi –'

'A pissy Prefect? Fuck sake!'

'She was real angry, I remember. Still is.'

Dad's face is now tinged by the fire light. 'Look, Junior, things just happen. Fate, I s'pose. Forget it.' He moves closer, grinning. 'Anyway, visiting time's up, but there's one thing I must do.'

I know what's coming again but can't stop him. Dad always wins the ear pulling game – like everything else. Yeah, I understand now it's always about Dad winning. And again, the ear bloody hurts.

Now, I smell the fire, the burning driftwood. 'Dad,' I'm pleading. 'Daad, don't leave us again!' I try to sit up further but can't. I continue yelling.

He's with the other men, as I always see them, standing in the shallows of Port Phillip Bay in their swimming trunks, their forms fractured by the flickering flames. Again, they're drinking and joking together, big beer bottles in their hands. Wives and kids are spread out around the bonfire, an island of light on the vast, otherwise-empty Seaford beach. One or two kids are asleep on blankets, others still play in the sand. Am I the only one who knows? Didn't they hear my warning just then?

One of the men challenges the others, grinning. 'Are ye' game?'

'Course we're fuckin' game.' They answer with finality. 'We did it after we won the Grand Final two years ago.'

'Here's to that bloody premiership!' It's Dad, shouting, grinning. A cheer erupts and together they drink the bottles empty.

Jeepers, I can see myself with Kenny and Kaye, still trying to finish that sandcastle. Mum is near us, and now gets up and goes over to Dad. She's wearing the dark green bathing costume and is still a good sort. She stands there brushing sand off her arms and legs, really asking him not to go. Perhaps Mum understands these are the last care-free hours of her life.

'Hey, Junior, your mum doesn't want me to dive off the Carrum bridge. Whatta ya reckon?'

God, now I watch myself get up and join them. 'Yeah, go on Dad. You can do it.' It's my nine-year-old voice. I watch myself give Dad a hearty wave. 'Go on Dad, you can do it. Take no notice of Mum. Dive. Dive off the bridge!' He gives me that special grin.

One of the men returns from the hefty ice box with more bottles of beer, their caps off. He gives the first to the oldest of their group. 'C'mon Hutchy, you're still the captain. Let's go.'

Then, together, they each take a pull of beer, and with Mr Hutchinson leading, begin to move towards Carrum. As they pass near the flames, the expression of finality on Dad's face again is imprinted on my brain. And then the night takes them. My Dad forever.

'No Dad. Don't go. Don't go again! I didn't really mean you to go!' I'm screaming from my hospital bed, but again it's a waste of time.

2.

He sat by the hospital bed, left arm and shoulder trussed up under his clothes, utterly devastated by the little ceremony taking place. He didn't want to be discharged – he didn't feel well enough to be discharged. And, it had all happened too sudden, too soon. Yet, approaching him the previous day, Sister Printie had been adamant; after almost a month in hospital, he needed to be up and about, and suitable accommodation finally had been found. But the staff were his only friends here in Scotland. It wasn't bloody fair!

Then there were these clothes Nurse Warhurst had bought for him to wear today – uncool baggy pants and a hairy brown jumper. He felt a real goose. Yet, he was thankful, as equally he was for the small radio someone had brought in, and the birthday cake and fuss they'd made when later it was realised he'd turned 21 while in the coma.

Sister Printie began again. 'Wee David, while all those lesions you collected in the accident have healed well, you do need to remain in the district for some weeks yet. The physiotherapy sessions we have arranged will eventually mend that immobilised shoulder and arm, but it's the effects of the fractured skull that are less predictable. Doctor Connor wants more x-rays of that precious head of yours. An interesting specimen, he says.' Her eyebrows, raised for effect, would normally have cheered him.

'Now, don't rush things; you have only been on your feet for some days after all. Be sure now to follow the instructions for your medical needs. They are all in your bag along with your camera, and those attractive foreign beads, which I almost kept for myself.' A short pause. 'David, you have been an excellent patient, and leave the Royal Infirmary staff here proud owners of the only 7ft hospital bed in Scotland.' The sister's humour had cheered him through those early painful weeks in Ward 4, but he couldn't find a smile today.

Still beaming, Sister Printie gestured to a tallish woman he hadn't noticed earlier, standing to one side with Warhurst. 'Mrs MacAdam here has kindly offered to provide accommodation until you are fully

19

recovered. I'm sure she will let you watch your cricket series on her wee television set.' The woman nodded towards him.

'Thank you, Mrs MacAdam, you certainly are a life saver.' Still smiling, the sister then indicated to Warhurst, who helped Dave up from the chair, lifted his backpack and lead the way out of the ward.

The young Australian woke as the car jolted to a stop in front of a low building. The woman helped him out, and then led him in through a doorway. No people, no one to greet them. Well, he just wanted to lie down for a bit – perhaps meet them all later. The strong odour of new paint was all Dave really took in as his benefactor put his pack near the bed and helped him sit down.

'You seem tired, Mr Lawson. Shower and toilet are just through that door there.' She indicated behind him, but he was too buggered, too sore, too sad to take much notice. 'Now, make yourself comfortable, while I prepare your supper. A good time for you to organise your medicines. Are you hungry?'

He nodded an answer, but she was already at the door. She looked back before disappearing. 'Chin up.'

He wanted to shout, *Bugger off. I feel bloody awful, and I'm bloody lonely!* Instead, he attempted a wave to show he was coping. But he wasn't really.

***

He lay in the foetal position, deep within a womb of bedclothes. He'd woken up in this strange place yesterday, alone, numbed of feeling, with no idea where he was: like the sole survivor of a terrible plague. And the full impact of the accident a month earlier on his overall travel plans had finally registered. More bloody weeks of recovery, the sister had said. Christ, by then the summer would be finished! To see Europe properly, he'd need to stay for the following summer, and that meant a job for the winter; probably bar work in London.

No real problem there, but he knew the thrills and memories of a summer raging on the Continent would have carried him through the coldest, darkest English winter. Instead, now it would be: *Hi, I'm*

Dave. I've been nowhere – a nowhere man. Like that Beatle's song. So, just hide. Stay here.

And it'd happened just when he'd really begun to enjoy himself. Burns Country hadn't been all that cool, but he'd done it on his own. And mixing with people, strangers, as he'd never done before had triggered a sense of release from his shitty past: the shame of responsibility for his father's death. Then suddenly, wham! All chopped off. Gone. Not only the summer, but his half of the Kombi van, the tape player, his music too! And where was bloody Picko now? Spitting out how the Spazzo had let him down again? Well, he shouldn't have come overseas – should've stayed at home and bought that red Monaro with the money after all. He was wallowing, he knew, but didn't care; being run over allowed you to be pissed off. He pushed further into the blankets.

***

Mr and Mrs Hutchinson have put Kenny and Kaye to bed, but they say I can stay up a bit longer. 'You're so like your dad,' Mr Hutchy says, stroking my hair. But he looks sad.

It's at least two hours since we left the beach. Mr Hutchy had to bring us home because Mum can't drive. Someone at the beach said Dad was missing, an accident or something. But I don't believe that, as sometimes he's really late getting home at the weekend. He's always there in the morning, right as rain, happy as Larry. Prob'ly asleep in the car again!

Suddenly, there's a knock on the front door and Mr Hutchinson answers it. There're two big blue policemen filling the doorway. They look real serious, like Mr Vanstone, our headmaster does at assembly. One policeman has a notebook in his hand.

'Mrs Lawson? Mrs David Lawson? they ask Mum. Funny how they say it, like Mum's first name is David too! She nods and they come in. They walk into the lounge and one of them tells me to go to bed now, so I can help Mum in the morning. But I always help Mum in the morning, with breaky and stuff.

Mum nods. 'Yeah, go to bed, Dubby, and go straight to sleep now. I'll come in later and check on you.' She kisses my head and turns me around. She pushes me softly towards the bedrooms. I remember now it was the last kiss for a real long time. The last time she called me Dubby, too.

The next morning, Mum's in the kitchen in her dressing gown staring at the toaster. She has a slice of bread in each hand, but it's like she's forgotten how to put them in. Kenny and Kaye are sitting at the table, and they're playing Ludo. Mr and Mrs Hutchy must've gone home.

'Morning Mum. Dad home now?' I ask as I go to the fridge to get the milk and jam and other stuff.

'No, he's not home.' She says it real slow and loud, like so the toaster can understand too. She turns and looks hard at me. 'He's dead!'

I stop, and the fridge door stays a bit open. I can see the light inside flickering on and off, like Dad's a secret agent sending me a message. Nah, I'm not dead – don't believe her.

'Close the bloody fridge door!' Mum yells. Then she does something funny with her mouth, like she's chewing in her next words. 'I said your father's dead!' Now, she's really yelling, and she does the mouth thing again for the next words. But I don't want to believe her. Can't be true.

'Bloody killed himself!' She's still shouting it. 'Broke his stupid, bloody neck in the Carrum Creek, be ... because you . .' Her mouth collects more words. 'Because you *bloody told him to dive.' The youngies look scared, with the yelling.*

Now, they're all staring at me, Mum's still doing that mouth thing and yelling. Kaye starts crying, Kenny's about to. It's like they're all pointing, pointing guns at me.

But now I can't hear them. Did someone turn down the volume? Mum's always telling me to ... .

I'm looking at Mum and the littlies and I can see they are real upset. Still staring at me. Mouths still going. As if they know who's done it.

Me. *Can only be me! Must be my fault – I ... I must have killed* dad.

I've killed my dad ... . I'm ... I'm a killer.

I feel so bloody awful, so ashamed. The ... the dunny. Quick!

***

The young Australian was eventually roused from this raw remembrance by more immediate sounds – irregular scratching. He raised his head from under the blankets to find a large tabby cat on the outside ledge of the big, wide window of his room, swiping intently with one paw at the glass. Peering further, Dave noticed on the inside a small white moth fluttering wildly, like a plane with a dead pilot, up and down, back, and forward across the pane. It seemed unaware of the deathly interest taken in its flight path, and the clawed swipes. Couldn't it see what was outside the thin glass?

Stirred by the unlikely interplay, Dave sat up to watch. The cat continued to follow the insect's random movements along the window, again clawing noisily on the glass when its prey appeared to come within reach. Yet, at times the tabby seemed uninterested, cleaning itself vigorously, but would suddenly strike with a paw if the small creature appeared close. Then Dave grinned as the cat, at the far end of the window, leapt again to swipe at its prey, landed awkwardly on the end of the ledge outside, and fell off, out of sight.

Now stimulated, Dave remained sitting, and took in his cavernous bedroom – the exposed beams, the drab, chunky furniture from another era, the faded rug. Then he noticed the view outside – a large, lush paddock, lots of trees beyond, and further, some low hills. Was this a farm? So quiet, just the occasional bird. So unlike the hospital. Yeah, no hospital smell either.

A sudden metallic sound made him turn to find a face peering in through the room's main doorway. Then, a young woman entered, carrying a tray. 'Och, you're awake, then?' She was of medium height and build. The face suggested friendliness. About his own age, he guessed. The bright blue apron over her clothes clashed with the shock of red, curly hair.

'Hello.' She stood looking down at Dave, who was struggling one-handed to pull up the blankets of his large bed, as if protection was needed from this sudden intrusion. 'I'm Pauline, and you must be

23

David. I was told to bring in your breakfast. You've been in a bad accident.' It was a bouncy tone.

She stood there, waiting. 'Cat got yer tongue, has it?'

'So ... sorry. You Mrs MacAdam's daughter?'

'Och, no!' The reply had that long Scottish *noooo* that Dave had come to enjoy. 'I'm her Ladyship's cleaner. Every Wednesday I come and do my best to keep the house clean. But you've seen it – a mansion! Can one poor soul clean a house this size in a day, can they?'

'Her Ladyship?'

'Aye, Mrs ...' She stopped, head turned, as if doubting his intelligence. 'Och, no, she's not really a Ladyship. A bloody tyrant, mind. *This is not clean enough; you have missed that, do it again.* Always complaining. Yet, I could do with more of the work – another day at least – but she just won't give it me.'

'Hav ... haven't seen the house yet.'

'Aye, it's big enough, you'll find. Once ran a staff of 10 or 12, they say, but now there's really only me.' She looked around. 'This room was painted out for you – must be someone special, I told myself.'

He stared at this bubbly apparition as she placed the tray on the nearby bed table. A rich voice to match the rich accent. Face attractive, cheeky, an aroma of perfume and sweat. 'Her Majesty said you were from Australia. Somewhere like that I'd say – you've had a lot of the sun, and you're wearing those fancy beads.'

Dave blushed. At least she didn't mention his short hair. He struggled to find more to say – and not stutter. 'Where am I?'

Pauline laughed. 'Were you delivered in a hearse, then?'

Embarrassed, he again tried to pull up the blankets, and like an unfurling flag the empty pyjama sleeve for his strapped arm flapped into view.

Open mouthed, the young woman stared at it. Transfixed, she sat slowly on the arm of the nearest lounge chair.

'Och, I'm so sorry. She didn't, um, explain your injury.'

He hadn't meant to shock her like this. 'Sorry ... too.'

24

'No, no, my fault. Friends tell me I gab on ninety to the dozen.' She hesitated. 'Aye, you must come and meet them when you're up to it.' Another pause. She pointed. 'When the arm's grown back, like.'

As Dave outlined the immobilised arm with his free hand, she began again, grinning. 'Well, as you ask, this is Glendaruel, a country estate that is well past it, but whose owner refuses to accept the reality. Her husband died in a war somewhere out there in Asia, but that's no reason to go on being miserable, is it now?'

Stimulated by this girl, Dave answered a few questions about his accident and treatment in hospital, and for the first time in weeks, began to relax. They were talking music groups when a distant voice called her name. 'That will be madam wanting me to paint all of the rooms on the top floor next.'

'Oh,' he answered, then smiled.

'I'd better go before she gets her knickers in a twist. Nice to meet you, David from Australia. Make sure you eat this breakfast I've prepared, now.' She picked up the untouched tray from the night before, spun on her heels and was gone.

He sat grinning for some moments. Hey, suddenly things were looking up! He was hungry. Hang on, some pills have to be taken with food. He began to get out of bed.

3.

Invigorated by the combined antics of a grey tabby cat and a red-headed girl, Dave Lawson ate some breakfast and dressed himself for the first time, despite the useless arm. Feeling somewhat back to normal, untied shoelaces aside, he ventured out into his new world.

The first surprise was to find his room stood alone, separated from the house by a short distance. Renovated stables perhaps. The second, was the house itself – like Pauline said, a bloody mansion! He had to stand back to take it all in – three floors high and an attached tower, round and even taller. Built of grey stone with reddish stone edgings, the vast, chunky house looked quite old. The area around it was clear and grassy but needed cutting. Distant vehicles could now be heard – cars, tractors?

The entrance to the house adjacent to his room had a paint-flaked door. Had Pauline come this way? Should he knock?

He rapped on the door and waited. Nothing. Knock again? Louder this time, but still nothing. After further hesitation, he opened the door and saw into a wide, cream-painted hallway. An appealing cooking odour drew him inward until he stood beside a dusty, wall-mounted glass panel of indicator lights. They were in three rows, with names below each one: drawing room, parlour, morning room, many others. And a whole row of bedrooms! He was counting them when a sharp voice interrupted.

'Is that you, Mr Lawson? You are looming out there. Don't loom.'

Drawn to his left, the young Australian saw off the hallway into an expansive kitchen. The room was also cream and had a flagstone floor. It was about five times the size of their kitchen at home and was well lit by high windows above wall benches. A tall woman in blue stood behind a hefty, dull-varnished table, holding a rectangular baking tin with oven mitts. Mrs MacAdam?

He was reminded how his mum seldom baked cakes.

She looked at him a little longer. 'Well, come in. I *am* pleased to see you are up at last. I was concerned. Can't understand why a young fellow would wish to remain in bed once discharged from hospital.' In contrast to their first meeting, Mrs MacAdam seemed unkempt – a dirty-white apron over old clothes, sleeves pushed up, hair tied back in an unruly bun. She wore wavy-framed glasses, like his mum's.

She freed a hot cake from the baking tin and placed it next to others on a wire tray. 'For the jumble sale at St Georges' tomorrow, Mr Lawson. We will deliver them whilst driving to your first physiotherapy session. Ten am, I believe.'

'Yeah ...' Jeez, he'd completely forgotten the physio.

'Now that you are up and about, would you like a cup of tea? We have much to discuss in relation to your stay here, however short, and this seems a suitable time. A fresh pot on the sink there, crockery as well.' A gloved hand pointed. 'Milk in the fridge. Oh, here is my cup – no sugar, thank you. You'll find the short bread tin in the pantry behind us. Second shelf on the left.'

He waited. His disabled arm? She looked up. 'Yes?' A pause. 'Not too much milk, now.' She began stirring a bowl of cake icing. Unsure, he walked over to the sink, and after some hesitation, poured the teas and added milk. Then, with his free hand Dave carried each cup separately, rattling in its saucer, to the table. Next, he found the shortbread tin, but with only one hand couldn't get the lid off.

'Och, give it me here, Mr Lawson.' A light voice, but a not-so-light manner, he decided. Again, like his mum.

Settling at the far end of the table with his cuppa and some shortbread, he watched Mrs MacAdam spread icing onto each cake with a broad-bladed knife. He thought to say something. 'Your ... your cat. I saw your cat ... This morning.'

'Ah, that will be Sergeant Major. He's quite active for his age. Now, Mr Lawson, I first ...'

'Da ... Dave, Mrs MacAdam. ... Or Henry. Everyone calls –'

She cut him off. 'I first want to say, Mr Lawson, I am so pleased you are up and about, for this means your health is improving and you soon will be on your way. Also, I am very busy, with this large house and estate to run, charity work for both the parish and further afield, and lay responsibilities at St George's kirk. So, it would no doubt benefit us both if you were able to tend to most of your own needs.'

No more laying in bed feeling sorry for yourself, Henry, she was saying. 'So ... sorry. Painkillers ... sleeping a lot.' Watching her, he decided that Mrs MacAdam didn't look all that well either. At least he had an excuse. Shadows under her eyes behind the glasses, and dandruff on the shoulders of her dark blue cardigan. Crabby, and up herself, he decided. Is that why she's alone?

'I understand, Mr Lawson. Now, first, we need to discuss the toilet.'

'To ... toilet?'

'Aye, the toilet. I recently have had to spend considerable money on the septic system. It had become blocked, which is inexplicable when you consider I live here alone.' Dave stopped himself from smiling. 'So, to help prevent a recurrence, could you please restrict your use of the toilet to a minimum.' She looked towards the fridge. 'Now meals. For breakfast and lunch, you may help yourself to ...' She began a tirade of information. '... and this way you can come and go as you please ... crockery in the cupboard there.'

Dave had taken little in when she stopped, his mind still with the toilet – should he pee in the garden?

'Now, for the evening meal, I prefer ...' Then, another gush of words; like listening to the Melbourne Cup, he was missing the detail. '... is washing day, Mr Lawson, so have your dirties ready. I will have the cleaner change your bedding then, as well.' He pictured Pauline – her cheeky face.

The woman had stopped, eyebrows raised for some sort of conformation. 'F ... Fine, Mrs Mac. I–'

'Please do not call me that. You will address me as Mrs MacAdam, as I address you as Mr Lawson. Save that for your rough Australian friends.'

He sat back. Yeah, definitely up herself. 'Tea and coffee things are ...' She began again, nodding, when necessary, towards the sink area or pantry. When finished, she asked him if he smoked.

'Sometimes.' He'd really only started a few years earlier to look cool; hadn't done him much good though.

'Please do not smoke in the house, especially your bedroom. I suggest you give it up completely – better for your health.' She was wearing him out. He drank the last of his tea and decided not to risk a second piece of shortbread.

'Now, we must discuss your physiotherapy sessions. Only one this week, Friday, but then it's every Tuesday and Friday. As this will consume a considerable amount of my time, I will ...' Now quite tired, Dave let the next tidal wave of words wash over and around him.

She must have noticed his oh-shit-not-more look. 'Lecture almost finished Mr Lawson. Unfortunately, my television set currently needs repair. I am sorry. However, there are pleasant walks along the laneways surrounding the estate. I do have a wee map which indicates Ellisland, and other district Robbie Burns sights. You may wander about the estate freely, but understand Mrs Duffy lives in the gatehouse, and will not wish to be disturbed.'

It was like she was trying to do good but just wasn't good at it. She gives a useful comment but follows it with a condition. 'Now inside the house, please restrict yourself to the kitchen, and the library, off the hall on the first floor, if you wish to get yourself a book. Do you read, Mr Lawson?'

To that, Ric would have said, *Nah, books haven't reached Australia yet, Mrs Mac.* In fact, being such a loner, Dave enjoyed reading: Agatha Christie, Alistair McLean, Graham Greene, and lots of history. Always did well in history at school. But already she was away, again.

'I am sorry if that sounds stuffy, but I do need to consider both the cleaning and my privacy. Now, the estate name, *Glendaruel,* is from the highlands, and means glen, or valley, of blood. The house itself is mid-nineteenth century, although the MacAdams have been here considerably longer. And, it is of some historic interest, as Lord Kitchener stayed here overnight whilst travelling north in 1916 for that fateful voyage. If you are able to constrain your curiosity, Mr Lawson, I promise a personal tour before you leave. Is that a deal?'

He nodded. But there it was again – this time a friendly offer but on condition of being good. Yet, he did want to climb that tower.

'Um … thanks.' Rising from the table, he noticed behind her, hanging between two windows, some framed poetry sewn on fabric.

Look up, Give thanks:

Look forward, Take courage.

Although uninterested in poetry, the simple lines did make him think. Yeah, *give thanks*, Henry. At one low point, Sister Printie had explained how that initial swelling of his brain could easily have been fatal. But he would fully recover, she'd said. So, *take courage*, he told himself again.

Sitting out his holiday, injured, in this place with a woman as grumpy as his mum hadn't been part of the plan. He smiled. Although more of Pauline would be great, he was already *looking forward* to leaving!

4.

In early exploration of the estate, Dave discovered a hedged sun garden that was tucked in behind his bedroom and part of the big house. Despite neglect, it offered privacy, and caught any warmth the reluctant Scottish sun had to offer for both his low spirits and damaged shoulder. When not away for treatment, he was at the weathered garden table there, listening to music or cricket on the small radio from the hospital. Sergeant Major was soon a constant companion, seeking attention, or camaraderie, or like himself, the sun.

Back home, there'd always been a radio going – on the fridge in the kitchen, or the portable at work. In the summer crowd on the beach near home, there'd be 3UZ or 3AW or 3KZ playing. And he often sang along to music, despite teasing from old Charlie, or young Kenny; they didn't understand. Joe Cocker, The Doors, Janis Joplin, and Jimi Hendrix had been played around the clock on the ship to the UK, and he'd bought their music and the tape player during that port call at the Canary Islands. All bloody lost now, in the Kombi van in Europe somewhere! Still, with Radio 1 by day and Radio Luxembourg at night, he could follow the latest groups like Creedence and Led Zepp. Yeah, the music, the sun and Pauline's flirting on Wednesdays together began the process of healing.

Now with time to go over the events that found him at Glendaruel, Dave came to understand he'd had a lucky escape. Yeah, he's suffered serious injuries that still gave him hell some nights. And of course, it'd been so great to hear the family voices during that first long-distance call to his hospital bedside only a day or two after having regained consciousness. But, by then the police had told them the worst was over, no need to rush to his bedside, which probably saved them considerable worry and cost. And saved *his* freedom. Okay, a big bloody hole had been blown in his travel plans, but he still had some travel money, and he was still here – in Europe. Like the poem in the kitchen said: *Give thanks*.

Dave pondered on his relationship with his mother. He didn't get on well with her. He didn't hate her, but he came to understand he'd left Australia principally to escape her, and her constant judgement of him. She didn't understand him – didn't seem to want to, like she did with young Kenny and Kaye. Perhaps being a nurse, she was always desperate to find a label, a 'condition' that explained his *unusual behaviour*, his silences, his remoteness, his resentment. And yeah, after his father's stupid death, he *had* worn the blame blanket she'd thrown over him and had retreated into himself to numb his inner feelings of shame, guilt, and sudden loss of a hero dad.

What's the Spazzo gunna do next? was a burden he'd suffered right through his teenage years – through bloody Picko, it had even followed him to Scotland! But his mother hadn't seemed to view any of that as punishment enough and had had him treated with drugs for *avoidant personality disorder* and *acute depression*, none of which, despite knocking him out for weeks on end, had done much bloody good.

It was Ric, Dave knew, who had kept his youthful head above water. Moving in with them a few years after his dad's accident, Ric had provided an understanding ear – *Your mum blames you for your father's death, because she can't admit she married a drongo. But remember, young Dave, you're not a drongo.* In time, he'd helped his grandson find a job, the one with Charlie, and later encouraged him to travel. During that last call home from the hospital, while his mum had begun to shape the road accident as the latest of Dave's failures, old Ric had told him to stick to the physio so he could travel again, *perhaps even to Berlin, young Henry, as I did after the end of the war.* And a week or so after that, he'd forwarded $250 to his grandson, unannounced, of course. Dave was sure his mum didn't know. Typically thoughtful, encouraging Ric!

Always thoughtful, always accepting Ric.

***

I'm standing under the big back porch at the Sellars' house. Wipeout starts playing – the Surfaris from the USA, number 7 on the Top 40 last week. How many songs begin with a laugh like that?

Ric says it's good to get out and mix with other kids. He says they are real nice people to have kids around one Saturday night each month. Anyway, it gets me away from Mum for a while.

Looks like there's about 14-16 kids here tonight. The boys are standing in the dark near the clothesline, so some of them can sneak a smoke. The girls are under the carport lights because Mr Sellars has put his Vanguard out the front. The mob here usually leave me alone, and I just stay quiet and listen cos I need answers too.

I know the boys here from Tech School or the beach. The girls are Joycey's friends. She's Mr and Mrs Sellers' daughter. I wish I was part of their family, with a dad, and a Mum who's always home and cooks nice cakes and things. Joycey's too tall like me, but she never laughs at me. She's the only girl I feel okay with.

Lionel is Joycey's brother, and he's got lots of records and other music on tapes. He and Blacky play the music like they're DJs from 3DB or 3UZ. They're a bit older than the rest of us.

Mrs Sellers is bringing sandwiches and cordial out through the back door. She's having trouble with the screen door, so I hold it open for her. I often do stuff like this, so I don't have to stand with the others.

'Thank you, Dave. You're a great help.' Mrs Sellers smiles at me as she puts a tray down on the trestle table. She goes back inside again.

I'm still holding the door for Mrs Sellers, so I sneak a look over to the girls. Especially Susan Bright. She's about 14, like me. She's got beautiful long golden hair, and she's um ... grown ... a lot now. She's smiled at me a few times. I know that doesn't mean she likes me – prob'ly smiles at everyone. But I'm pretending her smiles to me are different. I've dreamed about Susan a few times.

I see Lionel stand up and raise a hand. 'Hello to you all out there in Listening Land. I'm Lionel, your 3DR DJ.' His other hand holds the record player arm ready to play. He's always good fun. His voice is already deeper than ours.

'Here's a new record called From Me to You. It's by a new group, the Beatles. Funny name, eh? But the music's alright. Now listen.' Everyone looks at him as the song begins.

I already know most of it and sing along. But only to myself so people don't look at me. Some of the girls in the carport start jiving.

'Radio Land listeners, that's John, Paul, Mick and ... . Um, John, Paul, Mick and ... -' I see Lionel look at Blackie for help.

He's mucking it up. I don't usually say much cos its safer not to. But Lionel's okay. Then I hear my own voice. 'It's um, ... John, Paul, George and ... and Ringo. Mick, um, ... Mick Jagger, he's the singer for the Rolling Stones, an ... another new group.'

Lionel looks across at me, surprised. 'Ah, yeah. Thanks, Dave. John, Paul, George, and Ringo!' There's a slight scratchy sound before the Beatles begin again.

When the song stops, a hard voice I know starts. It's Bill Killen, and he's pointing at me. 'Hey, everyone, did you hear that? Bugger me dead, if it's not old Spazzo himself talking. Hey Lionel, make an announcement to Radio Land that Spazzo Lawson is talking tonight, will ya. And look! He's talking without throwing a wobbly like he does at Tech.'

Bill grins around to the others. I just stand there. I'm so bloody tall I can't even hide in the crowd. I begin shaking. I'm trying to ... stop.

But then another record begins – Del Shannon – and now I can't hear what Killen is saying. Has Lionel got it louder on purpose? Then he comes over, smiling. 'Hey, how come you know all the Beatles' names, Dave? They're new.'

'I ... I always listen to the DJs on the radio, new ... new groups 'n stuff.'

I'm starting to calm down. Dad used to write down the rock 'n roll stuff. I do too. Stan Rofe, Stan the Man, on 3KZ is the best. Mum doesn't like it, but Ric says as long as I've got my homework done its okay. I'm feeling better now. I could talk about Top 40 stuff all night.

'Hey, Blacky, looks like we've got an assistant at 3DR tonight, so le-' His words are drowned out by the really loud rattling of a train going past the back fence. It's heading for Frankston.

It's after 10 o'clock, and Ric'll be here soon. Suddenly, there's a scream from inside. Lionel and I look at each other. Yeah, from inside, and there's more – people talking loudly. Now there's more screaming. I hear Joycey call, 'Mum, Mum.'

Then, someone comes rushing out through the back door. The door hits the wall with a crash. It's Susan. Her face is strange – really wild, and it's her screaming. Other girls follow, and then Mrs Sellers. She says, 'Susan. Susan, stop. Let me handle this.' But Susan doesn't stop. She sees me and rushes over. She begins hitting me with her fists. Her lovely hair is all over the place, and she is screaming at me.

I step back as she hits me until I bump into the clothes hoist. I begin to understand her words. 'You pervo! You weirdo! I hate you! I hate you, Lawson.' And she's crying-screaming again. Now, Mrs Sellers has got hold of her.

'Susan. Susan! Stop it. Let me handle this.' And it's just Mrs Sellars and me. I can see everyone behind her in the porch light. They're all watching – waiting.

Mrs Sellars holds up some notepaper and says, 'David, how could you? This is filthy stuff you've written. From a perverted mind.'

She stands there with her arms crossed. I'm tensing up quickly. I try to say something. 'I ... I don't know ... what ... you're ... talking ... abo ... Mrs Sell–.'

'I'm talking about this terrible, filthy note that has your name on it. It was tucked inside Susan's purse. No doubt so she wouldn't see it until she got home. What a filthy trick to play.'

'But I ... I try to speak again. 'I didn ... Did ...' The words can't come. I'm starting to freeze up. Like the other times. They're all still looking.

Someone says, 'Did he just say he wrote it?'

No. No. I try to talk but there's no voice. Nothing.

'Do you admit this, David? Writing this filth?'

I just stand there, looking inside me where it's safe. Then, I feel my crutch get all warm.

'Ugh.' I can hear the voices. 'Look at that. Yuck. He's pissed himself.'

It must look like proof that I'm guilty.

'Imagine a 14-year-old doing that. Give the Spazzo a nappy.'
There's more talk ... I can only stand there.

The next Thursday night after dinner, Ric asks me again if I'd
written the note. The police came twice after Saturday, but I froze up
each time. They thought I was real looney. I heard them say to Mum
about me going into a <u>nut house</u> *for treatment. And when she began*
to agree, Ric got real angry. "Over my dead body," he said to 'em.

I can talk about it now. Tell him it wasn't me. I'd never do that to
Susan or anyone. Ric asks me if I ever liked her, had a crush on her.
And after a while I nod.

'Well, nice to see you've got a healthy teenage libido, Lad.' He
roughs up my hair, and I know he believes me. Not sure what libido
means ...

'Now Dave, you always get top marks for spelling. So, let's see if
you can spot the spelling mistakes in this.' He gives me some scruffy
note paper.

Soosan

I want to rute you and rub your titts

I luv you

Dave

***

The young Australian needed something to read by the end of that
first week at Glendaruel, so he went searching for the library. The
steps leading up from near the kitchen brought him into a vast,
panelled inner room, or hall, its walls much decorated. Away to the
left was what he assumed was the front door, framed by panes of
tinted glass that allowed diffused, coloured light into the chamber.
Above this was a mounted black cat's head: a panther?

Between him and the front door hung an immense gold-framed
portrait of a stern military officer. Both the man's soup strainer
moustache and battery of medals were impressive.

Dave knew about war medals, having worn his father's on many Anzac Day parades. Would Kenny wear them next year?

The other end of the hall, to his right, was dominated by a wide, ornate staircase with a faded maroon runner. His eyes followed it up to the second floor – enemy territory. However, his attention soon returned to the bottom of the staircase where the word *LIBRARY,* written in capitals on white paper, was pinned to a door almost opposite him. Was it there to steer him away from the rest of the house?

Floorboards creaked as he stepped across to the library. Once inside, Dave found another portrait of a senior officer, though perhaps of an earlier time. First World War? On other walls, framed black and white photos of what looked like colonial hunting parties were intermixed with spears and an oblong leather shield that was quite tatty. Nearby, mounted above an empty fireplace, was a brassy shotgun with ornate inlay, no doubt ready for the next foolish panther to enter Glendaruel grounds, he joked. An attached brass plate said thanks from the Maharajah of Bikaner. Maharajahs – India? On shelves, dusty piles of *Country Life, Punch* and other magazines sat with dusty books, suggesting neither Mrs Mac nor Pauline visited here very often. He eventually found some paperbacks and chose *The Day of the Triffids* by John Wyndham. Someone in a hostel had recommended him.

Sounds of movement on the floor above reminded Dave of Mrs Mac – he was determined to call her that privately – up there somewhere, alone. Was she doing her charity work? Yesterday, returning from the Royal in her Morris Traveller, they'd delivered finished children's clothing for Christian Aid. He was learning to ignore her impatience and silences, and often tired from physio when they drove home, he was happy to fall asleep. But, now understanding the need to remain in the district for the full course of treatment, he had to concentrate on the physio that would eventually get him out of here. Only a few more weeks?

***

In the kitchen to get his lunch, Dave heard the desperate voice calling from the servant hall. 'Hello! Can someone help me? Is there a *toilet* here?'

Almost immediately, a small face peered around the edge of the kitchen doorway. As might a pixie in an enchanted house, Dave decided, controlling his initial surprise. 'Arrr … aren't you supposed … outside?' He had been ordered to remain indoors today while the Thornhill Brownies picnicked in the wood at Glendaruel.

'Aye, but I'm *busting. Quickly*!' She must have been nine or ten, and wore the yellow brownie scarf his sister once had. To avoid an embarrassing disaster, he immediately led her around the corner of the hallway to what was once the servants' toilet. 'I … I'll wait … the kitchen.'

Just another strange thing in this strange place, Dave decided. Like yesterday – outside, reaching the grey-stone gatehouse along the gravel driveway, he'd found a little old woman he assumed was Mrs Duffy sweeping its front doorsteps. She had an equally aged straw broom.

Before he could retreat, she'd waved vigorously and called out to him. 'Och, it's you, Master James! And look at that poor arm of yours!'

Master who? Stooped, and of also of pixie-ish proportions, she continued, 'Miss Catherine must be so pleased to have you home again, safe and mostly sound.'

Dave had looked behind to see if perhaps she was addressing someone else, and turning back, he found she and the broom were gone. Had he imagined it?

The other pixie returned to the kitchen a few minutes later. 'Thank you, Mr er …' She stopped, looking up at him. 'You're so tall. And you only have one arm.' She paused. 'Are you Mrs MacAdam's son?'

'No.'

'Och, that's great. I'd feel so sorry for you if you were.'

5.

Returning to the kitchen one evening to tidy up, Catherine MacAdam was surprised to find her boarder still sitting at the table. He had a novel with him.

'Yes, Mr Lawson?' She remembered he never normally remained here after his dinner.

'I … I saw the TV repair van … leaving this morning. The cricket …'

Now he wants access to the television to watch his cricket, she concluded. Tsk, more intrusion. 'Don't understand why it has taken so long. Are valves really that difficult to get in this day and age?' She spoke to hide her embarrassment at his request, because she'd also followed the cricket scores during the summer, cricket being the only interest she'd ever really shared with her father. But of course, it wouldn't do for her to be sitting watching it with a young stranger.

Now at the sink, she ran hot water onto the evening dishes. 'The television, only black and white, I'm afraid, is in the parlour along from the library, which I see you have already found.' She had noticed the green triffid on the cover of his book. 'A Wyndham fan, Mr Lawson?'

He looked up. 'Well … good, so far. I … I saw the portraits of military officers in …'

'Yes. That's my late husband James' father in the hall, the lieutenant colonel, or half colonel. James' grandfather, the young colonel, is in the library. Both were commanding officers of the Kings Own Scottish Borderers, or K.O.S.Bs, the family regiment.' She returned her attention to the sink, willing him to leave. 'Is there anything else, now?'

'Ye … yes. Need to talk about … about money.'

She arched back as if he had threatened her life. 'Money?'

'Yeah, money. You see, I–'

'You … you want money from me? N … now?' Panicked, she scrambled for words. 'Money?' How did he find out? 'Money … because of your accident?' Someone at the Royal must have told him. Was this boy attempting to blackmail her? And after all she'd done for him!

'Uh? … N … no. Thought I'd give you money for … for staying here. Weekly board. You know.'

'*Oh.*' She hesitated, struggling to keep up. Bloody hell. Board money? 'No, you certainly cannot give me money. You mustn't.'

'Only want to pay my … my way.' God, he was watching her. 'Good of you to have me … for so long, on … on your farm.'

'This is not a farm, Mr Lawson. Glendaruel is a family estate! With a stately home!' Like a savage dog kept in the house, the pompous remark had leapt out before she could control it. Oh, Cathy, stop being … yourself. The poor boy.

The lad dropped his eyes. 'So … sorry. Stately home …'

'But you mustn't give me money.' The sudden realisation of the boy's intent had clouded her usually clear logic with embarrassment. And, attached to that, like thunder with lightning, came a sudden sense of shame, something she'd not felt for years. You must tell him. Explain. And, well, hopefully …

She dried her hands and moved to sit opposite the lad at the kitchen table. She looked directly into his face, something else she seldom did, and realised that if anyone had asked for a description of her boarder, she could only have offered *Australian, very young and very tall*. And, Cathy, *very injured*. Shamefully, she knew nothing of this young person in her charge, this person she had almost killed. 'You truly are unaware!' Bloody hell, where to begin?

He shook his head, his face a question.

'You, um, have no idea of why you are here, … *really* why. Have you?'

'Su … suppose the hospital asked … for volunteers, and you … you offered. Very good of –'

'No, it wasn't the hospital.' She paused, searching towards the ceiling. 'It was the police.'

40

'The … the police?'

'Please listen … ah … .' She couldn't recall his Christian name! 'Mr um … Lawson.' She steeled herself. 'When your need to remain in the district became apparent, Sergeant Mackay, an old friend, approached me about providing you with accommodation.'

'The sergeant found my … my passport wallet in … grass, where the accident … They … they didn't know who I was. A week or so.'

We didn't know, she reminded herself. Her hands were clenching and unclenching, and she tried to make them stop. 'Well, it was me. It was me who ran you down, who … who nearly killed you.' Don't stop, Cathy. 'On Burnhead Lane, just away down from here, where … where it meets the main road … the A76 … Off to the kirk. Raining … it was raining … somewhat. Um … you were left impaled on the tree.'

The lad shot bolt upright. 'Impaled?'

'Er … yes, impaled. That branch stump … Through your shoulder.' She raised a hand to her own shoulder area, while looking across at his, still bandaged and trussed under the shirt. She noticed now its buttons had missed a buttonhole. Oh, poor young man. 'Your head had struck the trunk, but … but you were hanging there. Feet just touching the …' She lowered her head in a mental attempt to hide her shame. Indeed, to hide all of herself.

***

This news was so shocking, yet so surprising to Dave Lawson that somehow, he felt no initial shock. Indeed, he was more curious than angry as he looked across the kitchen table at the woman who'd just explained how she'd caused him to be impaled on a tree. That it was Mrs MacAdam, with her unstated intimidation and mixed messages, made little difference. He'd read Bram Stoker and watched enough vampire films to understand *impaled*: a specific word for specific situations, seldom used. Could it have really happened? In that accident? Well, no wonder his shoulder and arm were still so bloody useless. Then it hit him.

'*Impaled? Fuck!*' Shit, he hadn't meant to say that. He never swore much out loud, especially with adults, but yet … 'You? It … it

41

was you?' He stared at her. Until now, he hadn't really bothered to ask who or what had caused the accident; one small part his fault, that copper Mackay had said, and the rest just bad luck. But, this woman, scary, superior Mrs Mac, now was saying it was her! Yet, sitting there hunched over, she looked as scary as a shrivelled old lady, tucked up in a wheelchair and parked out of everyone's way.

And then, he made the connection; just down from here on the A76, she'd said. Each time they'd driven to physio, they passed the trees where he'd tried to shelter that afternoon. He hadn't really thought about *where* before either. Despite the trauma of the past five bloody weeks.

So much to take in. 'So, the … the police told you to … to give me accommodation.'

'Yes … Well, no, Mr Lawson. No, there's more.' She took a deep breath. 'And it's better you hear it from me. You … you see, when I struck you that evening, I had had a drink. Only two, … I … I think. I was … I nearly killed you because I had been drinking.'

She paused. 'I was … Oh, I am so sorry … so very sorry.' Her eyes, normally so penetrating, so all-seeing, now were pleading for forgiveness, understanding – anything. Then, head again lowered, she began sobbing noisily, as if fighting for breath, her everyday decorum, her self-control having fled the kitchen.

Again, the shock of this latest information was slow to take hold. He should hate this stupid woman who'd nearly killed him. Because she'd been pissing it up, his holiday, the one he'd planned for over 18 months, and worked so bloody hard for, was now buggered. Yet, instead, he sat there running a finger around the green triffid on the cover of his novel, unsure what to do with his emotions. Triffids could also be lethal.

After some moments, Mrs MacAdam took a handkerchief from a sleeve, removed her wavy glasses, and attempted to dry her eyes. She looked awful. 'You see,' she began again between sobs, 'when the police arrived that afternoon …' The face was screwed up, no doubt reliving the accident. 'The shock of having to take you down from …' Another sob. 'I … I was covered in blood – your blood, all over … By … by the time they arrived, I … I was quite sober. I hadn't been rolling drunk, but I shouldn't have been driving, I know. Somehow,

Mackay suspected ... Another, a smaller incident, about nine – ten months earlier. This ... this time though, a ... a new mudguard ...'

But Dave was only half listening. That the person sitting opposite had nearly killed him – had impaled him onto a bloody tree – was increasingly difficult to digest. And somehow, he could recall the smell, the oppressive odour of blood, his own blood. She'd said Glendaruel meant *valley of blood*. How bloody appropriate.

She wiped her nose. 'When ... when they realised you would need to ... to remain in the district after discharge, the sergeant drove out here ostensibly to, um ... say there would be no inquest into the accident. Luckily ... no fatality, and evidence had been given by a farm labourer on a tractor of you standing almost on the laneway when ... Later corroborated by yourself in hospital, it seems.' He remembered now the policeman's questions.

'... And, it was thought I had stopped your bleeding ... which may have saved your ... My cardigan ... have had to throw it ...' She was speaking in spasms. 'However, the sergeant suggested very strongly ... I offer you my hospitality. Not simply a local Jock run down wandering home ... pub for his supper, he'd said. You a foreign tourist ... Didn't seem right ... and of course, he was correct.'

Her voice was steadying. 'Mr Lawson, I ... I may have offered that anyway, I don't know. I did visit the hospital daily, until you regained consciousness and they said you would recover. The staff knew to contact me regarding any expenses. I ... I haven't had a drink since.'

Expenses! The clothes, the radio, the long-distance calls home – even the 21st cake! That's why they wouldn't take money from him. The Ward 4 staff must have known all the time.

'This will be a great shock to you, Mr Lawson – the victim confronted by his assailant, so to speak. I am so sorry. You must be very angry – of course you are. Understandable. However, I do hope you will eventually forgive me.'

She was wasting her breath. He wouldn't shout or rage openly. That was a former Dave – years earlier when others were always stirring him, taking the piss about his height, his stuttering, his quietness, even his long dick – *bloody wasted on a spazzo!* – anything. Before he'd learned control, thanks to Ric. And old Charlie.

To take responsibility, which, he grudgingly understood, *she* now had. He began, instead, to explain how the summer of 1970 was to have been the best of his life. How he'd had to save hard for well over a year – a second job in a pub with a mongrel boss – for enough money to get to Europe. Cheaper by ship, he'd discovered. How they'd met the girls by chance in Glasgow and made their plans. About his lost tape player, and the lost Kombi van that'd cost him a big chunk of that travel money. And Picko and the girls, now enjoying themselves in Europe. Somewhere. Gone.

He was tiring fast, losing his flow, but he had to finish. 'My … family's not rich … like this.' He gestured about him. 'You … you can take things for granted that I … I can't. And … and fuck it, now I'm stuck here with you.' He glared at her, and for once, demanded a response.

However, she said nothing, and they sat there, avoiding each other's gaze, two lonely people, in a lonely kitchen, in a large, lonely house. Only the ticking mantle clock offered company.

It was the first time he'd spoken of his frustrations, his anger, since the accident, although that big chunk of disappointment about the lost summer on the Continent had always sat in his guts. Dave hated confrontations, and since the tantrums had stopped a few years earlier, he seldom really got angry. However, this time it remained, probably encouraged by the ache now in his shoulder. He stood up, jolting the table as if in a last show of resentment.

Her still-wet eyes followed him. 'Mr Lawson, this is a desperately unfortunate situation; all my fault, I understand. But now we must put everything aside and put up with each other until you are fully fit. Then you may be away and hopefully enjoy the rest of the summer with your friends.' She picked up her handkerchief. 'And, please, no more mention of board money. You said my world is different, but if only you knew. Stately home indeed – who am I trying to fool? I wasn't very stately the evening I almost killed you, Mr Lawson.'

To match her conciliatory tone, he forced out a *good night*, before heading outside into the growing darkness. Well, he now knew everything about the accident that had nearly killed him, but it brought little consolation. However, the thought of leaving here in only a few more weeks certainly did.

44

6.

(Yeppoon, Queensland – 30th December 1999)

Still seated at the patio table, Dave Lawson had begun to calm down. Out to sea, there were lots of islands today – he'd often counted them. Above and beyond the terrace, he also noticed a pair of mottled kites floating, heads down as if tasked to keep an eye on him, their soft whistling just audible. Riding the air currents in ever-broadening circles, they eventually drifted away to his left, seeking other prey.

Soon, the easing of Dave's anguish prompted a measure of clarity. Which enabled him to begin to seek answers to that shattering phone call. Those islands out there that came and went on different days weren't under some ancient curse, like in the Greek legends. He knew light waves and weather patterns caused the disappearing effect, so equally his name turning up in a celebrated Scottish person's will had to have a logical explanation.

Now, he wondered, had someone set all this up to expose him, humiliate him? But who? Who else knew the details of her terrible death? And then there was why – why would someone – anyone – want to do this? What was in it for them, especially after so many bloody years?

Then, his anxious mind grabbed onto a more obvious explanation. It was a simple mix-up! The wrong Kat Cale, or the wrong Dave Lawson. Yeah, that had to be it! Relieved now, he felt the need for another beer, but that'd mean going into the house. Sort this out first. Before Terri, or their other friends arrived. And misunderstood.

Proof of this explanation, he knew, was in his shed, so he got up and headed there, across the brick-paved area and past the raging-red flame tree. Once inside, he stepped around landscaping tools and materials on the floor to reach the rusty rubbish bin. A cloud of fine dust wafted from a disturbed bag of cement, as if in sympathy with his own disturbed ghosts.

45

He found the UK courier envelope scrunched under some timber off-cuts, then sat down with it on a large, upturned garden pot. It was hot in the shed, but he didn't care.

This time he read the typed letter with some intent. The letterhead was of *The Kat Cale Foundation*, and yep, it informed him of his listing as a beneficiary of the will of Ms Kat Cale, who'd passed away on 27 May 1999. Over six months ago. In formal jargon, the letter stated its purpose was to advise him of this, to confirm his existence and to ascertain his whereabouts for future communication. It requested he respond, either by mail, phone, or email. Well, he'd done none of that. No wonder, as Maggie said, the lawyer had been pleased to find him. He just couldn't share the sentiment.

But now, he noticed another sheet inside the crumpled envelope, a photocopied obituary from the UK *Guardian*. Ah, would the answers to the other Kat Cale be here? With as much objectivity as he could muster, Dave began to read.

Kat Cale:

Enigmatic photographer who captured the essence of a changing Britain

He understood *this* Kat Cale must have done exceptionally well to be remembered in a UK paper. Desperate for more information, for confirmation of the mix up, he read on in thirsty gulps.

The pieces for Counterview in 1984 on the divisive UK Miners' Strike can now be seen as Kat's breakthrough moment, for not only did this thrust her images into the public domain, but it also saved the once trendy magazine from oblivion. That series of photographs began a long partnership that was to profit both parties, with respect and royalties. The set that followed, capturing the human cost of the 'de-industrialisation' of the Clyde Basin, took Kat and her probing photography ...

He jumped ahead quickly:

... somehow always one step ahead of social commentators half her age, she had been a long-time member of the Campaign for Nuclear Disarmament in Scotland.

Then again:

... she seemed not to need human company, preferring instead the solitude of her home near Dumfries ...

It stopped him dead. 'God – *Dumfries*.' He tried to fight off an emerging image, as one might repel belligerent bats in a blackened cave. He shook his head and read on. He couldn't stop.

From the obscurity of a gentrified widowhood, and with little professional training she rose to become one of Britain's leading photographers and social commentators. But what had been the catalyst for this meteoric rise, what actually had enabled her so skilfully, so thoughtfully and so thoroughly to capture and record a country, a world, and indeed a time, the 1980-90s, in transformation? Retiring to Glendaruel only months before ...

Dave didn't finish the neat, clinical paragraph.

Glendaruel, Jesus! Like an unsure second language learner, he haltingly tried the word, *Glen ... da ... ruel*. Then, whispered it. '*Glendaruel.*' It still couldn't be her – his brain, still clinging to reason, refused to believe it. Why die twice? He, Dave Lawson, knew his history, *the* history of what had happened in 1972. At the big house. None of this photography stuff could have happened! He knew because he'd been responsible for her ... her ... *death*. Like with his own bloody father, all those years earlier.

And, sitting there, again reading these last phrases which together defined the death, yet *life* of Kat Cale, Dave's emotional barriers began to collapse. As if inexplicably fossilised, he remained there motionless, sightless, the perturbing piece of paper in his hand. Even the crash of a dead palm frond onto the shed roof failed to stir him.

PART 3

Scotland – August 1970

1.

One bright Scottish Tuesday morning in mid-August, Dave Lawson received Dr Connor's medical clearance. With the return of that biting excitement he'd experienced upon first arrival in Britain three months earlier, his immediate decision was to leave Glendaruel in 48 hours, on the Thursday. In between, he'd catch Pauline at the house. She'd hinted a few times of a night visit to his room and perhaps some travel together. Returning home in the Morris with Mrs Mac, he informed her of his news, and she offered subdued congratulations.

Dave sat outside after dinner enjoying the mild Scottish evening, with music from Radio Luxembourg, and his large Europe map spread over the garden table. Sergeant Major was asleep on most of Scandinavia. However, Dave's euphoria deflated somewhat when he noticed Mrs Mac approaching through the garden with a tray of refreshments. She'd never done this before.

'Ah, Mr Lawson, I do hope you don't mind.'

Caught out, he stood up, conjuring a smile. Her confession weeks earlier about the accident had left him with mixed feelings towards the woman, as with his favourite teacher at Tech school, Mr Jennings, who'd later been investigated for molesting other boys. Yet equally, it had acted to clear the air somewhat. If seeing each other outside, he and Mrs Mac had shared a casual wave, and when in the car, both had been more willing to chat.

Joining him at the table, she poured out tea, then produced an envelope from under the plate of cake, passing it to him with a simple, *for you*. Inside was a British Railways combined rail and ferry ticket, Dumfries to London to Dover to Calais. 'Mr Lawson, you deserve to recommence your travels on Thursday in some style. It's an open ticket, and of course, I shall drive you into Dumfries.' An embarrassed smile. 'A final opportunity to express both my relief and pleasure at your full recovery, and my apologies for your lost summer.'

More attuned to laughter and piss-taking than expressions of regret and thoughtful gifts, Dave was lost for words in the swell of gratitude. On one level, she *did owe* him. But on another, he was touched, embarrassed even, that she would think to drive back into Dumfries to get this ticket. Moreover, he had come to understand her apologies were genuine, but equally comprehended that after he'd left Glendaruel she might continue to bear a burden of guilt, similar to his own sense of shame about his father. 'Are … are you sure?'

She nodded. Humbled, and understanding the poor woman would be alone again soon, Dave encouraged her to stay a little longer. He used the last of the evening light to indicate on the map his anticipated travel route to Paris first, using her ticket, then on to West Berlin, as Ric had suggested. It gave him some focus. He didn't mention the planned diversion from London to the Isle of Wight for the big rock festival starting in a week. It'd been one of his reasons for coming to Britain. She wouldn't appreciate the opportunity to see The Doors, The Who, Hendrix, Chicago, Donovan, Sly Stone, Moody Blues, Free and Melanie. Or that Pauline might come that far with him.

'Well, Mr Lawson, I really do wish you good luck in your travels. You deserve it.' Again, her sincerity embarrassed him. 'Och, well, I'm away to catch *Dr Finlay* on the box.' And, with a courteous good night she was gone. He stayed longer, watching the moon climb up through the top branches of the wood out across the fields. The realisation that those in isolated West Berlin might be watching the same moon made his shaky plan seem somehow possible. *Ticket to Ride*, he hummed, moving inside.

It was well after midnight when he sensed someone else in the room. Yes, touching him – his bare chest.

'What …?'

'It's me.'

49

Pauline?

'I ... I am sorry to ...'

The word *Pauline* was in his throat when the light accent registered.

'It's Catherine ... MacAdam, Mr Lawson. May ... may I be with you?'

Mrs MacAdam? Dave was stunned. This was the last thing he expected. Or wanted. He left the hushed, hesitant request hanging, yet, as she joined him in the large bed, the weak light revealed a softened face and long, long lustrous hair. Unsure what to do, he simply lay there.

Soon, however, the perfume, the tingle of that hair on his face and chest, and the touch of her body through the thin nightgown combined to begin a for-once unwanted arousal. Embarrassment came as he hardened. Oh, no, she'll have to notice! Then, she kissed him – his shoulder first. Then, his cheek. And, as further resistance melted, he returned the kiss. And all the others.

They coupled clumsily, more fumble than fondle, more pressure than penetration.

Later, he remembered fighting off sleep.

Breakfast was far from Dave's mind when he awoke, alone, the following morning. Had that really happened? Could his nocturnal visitor have been a younger, crazy sister of Mrs Mac who'd escaped from captivity in the tower? Didn't strange things like that occur in big, spooky old houses? *Especially* this big, spooky old house, Master James? Yet, inexperienced in sex, apart from a few drunken backseat scramblings, for him it was momentous.

He knew he should be full of tomorrow's travel plans, London, Isle of Wight, Berlin, but like a happy family celebration overshadowed by a suddenly offered free fishing expedition with good mates, it now seemed less important. But, what to do? Should he avoid Mrs Mac until he left tomorrow, and save them both embarrassment? And what about Pauline? He was staying this extra day at Glendaruel because of her. Yet, if she found out about last night, she'd probably laugh at him. As she did at Mrs Mac.

Eventually, Dave got dressed and began sorting his things, although now too late to start travelling south today. He could hear Pauline's voice somewhere in the house, so to avoid her too, he left the estate, indirectly via the autumn-tinted wood and the broken bridge, onto the Dumfries Road.

Walking a few miles towards Dumfries took him to Ellisland, Robbie Burns 18th century farm. There, the friendly staff made a fuss of him being this week's *first Australian* and convinced him to try Burns' *authentic* haggis for lunch. He also wandered the historic buildings and grounds and exchanged greetings with other visitors.

Later, with some therapeutic Tennent's Lager at a shaded farm bench beside the Nith River, he tried to sort through the muddled residue of emotions from Mrs Mac's nocturnal visit. Since arriving, he had found her strict, set, and straitlaced. But last night he'd seen, indeed experienced, a different woman – younger, softer, vulnerable. Perhaps the third can of Tennent's triggered it, for now playing and replaying inside his head was the caress of that amazing hair: the waft of alluring scent: the pressure of her breasts: the gentle groan: the orgasm. The orgasm.

She came again that night, this time removing all nightclothes. Sight of her shapely figure gave immediate arousal, and any uncertainties were dismissed as they began their love making, unhurried, yet passionate. Complete. Spent.

Later, as they lay together enveloped by that wondrous hair, as young Dave Lawson felt might happen in an enchanting fairy tale, he asked this woman to stay and sleep with him.

2.

Forced from sleep by shoulder twinge, a sleepy Dave initially was stunned to find Mrs MacAdam's head and arm upon his repaired upper body. Again, it took some seconds to comprehend the situation – the transformation of an intimidating widow into the alluring woman he'd had wonderful sex with only hours earlier. With that riot of shoulder-length hair and minus those glasses, she certainly looked younger, and, yeah, attractive.

But he hadn't given her the come-on, had he? He'd desired Pauline, and that pretty girl in the post office at Dumfries. But never Mrs MacAdam. Bloody inconceivable! Yet, here in the early light her new appeal was again obvious.

He felt Mrs MacAdam begin to stir. Then stiffen. Then her body pulled away into the bedclothes. Was she regretting it already? Soon, she raised a frowning face, a hand drawing hair away from it. 'I ... I shouldn't be here. I shouldn't have come here at all. I'm sorry.' She rose to leave the bed but was prevented by an entanglement of bedclothes and legs. She tried to kick her way free, but without success.

Dave moved to one side to ease her anxiety, yet he wanted her to stay. 'Don't ... don't go yet ... *Please.*'

There was a hesitation. 'Oh, I feel so embarrassed being here ... like this.' And she did look embarrassed as she moved into a defensive position, knees drawn up, bedding up over the shoulders.

'I ... I asked you to stay ... Remember?'

There was a slow nod. 'Mr Lawson, I ... I have never done this before. I ...' She frowned again. 'I'm concerned you may think I have taken advantage of you, of my position as your temporary, um, carer.' She looked so serious.

Would it help to say it was his first real time too? 'N ... no. I don't ...' He stopped. 'Your hair ... lovely.' He reactively reached toward hair strands on her nearest shoulder, now bared.

The woman jerked away as if threatened with a dagger. 'Mr Lawson!'

'So ... sorry.'

She shut her eyes. 'Och, me too.' There was a long sigh. 'Um, no doubt I owe you an explanation as to why this has happened. But then, I cannot really explain it to myself. Nothing planned ... Um, purely impulsive behaviour. I simply found myself wanting to be ... with you. I'm not normally spontaneous as ... as you no doubt are aware.'

He gaped at her words – *wanting to be with you*. Him, Dave the Seaford spazzo? No one, much less an attractive woman, had ever said that to him. But she was talking again.

'Oh, my actions sound almost sordid. Please don't be vexed, Mr Lawson ... or judgemental of me.'

A worried face, then thoughtful. 'Ah, should I call you David?' *Dearvid*. Another hesitation. 'Considering all.' Now an awkward smile. 'Um, may I?'

Christ, another surprise. Well, of course she could. 'Un ... understand, Mrs ... MacAdam.' Yet, he didn't understand at all. And he was struggling to answer and struggling not to look at the ample breast that somehow had gained release from the protective bedding, as if wanting to be seen.

'Please call me Catherine.' She spoke softly, with a slight lift of the face, as if to guide the words across to him.

'Ca ... Catherine.' And, his hand, again acting alone, touched her arm in acknowledgement. This time she didn't react.

That subdued voice, still full of concern. 'David? I haven't taken advantage of you, have I? I would certainly hate for you, or anyone else, to think so.'

How should he console her? How to explain his pleasure, his gratitude even, that this has happened, without sounding like a sleazebag? 'Suppose ... a bit ... surprised.'

'Well, it is different for men. They are almost expected to do such things – to sow their wild oats. But never women. And, well, you are somewhat younger than I am, and ... and I'm already in the bad books with the police.'

There was momentary silence. She gave an apologetic grin, which turned into an awkward smile, and soon an unabashed beaming face, which he matched with a cautious grin. 'I think that's my first joke for … for … Well, certainly for 1970, Mr, um … David.' She looked down. 'Sad, isn't it. I'm not known for jokes, as you well know. For laughter either, if it comes to that.'

Her concerned face returned. 'What are you thinking, David?'

And he *was* thinking – still adjusting to her dramatic change, his mind performing a recalculation of her age – 35-40? He wasn't sure, yet it wasn't only the hair. Or the nakedness. Or the scent. Her expression, her behaviour also had altered; now more relaxed than the perpetually tight, defiant Mrs MacAdam face and manner he'd come to know. And avoid.

Vulnerable – was that it? As if she'd been humbled. 'You're … different. Happier.' He could have added *attractive, naked, alluring, sexy, turn-on,* for now he could see both her boobs in his peripheral vision.

She smiled at the answer and reached up to run a finger along his nose. 'I am only beginning to absorb that change myself, David.' She moved position, and that striking auburn hair wafted across her bare shoulders like a fine curtain answering a breeze. He studied her face anew. Her eyes – also soft, light brown, like her silky hair; he'd never noticed before. Now in better light he could see the complementation. Yep, attractive.

She gave another smile, a now younger smile. 'I haven't, err … done this since … James, my husband. Gosh, 12 years, more – and yet my body seemed ready for you. Primed, so to speak. It wasn't difficult at all – quite the opposite. Most … um, gratifying, in fact.'

He thought so too. But could women's bodies do that? They grinned sheepishly together, then lay back, both with their thoughts. Now past dawn, the room was filling with light and warmth.

Her hand found his and squeezed it. 'David, this is the first time I've seen you really smile. And it is a lovely smile.' She squeezed again. 'Do you really have to leave Glendaruel today? Now, it seems it's my turn to ask *you* to stay. Just for the weekend?'

Leaving? God, he'd forgotten. Again. Of course, the train ticket. London tonight. What should he do?

Catherine stifled a yawn. Sex or travel seemed his choice. But was it really that simple? Sure, these last two nights had been terrific – Christ, he was still aroused! He certainly wouldn't stay for Mrs MacAdam, but this other person now beside him was different. He was somehow touched by her. That vulnerability, perhaps. He knew vulnerability … well.

Sitting up, he turned to reply. 'Catherine, I …' But she was again asleep.

He looked down to study her, and his eyes readily moved to her breasts, mostly clear of the bedclothes. Well rounded, they were as white as the sheets, except for the wide circle of brown pigmentation around each nipple. He understood he was staring, perving – he'd not seen naked female breasts before last night. He wanted to touch them, feel that unexpected softness again, but somehow now that would betray the trust she'd demonstrated by simply being here.

He examined her face. High cheek bones and a longish chin. Nor ponderously sultry like the renowned Mrs Robinson of *The Graduate*, but definitely attractive. The eyes he now knew, and that wonderful hair, again claiming both pillows. The mouth, earlier so terse, so tight, seemed more relaxed. In all, a face now of peace, of trust. Gone were the worry lines and permanent middle-age frown that had been Mrs MacAdam. Were her barriers really coming down? Should he stay for the weekend? He smiled to himself; he was enjoying smiling. Now, what would Dustin Hoffman do?

3.

Still grinning, still trying to absorb this latest episodic change, Dave remained in bed after his visitor left. He felt like a balloon floating up among the exposed beams of the bedroom ceiling, bobbing forward and back through the totally unexpected, yet highly sensual experiences of the previous 36 hours.

Sleeping with an older, well-to-do woman was something young blokes at home fantasised about, and, out of the blue it had happened to him! Like winning the Tatts jackpot without even buying a ticket! The travel buzz that had so recharged him on Tuesday now ran a distant second to a more powerful, more physical pleasure he'd never really experienced before. Jesus, worth being run over for!

That name – Catherine … Catherine – God, it felt … so special, so stirring, as was the whole bloody situation. *Catherine* sounded a million miles from Mrs MacAdam, as *she* was now from the bitchy Mrs Mac. And he had become *Dearvid*: her accent, of course. *Dearvid, must you really leave Glendaruel?*

However, questions soon penetrated Dave's reverie. What had brought this on? Did she just want company? Someone to mow the lawns? Or simply more sex? Nah, she didn't seem that type. Was it about the accident, then? A guilt release thing, a sort of payback, or perhaps an attempt to prevent him from suing her. He didn't know. Further, would she be able to stay as Catherine, or perhaps revert to Mrs Mac when things went wrong?

And if you did stay longer, Henry, you stud, what then? Again, he wasn't sure. However, a recurring mental image soon made young Dave Lawson's mind up – Catherine kneeling naked on the bed, long auburn hair everywhere, slowly pulling the nighty down over her bare shoulders and breasts, before leaving, just a short while ago.

***

The widow of Glendaruel Estate returned to her big bed in the big house, chastened by her own behaviour. With blankets pulled up to her chin, as if to stifle resurfacing urges, she also contemplated the bizarre events of the previous two nights. Thoughts of her own unexpected and unprecedented behaviour ignited initial shock and confusion, yet she could not ignore an underlying, almost embarrassing sense of gratification. Shock, confusion, gratification, and … and raw pleasure – bloody hell!

Throwing yourself at him like that, Cathy, does suggest a measure of desperation! Climbing unasked into a stranger's bed is perhaps the most carnal of acts. Which should never have occurred a second time because, here, just yesterday morning you scolded yourself for that first indiscretion and promised to keep away from the boy. Stay away from him, you said, and he'll be gone out of your boring, lonely, self-opinionated life on Thursday. Today. But instead, you've done it again, this time with requests to stay. Only till the weekend, aye, but perhaps contemplating longer. Well, aren't you?

She needed to move, unable to keep still, as if tormented by hives or microscopic mites. She rose from the bed, put on a dressing gown, and sat, as she so often had, before the large vanity unit and mirror, in place since her married days. But, regarding herself this time, she sought to see beyond the reflection, to delve deeply into herself, further than she was normally willing to probe.

There entombed were the painful memories of her life – the contrived marriage, the miscarriages, James' malevolent mother, his untimely death, her own maladjusted family, and the almost comforting bitterness that had ensued from her life's injustices. As a result, being rude and remote had become daily practice, a temperament ideally suited to the role and burden Scottish society expected of a lonely gentry widow with a husband killed on active service. And, since someone had labelled her the *new widow MacAdam* at the funeral of James' mother, seven years earlier, she had taken on the role, the responsibility, as if it was a position of privilege.

Yet, Cathy, what's happened these last few nights has only a little to do with all that, so the question remains. Why this man, this very young man? And why the smile? You've had no real interest in men since James' death, and you've had little trouble fending off the

57

attentions of William Boyle, or Mr Andrews at the kirk. So, why young David? Is it a misplaced show of obligation stirred by the accident? Your age, perhaps? Your 38th birthday arrived unannounced, and uncelebrated last month, July. So, then only a little over mid-thirties! Go on, smile at your wee joke, Lass, but that now is a smirk. Stop it, Cathy, we have to solve this. And put that brush down.

Unwittingly, she had begun to brush those long, lustrous locks, her one semblance of physical vanity, that, from James' death until Tuesday night had been her secret alone. Now, hardly daring to admit David might find her hair attractive, she did remember his comment. So, you do wish him to be attracted to you. Hmm? Now, we're getting somewhere. And are you attracted to him? He's tall, very tall, has blond hair, a solid suntan, and … and is certainly young!

Now, despite a stutter, a hesitant voice, he has that shy, boyish smile. Right, but be honest, girl, what you've seen in him from the start is not his immediate looks, but … but tragedy, buckets of tragedy. It's in his eyes, his demeanour – a fellow sufferer. And, Cathy, although you've never really wanted him here, the company has been pleasant, hasn't it? Someone to be concerned about, apart from your own miserable self.

Now stop grinning like a silly schoolgirl! And stop admiring yourself in the mirror! Go on, have a shower, clear your head. Wash him off you. She stood up. But, it's more than the company, isn't it? After he'd shared his travel plans, you realised what drives him is exactly what you lack, what you must find if you are to survive. Courage: quiet, unassuming courage. It's written up on your kitchen wall, Lass: *Look forward, Take courage*! Cathy, young David is fresh and uncomplicated, as you once were. Yet, although quite shy, as you know you were then, and despite the physical setbacks of his accident, he is ready to head off onto the Continent. To anywhere at all really.

As you once were. Remember all those years ago, that initial courage *you* summoned after Father cancelled your placement at Edinburgh University? Remember dragging yourself out of that crushing disappointment of a lost professional career, refusing to accept the expected role of girls of your situation and social standing as a 'wife in waiting', down to the Gifford Castle Golf Club.

***

What do I say to the two club officials sitting opposite me? You see, I know nothing about golf. I don't really know why I'm here! And it's all wrong anyway. Why would an interview for an assistant club secretary be held in a kitchen, clean as it is, across an old wooden table with a gingham tablecloth? Is the ceiling of the Secretary's Office really in danger of collapsing? And now they expect me to be an experienced golfer. My handicap? My father, *I want to blurt out!*

Always respectful to my elders, I do, however, wonder if the old fellow here, Mr Wood, is under the influence of drink, or suffering from its effects. Shaky hands, reddened eyes, poorly shaved, collar askew. And the woman, Mrs Stillie, I suspect is a cook – the club cook – though she has been introduced as Mr Wood's temporary assistant.

His voice again. 'My dear, your handicap?'

'Oh ... oh, I'm not sure.' A handicap? I can't even guess an answer!

The cook is staring at me – glaring at me. 'Well, girl?' Despite the small frame, she is intimidating.

'Now Miss. Your most recent position?' Mr Wood again.

I had planned to say Jenners Department Store, in Edinburgh. It would sound impressive, and that's where father, after reluctantly granting permission, thinks the interview is today. But ... no more lies. Get it over with. 'Um, I've never had one. I haven't really worked at all.' I must sound so pathetic. Another sigh from Mrs Stillie.

I watch them confer for a moment or two, waiting for the dismissal.

'You do know you've wasted your time coming here to the club, my dear.' The old chap is gently stating the obvious.

'I know, Mr Wood – Mrs Silly.' Almost immediately I realise. Silly! God, what have I said? 'Och, I'm sorry, Mrs Stilly.' What must she think? 'I'm so sorry.' Oh, no, this is getting worse. Too disconcerted to look directly at these people, I try to focus on a rusting tea caddy on the bench behind them.

59

The man points an accusing finger at my resume on the table before him. 'No, I mean I am impressed to read you have attained five Secondary Highers, which suggests you must be an exceptionally bright lass. Thus, I am somewhat surprised your parents haven't sent you off to the university – any university. It's obvious that's where you should be.'

Mr Wood's conclusion is totally unexpected, and his words penetrate my self-pity. 'Of course, you have the compulsory Latin, which I assume the educational board continues to demand of students on the off chance that Britain is again invaded by the Romans. No Roman members currently at the club to practice your Latin on, I'm afraid, Lass.'

Kindly meant, his joke is too late; tears are already on my face. I can't stop them. I'm not blubbing or bawling; I just can't stop the tears. I must look a wreck. I try to muster what's left of my self-possession. 'I'm sorry,' I mutter, almost to myself, 'I've wasted your time.' I try to smile across to my interviewers through the watery blur. Someone presses a handkerchief into my hand. I drop my head and continue to sit there, quietly weeping. Me, an Assistant Secretary? Whatever was I thinking?

I hear the reassuring rattle of crockery behind me. Then the woman's voice, gentler now. 'How do you take your tea, dear?'

***

Such a disastrous start, Cathy! Yet, your courage and capability that day did produce by mid-afternoon a sound, original and much-needed brain wave that gained you that position of Assistant Secretary, and ultimately saved the failing Gifford Castle Golf Club from oblivion.

Brrr – the tepid shower! Well, memories are fine, but the shower has made little difference. Indeed, in desperation to regain that inner courage, you've lost control and thrown yourself at young David. Um, twice! Anything else, Lassie? Aye, admit it. Despite the accident, and, yes, your haughtiness, he holds little bitterness, and doesn't laugh at you, as others have … and still do.

He's an innocent in many ways – as you were with Mr Wood and Mrs Stillie. Now, David may be somewhat confused just now. Continue if you must, but don't hurt him. And ring Cheryl.

***

With shy grins, they met in the kitchen, the rays of sunlight through the windows accentuating Catherine's auburn hair, as if in congratulation. Together, they mollified Sergeant-Major's demands for food, which, unusually loud, suggested he sensed a new order at Glendaruel. Then, over a late breakfast, the first meal they had really shared, Dave announced his intention to stay for the weekend. She rewarded this with a big smile and the promise of a surprise.

And after dishes were done and some laundry under way, he *was* surprised to find himself entering the cobwebbed ground-level interior of the tower, unvisited, she explained, since her husband's time. He was reminded of the Famous Five as, holding candles, they edged their way up shadowy, spiralling stone steps, eventually to emerge onto the high round tower top, with its chest-high parapet and 360-degree view.

To the young Australian, the rural countryside that surrounded Glendaruel estate seemed picture perfect. Under the semi-gloss sky, working farmland stretched in all directions, apart from isolated, but well-defined stands of trees, or wood. Again struck by the orderliness of the British countryside, the landscaper in him explained to Catherine how it seemed all accounted for – tamed – so unlike rural Australia, where vast tracts of native bushland, some the size of small countries, still existed.

Equally, he could sense the sharpness, the depth in Scotland's colours, a marked contrast to the seductive dun pastels of native Australia. Catherine, in turn, indicated the boundaries of the estate, the small family mausoleum near the wood and the walled garden below them behind the house, which, she explained, just years earlier had sustained the whole estate. From this vantage point, Dave took his first photos since June, including one of Sergeant Major sitting unruffled atop the exaggerated crenelations of the tower parapet.

Later that afternoon in the sun garden, Dave Lawson tried to separate his conflicting thoughts. Yeah, he'd agreed to stay longer at Glendaruel, and, yeah, they'd had a good day together, and she remained as Catherine. But old Charlie would say, *Dive, you're thinking with your cock.* Staying for the sex, when he should be on the road south to London, Paris, Checkpoint Charlie. That's why he'd come to the UK and Europe. And that's why Ric had sent that extra money. Well, wasn't it?

Yet, he remembered how hopeless he was with girls. While some at first went for his blond hair and perpetual tan from landscaping, nothing much ever followed because he never knew what next to do. Like with Joan on the ship coming to the UK.

But it felt different here with Catherine and her massive, mystical house – she was unlike the chicks at home, teasing and laughing at him. Yeah, she was older, and yeah, Picko would say she was desperate. But Dave wasn't so sure. Did he just feel sorry for her then? Nah, he wouldn't give up his travel plans for that, and anyway, he hadn't yet. Now she was suggesting they go to Edinburgh for the weekend for some Scottish festival. Well, a few extra days now was fine because the Isle of Wight rock festival didn't begin till the following weekend.

4.

They stood looking into the much-polished front window of the small village pharmacy. It was Friday afternoon.

'Shall I wait here, David?' Catherine thought to ask.

'Sh ... shouldn't you buy them? Being ... being older?'

'Och, I'm not sure it is considered the woman's role.'

'Oh, but ... but I've ...'

... never really purchased contraceptives before, she decided, but was unwilling to embarrass him more than her suggestion of buying some *protection* already had. He could travel the world alone and survive being impaled but couldn't face the wee slip of a lass they could see inside behind the pharmacy counter. It amused her until she realised the opposite applied to herself. 'Och, I'll go in.'

Catherine's friend, Cheryl, while shocked to hear she had indulged in sex with a *sheath* from the 1950s, had said to purchase some new ones – ask for Durex – plenty if you want him to stay longer. Catherine squeezed Dave's hand, then with the felt admixture of apprehension and anticipation, she entered the pharmacy.

***

Once in Edinburgh's New Town and booked into the Gardens Hotel, Catherine made another surprise suggestion, and Dave soon found himself at the Abbotsford, on Rose Street, for dinner. With its large, decorated island bar, ornate ceiling and mirrors, and a mixed odour of smoke and furniture polish, it was his ideal British pub. Taking drinks to a corner table, he heard above the Kinks singing about *Lola,* and youthful adventures in another bar

Dave was still grinning about the song when Catherine reached across the table and squeezed his hand.

'Now, David, I must explain that this glass of wine is my first alcoholic drink since that evening of your terrible accident.' She squeezed it again. 'You are a very forgiving person to be sitting here with me now. Thus, I wish to pay for all expenses while in Edinburgh.' She hesitated. 'However, I would be upset if you thought that I was ... err, buying your company. Or your forgiveness.'

'But ... but the British Rail tickets.'

'The least I could do. Now, my friend Cheryl in Harwick has given us the hotel room and the festival tickets for this weekend because she and her ailing mother are now unable to attend this year. Also an ex-K.O.S.B. officer's wife, she perhaps is my only real chum, and has refused any money, so, I must pay for other expenses.' She took his hand again, and stuffed notes into it, as might a favourite, tipsy aunt. 'Moreover, people are less likely to notice us if you are paying.'

Embarrassed, Dave quickly pocketed the money. Despite her words, he did feel under some obligation, but for now, it was easier to go along with things. And he wondered what Catherine had told her friend about him.

Then the song now playing, registered. It was *After Midnight*. Eric Clapton ... 'Cath ... Catherine. Listen.'

She straightened. 'Oh, what am I ...? Oh, yes, but what song is it?'

'After ... Midnight. You ... you know, like us. Let ... letting it all hang down.'

'Are you being crude?'

'No ... *no*. Didn't mean to be.'

Somewhat subdued, they ordered meals and another drink, and while eating Catherine gave detail of the festival – the famous Military Tattoo, the Fringe collection of unofficial acts, and this year the Edinburgh Highland Games. Cheryl's tickets included a Beethoven performance and a World Premier play, if they were interested.

'Cool.' He was up for anything. 'How ... how do you know the Abbotsford?' She didn't seem the pub type.

64

***

How does she know of the Abbotsford? Catherine wasn't sure if she wanted to share the answer. But she could understand David's curiosity.

'Well, I came here many years ago, while visiting Vicky – my sister Victoria – a student at Edinburgh University, in preparation for attending there myself the following year. You'll notice no Morags, Kylas or other quaint Celtic-Gaelic names for our family – had to be stout British labels that would trip over a draught horse – Victoria and Catherine, for example. Still, it was quite exciting then for a bursary girl to be in a pub with her big sister and her friends.'

***

'Vicky. Victoria! Over here.' A group at a table to the left of the central bar are waving to us.

'Ah, there they are, Cathy girl. Come and meet my crowd.' Walking towards her friends already in the Abbotsford, my emotions zig-zag! Is it excitement or anxiety? I'm not sure. Inside, the pub is nothing like I'd imagined – I'm walking into a work of art! Already, my head is reeling to keep up with events – today, my first university visit, my first placement offer, my first outing with Vicky, now my first visit to a pub and soon perhaps my first alcoholic drink!

Chairs are pushed outward, inviting us to sit. 'Everyone, this is my sister Catherine. She's visiting Edinburgh to decide if the College of Art is up to her standard!' Vicky rattles off names – 'Rose, Morag, Ronny... mostly Masters' students,' she said – but my nervousness prevents them properly registering.

I try to smile as I shake hands. 'Hello.' I'm aware of my school uniform hidden beneath Vicky's borrowed overcoat.

'Your sister? Well, this is a nice surprise.' The girl on my left, faded purple scarf – Rose? 'You're an artist, eh? What's your discipline, Catherine?'

Caught out, I stumble over an answer. 'Oh, oh, photography.' Not a commonly acceptable form of art, but Vicky's chums greet my

65

words with thoughtful nods, as if we are discussing the nation's performance at the Olympic Games in London the previous year. They suggest a few contacts at the College for my future use, and generally wish me well.

Another friend now arrives from the bar with a heavy tray of drinks. Vicky introduces us. 'Cathy, this is Steven, the birthday boy, and our reason for being here. Steven, my sister, Cathy. She represents the creative arm of the family, and with her talent should do well.' Steven smiles as he says hello, and also welcomes me. He has the soft Edinburgh lilt, as do most of the others, and wears the loose casual trousers and jacket of his male contemporaries. I sum him up in three words – kind eyes, handsome. Are they a pair already?

Vicky's praise seems genuinely offered, so I determined not to let her down. Waiting for others first, I pick up a half pint glass and take my first ever sup of beer – a large one. No reaction, no spluttering, and I later wonder what all the fuss is about.

'Well done, you,' says Sandy. More friendly comments come my way – 'Vicky seldom mentions her family – what a lucky father to have two tall, bonny lassies – love your hair, such a nice, light colour – suits your complexion – do you often wear it out?' Are they being polite? I've always considered Vicky to be the attractive one, but the thought of now being paired with her causes me to blush.

'So, why photography, Cathy? Is it simply that you have a talent with the camera?'

I understand Rose's questions are genuine and the beer has loosened my tongue. So, I answer yes, but also explain how many of Britain's successful women photographers have been exemplary role models. I mention my heroines, Christina Broom, Olive Edis, Julia Margaret Cameron, and of course, the controversial Madame Yevonde.

***

Successful women photographers … Bloody hell, the career, the friends, the life she'd missed … 'Oh, David, my apologies! I'm away in dreamland here.'

'Good … good dreams, I hope.'

'Not really, no.' She found she was still angry at the memory of it all. 'You see, later that year when Vicky refused to stop her relationship with Stephen, a fellow Masters' student, but who was Catholic, our staunch Protestant Father disowned her, and cancelled *my* university placement. I may equally have *disgraced the family*, as he put it. That Stephen was also kind, charming and intelligent, as I had found him, mattered little. They eventually eloped to South Africa, and remain there today, happily married, and successful. However, that effectively ended my education.'

'Oh, sorry, Catherine. O … okay?

She nodded.

'So … your dad, … he probably wouldn't approve of me either?'

'Err, no.' She found herself grinning. 'To Father, my, um, friendship with a much younger man would seem as scandalous as Vicky's situation, and I'm yet to discover your religious denomination!

He held that boyish smile. 'I … I'm a Bush Baptist.'

She understood his attempts to cheer her and looked towards the ceiling. 'Father, you'll have to be satisfied with that.'

However, her sour mood returned when she turned to the large mirror on the wall beside their table. There, they could see themselves and each other. 'Oh. To the eye, we are quite different, David. No wonder people are noticing us. The couple near the door have watched us since we arrived. The barmen too. Despite your kind remarks, I do look somewhat older than you, and will continue to do so. And there's our contrasting complexion; you with that youthful Australian tan, whilst I remain Scottish porcelain white. And my glasses; they are not flattering at all. Unfortunately, I need them.'

'Does … does all that matter?'

He was trying to be kind again, she knew. 'Well, it does seem to matter to other people, David.' She grabbed her drink. 'Then, of course, is our clothing.' She looked down at herself. 'This twin-set may suit the St Georges Ladies Guild, but definitely not here with you, who, in contrast, are informally dressed, as young people are these days.'

'But … but, my clothes … not right for … for Beethoven.'

'David, there's more than our obvious differences.' She felt her emotions, her voice, raise a level. 'You see, it's many years since I've had an intimate relationship. Thus, on one hand, I am excited simply being here with you, yet on the other I feel so inadequate – um, not quite sure what to do next. Now aware of people watching us, I'm not altogether convinced I can go through with this. It all seemed easier in the privacy of Glendaruel where our differences mattered little. Am I better to stop before making a total fool of myself?'

Was that panic she could feel? Had she drunk too much? 'David, I wish to go now.'

He nodded; the smile gone.

Her fears were confirmed when she overheard a barman jibing Dave as they left. 'Into the gentry, are we?' She wanted to slap the man's face. Oh, what had made her consider any of this would work?

***

Surrounded for much of Saturday by European and American accents, and other international language speakers equally drawn to Edinburgh's festival, Dave came to understand that his much-cherished travel plans had, in fact, restarted. Not quite West Berlin, but at the Celtic Exhibition in the Old Town, or touring stately Hollyrood Palace, or absorbing the diverse colour and clamour of the Fringe in and around the city, he felt he could have been anywhere on the Continent, despite Catherine. Or was it because of Catherine? He wasn't sure.

Her mood swings and sometimes starchy personality aside, Dave found she shared a sense of discovery that he'd never experienced with Picko. And often her ups-and-downs bought great amusement, as with their lunchtime visit to Jenners Department Store. There, Catherine was determined to buy him suitable clothing for their evening shows, but when the prematurely-balding departmental head became noticeably amorous towards her, she overcame initial embarrassment to give her surprised *son* a most un-motherly kiss on the lips to avoid further misunderstanding.

68

Jenners! she snorted as they marched back out onto Princes Street. Despite initial awkwardness at having clothes bought *on the Glendaruel account*, Dave laughed out loud. And it felt good! Yeah, he was quite enjoying himself, and his new travel chum.

That evening, they soaked up the world premiere atmosphere of *Lovecraft's Follies,* sipping complimentary champagne together and mingling with other well-dressed people at the Church Hill Theatre. Finding the play a little confusing, they sought out another champers at intermission to get them through it. As he would with any travel mate, Dave realised. But Saturday still had a final twist when a misunderstanding by the sleepy hotel reception clerk about them sharing a room sent Catherine to bed alone, again. On again, off again.

Catherine's suggestion at Sunday breakfast to spend the day at the Highland Games surprised Dave, for he'd assumed she was about to call it all off. A chilly morning, they quickly dressed for warmth, he in his Jenners' Fair Isle jumper, and she, looking smart in family clan rig, with its striking mix of sharp and muted tones.

Once at the Meadow Bank games grounds, Catherine bought Dave a matching MacIntosh tartan tam-o'-shanter and scarf. Wearing them, he did begin to feel part of the huge throng of people gathering there, fully, or partly clad in national costume. To Dave, it was all very entertaining; huge sweaty men in singlets tossing cabers and big hammers, serious yet unbounded Scottish country dancers swirling up onto their toes, pipe bands marching and moving as one and the inescapable, yet contagious drone of the bagpipes.

It was an easy, comfortable day together and driving back to the city for the Tattoo that evening, Catherine pulled another of her surprises, when stopped at traffic lights on Lothian Road. 'The MacIntosh tartan does suit you, David.' Her face was indecipherable. The lights changed, and they moved forward. 'At least I've given you a real dousing of culture and ritual before you leave Scotland.' Was tonight the end?

***

Edinburgh Castle itself was still silhouetted against the last of the day's light when a shrill fanfare of trumpets focused the audience. Then, one by one, eight military pipe and drum bands, resplendent in ceremonial uniform, emerged from the castle, to fill the enclosed Esplanade with controlled sounds and spectacle to begin the Tattoo. From their seats high amid the appreciative crowd, Catherine pointed out the K.O.S.Bs, the family regiment, notable in dark green and reddish-purple kit. Within the confined area, the strident skirl of the pipes and the sharp staccato of the drums seemed overwhelming, but just when her ears neared bursting point, the bands marched off, as smartly as they had arrived.

The next assemblage of bands moved in unison to a set of popular tunes, and watching, Catherine felt herself begin to relax. Now quite dark, eddying firebrands on the castle ramparts cast an eerie, yet dynamic backdrop as spotlights roamed the phalanx of massed bands and the appreciative audience in the stands. Next to she and David, a middle-aged man also wearing a tartan cap stood up, clapping, and whistling loudly. Then, as if suddenly aware he wasn't alone, he nodded apologetically to Catherine and explained that his son was down there, a drummer with the Canadian Fusiliers. To her surprise, he offered a hip flask. 'Here, you and your guy have some Canadian. It's a damn cool night. Name's Ben.'

Not one readily to interact with strangers, she was surprised at herself. 'Oh. Um … hello, I'm Catherine, and … thank you.' She accepted the flask, took a careful sip, and nudged David. 'David, Ben here has offered us a wee nip.' The crowd around them continued with bursts of applause.

'Cheers, Ben. I … I'm Dave.' Almost shouting, he shook hands, then swigged at the flask.

'Nice to meet you both. Wait … Ellen, Honey!' A woman with a friendly, ruddy face, a little older than Catherine, turned towards them. Strands of blonde hair had escaped from under her red head scarf.

Dave began coughing. 'You okay there?' Ben glanced at Catherine, concerned. 'He doesn't handle the rye like you.'

A little embarrassed, Catherine slapped Dave's back. 'Um … no. I seem to be our whisky expert.' Nothing to be proud of there, Cathy.

Ellen indicated towards the bands. 'That's our son playing now – the one outa tune.'

'It must be quite a thrill for you.' Catherine had to shout over the enveloping din.

'Sure. He's such a great kid.' Ellen was yelling at them. 'About the same age as you guys. I hope you meet him sometime. Hey, are you from Australia or New ...?' She stopped, and Catherine noticed her peering more closely. 'Oh! ... Oh, I'm so sorry.' Ellen slid back behind her husband, as might a bashful child.

Initially unsure how to react, Catherine decided to grin. 'Oh, no, don't be. It ... That's my best compliment today.' There was a moment's pause until they all laughed, Ellen, she was sure with relief.

Perhaps it was the unintended compliment, for despite the penetrating military noise, Catherine was overcome by a sudden realisation. She was treating young David poorly. Herself as well, if she was honest. Part of it, she now understood, was being out of her depth, away from familiar territory, having to interact and be pleasant with strangers. Normal people. Like these friendly Canadians, sharing their drink and good will. Ordinary people, simply going about life, loving each other, their son, their own. That's your model, Cathy – not ageing, embittered Mrs MacAdam, who is still hovering about you like a vengeful wraith, tempting you to over-react to situations, which, if thought through, are only trivial: the nosey people in the pub, the sleepy hotel clerk, the randy salesman in Jenners.

Your companion David – it was suddenly so clear – now, he really is a solid one. Despite everything, he is still without judgement, fitting in, doing his best for the relationship. And you have repaid him with complaints and caustic remarks. Cathy, you once were better than this; a sudden vision of the Member's Lounge at the Gifford Castle Golf Club, solving problems with Mr Wood, and Mrs Stillie. How they had welcomed her, the fun they'd had working together. You can be better, must be ...

A hand shook her. 'Ca ... Catherine! You okay? You've ... gone so quiet.'

It took a second or two to register the place, the din, the very Scottish din! The Tattoo, with David – who could be, should be, *her* David. She answered with a sheepish grin, as if just reminded how the

71

Tattoo had been put on for her birthday. 'Och, I'm fine, thank you, David. Couldn't be better.' The Canadians were pointing down at the bands. 'Um, would you mind if we, um … were to leave?' Her hand somehow had wandered onto his thigh.

5.

They sat at the hotel table grinning at each other, unaware for some moments their breakfasts had arrived. Eventually, Dave felt a hand on his.

'David, last night … and well, this morning also … was just *so* wonderful. I still feel wonderful, tingly even, as if my body's sensors have just been reactivated after years of malfunction. Is it silly for me to say I can see and hear more clearly than yesterday – perhaps more than ever before?'

'I'm … I'm …' He also was blown away by their impassioned night. 'Feel … feeling pretty terrific too.'

'It's as if I'm going through a second puberty, as Madam Bovary described.'

Second puberty? 'Madam … Bovary?'

'A friend of Cheryl.' Catherine nodded, as he stared at her. She broke into a grin. 'No, no, David. It was something Cheryl mentioned.'

Ha, like Charlie Silvagni. Last night, while quickly showering, Dave recalled perhaps the only piece of sexual wisdom ever offered him. It had come from the unlikely character of his boss, Charlie, a usually gruff, reticent individual. One wet Friday afternoon in the Mornington pub, they'd overheard two young blokes bragging about their sexual conquests.

Sitting down with two more beers, Charlie had said quietly to him: 'That sort of blokey talk is just bullshit, take it from me, Dive. I know I'm no Romeo, though I be Italian, but I do know how to satisfy Mrs Silvagni. She love our sex life and love me too. Shit, in a caravan park near Mildura one night, I had her groaning and shouting so loud, next morning the neighbours asked if she have an attack, or a snake in the bed. Fucking snake! Jesus, Son of Mary, I laughed. A big one! But, seriously, Dive, sex is about *both* of you enjoying, coming, err … off, you know what I mean. Wait for her, wait until she is satisfied too, and she love you forever. Remember that, young Dive, when you get a nice sheila. Don't mention to anyone now … Especially Mrs Silvagni.'

And, difficult as it was, Dave had waited for Catherine, until together they had groaned and thrashed on their joined single beds. Now, at breakfast he wondered if *their* love making had disturbed the neighbours. He wanted to giggle.

Catherine must have read his face. 'David, I feel as if everyone is watching us. But, for once I really don't care.' Surreptitiously, they looked around the bright, busy cafe, expecting to find all eyes upon them. But instead, people were quietly starting their day – businessmen and tourists, alone and in groups – reading and chatting, eating and drinking.

With breakfast finished, Catherine produced a festival map and placed it between their empty plates. 'David, Cheryl has a long-standing hair appointment, with nearby HERS Salon, booked for 9.15 this morning.' She pointed at the map. 'See, only a few blocks from here.' Her finger continued onto the back of his hand. 'I do want to look more *with it* for you. Should I take the booking?'

Surprised but pleased to be asked, he agreed, and within 10 minutes they were looking at the imposing red letters, HERS, in a salon window on Hanover Street.

'I'm sorry, David, but I realise now this may take a few hours. New clothing, perhaps, as well.' She dipped into her bag. 'Here are the Morris keys, if you wish to drive to a museum, or perhaps a gallery.' He accepted the bulging bunch. The keys to Glendaruel, indeed, all the keys to her world, were there.

***

A glamorous girl guided Catherine to a secluded chair in the otherwise busy salon. She then arranged for a cup of tea, glossy magazines, and some towels, and stayed a few minutes *to help you settle down, Missus*. Next, the girl explained how she held the significant role of welcoming first-time customers. Although perhaps over-confident, especially with that only marginally-suitable Afro,

Catherine decided, the girl carried her responsibility with ease. As she, herself had done once.

***

The throaty growl of a sports car intrudes into the welcome quietude of the mid-week morning. It's our first full Spring day – bright and clear, with the country lanes now enlivened by flowering white hawthorn and minted myrtle. So lovely to be alive. And one knows this is only the first week of April, with months of warmer, brighter weather ahead. Indeed, as we discussed last evening, this year, 1950, indeed the new decade, holds so much promise of renewal, of regeneration after so many years of destruction and distress.

A well-dressed middle-aged couple soon appear at the office counter – him notable in a tweed flat cap, she a cream silk scarf – sports car types. 'Good morning,' I begin. 'May I help you?'

'The Gifford Castle Golf Club?' the man asks. I nod in reply. 'Our name is Murray – from Musselburgh.' There is a pause, which I suspect is to encourage some indication of recognition.

Instead, I offer my working smile and a polite 'yes?'

Mr Murray clears his throat. 'Well, we're here about the Great Triumvirate rematch the club is holding next month. Is the Club Secretary about?' He looks past me into the office.

With Mr Wood still in bed, perhaps under the weather, I know the form. 'He's over at Dunbar for an inter-club meeting. May I help? I'm the Assistant Secretary. Acting Secretary today.'

The man smirks and leans forward on the counter. I sense his assured manner. 'Well, a female Secretary! Unusual.' I retain my bland look. Behind him, Mr and Mrs Douglas across from Aberlady have completed their early round and give me a wave as they leave. I wave back, beaming.

'Do ... do you have something printed?' Its Mrs Murray, and I understand she is quite shy, or dominated by her husband. Or both.

'Aye, of course. The rematch is the highlight of our spring season.' I give them a green and yellow pamphlet from the neat stack

75

at the side of the counter. Our own triumvirate of Mr Wood, Mrs Stillie and I have had considerable fun putting these together.

Should I further shock these two by revealing how it had been my idea to organise the rematch?

Friendly hubbub fills the lounge. It's the Davies party from Culross Estate arriving for a 10am tee-off. They returned to the club after the full restoration of the clubhouse, and now play most Wednesday mornings. Organising those renovations had been my first project as Assistant Secretary. I call from the counter. 'A cup of tea before you start, Mrs Davies?' I know she and her guests enjoy being indulged. She grins an affirmative.

Mrs Stillie's antenna is well tuned this morning, for she soon appears with a tray of hot refreshments and arranges them on the Davies' table. Returning to the kitchen behind the office, she glares at the Murrays, but gives me a quick wink.

'Now, remind me. Who were the Great Triumvirate, Miss?'

I explain how Scotsmen Harry Varden, John Taylor and James Braid between them held the world golfing Open Championship from around 1890 to 1910. In 1921, I add, the then Club Professional, and our current Secretary, Mr Angus Wood, had made up the foursome for an historic triumvirate game played at the club. And almost thirty years later, they have again agreed to a rematch to help save the Gifford Castle club. 'And lucky they'll be to get away with their reputations intact again,' Mr Wood had quipped as we had selected the most suitable original photograph to include in the advertising.

'Are you both keen golfers?' I ask.

'No, it's my father, Major Murray – a life-long player. On our way to Berwick for a ceremony and so told Father I'd call in.'

'Ah ... excuse me, Miss. May I take a second pamphlet?' Its Mrs Murray, and I feel for her, as my own shyness only lifted some months earlier. I give her an encouraging smile.

I have about five minutes before the next booking arrives – a new group to be registered and given the tour. Time to finish it.

'Tell the Major to ask for me, Catherine, when he arrives.'

He didn't see her at first. The busy salon, deceptively large inside, was loud in both human hubbub and psychedelic shades. Haughty hairstyle posters adorned the white walls, and chatting staff and customers crowded around hair driers and mirrors. He hoped to remain unnoticed as he took a furtive step inside, as if an apprentice lion tamer on a first solo run.

But the pride had noticed him, and they turned his way, leering. An angular woman in her thirties with outrageously coloured hair and clothes, and an accent to match, came forward. He felt her deep, penetrating eyes appraise him, as if he was to be her next meal.

'You are David, then; I'm Nonie McKenzie. We've expecting you, aye.' A hesitation. 'Almost ready, and bonny she is.'

Moments later, a tall, elegant woman in a bright-green patterned shift separated from the crowd. It was her, stunningly transformed. The long auburn hair, now gleaming, bouncy and curled below the shoulders, a leather shoulder bag, a touch of make-up and an intriguing perfume completed a younger and more fashionable Catherine.

'Well, what do you think, Davie?' Nonie's eyes still held him.

He had trouble finding words. 'Ter … terrific. She … looks … terrific.' Thank goodness he'd dressed in his Jenners' clothes.

'Och, is that all you can say to describe this beautiful creature?'

At a nearby tea shop, they ordered, sat down and, like over-excited sports fans, began talking simultaneously. They stopped, laughed out loud, then took each other in. Dave waited to let Catherine speak first.

'What a wonderful experience,' she eventually said. 'Those women at HERS were *so* helpful, *so* friendly and with *so* many clothing connections. I now understand why Cheryl visits there whenever in Edinburgh.' She stared out the shop-front window as if to study the busy traffic outside. 'I've been out of life too long, David. Cooped up at Glendaruel. Frozen in time.'

She gave a cautious smile. 'Now, be straight with me. How do I look? Really?'

He said it immediately. 'Hon … honestly, Catherine, you look … gorgeous.' And he meant it. In just a few days, he'd seen the intimidating, older widow become a gawky, insecure lover with striking hair and eyes. And she'd transformed again, now into an elegant, attractive thirties-something woman. He felt really happy for her.

'David, I suspect you are biased. Please explain *gorgeous*.'

What does he say? 'Your … your dress, hair style and perfume, suit … suit you. *Really* suit you. The colours and … and …' He stopped as an intense girl in white, possibly not long out of school, brought their drinks.

It was difficult to put it all into words, for he could see now that Catherine held a natural elegance, earlier hidden behind Mrs MacAdam's gruff exterior. He waited until the waitress left. 'Younger … look fashionable, and … and happy. Yep, happy.' He smiled awkwardly. 'Your … your legs … look good too.' Did he sound like a perve?

Blushing, Catherine leaned forward to run a hand along one shin. 'David, thank you. Don't think anyone has admired my legs for a long time, apart from Sergeant Major, of course.' She lowered her voice. 'Well, I'm wearing pantyhose. For the first time.'

Pantyhose, eh? It was like being let into a deep female secret.

'David, you are so good for me – for my confidence. Do you realise it's you who has given me reason to dress like this, to want to change? But it's more than that.' Her hands were on his arm. 'Some of those women were envious of me when you came into the salon, looking so smart.' She beamed. 'Thank you.'

They chatted until Catherine touched her watch. 'Drink up, David. Sorry, time to go. Beethoven, at Leith Town Hall in 30 minutes.'

He felt ready for anything – stage play last night, now classical music for lunch. Yet, getting to his feet, he understood that unremitting urge to catch the Isle of Wight rock concert the following week remained. Roll over Beethoven, as Chuck Berry would demand.

The solid woman behind the counter punched the cash register, then fixed her eyes on Catherine. 'You are so bonny, Missus. My daughter here has been admiring you. Especially your hair. She has the length, right enough, but she has to earn some money first. You tell her, now.'

While Dave paid, Catherine smiled solemnly at the young waitress. 'It's true what your mother says. When you have the money saved, take yourself to HERS Salon, just along the street here, and ask for Nonie. She'll look after you.'

'There. If you won't listen to me, take it from this modern Scottish woman.'

Exchanging glances, they left the shop.

***

Reluctant to leave Edinburgh before evening, they parked the Morris down behind the Old Town and returned to the Castle-Lawnmarket area, now buzzing with tourist groups, incessant live music and clashing culinary aromas. The afternoon was warm, yet to Dave, Catherine looked cool in her new outfit, its tones and style blending easily into the colourful crowd.

'I'm sorry you haven't the chance to tour the castle grounds in daylight, David.' They had begun moving down the Royal Mile. 'So much to see there, and clear views out across the city to the River Forth. We must visit it next time.'

He stopped, and like a diligent tour leader spoke aloud to be heard above the din. 'So ... so, you think there ... will be a next time?' However, an unexpected lull in the clamour of the crowd around them gave his words a barked, brash tone, like a doubting, throwaway line – not at all the friendly, affirming statement they had meant to represent.

She turned quickly, her face a question. 'Well, um, ... I hope so, David. I ... Don't ... don't you?' Those hazel eyes, so recently sparkling at the label of *modern Scottish woman*, now implored an affirmation.

Reacting quickly, despite the pressing crowd, he pulled her into his long arms, then held her face and kissed her, and kissed her again. 'Yes, I … I do, Catherine, I … I really do. We have to make … make sure that we do. Sorry, it came out all wrong.' He continued to hold her; his face buried in that wonderful hair.

'I so hope we do too, David.' She was barely audible.

They stayed together as one on the cobblestones of the Royal Mile, people, and music surging about them. Until they were jostled sideways, almost into a nearby shop window. They giggled together, but Dave remained annoyed with himself. Was she angry?

'Och no, David.' Smiling, Catherine straightened her hair and shift with as much exaggeration as a film star.

Grinning both with relief and at her pantomime, he relaxed against the shop front. Yet, an irritation remained. An unrelated urge still pricked at him – *the rock festival.* Yep, he was enjoying the fringe benefits of their relationship – the good company, his new clothes, the sex, and … and considerably more to come, as suggested by the six dozen frenchies he'd discovered in their luggage last night!

But he still hadn't fully committed himself to her. One original reason for coming to the UK had been to attend a rock festival, and the *New Musical Express* had described the talent line-up for the Isle of Wight next weekend as the best ever assembled. He didn't want to miss it. Until a few moments ago – until he'd seen that vulnerability in Catherine's face. That look which said I've sent Mrs MacAdam on her way, *Dearvid*, but I'm going to need your help with this. I've now put my faith in you. Totally.

It had jolted him. He now understood he alone was responsible for her happiness, whether he liked it or not. If he left Catherine now, it will no doubt crush her. That newfound attractiveness he was so drawn to, was no accident – it was because of him, she'd said so in the tea shop, but it was also *for* him. For a woman of her background to walk into that beauty shop and, as Nonie related, explain to strangers she had a young boyfriend she wanted to look smart for, would have taken a lot of guts.

Sure, he wasn't responsible for how things had worked out, but hey, did it matter? What had Ric done after Dave's dad had gone?

Moved in to take responsibility for his suddenly widowed daughter and three fatherless grandchildren.

'David, you are so quiet.' She was touching him, holding him.

'Yeah ... sorry, Catherine. Day ... daydreaming.' He was emotionally choked up, but he couldn't tell her that. 'I'm fine. Cool. Could ... couldn't be better. Um ... home?'

'Not yet, David, I've one last surprise.'

Oh, oh.

***

Drinks in hand, but this time oblivious to other pub patrons, they again inspected themselves in the Abbotsford mirrors.

'Well, I still appear older than you, David, but we have reduced the obvious differences, would you say? My complexion has improved, both from Nonie's rouge and a touch of sun. And this lovely frock and my wonderfully styled hair certainly make me appear more fashionable, and thus younger. I certainly feel younger than my 38 years.' There, she'd said it, and with the elation not felt since a young bride, she took his hand and squeezed it. And in doing so realised she now could squeeze him as often as she liked!

They discussed the maturity his new clothes had given him, and how they now appeared more relaxed together. She was trying to be adult about all this, as if one of them should remain so, but her happiness was now so splashed about.

She smirked. 'Aye, I begin to understand that people don't really care what others do, within reason, but it has to look right. It has to please their sensibilities, if you like. We must have seemed an odd couple on Friday!' She absorbed his answering grin; so magnetic! 'But hopefully, not so *odd* now. Many couples have the inner strength to ignore what others think. David, we must just be patient.'

Bloody hell, could the new Catherine be patient?

Now sipping her wine, she watched him nod in agreement. Still a serious young man, but a very special young man. An hour earlier, he had said *home*, meaning Glendaruel. Home together! Gosh, what was happening?

81

6.

Perhaps the riotous yellows, oranges, reds, and browns of Dave Lawson's first European autumn had been deliberately splashed about to heighten his physical and emotional senses. Perhaps he and Catherine had returned from Edinburgh in their own enchanted fairy tale, set in the wonderful world of Glendaruel. Perhaps they over-absorbed themselves in exploring the estate and each other, picnicking and catching the autumn sun with Sergeant Major in tow, lying in bed for hours talking and caressing, having sex or food when the desire demanded, reading books, or writing letters up on the tower or poking into disused rooms and forgotten spaces of the big house. Perhaps, unwittingly, they were postponing the inevitable post-Edinburgh clash with reality.

In those early weeks, while Dave wafted about this bewitchingly romantic cosmos, Catherine found she was, for the first time, actually discovering and enjoying her bridal home of nearly 20 years. When she and husband James had moved into Glendaruel, it had been his mother's home, and, until the old besom died, she had reminded Catherine of it every day. Now, on one hand, she was desperate to tell all of southern Scotland of her bursting happiness.

Yet, the only person Catherine knew she could admit into their secret, apart from Cheryl McCann in Hawick, was Mrs Duffy in the gatehouse. An eccentric octogenarian, she had lived her own fairy tale; arriving at Glendaruel in 1912 to marry the young, handsome estate forester, within two years she had lost him to the Great War, yet later gave a measure of God-motherly protection for Catherine from the evil mother-in-law.

The young Australian's life in general and focus in particular had changed so dramatically since he landed in Britain that at times it was too difficult to absorb. As if suddenly, he'd been picked to open the batting for Australia! The initial thrill of travel and adventure that had brought him halfway around the world had been supplanted by an intense sensual relationship with its delicious surprises.

Moreover, he now had a companion he felt he could trust. At first, it was both the sex and her acceptance of him that so boosted his almost non-existent self-esteem. The grand house itself, and the titillation of the *Mrs Robinson* situation also played their part. Yet, in contrast to the famous screen seductress, he understood Catherine's mature exterior masked considerable vulnerability and self-doubt.

Later, as her crusty demeanour further fell away, and Mrs MacAdam became a very distant relative who was never expected to visit again, Dave came to understand that Catherine's needs and desires – nurturing, acceptance, fulfillment – were very much like his. It was as if each of them was starting out on new lives – together.

But, what for Dave made Catherine so enjoyable to be with as September stretched into October, was her increasing approach to him as an equal. She seldom played the older adult, or more experienced, or gentrified role that another in her position might have assumed or may have fallen back on when pushed. Nor did she attempt to be a pseudo-youthful Carnaby Street-type counterpart.

Yet, here she was, in her established family estate, a paid-up member of the Scottish gentry and somewhat older. Despite her now rare fits of doubt or anger, he felt comfortable with her. As colder weather found them increasingly inside together, Dave came to understand that their relationship had moved on from the glaring yellow of mutual infatuation to more temperate tones.

On a practical level, they both were kept busy. Dave found plenty to do on an estate suffering from years of neglect. Despite a certain grandeur, both the house and the wider estate were down at heel, and he came to see repair or maintenance problems that Catherine couldn't. And, fixing those leaky window frames and broken roof slates, and mowing lawns and tending to the overgrown gardens of Glendaruel enabled him to justify his continued existence there.

For the present, with Pauline accepting the work transfer they'd organised after returning from Edinburgh, Catherine took over her duties, while continuing with the ongoing community obligations somewhat expected of her, though with reduced time and enthusiasm. And she came to enjoy shocking social contemporaries, as increasingly did her youthfully-styled clothing and hair, and new John

Lennon glasses, as someone commented, at the St George's Harvest Thanksgiving service in late September. Moreover, the few visitors that came to see Mrs MacAdam now risked being met by a modern version in Levi jeans and one of Dave's flannel shirts. As did the Reverend Donald Bullpit, whose middle-aged libido must have been aroused by the unexplained change in deportment and poise at the kirk of the esteemed Mrs MacAdam. Over tea and scones in the sun-filled parlour one stimulating Tuesday morning, he was unable to complete his prepared speech about setting examples for society, or to totally hide indication of his physical attraction to her.

Some evenings, Catherine and David delved into old gardening books for ideas of future planting in the walled garden, or propagation in the repaired glass house. Often, Catherine would set off for her social obligations with lists of repair materials and tools, or seeds, to buy.

Yet, although now busy and highly contented, Dave began to contemplate a proper job somewhere; bar work perhaps until he found some landscaping. He explained his need to remain economically independent, although he still had Ric's travel money, but Catherine's concern was for privacy. Glendaruel, she argued, would provide, and later he could help with its running. By mid-autumn, the only cloud on Dave Lawson's happy horizon was the unexpected deaths of pop idols Jimi Hendrix and Janis Joplin, and the understanding that by missing the rock Festival in August he'd foregone the opportunity ever to see the famous guitarist in the flesh.

7.

Today's sudden cold, wet weather had them both inside, David starting on those collapsing Victorian-era shelves in the laundry and Catherine finally facing the much-needed de-clutter of the big house. She had begun in the morning room, now seldom used, when the hall phone rang.

Following the call, she returned to the room to think this out alone – the first major hurdle in her new life. That it was William Boyle who had just rung to say he was on his way to Glendaruel made it doubly difficult. An old K.O.S.B. chum of James – indeed, present when her husband was killed in Singapore – William had visited Glendaruel over the years, sometimes helpful, often obsequious, habitually nosey. She had never quite known how to take him. Or whether to trust him. But now, of course, David was here … Bloody hell, she wasn't prepared for this. Not yet.

The thought took her to another dismal day, in spring 1960 – two years into her widowhood – again waiting in the morning room, again in an anxious state. The second of William's visits.

***

With relief, I hear a car arrive outside. That'll be them, the solicitors. Hell, here goes.

However, once out on the front steps, I find a stranger, grey suit, plain tie, road map in one hand. Someone lost? 'Oh, hello. May I help?' Now, the face is familiar.

'Mrs MacAdam, it's you! I'm sorry for the intrusion, but I'm trying to find …' The voice holds uncertainty. Light rain has begun again.

'Oh, Lieutenant Ball, a surprise! My apologies, I'm expecting someone …' The boyish face, some Glasgow in the tone, he had

visited Glendaruel with the sad circumstances of James' death in Singapore. Two years ago?

'It's Boyle, Mrs MacAdam, ex-Lieutenant William Boyle.' He begins again. 'I'm so sorry to disturb you when you're busy. I'm actually looking for Cairnhall.'

I'm sharing a cup of tea with Mr Boyle in the kitchen, fulfilling a sense of obligation. One ear remains on duty, listening for McCrindle's vehicle. Mr Boyle has explained in detail his metamorphosis from military officer to real estate agent. He now asks of my widowhood, but I don't wish to discuss it – crushing, of course, but kept too busy to miss James really, not that he was ever much at home. K.O.S.B. battalion duty always called. So, I raise the topic which I suspect is puzzling him. 'Well, as you may notice, Mr Boyle-'

'Call me William, Mrs MacAdam.'

'Oh, sorry, ... William.' *I don't wish to reciprocate with first names, however.* 'You will have noticed some changes since your previous visit.' *I indicate the unwashed breakfast dishes beside the sink, the clothes drying around the combustion stove.* 'My first tasks after you leave. The staff have been let go – we more or less fend for ourselves now. Welcome to the modern world, eh?' *At least they were paid, I want to add. I've had no money of my own since James' demise.*

'Oh, I am sorry to hear this, Mrs MacAdam. Am I able to ask why?'

'Well, . .' *I stop. Should I open up to a relative stranger? Ah, well.* 'Death duties.'

William offers an apologetic face. He finishes his tea, then nods, as if having reached a decision. 'Would ... would it be possible to pass my regards personally to Mrs MacAdam senior? I remember her as a kindly, matronly woman.'

I find myself staring at him. Are you joking I mentally ask? There is nothing kindly about that old harridan – especially toward me, her son's widow. Indeed, never having approved of me, with my vast list of insufficiencies, she has made my life at Glendaruel a living hell. Especially, since James ... Of course, she blames me for that as well.

86

William is watching me, waiting. 'Oh, no,' I say, recovering. 'She never sees visitors, now. As you would imagine, she was totally devastated by James' death, so soon after that of her husband, the colonel. And now other matters ...'

You've said enough, Catherine. *'Now, William, you were in search of Cairnhall. Well, turn left at Burnhead ...'*

The growing growl of a vehicle halts further conversation, as might a wailing police or ambulance siren. I rush to the rain-flecked window facing the carpark.

'Oh, it's the solicitors. Finally!'

'I'd better be getting along then. Thank you ...'

My visitor. How to keep him out of the way? Up in the house, the front doorbell dings with indignity.

'Wait, please, William. Mr McCrindle and his son are here to consult with Mrs MacAdam. Just give me a moment to organise this.'

He nods a reply. 'Of course.' Relieved, I turn and head up into the house proper, calling for the Conagher woman, the old lady's cunning companion.

'That's done then. They're settled into their business.' I'm back at the table with William. 'Thank you for your understanding.' I reward him with a smile, although I cannot dismiss the feeling he has had a look around downstairs. His eyes are still wandering. 'And I am pleased you called today.' Aye, I have enjoyed the distraction of his visit from the day-to-day drudgery of Glendaruel.

'Me also, Mrs MacAdam. I've always felt a deep duty towards your husband James, for he took me, a young national service officer, under his wing. That duty also includes Mrs MacAdam and yourself.' Is this a genuine sense of obligation I wonder? *'Now, my firm is one of the largest in the Lowlands. If I can ...'*

'Thank you, no. Done and dusted, as they say.'

He stands up to leave. 'Without meaning to intrude, Mrs MacAdam, you haven't thought to move on yourself? Back to your own family in ...'

'Milngavie. Well, I can't really. You see, I'm now the owner of Glendaruel.' I don't add that McCrindle is up there now, explaining to the Old Harridan why she cannot challenge British Law. And why the bank accounts must be transfered into my name. Today.

'Oh,' he says, perhaps as surprised as initially I was at the news. 'Are congratulations in order, then?' The grin is back.

'Thank you, no. It is proving to be a burden, and legal matters are still to be concluded.'

I lead him out through the back door and around to his well-polished sedan. Perhaps sensing better times ahead, the sky is attempting to clear. William seems deep in thought and is not really that interested in my directions for Cairnhall after all.

William's last visit had been some weeks before David's accident – early June? She couldn't remember much of it, another blur in that period of her lowest ebb – loneliness, deep depression, alcohol. Of course, since then the man had totally slipped from her mind in the whirlwind exhilaration of her new life. However, William was an acquaintance who had offered help at times, and so deserved some sort of explanation for this colossal change in her life. And hopefully, he would give her relationship with David his blessing. But she hadn't mentioned it to William in that short call. Hadn't known how to. Well, he'll be here soon.

'David!'

***

Shaking off the rain, William Boyle opened the back door into the servant hall. 'Catherine, it's me!' What'll she be like today? Tipsy again? Still moping? He moved into the kitchen expecting to find her alone and needy, but instead she and a tall, skinny young feller were organising crockery on the table. A workman? 'Catherine, who's this?'

She answered, startled. 'Ah … William! How … how nice to see you. We're just preparing some morning tea.'

We?

'Um, this is my nephew, David … from South Africa. You know of my sister, Victoria. Well, this is her lad. Quite … quite tall, like his father.'

The solemn boy offered his hand. As if he'd never done it before, William thought.

'Yah … Yah,' the boy began. 'I'm Dave … David. Nice … nice to meet you, man.'

Boyle gave him a strong Scotsman's shake. 'I'm William Boyle, a personal friend of your aunt. Welcome to Bonny Scotland, if I'm not too late.'

The boy's reply was a stupid grin.

'William, you are wet, and no doubt cold. Stand near the combustion stove while I get you something.' Catherine went out into the laundry and returned with a wide, striped towel. 'Here. Now, a cup of tea?'

The Scotsman began drying his hair. 'Thank you, aye.' Hmm, she's different today.

When finished, he sat and watched her pour the tea. Time to take charge. 'What's that bloody noise?' He pointed towards the radio on the shelf above the stove.

'Led Zeppelin,' said the nephew as if he, William, would appreciate this. Never heard of 'em. Never likely to, aye.

'Turn it off! Never heard raucous Radio 1 playing in this house before.'

'So … sorry.' The boy reached up and quietened it.

That's better. Accepting a piece of chocolate cake from Catherine, William wondered what had happened to the soused, depressed woman of the previous year or so. Something not right … Aye, her hair is out, and down, quite bonny, mind, like the old days, before … she'd banished him from Glendaruel. Before old lady MacAdam died. 'Now, Catherine, beautiful as ever … but more colour in your face … quite …'

She gave that silly grin again. 'Well, we've been out seeing the sights, eh David? – Edinburgh, Glencoe, Dumfries.' The boy nodded away like a puppet.

Hmm. Is her improvement because of the boy's visit, to stop rumours reaching his mother? Or …? And why is he here? Find out. 'What brings you to the UK, Lad?' She'd mentioned nothing about family visitors on the phone earlier. Or in June. But he'd been unable to visit since then – always so bloody busy at the pub now, with Elaine … with Elaine gone.

'I … I came for the cricket. The … the England tour of South Africa … cancelled and … and wanted to see D'Oliveira and Sobers.'

Does he have a speech problem? William wondered. Anything possible in this family.

'And … and, yeah, to visit … auntie here.'

Right. A few questions will sort his story out. 'Laddie, have you visited your mother's family home yet?' A deliberate pause. 'Edinburgh, isn't it?'

'N … no, I think … Milngavie. Auntie Cathy?'

'Aye, Milngavie.' She's nodding away like an idiot. 'Not yet.'

'Laddie, she doesn't like to be called Cathy. It's Catherine.' Boyle watched them both for a reaction. But nothing. 'So, what have you been doing since the end of the cricket season? The last few months?'

'Yah … well, the Isle of White Rock Festival in August. That … that's why …' He pointed towards the radio. 'Then, I went onto the Continent. First to Paris, so … so much to see. Then, Rome, and … and West Berlin.'

'Fine. Right, stop. We don't have all day.' Christ, thought William, he can't string two sentences together. Makes you wonder how he can travel alone. 'Well, we hope Bonny Scotland is one of your favourite places, Lad. So, which one of the many bedrooms at Glendaruel did you choose to sleep in?' He asked the question as if it really didn't warrant an answer.

The lad turned and pointed towards the old studio outside. Ha, she's put him outside there! Can understand with that 'effing stutter! 'Close … close to the fridge … man.'

'Now, Catherine, driving in I noticed considerable garden work along the driveway. Also, some touch up painting on the front windows.'

'Och, that's David here – a landscape gardener. Bonny work, don't you think? And he's repaired that troublesome front doorbell too!'

You're jokin', William thought. He had to stop all this. Such maintenance work undermined his little plan for bloody Lady Catherine and the estate. That toilet blockage, the electrics short upstairs, the car engine too, all were problems created to make himself indispensable. And they'd also bitten deep into her bank balance as expected. Cousin Jimmy at the bank had confirmed this.

She and the estate were now his for the picking, and he'd come today to set up their future – together. She had no choice now but to come across – in more ways than one! So, warn this nephew off.

William downed the last of his tea. 'Look, Laddie, there's no need to spoil your holiday working at Glendaruel. I attend to any maintenance requirements, here. So, just relax for the remainder of your stay.' He offered an affectionate face. 'Now, returning home soon?'

'Yah … yah, time to book. Getting cold in Scotland.'

Then the boy stood up. 'If … if you don't mind, I'll split. Afternoon nap. Nice … nice to meet one of auntie's friends.'

'And pleased to catch up with someone from Catherine's family at last. Quite alone here, with no relatives now in Scotland. Inform your mother William Boyle is keeping a strong eye on her sister.' He wanted to demonstrate some of that we're-all-family shite. 'Now, away with you, Lad.'

They shook hands again. That's a better one. Harmless enough. William watched the boy leave the kitchen and waited for the outside door to close.

***

Catherine stood watching David asleep on the bed in the studio, Sergeant Major, as usual, up beside him. William's visit had quite unsettled her, particularly his assumed position in her life. He had never really articulated this before. Or had he, and she'd somehow missed the signs, when … when she'd been under the weather.

91

However, today she was sure he hadn't noted anything amiss, and David had done as she'd asked – gosh, that South African accent! – despite the man's aggression.

She closed the studio curtains on a darkening world as David began to stir. She sat on the bed beside him and the cat. 'Darling, William's gone now. He stayed for more tea and remained inquisitive about your presence here.'

'He … he seems okay … suppose. Bit up himself, though. Who is he, again?'

'An old military chum of James.' She briefly explained William's early connection to Glendaruel until around 1962 and how, about two years ago the visits had begun again. Today was the first time he'd rung first, she understood. But, why?

'Darling, listen. I cannot remember ever feeling so happy, so contented as I am now.' She ran a hand through David's hair. 'Yet, there was a time, not all that long ago when I thought I'd never be happy again. That may sound somewhat melodramatic, but for me it was real enough. Mrs MacAdam, James' mother, was a cantankerous old bat, but for some years she was my only company, and my final connection with James. Her death, soon followed by that of my own parents, left me suddenly alone and frightened; frightened of the loneliness, but equally of the responsibility.' She waved a hand towards the house. 'I was left with an estate to run, and … and a prescribed societal role, that of the landed widow, the new MacAdam widow. I had had no preparation for any of it.'

'When William reappeared after some years, I had already slipped into a desperate state – frightened, depressed, and drinking to allay that fear. Thus, initially I was pleased to see a familiar face, which I now understand William interpreted to suit himself.' She ran a finger down Dave's nose. 'However, thanks to you, Darling, I am now back to normal. Better than normal!'

'What … what does he do? Where does he live?'

'He runs a pub over at Galashiels in Selkirk. Quite a way from here, thank goodness. He has been married, I think, but is always vague about these things.' She raised her hands together, as if in prayer. 'David, there's something unnerving about him, like his questions to verify your story.'

'An existing admirer, eh?'

She wasn't amused. 'Please David, don't joke about this. I've always had reservations about the man. He acts the concerned friend of James to maintain a connection, I'm sure. Aye, he can be helpful, as when the Morris broke down, and … and with those electrical problems last year. Yet, he has the propensity to be over familiar, like today. And I sometimes wonder if it's me that interests him, or Glendaruel itself.'

'But … but, surely once we make it obvious to everyone that we … you know.'

'Aye, I understand that's the problem in front of us. I know I should have said something today, but …' She hesitated, concerned. 'But William Boyle is a special challenge, as I do believe he could be ruthless.' She kissed David's forehead. He, she knew, offered positivity, stability, the future – William, in contrast, was negativity, pain, the past.

8

'Why is no one living here?' Dave asked. 'Not big, but … but seems solid enough.' She watched him gaze around the empty, but undamaged interior of Wright's Cottage.

'This and two other cottages situated behind the walled garden of the big house, Darling, became vacant in 1958 when the estate and it's staff shrank dramatically.' But, why indeed, she concurred.

The cheery, early November morning had offered Catherine an opportunity to try David's Yashica camera, capturing the last of the autumn leaves in the wood. They had wandered across the broken bridge towards Wrights Cottage that faced the Dumfries Road when a rain shower caught them. Abandoning that early cheer, they had rushed into the cottage for shelter.

Catherine later rang reputable estate agents in the district, and they acknowledged an ongoing need for good rural accommodation. During dinner, she proposed a scheme to David to repair the three empty cottages to prepare them to rent, which would enable him to contribute to Glendaruel's land-rent-based economy yet remain largely anonymous. Catherine's calculations suggested Glendaruel would gain almost £1000 profit from the project in the first 12 months. This convinced him this was more than a token project. In the days following, she organised legal and financial arrangements, which necessitated a trip to Glasgow.

Within a fortnight, all three cottages had been inspected and priced to repair, and building warrants and tradesmen organised. Then, work began. An irritating phone call days later from William Boyle, ostensibly to say he'd broken his leg in an accident, failed to deflate Catherine, and she and Dave's combined excitement at the progress of the project work remained. Most external cottage repairs were completed before wintry weather moved the focus inside, where Catherine helped out with painting.

They were exhausted some evenings, falling asleep while watching the television. That their love making now took second place only acted, for Catherine, to make it even more special.

***

It was drizzling outside, and Dave and Tom King were sitting on paint drums inside one of the empty cottages behind the big house. He had come to like the stonemason, his careful work, his gruff humour, and was pleased the man had stayed to enjoy the Friday afternoon crate of beer. The other two tradesman had left after a short while, but Tom seemed in no hurry.

He grabbed another McEwans and pointed it at Dave. 'Aye, you'd have to be bonking her, you would.'

Initially stunned, Dave felt the man's eyes holding him, teasing. 'Wha … what do you mean? Who am I bonking?' He attempted a man-of-the-world grin.

'Her! The lady of the big house – Mrs MacAdam. Your *auntie*.' The words were drawn out in accusation. 'C'mon, Laddie, I didn't come down in the last shower. It's all over yer faces, and she's a woman transformed. Last year when young Tommy and I repaired the front steps of the big house, she hardly spoke, and we never got so much as a cup o' water. Now, it's good morning, Mr King; how is Mrs King; more cake Mr King? And,' he leant forward, 'you've both got yer initials in that bit of leftover concrete we laid in the sun garden!'

'Um … I …'

'She's in love … with yooou.' He leaned forward and poked Dave in the shoulder with his now half-finished bottle.

'No, you're making a …'

'And you're no more one of them South Africans than I am. You're a fuckin' Aussie. You sound Aussie. Like Rolf on the television.'

A sudden voice made them both turn. 'David! Darling, have they gone?' Catherine appeared through the back door, cleaning rags in one hand, and stopped when she saw the two men sitting together. 'Oh, Mr King!'

Despite the working clothes and long hair held back with a faded scarf, she still looked attractive, and Dave could see that Tom thought so too.

'Afternoon, Mrs MacAdam.' Tom raised his bottle. 'Young Davie here is just telling me about life in Johannesburg. Aye, plenty warmer than chilly Dumfriesshire, I'd say.'

'Oh … yes. My sister always says so.' She looked towards the front door. 'I'm … I'm sorry to disturb your refreshments, Mr King, but I thought I'd heard your vehicle …'

'That'll be wee Tommy backing it up to the other cottage to drop off the mixer. Drink up, young Davie, and we'll help him off with it.'

'Mixer?' Dave was puzzled. 'But haven't you finished your work here?'

'Aye, but *you* haven't. You'll be needing lots of cement for the render repairs there we talked about, and for all that drain work too.' He downed the last of his beer and stood up. 'Come on now. Tommy will be waiting for us.'

'Mr King,' Catherine spoke as the men headed towards the front door of the cottage. 'Thank you. It's very thoughtful.'

'Your nephew's okay, Mrs MacAdam. He's not afraid of a challenge.' He slapped Dave hard on the back as they went out through the doorway. 'Any challenge!'

9.

They stood together on the edge of the pavement, the suitcase between them. A small, weathered sign, *Hotel Ches Marie*, was on the frontage that faced them, the second of four buildings wedged together in the small grimy block.

Could be the start of a cheap horror film, Dave thought, taking in the tired facade. Even the shuttle bus had quickly left, as if reluctant to be seen here. He felt Catherine's disappointment as she leaned in closer. Then, as if to forestall any thoughts of escape, a chilly Paris wind scooting down Rue Lepic, drove them into the tiny, dingy foyer of Hotel Chez Marie.

***

The receptionist behind the counter peered up from a fashion magazine. Almost grudgingly, she acknowledged their booking query with a curt '*Passeport?*' Catherine took in the hair, of similar length and style to her own, but any resemblance ended there, for this young woman looked pale and underfed. When she stood up, her cardigan hung from her thin frame like a much-used hessian sack.

The booking-in formalities were performed in silence. Then, the receptionist crashed a large room key with an even larger brass name tag onto the chipped counter, as if to further underscore a general reluctance to have them at her establishment. 'You have a booking for four nights, *oui*? Your room is on the third floor, Monsieur Law-son and Madam … err, Madam MacEdam.' She barked out the information.

'MacAdam,' said Catherine, leaning forward.

'*Oui* … what I have said – MacEdam. I will return the passports after. The hotel bar, and the restaurant – there.' She pointed behind them. 'Luggage?'

'Of … of course.' Dave nodded down towards the suitcase.

'Hmmm …' The woman seemed to doubt him. 'The lift is not operating these days. You will use the stairs. You will want romantic city tours and other attractions, hmm? This hotel can organise such. The brochures – there.' She thrust a hand towards an untidy collection of pamphlets and maps spilling out of a damaged wooden stand near the front door. '*Merci.*' She sang the word, and returned her attention to the magazine, still open in front of her.

'Welcome to Paris, Madam MacEdam,' Dave said as they began to negotiate the narrow stairs.

Cathy muttered. 'Not even a French cheese.'

Her humour didn't improve when they entered their hotel room. The bright, swirling wallpaper design was quite overwhelming in a small room. And it was peeling in places. A grubby wash-hand basin in one corner was the only indication of plumbing.

'Oh David, this is too much. I specifically requested an ensuite. And look at the state of the room. It's filthy.

Back at Reception, the young woman loudly declared her ignorance of the ensuite stated in their Christmas holiday package. 'Of course, the Hotel Chez Marie does not 'ave private bathrooms.' She spoke as if this deficiency was the latest in *chic*.

Catherine felt David's reassuring arm envelop her. He led her from the counter, and gently suggested they explore nearby Montmartre before dark; perhaps they could find somewhere more romantic for dinner. She nodded and gave a weak smile of thanks. Yet, she understood the state of the hotel had little to do with her agitation. But she couldn't yet bring herself to tell him the real reason for their sudden holiday in Paris. Or how it had been paid for.

***

Once out wandering the cobbled streets and steps of Montmartre amid French voices and language, Dave and Catherine began to experience the Paris they'd expected. With the aid of his guidebook, Dave found the nearby *Basilique du Sacre Coeur*, and they sat in its pews to absorb the ornate interior.

Outside again, they asked an American tourist to take their photo together near the entrance, and later, in the growing winter gloom, they watched the lights of Paris appear below.

They retraced their steps to the still busy Place du Tertre and browsed the art galleries and tourist shops. Soon, the evening chill and an enticing advert for hot chocolate in a modest café window drew them indoors. Settling at a table near the cast iron combustion heater, Catherine gave Dave another surprise when she ordered in French. The waiter left them with a '*mais oui, Madam.*'

'Hey … cool.' Impressed, Dave asked when she had learnt the language. Why hadn't she mentioned it before, or used it with Madam Grizzle-Guts in the hotel earlier?

'Hmm, she wouldn't understand me. I speak only High French, while she, of course, is a peasant.' There was that hint of a smirk. 'Further, you must call her Mademoiselle Grizzle-Guts.'

'Why?'

'Well, no wedding ring, of course, David. Which does not surprise me.'

'Oh … yeah.'

'To be honest, Darling, when we arrived at the hotel, I was tired and somewhat disappointed, as you know. Not a good time to trial my high school French. So, it was a surprise I was saving for you.'

Relieved to hear Catherine more cheerful, Dave scanned the austere yet intimate café to find they were a topic of conversation for the locals sitting at the high wooden bar towards the rear. A similar reaction had occurred that morning at Glasgow airport as fellow travellers took in the tall young man and his elegant older partner joining their flight. It didn't really bother him anymore.

Soon warmed in body and spirit, the pair drew comparisons with their Paris hotel room and the one months earlier in Edinburgh. Catherine leaned forward conspiratorially. 'Do we trust the cleanliness of the sheets and sleep *au natural*, – this is Paris, after all – hmm?' She raised her eyebrows.

Dave laughed. He was finally on the Continent, finally in Paris, and finally with someone who liked being with him. And he with her! And already, they had the buzz of shared memories and history.

For a history of sorts with Catherine had begun. Edinburgh, the cottages, their sneaky trips to the Dumfries cinema, disguised and entering separately, yet sitting together and snogging like teenagers! And now this unexpected but exciting holiday in Paris which would add to that shared history – become part of them – even the crappy room at Hotel Chez Marie. Especially the crappy Hotel Chez Marie! They'd laugh about it, later. And they'd had their first photo taken together!

'Darling.' Catherine took his hand. 'Being in Paris now is second time lucky for me.'

'Really?'

'Oh yes. Paris was the initial destination of my honeymoon in 1951. I had talked James into it, and I was excited. However, at short notice his regiment was ordered to Korea, and so the honeymoon became a few frantic, unromantic days in London instead. God, there's that word again – romantic, unromantic. That was my first taste of life as a military wife, and once hastily deposited at Glendaruel, I became the property of my malevolent mother-in-law.'

Catherine sighed, and sat quietly, sipping her chocolate. Watching, Dave felt a bubble of guilt. Though careful not to wallow in the confusions of his own life, he had come to assume other people generally led pleasant, uncomplicated lives. 'You ... you've never said about that, or Glendaruel. So much to learn about you.'

'David, we have so much to learn about each other.' She looked about the cafe before continuing. 'It's warm and comfortable sitting here, don't you think? So, what say we stay for the house soup and entrée, and perhaps some wine. And just continue talking – sharing – filling in the gaps so to speak. Like why you want to take me to a *terrific* film called T*he Wild Bunch* now showing at the ABC in Dumfries when we return.' Her smile slid into something saucier. 'And later perhaps – ahem – in the privacy of our wonderful bedroom, I may perform the Madam MacEdam adaptation of Moulin Rouge!'

Ha, another surprise. More and more he loved being with her. Was that love? Was that possible with an unpredictable woman almost twice his age?

10.

Their first Christmas together was special simply because they were in Paris. Catherine had studied the French Revolution at school, and after they exchanged gifts over the hotel's meagre continental breakfast, she led a rugged-up David on a loose excursion of relevant historic sites, despite most venues being closed. In a sense, it was a tour of the living museum of the Paris streets and gardens, still vibrant, despite the cold weather and this being the most august of holidays.

The Eiffel Tower is one of those world-famous landmarks that, no matter how well you prepare, always astounds when seen close up for the first time. Approaching it unsighted, both Dave and Catherine were finally confronted with the enormity of the elegant metal structure. The entirety of its blue-grey steel construction, still damp from overnight rain, glistened proudly in the morning sun, as if having carefully cleaned and preened itself for another demanding day of visitors.

Catherine left Dave in the queue for tickets, which despite the holiday was long, while she attempted to catch the tower complete in a single photo. It was no easy task she soon realised.

Sometime later a packed lift delivered them to the highest level open to the public. A cold but clear morning, thin ribbons of cloud still hung over the northern reaches of the city. Despite the noisy, excited crowd moving and gesturing on the viewing platform, they absorbed the expansive view of the city below them, taking photos and identifying the Arc de Triomphe, Champs Elysees, Notre Dame Cathedral, and other famous landmarks on their list. Before descending, she indicated the size of one of the many thousands of rivets that held the steel structure tightly together – its diameter was wider than her fist.

***

It was easy for Dave to describe Christmas at home, when Catherine later asked in a smoky cafe on the Right Bank. Until then, he had been reluctant to discuss what he considered was his humble family and home in Ti Tree Crescent, Seaford. Christmas Day, he explained, was the one time of year when his mother went out of her way with the cooking, and the Lawsons acted as a normal family. There was always a decorated tree, an exchange of gifts, a big roast and trimmings, steamed pudding with coins and brandy custard, bonbons to be pulled, and lots of drinks and genuine good cheer all around.

After dinner, on Christmas afternoons, and despite the unpredictability of Melbourne summer weather, Dave and his siblings would wander across the busy Nepean Highway to the beach. With Ric, they would unhurriedly set up a family base back from the water with the beach umbrella, blanket, folding chairs, and Esky. Around 6 or 7 o'clock, Mrs Lawson would find them, bringing a supper of dinner leftovers, cordial, and a surprise cake or slice, held back from dinner.

Catherine related Christmas stories too, of opulent meals, formal dress and expensive gifts, visits to other estates, but all, it seemed, with a large measure of ostentation, regimentation, and argument. For all the grandness of a Glendaruel Festive Season, Dave felt that they hadn't left her with particularly happy memories. Curious.

In the afternoon, standing just inside *Notre Dame de Paris* and facing the grandeur of its vast vaulted nave, Dave felt overwhelmed for the third or fourth time that day. Was this why he had stepped out of the relative comfort of Melbourne suburban life – to be humbled by history and grandeur? Yeah, the Tower of London, Westminster Abbey and other famous sites in London had been exceptional, stirring his sense of adventure in that first week in Britain.

However, he had understood the felt familiarity they had radiated – as if embedded in the Australian psyche, despite being on the other side of the world. That familiarity was absent in Paris; here he sensed he really was in foreign lands. Of course, language and culture would have much to do with this, and the few French people he had encountered so far had been standoffish. Yet, it was all so exhilarating.

102

Cramps – sudden, sharp stomach cramps. The psychedelic wallpaper – it was attacking him! Then, Dave woke in a sweat with more cramps. His watch said 11.13, but another bout of cramps prevented a return to sleep. Catherine, now awake, suggested an age-old MacAdam cure, whisky, and soda at the hotel bar. Lots of soda. And perhaps a second. He got out of bed, the cold jerking him into full wakefulness as he dressed. Before leaving, he kissed her forehead. 'You … you okay here alone?'

'Of course, Darling. Now off with you for that wee dram.'

There were still some people in the hotel lounge-bar. A wooden counter ran the full length of the room on one wall, while cheap metal tables and chairs were scattered, like grazing cattle, about the black and white tiled floor of the rest of the room. Apart from a faded advert for *Gauloises* cigarettes, he could have been anywhere. Even the background music was indistinct.

A heavy-eyed barman looked up. 'Monsieur?'

Dave ordered the whisky and soda and rode a few more stomach cramps until his drink was ready. 'American, Monsieur?' the barman asked.

'What? Um … no. Australian.'

He had begun a cautious sip when the voice interrupted. 'Hey, Aussie.' Turning, he saw three young women sitting at a near table looking his way. One had a hand raised. Surprised, and unsure, he gave a hesitant smile. She called out. 'Come and join us, if you're on your own.' He took in her long blonde hair and easy manner. Another Australian?

He paid for the drink, and riding more cramps, walked over to the threesome. Well-rugged up, the girls were sharing a carafe of red wine.

The blonde girl spoke again as he approached. 'You were in Scotland, in … in Aberdeen, I think. In June, at the youth hostel.'

June – youth hostel – another world, another time. 'Yeah, that's right.' He was baffled.

'You had a mate with you, right? He here too?' She pointed to an empty chair. 'Hey, join us for a Christmas drink.'

'Thanks, yeah, Um … Merry Christmas girls.' Sitting down, he lifted his drink, and they returned the gesture. 'No. Lost him along the way. Were … were you three together then – sorry, can't remember.' He sipped the whisky, as his stomach cramped again.

'No, with my hopeless boyfriend from home, Gazza. Funny how things seem different at home. We three all met on the Kontiki tour later, after I'd ditched him. Best thing I ever did, hey girls.'

'*Yayyy!*' They sang out together, which brought back more pleasant memories. Wonder what Gazza had done?

'Hey, like your Guilomine beads. They're so hard to get.' Pleased they were noticed, Dave grinned, masking yet another cramp.

'Stop talking, Trish.' Another girl spoke. 'That's Trish chatting you up. I'm Rosemary and this is Pam.' Pointing at Pam, she leaned in towards Dave. 'Pam's a bloody Kiwi, but don't say it too loud or we'll get kicked out … . Again.' She finished with a snigger. Kiwis always copped it. He could feel the travel memories returning.

'Shut up, Rosy. Jeez, you go on.' Pam, a friendly, dimple-faced girl, pushed at her friend. The three were obviously comfortable together.

'I'm Dave. Dave Lawson.' Another small cramp.

'Where you from, Dave?' asked Trish.

'Melbourne.' He hadn't said that for quite a while. 'Your … yourselves?'

'I'm from Wollongong.'

Rosy was next. ' Ya know, Wollong–bloody-gong. I'm from Perth.'

'Perff,' Pam giggled.

'Been in Paris long, Dave?'

'On … only a few days. And you?'

'Arrived yesterday afternoon. You staying in the hotel too?'

'Yep. Bit … bit rough around the edges, though.'

'Jeez no, it's okay.' Pam looked around the bar. 'Been in lots worse, hey, girls. Like that grotty place in Granada. Half the bus had the shits when we left. Funny, everyone you talk to says how great Granada is, but not great to have the shits in. You been there, Dave?'

'No … not yet. But have had the shits a few times.' No more cramps, and he was relaxing.

They all laughed together. 'Hopefully not right now!' More laughter. 'So, where've you been since Aberdeen? God, that's six months ago. I remember you because you were so tall and quiet, and your mate was such a wanker. He thought he was so cool, but the girls in the hostel there just laughed at him. Mr … um, Mr Available, they called him. Something like that.'

Dave nearly choked on his drink. So funny to hear the vain Picko described like this. But what does he tell them? He hadn't had to give a rundown of his travels, or of Catherine, to anyone until now. Would these girls understand, approve? They were waiting, genuinely interested to share stories, experiences. He finished his drink.

'Better a tall, silent bugger than … than an available wanker, eh?' They laughed again, and he told them about the night they'd been all locked out of the hostel at Fort William after a folk concert, his unexpected tour of Burns country and waking up in Dumfries hospital days later.

He wanted to tell them about Catherine, their easy relationship, and his happiness. But somehow, this was left out, as it was still in letters home to his family. He felt guilty enough about that extra travel money from Ric that was being used on anything but travel. So, as a diversion, he described the Edinburgh Festival and Fringe, and lied about working in Scotland to save for next summer's travels. This quick Paris trip had been a spur of the moment thing, he added, but again omitted Catherine.

As they sympathised over Dave's ruined travel plans, Pam topped up wine glasses and found another for him. Then began a series of silly stories of the Kontiki tour on the Continent. God, he missed this; yarning and drinking with other travellers, with little or no judgement made. Instant mateships, based on minor shared experiences, and often with people you never saw again. Sitting there, enjoying the company of these chicks, he was surprised at the level of envy rising within him.

He laughed again as they described a comic incident at the Hofbräuhaus in Munich – so different to how a bloke would have told it.

He was still laughing when a separate voice, a separate tone, joined the Kontiki cheer. 'David.' It didn't fully register.

However, another utterance moments later did. '*David*!'

Riveted, he spun around. Catherine was standing in the doorway of the bar. She must have thrown some clothes over her night dress, for her body shape seemed all wrong, and her hair was only half up – or down.

'Who's she?' Trish asked.

There was a hush in the room as Catherine gravitated to their group and stood, staring down at them. Long strands of hair were stuck to her face. She looked tired.

He heard Rosy snigger. He wanted to slide away under the table.

'David, are you coming back to bed?' The clarity of her voice drew all eyes in the room to them. Then, as might the top model of a classy couturier catwalk, Catherine turned, lifted her head, and strode from the room, sucking out all conversation.

11.

While earlier planning the Paris trip on the kitchen table at Glendaruel, the mention of a visit to the famous Palace of Versailles had really excited them both. Now inside its historic halls, with Catherine seething, silent and separated from him, Dave was left in a dejected shuffle behind the gregarious guide and his attentive tour party, as they explored expansive corridors and rooms of overpowering ornateness and stately splendour.

As with the morning Seine cruise and at the Louvre, she'd kept her distance from him, and every minute suggested this stupid quarrel would not end well. What happens when they return to Glendaruel? Would they return, or might there be a separation at Glasgow airport? Or at Orley? The very thought frightened Dave, yet equally within him was a rising sense of injustice.

The tour leader turned right into a vast, extended chamber and stopped, his tour party milling about him as might chicks around their mother hen. 'Ladies and gentlemen, take in this area if you can! The famous mirrors in this hall, all 350 of them, have witnessed many …' The guide began another enthusiastic speech, detailing the decoration about them. Dave watched, but took little in, his mind churning over other significant detail.

Sure, he had stayed a while at the bar. Yeah, he had accepted a drink from the girls, but no, it hadn't been planned, and no, he hadn't intended to pick any of them up. God, until then he and Catherine had had such a terrific time in Paris. Yet, she wouldn't listen, wouldn't even talk about it now. Suddenly their intense four months together counted for nothing, and she'd reverted to the Mrs MacAdam of earlier times. No doubt she'll call it all off. Perhaps she already had.

'Sure is a reflection of opulent times, ain't it?'

'Sorry?' Surprised, Dave looked around to find an older man grinning up at him.

'I said, sure is a reflection of better times. It's a joke, buddy. Get it? Reflection – Hall of Mirrors?'

107

'Yeah, sorry … miles away. Yeah, good one.' Dave's focus remained elsewhere.

The old man tilted his head. 'English?'

'Sorry? No, Australian.'

'Long way from home, son. Name's Ralph – from Florida, US of A. Been to Europe twice now, but never Australia.'

'I … I'm Dave.' He hesitated. 'From Melbourne.'

He took in the American, shortish, solid, around Ric's age, he guessed, with eyes to match the bright personality.

'Damn nice to make your acquaintance, Dave. Hey, did you come in through Orley?' The young Australian nodded.

'Did you notice the new terminal being built there for the arrival of those new Jumbo Jets? I read somewhere they'll carry 300-400 passengers – my God. Pumping more boring old folks like me into places like this.' He looked around. 'I watched you get on the bus this morning.'

'Eh?' Dave straightened.

'Um, well … I've become an old nosey parker since Stella went. But I mean no harm. We don't get many interesting people on these tours.' He indicated the group around them. 'Most of these folk here are old and boring, or old and rude, or … or, well, all three!' He gestured again. 'You do wonder why they leave home.'

'Oh.'

'So, when I saw you both board the bus –'

'Both?'

'Yeah, you and that attractive dame over there.' Ralph indicated Catherine, poised on the edge of the tour group, peering up at an ornate chandelier the guide had described. A moment or so later, she turned towards the two men, and produced a weak smile.

'You know, everything was right about you both, look so good together, classy clothes, out there, y'know. Yet, it was obvious the two of you were hurtin.' Something wrong, Ralph Amigo, I told myself. Something small got 'em going, I'll bet.' He glanced again at Catherine. 'But, buddy, you've got real taste.' Had Ralph said it aloud on purpose?

'Shhhh!' People around them hissed.

***

Catherine, while still riding a fug of righteous indignation over the previous night's events, had begun to experience an all too familiar sense of loneliness. Thus, she felt relief to see David and a well-dressed stranger smiling her way. So, when the group moved forward, she waited. However, as David introduced his acquaintance, she was determined to remain piqued, for just for a little longer. 'Hello,' she said.

'Pleased to meet you, ma'am. Enjoying the Palace? Quite something, ain't it?'

Catherine nodded, and together they followed the group out of the Hall of Mirrors.

Ralph began again. 'My second visit here, but on my own this time, damn it. Cancer had been eating away at Stella for years, but she never said. We did everything together, you know.' He stopped and refocused on the two of them. 'As I'm sure you both do.'

Catherine looked away before answering. 'I'm so sorry. It must be very lonely for you now.'

'Damn right it is. And I was angry with her for a long time until my son and daughter told me to shape up. Now, they make sure I'm generally fine, as do my pesky grandchildren, who are of great interest to me. Do you know, young Duane began at Johns Hopkins last fall, and … Oh, I'm gabbling on, and here we are in one of the most famous palaces in the world. Sorry, folks.'

Again, Catherine felt that cold loneliness of pre-David times in her bones. 'No, no, I understand.'

The three continued behind the tour group into the resplendent Queen's Bedchamber. The guide ahead listed the famous royal wives who had occupied the room, and as if national pride was at stake, he gave emphasis to those who had produced an heir within its over-ornate walls.

109

Catherine spoke, perhaps expressing what many in their group were thinking. 'That *is* difficult to imagine, the room being so opulent, so busy. The ornamentation, the gold …'

'Well, no doubt, inspiration behind the decor was to take their mind off things.' The American's response made her smile. 'Hey, did my hotel use the same decorator? The room is so … so brassy! Like the wallpaper is gonna take possession of me! Or eat me!'

Catherine smiled towards Dave. 'Aye, we know the feeling. Our wallpaper too. David?' They shared the grin, extending it to welcome each other back.

'Shhhh!' Again, people near them turned and glared.

Ralph beamed about the room in general. 'Well, no doubt this is the perfect bedroom for the ultra-rich. Not that it did 'em much good, ultimately.' He waved a hand across his neck, then looked at Catherine and Dave individually. 'I do hope you folks have an ideal bedroom at home. It is so important to a relationship. No sleeping children, no work desk – just humping, and a wink of sleep to regain your strength.'

Embarrassed, Catherine looked across at Dave who had found sudden interest in the parquet floor.

'Shhhh.' Again censure. Again, Ralph grinned and shrugged his shoulders at those near them.

Their final destination in the Palace building was the Salon d'Apollon, another chamber of overwhelming décor. Here, Catherine noticed Dave stop at the gilded portrait of King Louis XIV, the sun King, as if to honour the man who had initiated the world's most celebrated landscaping – the famous gardens. Now relaxing into the lavishness and complexity of Versailles for the first time that afternoon, she linked her arm into Dave's, and felt him squeeze it to his body.

'Is our bedroom ideal, Darling?'

That boyish grin. 'Course it is.'

She wanted to apologise, but he began, again. 'We should get outside to the Gardens before they close. Join us, Ralph?'

The surrounding crowd answered instead. 'Shhhhhh!'

110

12.

It was already late one morning in the new year, and they hadn't moved from the warm kitchen – nor Sergeant Major from the basket next to the wood stove. They were looking through photos from Ralph of the Versailles Gardens when the phone in the servant hall rang. Catherine answered, as was normal, then called to Dave. 'Darling, a stranger has appeared at the gatehouse, and Mrs Duffy is concerned he may be injured. Perhaps there's been an accident. I'll go immediately.'

Probably dangerous out there, Dave decided. 'No. I'll go.'

'But it's my responsibility.'

'Catherine, I'll go. Free … freezing outside. And, any problems, it's better I'm there.'

'Yes, but this is my …' He was already in the servant hall reaching for his coat and scarf, hanging near the back door.

'Well, be careful, Darling. Remember the television reports of black ice on the roads.' He waited as she reached up and pulled the thick knitted beanie over his ears, kissed his cheek, then opened the back door.

The bent, diminutive figure of Mrs Duffy, almost hidden under a bulky hand-knitted shawl, opened the front door. 'Hello, Master James. Certainly an icy start to the New Year.'

Dave grinned as she led him inside the gatehouse. While a measure of acceptance to be mistaken for Catherine's long dead husband, it never ceased to be a little spooky.

'He's in here, he is.'

In the small parlour was a thick-set man in a lounge chair shivering like a malaria sufferer, despite the cheery electric heater at his feet. 'Hello, I'm Dave.' He sat next to the stranger. 'Can we help you?'

The man turned, as if unaware of others in the room. 'Err … yes, perhaps you can. I … I seem to have lost my way.' Dave's first impressions were of tidiness and sophistication: refined speech, soft accent, trimmed beard, dark blazer, and matching trousers. Around 40-45? Yet, the man's eyes were troubled and the face florid, tiny red veins obvious on the nose and cheeks. Above the right eyebrow was a broad, reddened graze at the point of bleeding. Wet knees too. Had he fallen? And no coat in this icy weather?

'You … you seem to have had an accident – your head.'

'Have I?' The man raised a hand to the grazed area. 'Yes, painful, but I'm so damned cold.'

Dave made a decision. 'Mrs Duffy, could you phone Miss Catherine at … at the big house, and inform her we are coming. Say about 5-10 minutes. Ask her to prepare hot drinks, some soup perhaps.'

Dave returned his attention to their visitor. 'Mr …?'

'Rollo, Mungo Rollo.'

Do … do you think you can walk, Mr Rollo?'

'Well, if it's for the best, I'll certainly try.'

'Great. I have a car here. We're close to the big house. Be there in no time. Warm … warm you up with something hot. Okay?'

'Splendid.'

Dave smiled at Mrs Duffy, now at the telephone. 'Well done for taking him in.'

She twisted towards him, as might a disturbed bird of prey, receiver in one thin talon-like hand, her sharp little face at an angle. 'Och, nothing at all, Master James.' The tiny eyes held him. 'Aye, this reminds me of the time when Mr Nicol's leg was crushed by the harvesting machinery. The young colonel was making arrangements, just like yourself now.'

'Oh? And what happened to … um, Mr Nicol?'

The eyes swooped upon their unexpected guest. 'He died, of course.'

'Hmm. Encouraging, that,' mumbled the stranger.

***

Catherine rang Dr Black, the MacAdam family physician, who explained he was marooned in Dumfries by the sudden icy conditions across Britain. He did suggest, however, their distressed guest may be suffering from hypothermia or concussion, or both, and should immediately be put to bed.

This she did, and later, she went with Dave to find the man's vehicle in icy Burnhead Lane – a Triumph Stag no less. Hard up against a stone wall as if still hiding from a hunting party, the wounded white Stag was scraped and dented, its battery exhausted. Together, they coaxed the vehicle into the safety of Glendaruel's vehicle shed.

Now, some hours later, entwined on the couch watching the evening news with a warming glass of port, they were surprised when their enigmatic visitor opened the drawing room door.

'Oh, sorry to disturb you.' Mr Rollo did seem embarrassed as, like a pair of canoodling teenagers, she and David slid apart. 'I … I've woken up in a strange house, and unsure where to find anyone, I've followed the television sound to its source – and *voila!* But again, my apologies. Should have knocked first.'

Recovering, Catherine rose and switched off the set. 'No, not at all, Mr Rollo. Please come in and sit yourself by the fire.' They had put the man to bed in a pair of her late husband's red-striped winter pyjamas, and now with him also wearing the winter coat found in the Triumph, he could have been heading out to a fancy-dress ball, she decided. Yes, a big man, not as tall as David, but big bellied. Likes his food and drink.

David had pulled a lounge chair closer to the low flames, and their guest sat down, arms spread on the high, wide rests like a confident king on his throne. His face had regained human colour.

'Thank you. But you must call me Mungo.'

'Mungo it is then. Are you feeling better now, Mungo?'

'Well, on a physical level, my head still throbs, and I do feel a little weak. However, on an emotional plane, I am quite embarrassed

113

to discover you both know who I am, but I have no idea who either of you are. Or where I am, and why I am in your good company.'

'Well, you certainly look far better than after your car accident, Mr … sorry, Mungo. My name is Catherine, Catherine MacAdam and this is my … this is David Lawson. You are at Glendaruel Estate, twelve miles north of Dumfries along the A76. Now, would you like some tea – coffee perhaps? And are you hungry?'

'Pleased to make your acquaintances, and quite fortunate to have done so, it seems. Weak black tea with the smallest of sugar would be most welcome.'

Catherine left the room and returned some minutes later with a tray of refreshments. Pouring tea, she explained how Doctor Black had rung back, but while pleased to hear of Mungo's recovery, he had advocated the man remain the night at Glendaruel, staying warm and off the icy roads.

Their visitor offered a smile of embarrassment. 'No, no. I must be getting along. I dabble in antique documents and was driving to an auction in Carlisle. Foolishly thought I'd miss the icy conditions by taking back roads. Ha! But mustn't stay. One, Alex may be worried, and two, I don't wish to impose on your hospitality any longer. You already have been most kind. Perhaps, though, I could have that cup of tea first.'

Catherine stared at the teapot still in her hand, as if having spotted a leak. She then caught David's eye, who nodded. 'Mr Rollo, Mungo, it is certainly no imposition on me … on us, if you stay here tonight.' She put the pot down. 'Indeed, we insist. It is almost 7pm, and the icy weather hasn't improved at all. And, although you may feel fine, we cannot allow you to drive away on dangerous roads in your condition, and at night. You must stay here.' She finished with an open, beaming smile of welcome. 'And please feel free to use the telephone to inform your family. At least that is still working.' Was he uncomfortable with accepting charity from others?

'Well, you are very kind. And as you are so definite, perhaps I should stay. Sensible really. And I should inform Alex of my whereabouts.'

She took their visitor out into the cold hall to the phone on the table under the half colonel's portrait. 'Thank you,' said Mungo, and pointed up at the painting. 'Does he eavesdrop?'

She did want him to feel welcome, so she indicated toward the front door. 'Och, no. It's the panther you have to watch.'

***

At first, they found it difficult to ignore their visitor's presence in the house, tiptoeing around their bedroom and bathroom as if he was sleeping next door, and not at the other end of the second floor. Once in bed, they didn't immediately reach for each other as on other nights.

Dave eventually thought to speak. 'Interesting bloke.' He had liked their unexpected visitor.

'Darling, I'd feel better if Mr Rollo had asked questions of us. I'm left wondering what he really thinks.'

'Me too.'

'His business involvement with antique documents is unusual. Yet, must be millions of them stored in dusty places around the world. In this house, for example. And also, those documents relating to early Australia, he mentioned no doubt for your benefit, perhaps wishing to share something with you. As if he was already an acquaintance of yours.'

'Yeah. But is it that obvious I'm an Aussie?'

'Oh aye, my Darling, it is.' Under the blankets, Catherine abruptly rolled over, almost on top of him, her face now close to his. 'As Australian as a cuddly kangaroo. To we Scots, Australians seem amazingly free of the class strictures that permeate Scottish, indeed British society, even though Mr Wilson, Mr Heath and other leaders may deny this.' Lying passively under her weight, Dave felt his pyjama jacket being unbuttoned. 'Indeed, Mrs MacAdam has told me that it was your social innocence, or was it freedom, she said, that initially drew her to you.' Soon, fingers were playing with the hairs of his bared chest. 'Amongst other things.'

'Ca … Catherine?'

115

'Quiet now, Darling. As we spoke with Mungo tonight, it somehow registered that I see myself less and less as Mrs MacAdam. I am not yet exactly sure who has taken her place, but the new persona, the new me, is someone I do feel comfortable with. She is a person I like. And I do hope you like her too.' The fingers were now softly tweaking one of his nipples. Hey, this was new – and – nice.

Christ, other fingers were on the move, exploring downward, to his stomach, and now further on towards his groin. His body stiffened, but it was difficult to react further, Catherine and the heavy winter blankets were upon him. But did he really want to?

God, she's never done this before. Apart from that first time, she'd left him to take the lead in their sex life. Traditionally a man's role, and with traditional positions, James, she said, had told her. And she'd never experienced a proper orgasm before meeting Dave, assuming it too was restricted to the male species. Now, it was once or twice a week! Although obviously enjoying their sex, she'd initially been embarrassed at what she said was a demonstration of her loss of control, or lust. I prefer lust, he'd answered.

But she was talking again, almost a whisper. 'It's a strange experience to catch yourself in the act of … of, changing … altering dramatically. Regaining one's youth, perhaps. And it is you, Darling, who has given me reason to.' The fingers had begun a slow teasing tour of his crotch, his erection enlarging. He could only lie there.

'David, we've been together now for five wonderful months, but today, this evening, I felt we became a proper couple, a team, if you like. Confronted with Mr Rollo's sudden appearance, we acted together, despite our preference to remain anonymous. We played our separate roles quite naturally, and without discussion we did what was necessary, and it seems, did it well enough.'

The fingers were drawing small circles on his balls, the side of her wrist rubbing up and down his hard cock, electrifying him. Somehow, Catherine's toes were pushing-pulling his pyjama pants down – now around his ankles. His feet seemed tied; his body was pinned. It was building like a campaign. The fingers were back again, now up and down, up and down his erection. Would he blow early? C o n c e n t r a t e.

Then, with one sudden movement, Catherine pushed off the blankets and straddled him. And he could only lie there, as her body searched for him, then exhilaratingly enveloped him.

He could see her dimly above, shaking that long hair out like an unashamed teenager. She bent forward and kissed his mouth, and those magnificent tresses cascaded over his head and shoulders, sending more sensual jolts to his crutch. Then, she leant back, and with one deft movement, dragged her nightgown off over her head and flung it away into the darkness. He reached for her breasts, quivering with enticement above him, as she began, slowly at first, to move. Then, as if part of a practiced dance routine he took hold of her hips until his rhythm blended with hers, and together they began, slowly at first, to thrust and heave.

'David... oh, David, this is so, so...' It was building. 'I... I've never felt such... ' He was close to climax himself. 'I... am... am... ah, ah, ah, ah!' He further grasped her, to quieten her, to comfort her, to further entwine with the woman he loved. Yes, he understood, as spasms of pleasure further ripped through him, that he did love her – he had known that for a while. But now, now, it was okay to say it. Say it, Dave. But, his raging sensations peaked, and he began to ejaculate violently; again, and then again, pounding paroxysms of pleasure, it seemed for minutes. Until the 21 years of boyhood had pumped out of him.

Later, they lay together, quietly caressing each other. With her head nestling into Dave's neck, Catherine eventually spoke. 'I feel I've found my former self, a much younger Catherine, if you like. Now, just now, is the happiest, the freest I've ever felt.'

'Me too.' He grinned into the darkness. He knew he grinned a lot now. Hard to stop, really.

13.

Weak sunlight had penetrated the kitchen windows when Mungo found Catherine and David preparing breakfast. 'Ah, this certainly is a house to encourage one's senses,' he declared. 'Last night twas the sound of television that guided me down through your vacuous home, and this morning it's the sizzling smell of breakfast that's drawn my nose to the kitchen!' Outside, it looked as cold as the previous days, but that touch of brightness did reflect how considerably better he felt.

Catherine turned from the stove. 'We thought to let you sleep as long as possible. Hungry?'

'Certainly. Haven't really eaten for 24 hours.' He hesitated. 'Not that I really deserve to, after yesterday's debacle.' He found a place at the table, busy with breakfast things, and with an imploring look grabbed young David's arm. 'Please, please tell me my Stags is still alive!'

His hosts exchanged grins. 'Only if you eat your breakfast, now,' Catherine replied, and placed a full plate of bacon, eggs, tomato, and toast in front of him.

Mungo was intrigued by these two, an unlikely pair alone in a down-at-heal estate. She, an attractive widow, late 30s perhaps, and he a very tall young man from the other side of the world. Yet it was obvious they were happy together, and, reminded of his own quirks, he was reluctant to pry further. He began to eat.

Despite the warmth of both the kitchen and company, Mungo eventually felt the need to get on, so suggested he should check the Stag. David found both their coats and led him outside into the silent white world. Crossing the frosted sun garden, Mungo took in the considerable landscaping work begun there. He stopped and pointed. 'Someone has been busy.'

'My next project,' the young man answered, as if unsure.

'Hmm. What's your overall plan?'

Young David began to explain about expanding the garden area, while preserving its intimacy. He then pointed out, among the lines and pegs, its future boundaries, garden beds and pergola site. Perhaps even a small summer house, he added.

'A big job then.' Mungo was interested.

In the vehicle shed, with its battery recharged overnight, the Triumph started easily. Mungo also was relieved to find it drivable, the crash damage only superfluous. He grinned. 'So well done, young Davie. Now let's take the Beast for a test run.'

They drove out from the rear of the house, and down to the gatehouse. Upon return, they found Catherine, rugged-up and grinning down on them from the front steps, Sergeant Major at her feet, as if on guard duty.

'Despite the scrapes, it's a sleek motor car, Mungo. You must be proud of it.'

'Well, I was until yesterday, Catherine. Let me down somewhat. Grounds for trade in, would you say?' He got out and leaned on the roof. 'No, I'm very lucky to have such a beast. Alex always calls it my beast, no doubt with its raw power and the Stag moniker in mind.' He looked across at Dave with an exaggerated beaming face. 'Or could it be the beauty and the beast analogy?'

Mungo watched the pair laugh together. He liked them both: friendly, generous but modest. Practical too. 'Now, before I take my leave, I have a question.' He pointed to the disturbed flower beds around the front of the house, either side of the wide steps. 'You've had some serious garden work done; I see. Particularly behind the house where we walked earlier. Who is supervising you, David?'

'Only me.' Catherine joined them beside the Triumph. 'No, my clever David does it all himself, all his efforts and ideas.' Now Mungo laughed as she quickly grasped her young man's hand and lifted it high, as if presenting a new racing car champion to a rapturous crowd. Sort of gesture he'd make himself! 'He has also renovated the estate cottages,' Catherine added.

The older man chortled again, as Dave, obviously embarrassed, tried to free his hand, but without success. 'It's not much, really. Just

… just formed the beds, turned the soil, and planted some shrubs that can survive the winter.'

But Mungo had a special reason for his query and persisted. 'Yes, perhaps that is true for this, here. But I could see how that sun garden work will be a large project before it is completed. What's your overall plan, Davie? What are you trying to achieve?'

***

For Dave, unexpected questions usually triggered a stuttered answer. However, these five months with Catherine had injected confidence into his thoughts, his speech. So, he took a deep breath and in landscaping terms learnt at Burnley College, he explained how the general garden area surrounding the house needed definition and development. An attractive, historic house required this; indeed, it deserved it, he explained. Beds full of bright flowers and blossoming shrubs would transform the relatively plain front steps area into a memorable first impression for visitors.

As part of this greater plan, he wished to separate and beautify the sun garden behind the house where, with some thought, the sun might be enjoyed all year round. He stopped to find both Mungo and Catherine looking at him intently.

'My man, I have a strong feeling you've done this before. Am I right?'

'Well … not in Britain.'

'Interesting stuff. Renovated cottages, as well, you say?' He seemed momentarily in thought. 'Now, must go. It's still frightfully cold, isn't it? I thank you both again for your speedy action yesterday, and the kindness and hospitality since then. Including that smooth single malt last evening, and the bursting breakfast, Catherine.' He tapped his sides. 'I do hope we meet again soon, if only for those unforgettable pyjamas!' He shook hands, then climbed into the Triumph, and with a final wave drove off.

They stood there, hand in hand, as the car disappeared, its exhaust fumes holding in the still air.

120

14.

(Yeppoon, Queensland – 30th December 1999)

It was almost dark when Maggie Lawson found her husband. He was in the workshed. 'Come on inside, Sweetheart. There's lasagne almost ready and I've opened a bottle of our favourite Merlot.' She led him back to the house.

Once Dave had showered and was seated at the long table in the dining room, Maggie raised her glass. 'Now, Terri rang to say she's down in the town buying alcohol, so we only have about 20 minutes to sort this lawyer business out.' She smiled at her husband. 'But first, Sweetheart, let's drink to a successful Millennium do tomorrow night. *Cheers*!' She sipped the wine.

'Cheers,' he replied, but with little noticeable enthusiasm.

'Dave, today's phone call seems to have given you quite a shock. I don't need all the details now, but what's it about? Why such a negative reaction to what might well be a windfall for you?'

'Maggs, um … to be honest … it … it's really difficult to talk about. There are things I'm… I'm…' He stuttered to a halt. 'Can we just leave –'

'No, Dave.' She interrupted him, glaring across the table, the use of that pet name clawing at her. Was he being honest, or fobbing her off? It didn't matter. 'No, Dave, I've left *it* with you all afternoon. I've prepared one of your favourite meals, and I think I deserve an answer to this silly mystery. And before visitors start arriving!'

She prodded her lasagne, waiting, her anger rising with no response. 'Now I discover you've kept secret a letter that appears to have arrived weeks ago. Sweetheart, what's going on? If it wasn't that this Kat person seems to have spent all her life in the UK, and is now officially dead, I'd be justified in suspecting you of having an affair.' She decided a joke might help. 'Sister Liz said I often called out Mick

… Mick Jagger, in *my* sleep! But you've never mentioned a Kat, a Kat Cale.'

But he didn't smile. 'Christ, Maggie, you know I've never been interested in anyone else. No … no need to worry on that account.'

'Well, that's reassuring, Dave. So, simply tell me about this Kat Cale.'

Again, she waited. What *had* happened before they'd met? London and Paris, he'd mentioned a few times, but never Scotland. And this Kat Cale was Scottish – and famous. She's on the Web!

'Dave, Sweetie, this is not you – you, who are normally so solid, unflappable. Remember Darwin? And the problems with your mum's sudden death? Later bringing Ric up here from Melbourne? All these you took in your stride.' She sipped the expensive Merlot without really tasting it, her eyes, all senses, focussed upon him. 'Is this about a fling while overseas years ago, a silly fling that you're now a little ashamed of?'

His loud, loaded answer caught her out. 'No, Maggie! There wasn't a silly bloody fling. Fuck, what a thoughtless thing to say. Just like your stupid father, telling everyone I couldn't produce grandchildren for him.'

Maggie thumped the table, glaring back at him. 'How dare you swear at me. I agree Dad was as tactless as a yacht without sails. But that doesn't give you the right to shout and swear at me. Don't you understand how all this looks? Secret letters hidden in the bloody shed. And a relationship with a woman, no matter how long ago, you *did* not, and … and *will* not tell me, your wife, about.'

'Maggie! I'd thrown the bloody letter in the bin!'

'Shut up Dave, and-' The unmuffled rumble of an arriving car interrupted her. They exchanged knowing *here-she-comes* looks.

'It's Terrible Terri. Listen, Dave. You'd better get your story ready for the lawyer tomorrow, as no doubt she'll demand straight answers too. As will Terri, if she gets a hint of it. Now, let's go out and meet her.' Maggie offered a half grin. 'At least *she* speaks openly, if sometimes too often.'

They soon had their niece at the table, and with more wine opened caught up with her news. They answered her questions about the following night's big party, including available young males, and discussed some predicted negative outcomes to the millennium end. The topics, the chat was all rather formal and mundane, until Terri put up a hand.

'Stop. Stop!' She looked at them both. 'C'mon, you too. You're my favourite relatives…' She hesitated. 'apart from all the others.' A grin, another pause. 'So, what's going on? It's like we're three upturned turtles on a beach, brooding over how we're gonna be cooked!' Again, she scanned their faces, but got no reaction. 'What is it? What are you not telling me?'

Maggie scowled at her husband, prodding him to talk. 'Dave?'

'No, nothing, T T,' he eventually offered. 'Just a bit tired. Long … hot day in the garden.'

Maggie sighed, anger building again, then made a decision. She looked at her watch. 'Look, *Death in Brunswick* is on the TV at 8pm – about 15 minutes time. Terri, I know you wet yourself over Sam Neill, so go and grab a cold shower. And put your stuff in your usual room. Dave and I'll quickly clean up.'

In the kitchen with the dinner dishes collected, Maggie grabbed her husband's arm. 'David, I love you very much, but I'm not going to be lied to. Keeping me in the dark all these years, but particularly now since the lawyer's call, is the same as lying.' She squirted detergent into the sink water with emphasis.

She looked up, her eyes holding his for a moment, pleading for some sense. 'Do you know, Dave, the irony here is that tomorrow you may be rewarded handsomely for your deceit. Well, I don't want any part of your newfound wealth, if that's what it is.' She then stalked out to the kitchen, and deliberately made lots of noise tidying up the dining room. Yet, she was more worried than angry.

***

With a glass of wine to quench the angst, Dave moved to the study and sat down at his desk in the dark. He felt really bad about losing control – swearing at Maggie like that – just like the old days, the bad old days of the crap about his father's death and his mother blaming

123

him, when losing control was normal. Seemed normal. Maggie had brought him back to life after Darwin. She deserved better.

Out through the window he made out lights, perhaps the resort on Great Keppel Island, or some keen fishermen out in the Coral Sea. He envied their isolation. He heard the television go on in the lounge, and pictured Maggie sitting there with Terri, pretending to be interested. In here, he somehow was caught up with reruns of *Death in Scotland*.

Then Terri's voice boomed through the walls: '*C'mon, Dave, it's starting!*'

He ignored her, and eventually switched on his desk lamp and CD player. An Allman Brothers disc was ejected. He stood up to select something from his large music collection on shelves above the desk – a lifetime of CDs, tapes, and vinyl records – his one luxury. It was all there: from Bill Haley to Blondie; from Leadbelly to Led Zeppelin – decades of playing and listening. Except for the early '70s.

His eyes somehow focused on a CD he'd been given years ago – one he'd never played. Well, not since … Scotland: J.J. Cale. He looked at it again – and then a rush of memory, as if from a mental sluice gate, made the connection to Kat Cale and his past, that ponderous past. Naturally.

But why die twice? Dave again asked the universe. And he felt, as if in answer, something huge break loose inside his head, like an office block-sized iceberg splitting from a coastal glacier. He groped for support, then slumped back into the swivel chair.

Recovering, he spoke aloud, as if those fishermen out in their boat needed to understand as well. 'No, Maggie. The irony of all this is not what happens tomorrow. The irony is that Kat Cale's recent death is solid confirmation that I didn't kill her back in 1972. After all!'

And that's what he just couldn't come to grips with – why he couldn't talk about it – the letter, today's phone call, all arriving after so many years, after decades of guilt, of shame, of self-persecution. To be informed without ceremony, without warning, that you hadn't killed someone ages ago after all, was momentous. Really, really so hard to grasp, to believe, like the ceaseless and convoluted evolution of the planets that that TV professor had tried to explain the other week. Like escaping death bloody row.

But, the growing relief, the sense of release, didn't make it any easier to face the lawyer tomorrow. It didn't absolve his reprehensible behaviour back then. What does this woman know? What will she say? Will she be finished before guests start arriving? He reached for the wine.

15.

'*Catherine! Where are you*?' That distinct barking voice – loud, clear, demanding.

Still in bed on a listless late-winter day, Catherine and David sat bolt upright. 'God, that's William Boyle! Only he has the gall to come inside before being asked.' She quickly got up, Dave joining her at the open bedroom door. Down through the polished balusters of the staircase, they saw his thickset figure standing below in the main hall.

'Catherine, where are you? Catherine, it's me, William.' The figure turned and looked up the wide stairs towards them.

They shrank back, as might children almost caught stealing sweets. 'I'll go. See what he wants.'

Dave kept his voice low. 'This … this is stupid.'

'Oh, no, David. Listen to me.' Catherine pushed him back into the bedroom. 'He mustn't see you … us, like this … yet.'

'*Catherine!*' Again, the voice boomed up the staircase and into the bedroom.

Back at the doorway, she called down. 'William? I am sorry. I was asleep. Please wait there for me to join you.'

She promptly changed out of her bedclothes, and stepping across to the dressing table, gathered her hair into a Mrs MacAdam bun. 'I'm sorry Darling, but it is necessary.' She stretched up and kissed him on the cheek. 'Now, this may take a while. It's stopped raining, so I'll try to steer him outside for a walk. Please be patient. Just wait here till I'm rid of him.' With a final straightening of her jeans and cardigan, she left the bedroom.

Dave stood behind the closed door, like a cuckolded husband, listening intently, her voice still audible. 'You really shouldn't come inside like this, William. This is my home, after all.'

'Almost family, aren't I?' Another pause. 'Aye, you are looking well, more colour in your face. Now, Catherine, I called here on

126

Christmas Eve expecting a big welcome. Aye, phoned you late last year and said I'd be here. Remember? A broken leg wouldn't stop me, but found the house locked, and the car gone.'

'No, don't recall you saying that, William. An old friend in Hawick had invited me for Christmas and New Year. I've mentioned Cheryl, who…'

Back on the bed, Dave picked up the letter to his family he had started earlier. Yet, he couldn't settle, wasn't happy with this. Christmas in Hawick? What happened to Paris? How long would they keep this up? They'd been together now for about six months, and this was their home. It'd been fine with Mungo here.

After some time, he heard the front door slam – they would be outside now. He got up, quickly changed, and like a professional thief, crept out of the bedroom, stole down the main stairway and glided quietly into the servant hall. Propelled as much by curiosity as resentment, he entered the former butler's quarters near the kitchen, facing the front of the house.

From its small, ground level window, Dave could see Catherine and William standing outside, away from the main steps, near a silver Ford Zodiac. The man was dressed similarly to his previous visit, tweed jacket, corduroy trousers, and tartan cap, while Catherine, hands in pockets, now wore Wellingtons under her favourite gardening coat. Their voices were indistinct, yet Dave understood William's domination of the conversation, demonstrating the leg he had broken in November.

The young Australian smiled at Catherine's noticeable indifference to this display. She eventually indicated they should walk around the house, and together, Boyle limping, the two moved out of sight. Nothing untoward there, the man seemed harmless enough, yet remembering his pushy attitude, the young Australian felt the need to follow their movements. He headed towards the large study at the rear of the house.

***

Approaching the rear corner of the big house with Catherine, William Boyle assembled his thoughts. She's different, independent like.

127

Couldn't put a finger on it yet. Here at Christmas, he'd had it planned to declare his intentions, the whole kit and caboodle, of course. Only to find her out, away somewhere. Bloody Harwick, she now says. That saft old biddy in the gate house had told him Paris, but he'd laughed at that. Catherine hadn't an adventurous bone in her body.

Had she really forgotten his November phone call to book Christmas alone with her here? She'd become quite absent-minded, he knew. And there was the drinking – tiddly-like, sometimes when he'd called. But not today. No, she's quite definite, and unapologetic about her forgetfulness. His inconvenience. And there's that business of cottage renovations cousin Jimmy at the bank mentioned. Get to the bottom of it, he'd said. Coax her into marriage, then stop them. Bloody woman.

As they turned into the gravelled area between the back of the house and the long, metal-clad machine shed, William put his arm around Catherine's shoulders. He felt her stiffen, but he persisted, difficult as it was with his still painful leg. Well, get on with it. As a full-time publican now, it wasn't easy to get away. And such a long bloody drive over here from Galashiels.

Still, once he's living off the treasures of Glendaruel, he'd sell Elaine's pub. Jimmy will know where to park the proceeds. Now, get on and pop the question. In the shed there, perhaps, or more romantic back in the house? Just don't take no for an answer!

It was then he noticed the repaired and painted casement windows. And another set along from it. And another! Someone had repaired all the fucking ground floor windows here! Recently! He stopped and pointed at them, his hand shaking. 'Catherine, who's done all these fixings? You know I've … I've always taken responsibility for the repairs needed at Glendaruel.' What to fuck has she been doing? Spending money he knew the estate didn't have!

'Aye, I agree, William. It is all well done – no leaks now.' What? Did she misunderstand him? 'Who? Oh, David, of course. You remember him, my young nephew from Johannesburg who was here in the autumn. Desperate to earn his keep – so independent, as young people are these days.'

'But this would have taken…' He steered her towards the machine shed entrance, then stopped. More repairs! *'There!'* He shouted it, thrusting his arm up like a Nazi salute. 'There! More repair work up there, on… on the windows of your room. You didn't allow that boy into your bedroom, did you?' Fuck sake, that's reserved for him! 'I cannot approve of any man in your bedroom. Or staying in the house for that matter, Catherine. Aye, I can't at all.'

'Don't be so silly, William. David is my nephew, my sister's son.' She turned and faced him. 'And I find your assumptions offensive.' She crossed her arms defiantly, like one of those suffragettes. 'And, how do you *know* that's my bedroom? Have you been snooping about, watching me, perhaps?'

Of course, I've been snooping around and watching you, pompous Mrs MacAdam. And I'm soon to squeeze those still shapely chebs of yours. 'Catherine, you once told Jocelyn how much you liked me – I remember our weekend together, well. You know I've always cared for you and done my best for you. Remember the repairs in the house I've organised – the Morris too? I've a right to be concerned. And, because you've always seemed pleased about my visits over the last year or so, today I want to prop–'

But she suddenly cut him off, standing there, hands on hips. 'William, you disappeared for six, seven years after that weekend you mention – never a word. Then you swan back here as if I'd be … well, still waiting for you.'

'But I know you've been pleased to see me.' She'd said so.

'No, I'd become depressed and lonely, and initially I saw a familiar face … saw you as an old friend. Of James. But I understand now I was wrong.'

What's she saying? 'Catherine, I've only ever shown concern for you, of which I know James would approve. If you'd just damn well listen. The burdens of managing an estate and … and raising money for building renovation work are difficult for women. More so if they are alone. So, I've decided –'

Again, she surprised him, stepping back, eyes wide, as if he'd sworn at her. 'Building renovations? What do you mean, William?'

Right then, time to have it out, direct like. 'I noticed this afternoon while driving here how the estate cottage on the Dumfries Road has been painted out and has diggings around at the rear.' He pointed in the general direction of Wright's Cottage. 'And I –'

'Diggings at the …? William, I don't need to tell you anything. What I do is none of your damn business. How long have you been snooping around my property, making assumptions? What makes you think you have the right? How dare you!'

Where's all this come from? What's happened to the weak, vulnerable Catherine MacAdam? He'd never seen her so defiant. 'But, together, as James would –'

'And don't start any of that *James would approve of my interest* bunk!' She was singing the words at him now! 'William, he's been dead for 13 bloody years! But you've gone too far this time. Now, please leave. I want you to leave Glendaruel. Now!'

Leave? Be ordered off what's about to be his. Be fucked woman. Only one way to stop you, bitch. Leave? Let's begin with a kiss, and work our way down, shall we? He lunged at her.

Awkwardly propelling himself forward on his weak leg, William's nose collided with her hands that were half raised in defence. 'Ooww! Fuck!'

'William! William, stop it! Stop it this instant.'

He stepped back, holding his face. 'You've hurt me, woman. Fuck sake, if you weren't so damn stubborn. So 'effing proud.' His nose was now bleeding, his eyes watering.

She stood, open mouthed, perhaps as surprised as him. 'I … oh, I am sorry.'

Now he saw the blood on his hands, his jacket. His trousers! 'Look what you've done. To fuck with you. You're up to something, I know it!' He shouted, glaring at her. 'You've changed – something has changed! I've never seen you like this before. So … so defiant, so independent!' He pointed with a bloodied hand. 'And … and look at you, wearing denim trousers like a … a tradesman. And those glasses.'

She remained there, facing him. 'Like John Lennon. And how dare you swear at me. Is this demonstration of your caring, your so-called concern?'

130

John Len … John who? 'I warn you, Catherine. If anything unusual were to happen, especially in your fragile financial situation, only I could help.' Well, it's a waste of breath to say her bank manager is his cousin, the famous Jimmy Barr no less. She wouldn't listen now.

'William, as … as for suggesting Glendaruel is in financial trouble I can only assume it's wishful thinking on your part so as to make a Rob Roy of yourself. I want you to leave now. After today, I do not want you here again at Glendaruel. If you insist on returning, I'll ring the police. I will!'

Before he could react, she strode away towards the far end of the house. Astounded, he could only shout after her. *'Catherine! Catherine!'* She soon disappeared around the corner, only his words remained to reverberate between the buildings. *'Catherine! Catherine!'*

In utter frustration, the Scotsman continued to yell after her, his mind reeling. *'Catherine! Cathereeen!'*

What's happened to change everything? What happened to that insipid, pliable widow who'd seemed so thankful to see him? He couldn't understand it, couldn't follow any of it at all. The last time he'd been rejected like this was in Singapore – James bloody MacAdam. Always the fucking MacAdams.

His shoulders dropped, his hands began clenching: open-close, open-close. What must he do, how to regain at least a semblance of control? Open-close. He understood his chances of having any sort of relationship with her were now gone; she'd taken that away: open-close. No one takes things from him, especially a woman: open-close. She needed a lesson, like James, like Elaine at the pub: open-close. Then, he noticed the old garden pots and tubs stacked against the machine shed: open-close.

He walked across to the pile and picked up a large concrete tub with both hands. This'll do for starters. Stepping towards the house, he slowly lifted it up above his head and, once balanced, unhurriedly heaved it into the repaired ground floor window casements near him. Cop that, you pompous bitch, and all the fucking MacAdams.

***

Inside the rear study, crouched down near the windows, Dave Lawson experienced a sudden, loud shattering of glass and wood, and a painful peppering of shards.

16.

She found David in the servant hall. 'Darling, I couldn't find you! And what was that almighty crash?' She pulled him close. 'Oh, there's blood on your face! What's happened?'

As she bathed his wounds over the kitchen sink, David described how Boyle had smashed some windows in the study at the rear of the house. He had been in there to keep an eye on the man, but luckily ducked behind a cabinet in time to miss most of the damaging debris. Applying iodine to small cuts on his forehead and scalp, Catherine wasn't sure whether to be more upset about the windows, Dave's superficial wounds or the possibility of him having overheard mention of her *fragile financial position.*

It was cold and dark before they had the damaged windows cleaned up and covered with a tarpaulin. They then retired to the drawing room, and once upon the couch, a favourite spot together, Catherine leaned back into Dave's shoulder. His proximity, and body aroma calmed her somewhat. 'Warming up, Darling?' The chimney draft had encouraged an initially reluctant fire into long fingers of flame.

'Yep. Um, tell me about him … William.'

Aye, she pondered, time for some home truths. 'Well, after James was killed, old Mrs MacAdam and I had a formal visit from the K.O.S.B. commanding officer to inform us James had died bravely fighting the communists in Malaya, near Singapore. Next, Second Lieutenant Boyle arrived, unannounced, to offer us assistance, explaining how he and my husband had become close, as he still continues to remind me. Significantly, he made clear how James had instead died under an Orchard Road bus in Singapore itself, which devastated us both. And, of course, the house fell silent after that.'

'No more bawdy bachelor officers drinking till dawn up on the tower, or senior officers and their wearisome wives pontificating in the dining room, servants in attendance, just across the hall there.' She indicated towards the door.

'God Cathy, it … it's hard to imagine these rooms filled with people. Only 12-14 years ago.' Dave was behind her, refreshing their drinks.

Catherine accepted her glass. 'Thank you, waiter. Aye, another world, another time. Now, some months later, William returned, by then a civilian with a Borders realty company. In this and subsequent visits, he'd offer his help, which at the time seemed thoughtful. We were seeing considerably less of the wider MacAdam family because they were treating me, now the legal owner of Glendaruel, as *persona non grata*. No doubt the man came to see Glendaruel as a posh estate occupied by two vulnerable females.'

'Why did you become the legal owner with … with James' mother still alive?'

'Aye, a good question, but I often regret it.' Catherine looked thoughtfully at her drink. 'Briefly, on his deathbed, upstairs, the half-colonel transferred ownership of the estate to his son James, to avoid death duties. However, James never bothered to make a will, and once dead and childless, under British law his wife became the legal owner of Glendaruel. For me it offered a semblance of control over my own life, but the wider MacAdam family acted as if I'd deliberately schemed from birth to steal the estate from them. Moreover, because James was killed less than five years after his father, the bloody death duties still had to be paid. This ultimately cost more than half of the estate land!' She sighed.

'God, that much? Do you have much regret or bitterness about your marriage? How … how it worked out?'

'Well, David, it fits into that old conundrum of *what if.* I may have been happily married with cheery children's voices filling the house, or perhaps an aging spinster golf club secretary! So, no. No regrets or bitterness about a lost marriage. However, about children, about the miscarriages, perhaps …' She looked into the fire. 'Three in seven years was confounding, both in terms of self-esteem and popularity. The family labelled me the Barren-ess – could fall pregnant, but not deliver, so to speak. A cruel nickname. To have had a daughter …' Her voice dropped away.

Catherine began again, as if from a distance. 'The old lady had tried so hard to prevent the marriage, but she overlooked James' stubborn, conniving side.' She hesitated. 'As I had.'

***

'And now, it is my pleasure to pronounce you both man and wife. Lieutenant, you may kiss the bride.'

I can hardly believe it's over! Turning, my radiant husband takes that half step to his left. He lifts my veil, and kisses me, lingering with it, as if to defy formality. The ring, the dazzling ring we've chosen, seems to throb on my finger, as if it has a separate heartbeat!

Now, the chaplain smiles benevolently at us, cheeks puffed out like couch cushions. Best man Fergus is already pumping James' hand, and Father leans in from behind and kisses me. 'Congratulations, Darling. Or should I say, Mrs MacAdam!' The tone suggests my new surname deserves the felicitations, not myself. I mumble a thank you.

Next, bridesmaid Cheryl grabs me in a crushing hug, releasing the rose scent from her squashed bouquet. 'So well done, you,' she whispers, pecking my cheek. Behind her, in the pews smiling people are rising as one, tilting towards the central aisle, as might lines of careening yachts. Bright uniforms, dark suits, flowing dresses, angled bonnets, happy faces, excited voices – all so overwhelming.

James now has my arm and I mentally prepare for his parents, whom I've hardly met, standing straight and solemn in the first row. Yet, instead, he navigates towards the huge spinnaker of mid-afternoon sun slanting in through St Georges' open entrance doors – such a lucky portent in March! We drift out into a sea of gleaming uniforms – greens, reds, browns – a sniff of leather, barked orders, the bright blades of ceremonial swords. Confetti wafts like soft snow, as if to remind the sun of its unseasonable behaviour. And there ahead is the opened door of the Roadster to take us to the reception. I'm almost ... we're almost there.

Our wedding reception – the speeches, the toasts, the surroundings – is simply wonderful, and I feel so special, so privileged. The MacAdams have set aside the dining room at Glendaruel – our whole house at Milngavie would fit inside it. Mother and Father, and the other few guests from our side gape about as if on a tour of old Scottish mansions, adjusting to the plushness, the servants, the adorned walls, and the quality of food and drink in what are still straightened times in early post-war Britain.

With only coffee remaining, a servant girl quietly summons me. Ah, time to leave! I follow her out through the equally vast and decorated central hall, and down into the servant's area. I must learn all their names, I decide. Then, I am in a room marked 'Estate Manager', and surprisingly, my parents are there, as is Mrs MacAdam.

'–So, together, the three of you skivvied up a plan to trap James into marriage – the oldest trick in the book. And his unexpected posting must have seemed the opportunity to really hook him.' Mrs MacAdam is now quite agitated. 'Why else would he marry you, a mere golf club girl?'

I cast off the strictures of respect expected of a daughter-in-law. 'What a horrible thing to say. James and I are in love!' Father and Mother are sitting, open-mouthed, as if watching this on a cinema screen. "Support me," I want to yell! 'Why are you so accusative, Mrs MacAdam? I have hoped we could be friends.'

'Ha! We will never be friends!' She almost shouts it. 'And don't think carrying James' baby will make you any more acceptable.'

Now, Father is animated. 'Baby, what baby? He turns, mumbling. 'Ca ... Catherine?'

And Mother finally speaks, as if having just woken up. 'Catherine, what is Mrs MacAdam saying?'

'Please don't insult me with feigned surprise. Don't pretend you are unaware your daughter is expecting.'

'Well, no.' A hesitation. 'We don't know.' Father's voice has that quiver of someone attempting to re-establish control but doubting a successful outcome. 'Catherine, are you ...?'

How does she know? I'm not showing at all, and James and I agreed ... Yet, she is correct in one sense. There has been scheming, but only her son and I are guilty, using the battalion's suddenly announced posting to Hong Kong as a convenient cover for a necessary rushed wedding.

'Catherine!'

I sigh. 'Yes, Father. Mother. I haven't meant to withhold–'

'So, it is true. By God, Catherine. In ... in other words, you have <u>had</u> to get married.' *He doesn't wait for confirmation.* 'So, when <u>were</u> you going to tell us? Hmm?' *A small pause.* 'You are as immoral as Victoria.' *The pause again, with a glance towards Mother, demanding her agreement.* 'Well, at least Lieutenant MacAdam isn't RC.'

'Stop it, Father. That is not helping.' *I address Mrs MacAdam.* 'James will stop you. And ... and Colonel MacAdam seems a decent man as well. They won't put up with it.'

'Are you quite sure?' *She answers with disturbing smugness, before turning on my parents.* 'You two – I never want to see at Glendaruel Estate again. You are not welcome here. If you try, Masonic Lodges around Milngavie will hear of this.' *She is enjoying herself.* 'Make other arrangements to see your daughter and the child – Dumfries, Thornhill ...'

'Why are you so wilful, so heartless about this, Mrs MacAdam? Young people like these can make–'

'Stop! You have tried to gain privilege, advancement, from this wee scheme of yours. As it is, I only accept her presence here out of duty to my son, and my grandson.'

Out of duty to my ... ? Wait. Has James deliberately told her? Was that how he got her to agree? To ... to his own choice of wife? Has James had a scheme of his own that I've been unaware of?

'But... ' *Mother raises her hand, as if a child in a classroom.* 'But... what if the wee baby is not a boy?'

'For your daughter's sake, it had better be.'

James, what have you done?

A sudden, bright flame in the fireplace snapped Catherine back to the present. She forced a smile and raised her glass. 'Darling, you must try the Chivas; it's a 40-year-old single malt. The colonel labelled it 'old smoothie.' *Here, have an old smoothie with me, young gel*, he would say, and thrust a full tulip glass into my hand. He was an old gent, an old smoothie himself, in many ways. No doubt he was aware of James' shortcomings, but unlike Mrs MacAdam, seemed happy his remaining son had found a wife of at least middling Protestant Scottish pedigree and sensible outlook.'

'Remaining son?'

'Oh, yes. James had a twin, John, an artist who died climbing in the Himalayas, a year of two before we were married. Your old bedroom had been his studio. Only ever spoken of in hushed terms. Disappointed hushed terms, I felt. Lots of tragedy in the family, Darling, including my own.'

David got up and poured them both a whisky. 'Would James be angry about things now – you and me?'

'No, I don't think so, Darling. Despite his scheming, James could be kindly to others, which I am sure young Lieutenant Boyle took advantage of.' She nodded. 'Darling, this is why I feel no guilt about *our* relationship, despite considerable circumspection towards the outside world.'

***

Dave's mind was approaching their relationship from a different direction. Relieved that Catherine was okay after her confrontation with Boyle, guilt remained about the man's manhandling of her, and the windows being smashed. But then, how could he have stopped it?

God, he'd underestimated Boyle's interest. At footy club functions, he'd seen men scrapping over women, asserting their claims. Should he be staking a more visible claim to Catherine as William Boyle obviously was? Sure, she'd defended herself okay, but should *he*, Dave, have done something? Settled it there and then? But he knew bugger all about fighting.

Perhaps it was the second old smoothie that prompted the question he'd never really meant to ask. 'Did … anything ever happen between you and Boyle?'

'Yes!' Catherine twisted around, almost shouting. 'Yes, something did happen, if you are so damned eager to know. But not like you seem to have assumed!'

He hadn't seen her so angry. 'Around four years after James's death, William convinced me to spend a weekend with him, his sister Jocelyn, and brother-in-law, at a remote lodge on Loch Tay. I'd been really worn down by the Old Harridan, and it seemed an innocent, supportive gesture. That first evening, William plied me with drinks, and later, waited outside the bathroom until I emerged in only my night gown, pinned me to the wall and demanded I accompany him to his room. Aghast, I somehow found the strength to push him off.'

Her animated face reflected the anguish of reliving the event. 'I refused to see him again and didn't until about two years ago. Today is the first time since that weekend he has tried to lay a hand on me.'

Dave felt awful. 'God, I'm sorry, Cathy.' He remembered Boyle's pawing at her, just hours earlier. 'The bastard!'

She turned and ran a finger down his nose. 'And I'm sorry for shouting.' She began again. 'But, David, in such situations, the woman is left wondering if it's at all her fault. For example, had I led him on? Unknowingly given him tacit approval? It's never clear.'

He tried to absorb this. Christ, she's had heaps to put up with; a scheming James, a shitty mother-in-law, miscarriages, James' death, an estate to run alone, plus bloody Boyle. And now you, Dave, who doesn't know how to protect her.

They sat back together, each in their own thoughts. The much-depleted fire logs glowed like lines of expensive rubies.

'Darling, I understand now I made the mistake of greeting him like an old friend when he reappeared, 18-20 months ago. But I was just so depressed. Yet, with my failure to again be physically or emotionally attracted to him, William has, I think now, attempted a second line of attack – to create a dependence for the repairs of

Glendaruel. Now, we can only hope after his performance today that Glendaruel is shot of William Boyle.'

Catherine stood up, stretched, then stirred the fire with a poker. Eerie shards of light cavorting across the darkened ceiling and walls left her in fiery silhouette, like a professional illusionist deciding on the next trick. 'David, William's visit today was not coincidental, or motivated by simple curiosity. *Who* informed him of the cottage work? And *why* should they want to tell him?' She sat down again, picking up her tulip glass. 'I do think we should get ourselves a wee dog.'

17.

A few miles after Loch Doon, the gravel road came to a modest lookout overlooking another stretch of water, which Catherine guessed was the smaller Loch Deugh, their goal. They stopped and got out for a better view. Abruptly above them to the left was the brooding mass of the Galloway Hills, high, grey, and barren, deceptively close in the evening light. Also, to the left, and on around the far side of the loch as far as they could see, deep green plantation forest flowed like velvet staircase carpet down to the shoreline. In all, a valley of beauty.

Mungo's birthday invitation had arrived as unexpectedly as the man himself. They had, of course, discussed him often since January, even when seeking a name for their new dog, vying this weekend with Sergeant Major for Mrs Duffy's affections. The card had indicated a weekend at Pollcrayvie Castle on Loch Deugh in Ayrshire, about 40 miles from home, and requested both sports and formal attire.

Catherine explained to the intrigued Dave how such invitations had been common years earlier. Yet, she was initially reluctant to accept this one. Who else might be there?

On their right and below them, a spit protruded out into the loch, parallel to where they now stood. On it the dark roof lines of a tall building were visible among treetops. She pointed. 'That must be the castle – what a truly beautiful situation. Stunning for photography.' She held up her hands as if operating a camera.

From there, the road skirted the loch shoreline, then, with a sharp turn to the left, it took them through the gateway of a thick fortress-like wall, which suggested they were onto the spit proper. Lights appeared through the trees ahead, and they came to a wide gravel roundabout with cars parked on its far side.

Dave parked next to Mungo's Stag. Here, Catherine could see, was the castle, an odd throw-together of high medieval stone tower and Victorian mansion. And, coming down a set of well-worn, stone steps was the rotund figure of Mungo, smiling and waving.

'Catherine, Davie, lovely to see you both again, and welcome to Pollcrayvie Castle!' He joined them, kissing Catherine's cheek, and vigorously shaking David's hand, as if they were the oldest of friends. Compared to their last meeting, he looked bright and healthy, and slightly ridiculous in a brown-green tweed jacket and cap, and matching trousers that were tucked into long beige socks. Ignoring protests, he picked up their suitcase and ushered them towards the castle entrance.

'So pleased you have accepted my invitation. I do want to return your kind hospitality, but also wish you to meet my friends. And David, I am in need of your professional advice, if we could … ah, watch those smooth steps. Centuries of use.' Once in through an ornate doorway, Mungo led them on, as might an efficient butler, until they were in a room of impressive dimensions and decoration. He put their case down, and as if heartily thanking God for the safe arrival of these guests, thrust both hands above his head and smiled broadly. 'The Grand Hall – grand, aint it?'

Catherine glanced at David. The floor space of the room was of a good size, perhaps 20 foot wide by 30 long, but the ceiling was well above normal height: possibly 25 feet! On the walls hung a disparate collection of weapons, shields, flags, animal heads and large framed paintings. On their left was a massive fireplace with an equally massive log that, with imagination, could have been a resident sorcerer's somnolent monster lizard. The reflective interaction of the polished flagstones and chandeliers hanging high above added to the overriding ambiance of warmth and space. To Catherine, the central hall at Glendaruel seemed gloomy and inadequate by comparison.

Mungo next guided them to their first-floor room in what was the Victorian wing, plush with heavy 19th century red and gold wallpaper. He suggested they settle in, then come down to the sitting room for pre-dinner drinks with those who had already arrived.

***

Mungo was waiting for them, just inside the sitting room, the name etched into its frosted glass door panels. 'Now, for that well-earned drink after your long journey.' His tone suggested they had travelled from New York or Singapore. 'Come and meet the others.'

Hesitant at first, they followed him into a cosy room with deep green and polished wood décor, and a hint of smoke. People stood near a hearty fire; their faces illuminated like those of cheery campfire revellers. Dave felt Catherine's hand tighten. 'Help me with this, David. Please.' He squeezed her in reply, as Mungo began introductions.

'Everyone, I want you to meet Catherine and David, from near Dumfries. They are the kind souls who found me wandering incoherently about the countryside after I'd crashed the Beast during that icy week in January. I realise now that their quick action quite possibly saved my life. The Beast, however, still lives with the ignominy of having been towed by a Morris Minor. Please welcome these Good Samaritans.'

The now-smiling group were introduced as Mungo's uncle and aunt, Jim and Candice Rollo, and close friends Robert and Jean Nicholson and Paul and Chlodagh Harris. Jim Rollo was, Dave decided, an older version of Mungo, similarly well-proportioned, but with a friendly unruliness that included a riotous beard and a growling voice. Candice, in contrast, was short and thin, of Asian origin, and like the others, close to Catherine's age. Dave noticed, somewhat surprised, the Nicholsons could have been brother and sister.

Chlodagh, memorable in a lurid orange caftan, raised a welcoming hand. 'I didn't expect to meet anyone new this weekend. Well done, both of you, and welcome to Mungo's clan.'

Jim stepped forward to shake their hands, as Mungo organised drinks. 'Aye, Mungo has mentioned his wee adventure down your way. You shouldn't pity him – he's often to be found wandering incoherently!' Jim's accent was strong. 'But, as Mungo's uncle I'd very much like to thank you both. It's not everyone who'd accept a stranger on a grim night.' The conversation angled off to successful Australians who had taken up residence in the UK – The Seekers, Barry Humphries, others.

'And now we have an Aussie James Bond! Is nothing sacred?' It was Paul Harris, who, to Dave, had the colour and grace of a West Indian cricketer. 'You here to make a film, too, David? Another Bazza McKenzie, perhaps?'

'Ha.' Dave could only offer a nervous laugh to all these adults.

Luckily, Chlodagh helped out. 'Now, excuse my boldness, Catherine, but I do like your hair. It certainly suits you.' She ran a hand through her own tight curls. 'I'm never happy with mine!'

Blushing, Catherine had begun an answer, when a man of medium height and build, and dressed in black appeared at the door. His black hair was pulled back in harsh lines like those in a freshly ploughed field. Roy Orbison without the glasses, Dave thought.

'Hello Jim, Candice – everyone.'

'Alex, about bloody time.' Jim turned to greet the latecomer. 'Here, you must meet Mungo's friends from Dumfries, while I'll get your usual.'

The new arrival turned to Dave and Catherine and offered his hand. 'Hey, I'm Alex – Alex Hazzard. I've wanted to meet you both.' Shaking hands, Catherine introduced herself.

Dave's mind had locked up – he's a poofta. That … that means Mungo is too!

'David.' Catherine pulled at his arm.

'Um … sorry, I …' Dave reluctantly offered his hand. 'Pleased to meet you, too.' But he felt more awkward than pleased.

Alex took his hand and held it. 'Then, you didn't know. But, hey, I do want to thank you for what you did, Dave, Catherine. Mungo didn't sound at all well when he rang from your home that evening, but he did say he felt very welcome. Cheers again.' He continued holding Dave's hand, until he noticed the young Australian's glass. 'Ah, pleased to see there's another beer drinker among these whisky wallahs. You Aussies have a reputation that precede you, man, so I hope you haven't yet drunk all the beer!' Alex smiled. 'Look, I'd better go and catch the others.'

Dave watched the man move easily among the crowd, shaking hands, laughing. English perhaps, mid-thirties, out there. Mungo and Alex gave each other a one-arm hug and spoke for a few moments.

144

Then stepping back, Mungo looked around at everyone and raised a hand.

'Now we are all here, I can begin. Friends, I do thank you all for accepting this your first invitation to Pollcrayvie Castle for the weekend. As most are aware, I turned 40 some weeks ago, and so I've asked you here to help me celebrate it.' He waved an arm towards his partner. 'They say life begins at 40. But in modern Britain, as we begin the 1970s, and despite some archaic laws about indecency, I feel positive that life for me can only improve.' Some laughter. 'Despite the ruinous example of my recalcitrant uncle here.' He gestured towards Jim, gaining more laughs. 'So, raise your glasses to reaching 40.'

'To reaching 40.' The group chorused an answer, and then drank.

'I thank you all. And I also want to introduce you to my castle.' Mungo then explained how he had stumbled upon a rundown and empty Pollcrayvie while visiting Loch Doon and the fabled old castle there.

'Originally built in the 16th century, this was a classic Z plan fortified tower, but restored and extended in the 1860s by wealthy Glasgow linen merchants. The challenge of making Pollcrayvie economically viable, offering stately accommodation and a variety of leisure activities, fishing, shooting, tennis, for example, for another era of wealthy Glaswegians, quite appealed to me.' Mungo stopped and gestured towards his partner. 'Now Alex will tell you of an even more exciting proposal for the castle.'

Alex took a pull of his beer before speaking. 'Well, you all know of my involvement in the music industry, so basically, I wish to use the area outside the castle grounds, a natural amphitheatre really, to stage music festivals – rock concerts, if you prefer. And only yesterday I received the go-ahead from the council of the Doon Valley for the first one. So, friends, there's to be a Scottish rock festival held here in early June.'

'Oh, wonderful. I've always liked Jimmy Shand. Andy Stewart too!'

'Bugger off, Jim. I'm talking contemporary Scottish artists. I'm talking Marmalade, McGuinness Flint, Forever More, Writing on the

145

Wall, Nirvana, The Incredible String Band, Lulu. That new geezer, Rod Stewart. And wait for it … Donovan.'

In the silence that followed, Dave stared at the man. Did he say McGuinness Flint and Marmalade … and Donovan? Here, at the castle?

'Are you serious, Alex?' Paul perhaps spoke for all of them.

'Yeah. Mungo knows I've been organising this for months – musicians, caterers, transport. Now with official permission, I've spent this morning ringing group managers, and have them confirmed. Donovan is touring the US at present, but I have his verbal agreement.

'Have the McBeatles accepted?' It was Robert.

'They're finished, you silly twat.'

'Rolling Stones?'

'Not a Scottish bone between 'em.'

A buzz continued among the group until Mungo spoke again. 'Now, dinner is waiting next door. Meals this weekend will be self-serve, apart from the formal dinner tomorrow evening. But please remember the standard Victorian staff of 14 has been replaced by my caretaker couple, Bryce and Jean McCargo. So, introduce yourselves, have patience, and chip in where necessary. Later, we'll have a snooker match.'

He opened the dining room door, then looked around. 'David, is Penfolds a suitable brand?'

Dave's mind was still looping through the rock bands. Me – wine?

***

From their bed, Dave reached up to feel the texture of the heavy wallpaper. 'Cathy, you didn't say much at all tonight. Thought you'd like Mungo's crowd.'

'I'm sorry, Darling. Stepping back into society, so to speak, has been far more daunting than I imagined. Mungo is kind – they all seem nice, but I remain on edge. For one, they've known each other for years, Chlodagh, Robert and Mungo at university together, and they've all attended those nuclear disarmament marches. Second, I'm out of touch with small talk. Until you appeared, for years I had really only interacted with the Dumfries church set. And I think I had *them* somewhat intimidated.'

He felt that familiar squeeze of the hand – her need for reassurance. 'One reads of people who, having suffered major trauma, later must re-learn basic skills – eating, walking, or … or writing. Locked away as Mrs MacAdam for so long, Catherine needs to re-learn those social skills she once had – when she first met James – when she was acting secretary at Gifford Castle Golf Club.' She hesitated. 'God, I'd stopped being me for almost 20 years.'

Dave explained how it had been for him. Saturday nights at dances, and his attempts to get a girl – any girl – that always resulted in embarrassment or rejection, or both. Why didn't the brain just erase that stuff? Yeah, they have similar wounds, he concluded.

'You poor Darling. Yet, I am glad we've come this weekend. Are you?'

'Yeah, it's been good. And great news about the rock festival.' He'd thought of little else since Alex's announcement.

'And, Darling, I was unaware of your talents on the snooker table.'

'Thanks. I … I had a bit of luck tonight.' Yeah, the castle's professional snooker room had been a surprise, and he explained to Catherine his eye for the game, knowing what a ball would do on a good table – rebounds and things. Being tall helped – for once! Grandad Ric had often taken him to the RSL Club in Frankston where he'd played with older blokes who offered lots of tips. He'd loved it.

'A misspent youth some might say. Any tattoos I haven't yet noticed?'

18.

Despite initial grumbles at having to dress up, Dave Lawson did feel part of something special as, the following night, he walked down the main staircase of Pollcrayvie Castle in his hired dinner suit. Catherine was on his arm in a glistening black gown, shoulders bare except for pearls. Was that admiration on the faces of the other guests gathered below outside the Great Hall?

Mungo in full Scottish rig greeted them. 'Ah, Catherine, David, you do look so well together. Now, what's the tartan of the dickie bow you're sporting, Laddie?

'MacIntosh.'

'Suits you. Now, ladies and gentlemen, our dinner awaits – please follow me.'

All formally dressed, the group entered the Great Hall, now bisected by a long table with an elaborate dinner setting. The ornate name cards surprised and pleased Dave, yet he was disappointed to find his next to Jean Nicholson's; both he and Catherine felt she was over inquisitive. But happily, Jim Rollo, with a wink, sat down on his left, as head of the table. Good. Catherine, sitting opposite but further along and flanked by Mungo and Robert, momentarily caught his eye. Bryce McCargo, also in a kilt, filled Dave's whisky glass.

Jean turned towards him. 'You are quite a mystery, David. We don't often find young Australians wandering the roads of Scotland. Are you here to seek out family?'

'Err, no. Picko and I were doing a circuit of Britain when –'

'Picko?'

'Yeah, my mate Picko. He … he and I travelled together from Oz last year by ship.'

'And where is Picko now?'

Hmm, a bloody sticky beak. Dave reached for his whisky. 'I'm not–'

'Your soup, Sir.' He felt Mrs McCargo lean in from behind.

'Thanks.'

Jean again. 'Potato and leek – a favourite of mine. So, David, where is your friend now?'

All conversation stopped. Jim was standing, pinging an empty glass with a fork. 'Ladies and Gentlemen.' He now held up a full glass. 'For the first toast this evening, I ask you to raise your glasses to Queen Elizabeth II. The Queen.'

All at the table stood up. 'The Queen,' they chorused, and lifted their glasses, then drank. Dave, a few seconds behind, gulped down the rest of his whisky, and as it bit into his throat, began coughing. He felt all eyes upon him, as the hacking continued. Embarrassed, he slid back into his chair.

'Mr McCargo, the young laddie here needs a big glass of water.' It was Jim. 'Please.'

Further embarrassed, Dave drank some of the water when it came. His unfinished soup had gone.

'I must ask, David. How did you and Catherine become acquainted?' It was Jean again. 'You seem such an unlikely pair.'

Dave reached for a glass of wine. Bloody woman. 'A car accident – June … June last year.'

'Oh really? Anyone hurt?'

Careful Davey.

'An accident, you said?'

God, she's nosey. 'Yeah, ended up in Dumfries Royal.'

'Oh, gosh. Either of you seriously injured? You weren't in the same ward fluttering eyes at each other, were you?'

He looked at the creamy fish entrée now before him and smiled. 'Yeah, I suppose we were. In … in that amputations ward for weeks.'

'What? Amputations? Well, I …' Jean's eyes moved to scan his upper body. 'But, last night, today, you both …' She stopped, her face still finding a fitting look, then turned towards Paul Harris, her other neighbour.

About to congratulate himself, Dave again heard the fine *ping* of glass, and this time Alex offered a toast to Mungo on his 40th birthday. 'To Mungo,' the crowd retorted.

'Old tosser.' It was Paul, behind his glass. Laughing, they all sat down again.

'Now, cut out the *old* business.' Mungo grinned along the table.

When the roast beef came, more wine was poured, and Dave began to relax. Conversation around him focused on the Irish *Troubles*, and the three off-duty Scottish soldiers killed that week in Belfast. Then it was North Sea oil, or *Scottish* oil, as Jim corrected, to nods of approval.

Talk next drifted to the far-off war in Vietnam, and Dave confirmed, when asked, that young, conscripted Aussies were being sent to the war. He expressed relief that his birth date had not been selected, and when asked why, he hesitated, then began to talk about his one true friend, John Smythe. Two years earlier, he explained, Johnno had been called up for national service and sent to Vietnam as an engineer. He was killed there after only a few months, and a later enquiry uncovered a regime of poor training.

As the evening continued, they asked him about Australia's new Prime Minister hopeful, Gough Whitlam, but all he could really add was, *Gough'll change things*, as Ric had told him. During dessert, he noticed Catherine signalling, mouthing words. What was it? Toast what? Ah, *to Mungo*, but that's been done. She mouthed again – *to Mungo for inviting us*. But he couldn't do that here. This lot've been doing it all their lives. Yet, she was still at it, gesturing with that smile. Do it for Catherine? But what could he say? Shiiiit! Thanks for inviting us. Really good of you, Mungo. Great bloke, great car, um … great big guts. Something like that. He drank more wine.

Dave waited a few very nervous minutes until he thought everyone had a drink, and, shaking as if suffering from the cold, stood up and called for a toast. In the sudden silence, he blurted out a thanks to Mungo for including him and Catherine with these friends. Very thoughtful. 'And yeah, Gough Whitlam sends his regards,' he finished.

Laughing, with glasses held high, they all roared, 'To Mungo!'

Flopping back into his chair, Dave felt Jim's slap on the back. 'Good man yourself, young Bazza.'

He appreciated the approval; he was getting pissed, and in the past, he'd only ever gained disapproval when drunk.

Still elated, Dave watched small licks of flame, like just-hatched snakes, dart about in the glowing embers of the sitting room fire. A little earlier, and despite the booze, he'd again led Alex, Chlodagh and Paul to victory on the snooker table. And with back-slaps and whoops, they'd acknowledged him as their leader. Now, with Chlodagh on the sofa with Catherine and Candice, and Paul gone after only one victory drink, he found himself sitting alone with Alex – the poofter Alex. Yet, he'd decided that was okay too, for moments earlier the man had returned from the kitchen with some cold cans of McEwans.

'Cheers, Aussie.'

'Yeah, cheers.' They both swigged their cans.

'So, what's your graft?'

'Landscape gardening.'

'Here in Scotland?'

'At Glendaruel. Catherine's place. Sort of keep my hand in.'

'So, man, how do you pay your bills? Day to day things – food, clothes, beer?'

'Um ... money left over from last summer, and ...' Dave didn't feel like a round of *20 Questions*.

'And?'

'Well, I suppose Catherine pays for most ... But ... but we've renovated three estate cottages – to be rented. Yeah, also, lots of maintenance work around the place. Yeah, lots! Saves her money, I suppose.'

'You suppose? Another Lady Chatterley's lover, then?'

'Who?

'An aristocratic lady in a notorious novel who had a raging love affair with her game keeper. Scottish also. You're lucky, man,

151

Catherine's got class – could go for her meself, except … well. And she's willing to keep you.'

What's he saying? 'Hey, hang on. It … it's not like that at all. Those bloody cottages were hard work, and anyway, I want to work. I don't want to be just her *lover*, as you said.'

'But surely, you're enjoying it – the, ahem, benefits.'

Bloody Alex was starting to annoy him. 'Look mate, you don't understand. It really pisses me off not having a job. I want a job. I've always paid my way.'

'Not convinced.' Alex finished the McEwans. 'You're just sponging off Catherine.'

'Jesus, Alex, Alexandra, whatever your bloody name is, I'm not. Anyway, what about you and Mungo? Why are you with him? To sponge off him, too?'

'Had my music agency long before I met Mungo.' Leaning forward, Alex poked the fire with a blackened poker. 'No, you're freeloading, man.'

'Fuck off. I'm with her … I'm with Catherine because I love her. Yeah, I love her.' Dave emptied his can with some defiance, as Catherine, on the sofa, turned towards them, her face a question.

'And that's why I'm with Mungo. I love him.'

'But you can't love another bloke. It's … It's …'

'Unnatural? So, man, what's so natural about sleeping with someone nearly twice your age?'

A sudden visual memory of a night – many nights – when they'd had each other's clothes off before ever reaching the bedroom. Even had it off in the kitchen once or twice. Dave found himself grinning. 'Jesus, Catherine used to wear glasses like my mum's. That was scary. But … but, okay, you've got me buggered. And anyway, you said yourself she has class!'

'Sorry, Aussie, you're not my type.' But, before Dave could react, Alex had his empty can raised in salute. 'Hey, you're okay, man. Like your style. And take no notice of me. Yeah, I've a growing feeling you've also done it hard.'

152

The older man got to his feet. 'Now, before I come over all sentimental, we need more beer.' He stood there, a little unsteady. 'Hey … hey, I notice you wear the beads. Smoke joints, too?'

'So, man, what do you think of my rock festival?' Alex passed the joint back to Dave.

'Great, grouse, gerrific!' Now in the pleasant fug of booze and hash, Dave asked the many rock concert questions he'd been storing up – artists, logistics, chances of success.

'Success, ha! Now there's a thing. If the crowd goes crazy as the first poxy band play their first poxy number, I'll call it a success.' Alex smirked. 'Rock festivals never make money. They say the last two Isle of Wight gigs made bugger all, despite their fame.' He began to roll another joint. 'It's an extravagance, a total wank. I've warned Mungo, but he's cool with it.'

'Almost went there,' Dave said. Swigging beer, he explained how he'd missed out on the previous year's festival.

'You gave it up for Catherine, eh? Impressive!' Alex nodded towards the women on the sofa and held up his can. 'Here's to true love, man.' With a bent grin, the young Australian raised his beer in reply.

19.

'*Hoy!*' Mungo saw Catherine and David standing below on the jetty jutting out into Loch Deugh and shouted to catch their attention. They seemed engrossed in a photo shot towards the Galloway Hills now emerging from the morning mist and were slow to turn his way. Leaving the castle behind, he began towards them, waving.

'Morning! Morning all.' He was puffing as he joined them on the jetty. 'Sorry to interrupt, but too nice a morning to be inside. Saw you taking snaps earlier, Catherine. Certainly admire your energy and athleticism.'

'Aye, well, David keeps me young.'

'Lucky you!'

'No!' She retorted, red-faced. 'That's not what I meant at all.'

Oops! Mungo was embarrassed. 'Och, and me neither. My apologies. I mean it's always a pleasure to watch someone engrossed in their particular interest. And this is certainly a wonderful place for those who are artistically moved – photography, painting, sketching, poetry even – as you can appreciate. Are you, Davie?'

'Me? Don't think so.' He looked towards Catherine as if for help.

'There's your landscaping, Darling.'

Mungo beamed. 'And that, young man, is what I wish to discuss with you. I need your opinion about landscaping the place.' He pointed back along the tongue of land where the castle sat. 'Please join me for a tour of my tongue, and I'll reward you both with brewed coffee and some of Jean McCargo's sultana cake.' He broadened the smile to allay any doubt. 'The spit, I mean. Sounds like a Monty Python skit, don't it? Seen them on the giggle box?'

Smirking, they both nodded.

'And the exercise will be good for our hangovers, wee Davie. Now, we seem to have the place to ourselves. I know Jim, Paul and Jean kicked on into the wee hours with my birthday whisky, adding lubrication to the Scottish Home Rule and nationalism arguments.

Don't think it will ever come to anything. The English have us by the short and curlies, as Alex might say. Are you SNP, Catherine?'

'I was always expected to vote Unionist, but not anymore. Does my shady political past cut me out of coffee and cake.'

Mungo smirked. 'Ha! Follow me, children!'

***

'So, what do you think, young Davie?' They had walked the length and width of the spit with Mungo and now were sitting on the 19th century patio near the castle entrance. Jim and Candice joined them, but dull, distant gun shots suggested others were clay pigeon shooting beyond the castle wall.

Dave accepted a piece of the cake his host offered. 'What do *you* have in mind, Mungo?' Now, in his own territory, his own specialty, Dave felt more comfortable. Since arriving, he'd subconsciously scrutinised the castle landscape, a habit learned from Charlie, years earlier. But there was very little of the original gardens left – no obvious axis or focal point – only the odd damaged fountain or statue. Start from scratch he'd concluded.

'Have in mind? But that's what I'm asking you – your professional opinion. You demonstrated it during my adventures at Glendaruel.'

'Yeah, but that's fill-in work. Stuff I can decide on as I go.'

'Well, go on. Decide for me. Tell me what I should do. There's more cake in it for you!'

Jean McCargo's cake was good, as was the coffee. Dave's hangover was gone, his mind was clear, and he knew what to say.

'Mungo, you must have a good idea of what you want – what you want to achieve with the place. You need a vision, one that includes the castle, the loch, of course, and … and all the surrounding area. You see, those main hills over there,' he indicated towards the high Galloway Hills, now clear of mist, across the loch. 'They are part of your landscape too because they can be seen from here. Not always, but I reckon during the summer, they'll seem to be right next door.'

'Oh.' Mungo looked about him open mouthed, as if these significant natural features had been pushed into place overnight. Jim and Candice appeared similarly struck.

Another bite of cake. 'But landscaping has many uses. Yeah, beautification, to hide something ugly, or to feature stuff, like fountains or statues, or to create boundaries to divide an area.' He stopped, then added. 'Or simply to display wealth, like … like at Versailles.' Dave then mentioned the basic considerations before starting any landscaping, anywhere – soil, topography, weather, and budget. His conclusion, he told Mungo, was that a garden should flourish here.

'Well explained, David. So, where do I start?'

Yeah, where to start? Mungo just didn't understand the huge job in front of him, beginning from scratch. 'If you want to have tourists, the place needs dividing, natural-looking divisions that will create isolated places for people to play sport, or to explore – to add mystery.'

The big man smiled. 'Aye, I want mystery, and I want my tourism idea. Eventually want to direct all my business from here. So, not a whim, I'm in for the long haul at Pollcrayvie.'

'Then, you need the experts. Must … must be someone in the region who does large jobs, as this will be.'

Mungo pursed his lips. 'Hmm, not sure that's the best idea.'

As he answered, Alex stepped out through the main doors onto the patio, carrying a large tray of food. 'Dead quiet inside. Anyone for lunch?'

***

Later, Mungo waited until Catherine and David had sat down again with some soup and sandwiches and re-joined them. He felt strongly the young Australian would get him his dream garden. Too many stories about big gardening companies making big fuck ups.

'Laddie, two things encourage me to press you to take the job. First, when we spoke earlier you exhibited the ability to see the big picture, as they say. *The big picture*, God, it's one of those obnoxious

American terms that are vastly overused nowadays, but I am struggling at this juncture to find another.' He smiled apologetically. 'In giving me more than a general opinion as I'd expected, and not deciding *what I had to have*, I'm convinced, David, with you Pollcrayvie Castle will get the landscaping it deserves.'

Mungo hesitated to chomp the corner off his sandwich. 'Now, I can get you labour and equipment, and I'm willing to pay a top salary, with superior accommodation thrown in.' Smiling, he indicated the castle.

'I–'

'Another moment, please.' Mungo pointed the now half-eaten sandwich at young David. 'Second, and this now takes on the tones of a famous Shakespearean drama, but we are almost there. Picture two young Venetian merchants drinking late into the night in a seedy harbour bar. The tall one, Long Austral, confesses to the other, Musical Alexus, he wants desperately to gain employment to be worthy of the damsel, Hibernia. Our young Venetian even admits – the first time to anyone – his love for Hibernia. Alexus is so impressed that he ensures this tale of devotion reaches the ears of the indolent, yet affluent Pollcrave.'

Mungo sat back and finished the sandwich, his eyes flashing between the pair. He grinned as Catherine's face took on a glow of considerable pleasure. 'Bloody Alex,' young Davie eventually said, then moved his chair closer to Catherine and put one of those long arms around her shoulders. A soup spoon clattered onto the old terrace ceramic tiles, causing others to look their way.

'Control, show control now,' Uncle Jim grumbled somewhere behind them. 'No fornication on the patio, please.'

***

It would soon be dark. Dave had waited until the others had left Pollcrayvie before accepting Mungo's job offer, and now he and Catherine sat on the jetty, their legs dangling out over Loch Deugh. As they leaned together in their coats, Dave produced two part-empty bottles of Mungo's wine. 'Hibernia, I know it's cold here, but I ... I must teach you how to swig from a bottle.'

'David?'

He stopped, to calm his nerves, adjust his face. 'No, no, joking. Seriously, I need to talk …'

He started at the beginning and led Catherine along the convoluted commando trail of his life to date: his father's stupid death, the blaming by his mother, his resulting shame, and from that the incessant teasing and embarrassments of his teenage years. And just how much she was helping him to resolve it.

As it came out, with some tears and tough talking to himself, David Lawson began, by degrees, to feel release from years of twisted shame and emotional burden. At the end, he was somewhat drunk, but for once he felt emptied of shame and remorse.

20

It was getting late, and at first, he couldn't find her!

It was two weeks since the Pollcrayvie Castle weekend, and earlier that afternoon, Catherine had gone to the bank to request a loan for equipment for Mungo's landscaping project. Perhaps a work van too. Only had to ask the manager, she'd said. A formality. Dave had worked late to complete that final work on the cottages behind the big house, so was unsure when she'd returned home.

Now, after searching the darkening house, he was staggered to find her lying face down on an unmade bed in a seldom-used room on the second floor. And still in her town clothes! Only weak light entered through the doorway, and the smell of dust was strong. Was she crying? Why? Surprised when she failed to react to his presence, Dave sat on the edge of the bed and waited.

Eventually Catherine spoke, a muted mumble. 'I … I've ruined everything. The estate … I'm … I'm sorry David. What … what will I do?'

That hint of panic worried him. 'What is it, Cathy? What's happened?'

She began, slowly. 'I've never wanted to tell you, but the … the estate owes the bank considerable money … often spends more than it earns.' A long pause. 'Like, aye, like a stupid fool, I've hidden it. And … and, I've kept spending, desperate, so desperate not to lose you.'

He reached out to touch her, to calm her. 'And … and I didn't want to lose me … the new me, either. When … when I began to dress like, and really feel like Catherine again, I … I just didn't want any of it to end.' She began sobbing. 'But now, it … it's all gone! Because of my stupidity.'

He moved to the top of the bed and helped her to sit up. 'Catherine, please. Just tell me what's happened to make you so upset.'

Through more sobs and stops, she explained how Glendaruel had been on shaky economic ground for some years, but through increasing bouts of depression and drinking, she'd simply ignored this. How she should have taken notice when, about eighteen months earlier, and again just prior to his accident, she'd received bank notification that the estate overdraft had reached certain levels where considerably higher interest rates would apply.

'In … in short, Darling, I … I've been living beyond my means. Supporting us – the estate – on an expensive overdraft. Today, Mr Barr, the manager, refused the loan, and instead informed me of an audit concluded on the financial prospects of Glendaruel.' She paused, as if to gather strength. 'He … he said the bank has decided to call in the estate debts and, well … well, demand the sale of Glendaruel to recover the monies owed. Immediate bankruptcy, he said.' A hesitation. 'Bankruptcy.'

What? Glendaruel was bankrupt? 'But, in November he gave you the money, the loan, for the cottages. What's changed?'

She turned away. 'Well … nothing. You see, Mr Barr then had also refused me the funds, but … but because I understood the project was so important for you, for both of us, I decided instead to sell jewellery to raise the cash. And, well … when money also was needed for the Paris trip, I again drove to the pawnshop in … in Glasgow. Didn't want Dumfries people to know.' She dropped her head.

He remembered now those extra trips to Glasgow – signing papers and such, she'd said. Always brought home a small treat, a surprise for him. But selling jewellery! Bloody extreme – sounds dodgy.

God, hearing this he felt awkward … no, awful. 'Cathy, you should've told me. Discussed it with me. You've bought me clothes at the most expensive store in Edinburgh. You've let me live here free for over six months, and … and only allowed me to pay a small portion of that bloody holiday in Paris.' Uneasiness had given way to embarrassment. 'Do you understand where that leaves me? Feeling like a bludger, a bloody leech!'

'David. W … wait.'

'No, you wait.' His embarrassment had turned to anger – hot anger – not felt in years. 'You've let me become fully involved in the

160

cottages, and today – this evening, I finished them. Yippee. Yeah, the project's been great for many reasons, except, except we … sorry, you, can't bloody afford it. Bankrupt. And then there's Mungo's work. That was gonna be so … so enormous for us. Meant I could stay here forever, with you. Bring my family over here – sort it out with them. But now it won't happen. Can't happen, because we have no money to buy the gear, the van, I'll need to start such a large bloody project.' Other thoughts thrust their way forward. 'And, and how do I face Mungo, after his generosity and show of faith in me? And yeah, where will we live?'

Dave had to do something, react in some way. He stood up, and shook off his jacket, an old warm sports coat of James, allowing it to drop onto the bed. 'Have this back, for starters.' It was a petty, foolish gesture, but she'd left him feeling petty and foolish. He was at the staircase before he heard her desperate call. *'David … David!'* He tried to think it all through, sort something out, but it was probably too late. He started down the stairs.

***

'But what can I do, Darling? Since visiting the bank today, I've been consumed by an overwhelming sense of panic.' A bulky blanket was pulled over their nakedness to fend off the early April night chill. Dave wasn't sure now if he'd actually intended to leave Glendaruel, but he'd had to get out of the room and clear his head. Try to make sense of it all. He knew nothing about bankruptcy. About long term relationships either.

Somehow, canny Sergeant Major had again stepped in, this time sitting at the foot of the staircase demanding his dinner. And, as Dave fed his old friend on the kitchen table for once – no telling, puss! – he came to appreciate how Catherine had set out on her crazy, careless course because of him.

Yeah, perhaps because she needed him, but also because she loved him. If earlier she *had* confronted these financial problems, they wouldn't have attempted the cottages, or the sun garden landscaping, both of which have led to Mungo's momentous offer. Which was to anchor their future together. Nor would they have gone to Paris.

Indeed, would they have ever met? A sensible, careful Catherine would never have run into him at all, so to speak!

And later, as Dave put the Morris away, and moved about securing the large house that she'd probably lose, he became more convinced that each of those experiences had acted to make their unlikely relationship even more likely! The uncertainty now hanging over their future, he concluded, was a separate matter: just another problem to deal with.

So, feeling quite foolish for his overreaction and anger when Catherine instead needed sympathy and understanding, he had returned with whisky, tumblers, and the blanket, and with caring deliberation, made love to her. Her response was reassuring.

***

With further inducement from old smoothie, Catherine related the turn of events, which she had found herself locked into. The sudden holiday in Paris had become necessary because of a William Boyle phone call to announce he would be at Glendaruel for Christmas, as Mrs Duffy later confirmed he had. Again, postponing the inevitable confrontation perhaps, but postpone it she did. Accumulating stress, no doubt contributed to her serious overreaction in Paris to finding Dave with those girls in the bar. She had hated herself for it, she explained, behaving like an ageing *prima donna*.

She ran a finger down David's nose. 'It's difficult to admit to living a lie, but that's what I've been doing for many years now, isn't it?' In truth, this was a question to herself. 'Again, Darling, my deepest apologies for my lack of honesty, but I have been so afraid of losing you …. and me … and our wonderful relationship.'

She was on the point of tears again, when David asked the question she hoped he wouldn't. 'Cathy, just how much *do* you owe the bank?'

Out with it, Lass. 'Nearly £18,000.'

'Jesus, that's a lot of money.' She felt his shock, his surprise.

'Aye, David, it is, as the manager stressed in justifying the bank's need to declare bankruptcy.'

'But can they just do that? Can they just sell up a place as historic, as permanent as Glendaruel? It'd have to be worth a hell of a lot more than £18,000.'

'Well, yes, I would have thought so, too. But, Darling, do we have any choice?'

***

Once dressed, Catherine led David down to the former estate manager's office. It was at the far end of the servant hall from the kitchen. Yet, once at the door, she hesitated – as always, that sensation of dread. Here, her wedding night had been ruined by the marauding Mrs MacAdam. That encounter had set the tone for her marriage, and, she realised now, for her whole miserable existence at Glendaruel. Was having to deal with this room at the heart of why she'd let the estate finances slip? Or was that making excuses?

Catherine forced herself to enter. Once seated at the solid teak desk, she initially drew Dave's attention to an enlarged photo hanging opposite. It was a faded black and white aerial shot labelled *Glendaruel Estate 1952,* from which she indicated the original estate boundaries as a large prosperous working farm of seasonal crops and livestock herds. For over a century, she explained, the estate had provided generational employment for many local families. Mrs Duffy's forester husband, for example, had been born on the estate.

'And died somewhere in France?' David asked.

'Aye.' Catherine offered a rueful smile. 'Indeed, Glendaruel's laird, the young colonel himself, didn't return either. Killed at Arras in 1918.'

'That's him in the library?'

She nodded. 'Then the British Army's youngest ever full colonel from a Scottish regiment, and ironically the youngest to be killed with that rank.'

'And your father-in-law?'

'Died upstairs, in the room next to ours. Returned from Korea with what ultimately were fatal wounds, but not making full colonel, like his father, upset him more.'

'Oh … And your James just a few years later in Singapore in yet another war – the Malayan one. Jeez, that's a sad family history.'

'Aye. The MacAdams have done their bit for the British Empire.' She offered a cautious grin. 'You've met them all at the family mausoleum.'

Feeling a little better, Catherine explained what she knew of the estate finances. Following the death duties fiasco in 1958, the much-reduced estate should have survived on land rental to neighbouring estates, but James' mother maliciously chalked up massive bills, including her own funeral, despite being wealthy herself.

Then, the 1960s brought much increased costs of living, rising bank and service fees and changes to the land taxation system. Soon, a bank overdraft was needed, and more recent estate costs followed with major electrical and plumbing problems, and a new motor for the Morris. And, only months before Dave's arrival, came the need to increase the overdraft.

Next, from a dusty filing cabinet Catherine took out a buff file of bank statements, some still in envelopes. Once placed in order she and David were able to confirm how an increasingly upward spiral of bills, bank fees and overdraft interest continued to outweigh credits – land rental and Catherine's small military widow pension – by well over £150 pounds each month. 'With one thing after another, I'd stopped caring. Stopped living, really.'

She reached for his hand. 'Then you appeared, David, and … and, quite suddenly, I *had* a reason to live. I don't think you fully understand the consummate effect you've had on me, my life. Well … except in the area of financial management.' She watched him again, unsure of the effect of this admission, for despite his reassuring smile, feelings of guilt and stupidity remained, and nudging that, Catherine detected, the return of that sense of panic.

***

With Catherine finally settled into sleep beside him, Dave remained fully awake, dissecting the bankruptcy – everything. How long till they were turfed out of the estate? Should they somewhere salt away quality ornaments from the place, like stuff from those trunks from

164

overseas? Also, those paintings from Spain they'd found under the staircase when he'd first arrived – she'd once said they were valuable. But, where to stash it all, and … the big question, where will they go?

Eventually, Dave remembered something he'd overheard William Boyle say outside the colonel's study – about Cathy's economic problems, and his offer to help. Hadn't really registered at the time, but … but how could Boyle have known about any of this? Was there a connection?

21.

On the Thursday night before Easter, Mungo rang from London. He requested Dave be at Pollcrayvie Castle on the following Tuesday morning, as a local earth moving contractor would be arriving on site then. Dave could only agree to the request.

Both he and Catherine understood how Mungo's project offered them a focus moving forward, a distraction from the impending bankruptcy. Thus, with the last of his travel money, the sale of a diamond encrusted brooch and some dizzy driving around Glasgow, by Saturday evening Dave was satisfied. He'd bought a decent dumpy level, and laying out equipment and digging tools, all second hand, to begin Mungo's job. No work van, but with careful loading it would all fit into the Morris Traveller.

Rising at a freezing 5.00 am to head off to Pollcrayvie initially stirred Dave's sense of adventure. Despite other raging concerns, Mungo's job was an exciting challenge, in an exciting location, the dream of any young landscaper. That for the next few months he and Catherine would only see each other at weekends finally hit the young Australian as he put his luggage in the car. It was her small leather case and she'd packed it for him. Since waving goodbye to his family at Port Melbourne the previous year, he'd often felt guilty for not really missing them. But early gnawing in his stomach suggested this already was different.

Over an early breakfast, they kept up a cheery discussion of the weather forecast, Mungo's landscaping, rent money from the cottages, the new dog – anything but the bankruptcy. The small cross-terrier was a good yapper, at times almost desperate to prove her worth as a watch dog. Good company for Catherine, they were sure *wee Kenzie* was frightened of nothing – except Sergeant Major.

Catherine's got the shitty end of the stick, Dave realised, as he started the car. She was now left to poke around in the house that she soon would lose. They had decided she should make up a list of things that may be sold separately, secretly.

But, where to hide them before bailiffs came bursting onto the estate, yelling, and pointing? Although stating she was fine, Catherine didn't look fine at all, standing there on the front steps in the first of the morning light, a long, sad face, with arms wrapped around herself as if in a straight-jacket, the dog and cat demarcating territory at her feet.

Dave got out of the idling vehicle, and hugging her again, reiterated how the bankruptcy made no difference. 'Cheer up, Cathy,' he added. 'We're … We'll … we …' He stopped. 'Shit! I've forgotten what I was gonna say!'

He stood there, embarrassment rising up through his skull until he heard Cathy begin to giggle. Then laugh. And soon they were both loudly laughing, in each other's arms. Only stopping to kiss and wipe the tears of happiness, of love, away.

***

Arriving at the castle, the bankruptcy retreated to the back of Dave's mind. So did any initial hesitancy at finding himself working directly with Mungo, a man of considerable means, confidence, and personality. Given the freedom to run with his own ideas, the Australian was immediately absorbed in the work, measuring, levelling, and pegging out during the day, and drawing, and redrawing plans in the evening. Mungo proved a willing companion, running out string lines and digging where told, and keen to learn from the experience. In that first week at Pollcrayvie Castle, they drew up plans for the spit that satisfied Mungo's wish for both function and appearance. As earth moving began, they had already settled on a detailed works program that would have parts of the castle grounds completed for summer visitors.

By April's end, a web of string lines, boning rods and other markers designating new roads and walking paths emanated from the castle, and rows of newly planted shrubs, and fresh garden beds and mounds of soil and gravel also had appeared. Dave now understood his own role in the project could stretch well past Alex's rock festival and into autumn, if only he and Catherine could find a new home.

For Catherine, however, left alone to await bankruptcy and the bailiffs, this period was oppressive. Over some days, she drew up a list of saleable objects in the house – ornaments, paintings, furniture, boxes of old smoothie and other items of value, either unwanted or undetected by the MacAdam hordes, who, years earlier, had gone through the house and machine shed once the estate was declared hers by law.

Let them take some things, her then solicitor had said, and they won't demand *everything*. Said they were coming back for the colonels' portraits, but never did. Never came back at all, as if returning for more booty would have equated to stealing, as now making lists for secret auction or sale did, emotionally, for her.

And the conundrum remained: where to stash and/or sell valuables, once decided upon? Were they breaking the law in doing so? She almost wished the bankruptcy to begin, so as to stop the *waiting*.

Near the end of that first week, William Boyle arrived at the house, unannounced, and unruffled by loud and long attention from Kenzie. The man was all charm and smiles, as if his brutish behaviour in January had never occurred, and Catherine, though not allowing him past the central hall, adopted a similar attitude. His menace now took a poor second place to that of the bankruptcy.

Indeed, if bankruptcy bailiffs had walked in the door at that moment, she would have enjoyed the look on Boyle's face. He had begun his usual spiel, but she wasn't really listening. He offered assistance – from marriage to financial support – and three or four times used the phrase, *if anything should happen*. He also emphasised Catherine's supposed solitary existence; did she have his phone number, should he call in more often?

'No thank you,' was her clear reply, closing the front door. Yet, she was left wondering just what had prompted the visit. Only Mr Barr, and she and David knew of her financial frailty.

The following weekend, Catherine was happy to escape the gloom of Glendaruel to share the unclouded weather at Pollcrayvie Castle with David and Mungo. While there, the big man requested she take photos whenever she visited, and collect them, with previous snaps taken, into a record of progress of the castle grounds development. She was pleased for the diversion this labour of love offered.

Returning home recharged, she was determined to end the ever-gnawing uncertainty of a bankruptcy date and rang the bank for an appointment with Mr Barr. Surprised and irritated by a clear refusal of her request, she immediately drove into Dumfries and waited in the bank for him to go out to lunch.

When he did appear, she politely yet publicly pelted him with questions. Then, as she later related to David, with the attention of everyone upon him, the man pushed her away, yelling abuse, and bolted out the front door, more like a bloody bank robber than a mild-mannered manager! If nothing else, it had cheered her up.

***

'Mungo, why all the mystery?'

'Aye, apologies for the melodrama, but I did want to get you both alone. Before we begin the week's work, Laddie.' They had entered the aged walled garden behind the castle, skirted its forlorn flowerbeds, and now were inside an expansive, yet charming iron-framed glass house, bare except for a lonely wrought iron table setting, and some empty pots. Mungo indicated the chairs.

He watched Catherine and Davie sit down and look about, as if seeking clues to explain this unexpected development. It was a sunny May morning and they'd only just arrived from Glendaruel. He understood Catherine would soon return home and come back for Davie the following weekend.

Only his second time inside, Mungo again took in the glass house. Perhaps 10 foot high by 20 wide, it stretched away before them, empty wooden shelves down one side, its pebbled floor dotted with weeds. White paint was peeling off the metal frame in places like a major skin problem, but the glass panels of the wall and roof seemed intact. Before entering, Davie had suggested the extended building would have a north-south axis to catch the all-day sun.

'What a find, Mungo. It seems complete.'

Now unsure how to start, the Scotsman hesitated before sitting down himself. 'Righto.' He smiled sheepishly at them. 'Och, damn it, you see, I'm worried about you both. You can tell me to mind my own business, but I'm concerned for you.'

He watched them exchange glances, surprised.

'Tell old Mungo to bugger off, if you wish, but I feel I am allowed at least to be concerned with the welfare of my employee, my head man here.' He offered an apologetic face.

Again, they looked at each other. Then Catherine spoke. 'No, nothing is wrong, Mungo, but we appreciate you asking.'

He waited, looking from one to the other. 'Now, don't give me that tripe. While it is admirable of you, Catherine, to drive David back and forth from Dumfries, I am sure there are many other things you would prefer to do with your time. Do you really have to share the one wee car?'

He hesitated, but not long enough for an answer. 'But it's more than that. You see, David here is quite chirpy on the job, but at other times you both seem burdened, talking in hushed tones. Anxious, if you like.' He nodded at Catherine. 'Especially you, my dear. On Saturday, while I was praising the skin off wee Davie for his mighty landscaping and organisational efforts to date, you were totally preoccupied, mind elsewhere. Peru perhaps! So, unlike the *you* I've come to know and like.' He beamed across at her.

'Now, I doubt the problem is with your relationship, for your ongoing concern for each other is obvious. So, share it with someone who considers himself a friend, and who still feels indebted to you. What has happened to that nervous but happy couple who helped celebrate my birthday only last month? If it's societal pressures upon your relationship, I can fully sympathise. Alex and I also have suffered for daring to challenge the norms of conservative Scottish society. Chlodagh and Paul in a mixed marriage, Robert and Jean, close cousins, if you hadn't already guessed. To be different, well ...' He raised both hands.

He waited, conscious of the solitude of the glasshouse – no external noise at all.

170

'Please!' Mungo hit the table with both hands. 'Is it financial? Money?'

***

Catherine was jolted into an awkward smile. She really didn't want anyone else to know of this, her stupidity, her shame, but it was kind of Mungo to be concerned. She wasn't used to such consideration. 'Well, yes, it is money.' She felt David's hand grasp hers. 'I … I seem to have gotten myself, well, both of us, into quite a jam.' Here goes, and she began to explain it all to Mungo, starting with Barr's declaration of her bankruptcy.

'That's an awful lot of money, my dear – £18,000.'

'Aye, it is.' As she continued, he asked questions, and then focused on recent events. Does her mail ever go astray? How definite was the bank manager? What sort of fellow is he?

'You may know of him, Mungo: Jimmy Barr. Mr Barr to me, of course.'

'Jimmy Barr, the former rugby star?' Catherine nodded. 'Jimmy Barr, *everyone's friend*? Och, can't imagine him bankrupting anyone.'

'One and the same, though I'm now less convinced he is *everyone's friend*. I was quite taken aback by both my impending insolvency and his unusual behaviour.'

David looked up. 'Is the bank manager famous?'

'Aye, definitely in Borders rugby circles. Has a number of Scotland caps as well. Quite a character, by all accounts.' Mungo asked more questions, and as she answered Catherine felt the burden begin to shift.

The big man moved in his chair. 'I understand all of this must be difficult for you, Catherine. But let us now concentrate on what we are to do about it. More to the point perhaps, what *can* we do?' He was silent for a few moments, one hand on his chin. 'Now, may I offer some initial suggestions?'

'Of course.'

171

'First, today. It would not be sensible for you to drive back alone to Glendaruel, upset as you are. Stay here with us tonight, at least. There's more than enough room, as you know, and the McCargos would love the company. Second, you mentioned preparing a list of items to sell. Describe the significant pieces.'

He waited for an answer. 'Well, come on, Davie. Encourage her.'

***

That evening, during dinner on the patio, Mungo returned to the subject. 'I've made a number of phone calls and am now in a better position to offer advice. Hmm?' The faces of his guests brightened.

'First, Catherine, no bankruptcy order on Glendaruel Estate has yet been lodged with the Sheriff's Office in Dumfries. Perhaps the bank is still to do this, but I have now made arrangements to be informed before it occurs.' Grinning, he rubbed a forefinger on the side of his nose.

He poured Catherine and David more wine. 'Now, until the bank acts, you may pay off all or part of the sum owed. However, while raising money through the sale of heirlooms or antiques is legal, it does need a careful approach, with suitable catalogues, which I can supply.'

He wagged a finger at them. 'Important, Catherine, because it is likely you will need to repay some, if not all of the £18,000 owed to the bank.' He hesitated. 'Third, I want you to accept a loan of £4000 from me, to be transferred immediately into your account at the bank. Apart from providing a cash flow and reducing interest, it may trigger a *reaction* at your bank branch. A fishing expedition, you might say.'

'Mungo, that's very generous of you.' He watched them exchange cautious grins. 'Are you sure?'

Mungo sipped his wine – he was sure. 'If you agree to the loan, my dear, I will need both your passports, as surety.' He hesitated again, expecting a reaction, but nothing. 'More a sensible formality than a matter of trust, my friends. Now, the interest charge will be a case of Glendaruel's oldest single malt Chivas Regal. Old smoothie, I think you said.' His eyes lit up. 'A smooth drop, I remember. Hmm?'

He watched Catherine again look across at young Davie, who nodded. 'Thank you, thank you, Mungo. I agree. And I am *sooo* relieved.' She sat grinning for a moment longer, until she asked the one question that equally intrigued him. 'Mungo, why would Mr Barr have suggested bankruptcy was to be immediate?'

22.

'Is that Boyle's car, Cathy?' Dave stopped the Morris halfway down Glendaruel's long, shady driveway. They were returning after some days at Pollcrayvie Castle.

'Aye, it is.'

'What do we do? I can reverse back quickly before he sees us.'

'No, David, go on. This is my house still. It's … our home.'

He turned towards her, admiring her courage; he just couldn't match it. Instead, was rising anxiety – butterflies in the stomach. Butterflies? What a stupid expression – more like large, black bats flapping about inside him, screeching, and ripping into his guts. He was frightened of Boyle. It was stupid, he knew. The man hadn't done anything to him. But then Boyle was yet to see them like this, as a couple.

'Catherine?'

'David, I've have had enough of William Boyle and his visits. Reluctant as I was earlier, it's time to confront him with our relationship. I'm sure he'll see reason when we explain – your accident, everything. We've done nothing wrong. And, as I've said before, it really is none of his business.' Her resolve was clear.

Dave tried to understand his own fear, as reluctantly he moved the Morris forward. And all too soon they were parked next to the Zodiac. Once out of the car, they could hear distant barking, from the back of the house – Kenzie. 'Hear that?'

'Yes. Well, let's get your case inside.' Catherine unlocked the front door and stepped into the hall.

'*Catherine!*' The shout came from outside, yet Dave could sense its demanding tone. He stiffened further; the fear now entrenched. '*Catherine!*'

The raised volume in Kenzie's barking announced the man's approach. Together, they stood inside the shadowy hall, waiting. Dave felt like a frightened school kid outside the headmaster's office.

William Boyle came into view through the front door, his cap in one hand, perhaps to fend off the dog. They watched him mount the front steps, face stern with effort, and then shed the late sunlight to become a silhouette, a momentary malevolence that filled the doorway. Dave felt Catherine's hand tighten in his, then drop away.

William stepped into the hall, his eyes blinking. 'Ah, Catherine, thought I heard a vehicle. You are so difficult to catch these days, so have waited.' A hesitation. 'Who's that with you?'

Dave and Catherine spoke together. 'Hello, William.'

'Oh, the nephew. Well, a surprise to see you back here so soon.' The man stepped closer; his eyes narrowed. Kenzie was still barking outside.

'William, I must–'

'Catherine, what made you get that bloody wee dog?' He pointed back towards the front door. 'It's been trying to bail me up since I arrived.' His sharp eyes shifted to Dave. 'Laddie, perhaps you can talk some sense into your aunt.' He stepped forward again, offering his hand.

Catherine quickly moved between them. 'William, there is something you must understand. You see, David is not my nephew. He and I are … we have been living here together since August last. We love each other.'

The man's head turned, his eyes narrowing. 'But it's me you must love, Catherine.' He touched his chest with one hand. 'I'm the one who has looked out for you, watched over you – loved you, for all these years. No one else.'

'No, William. It's not like–'

'No, Catherine, you listen. I'm here today, like those other times, to offer my help, to support you, in any time of need. And I know you need help right now. So, it is me that deserves your love, no one else – not your nephew.' He gestured towards Dave.

'William, David is not–'

The man's voice rose. 'But I now know you have gained considerable help elsewhere. However, I can't imagine this boy having that sort of money.' He hesitated, head nodding, in emphasis. 'I can lend you … no, give you that money if it's what you want.

Catherine, that's all I have ever wanted to do – to support you and love you. But you have never let me – you are always so stubborn, so proud. So MacAdam. Others have welcomed my help – Elaine, at … at Galashiels …' He stopped and leant back on his heels.

Dave remained silent, fearful anything he said would only inflame the situation. From his position, he could see the half colonel's portrait up to their left. Come alive Colonel, come down off the wall and take charge. Order this bastard out.

Catherine was speaking again, her voice clear and earnest. 'William, please listen to me. First, *you* may have wanted to love me and care for me, but I have not encouraged this.' She paused. 'Second, apart from those helpful phone calls to the garages in Thornhill when the Morris broke down early last year, you have never really been around when I've needed assistance – never arrived with tools to begin repairs. And now you have the cheek to claim me, as if … as if somehow, I'm indebted to you, or … or waiting here for you. And, just what do you mean when you say *that sort of money*? What *sort* of money are you referring to? And just what gives you the right to inquire into my financial affairs?' Voice raised; she was visibly angry now.

Yet, instead of answering, William shifted his gaze to Dave. 'And what makes you think, boy, you can just waltz back here and stay on? You know nothing about Catherine, the Glendaruel Estate, the MacAdams.' A hand was again at his chest. 'Well, I do. I've made it my business to. Aye, I've been visiting Catherine since her husband's death, 12-13 years now. It was me at James' side in Singapore when he was killed. It was me here to help when Mrs MacAdam senior passed away.'

'William, stop it!' Catherine raised both arms, a bizarre reminder to Dave of a footy goal umpire. 'You did no such thing. Stop altering history to justify your needs.'

The man's eyes widened; his mouth hung open. His actions had slowed. Was there a momentary drop of his shoulders? Then, he burst into a large, friendly grin. 'Catherine, can we not discuss this over a cup of tea? Perhaps with a slice of that fruit cake you always make for me?' The grin seemed natural, relaxed, as if together they were sharing travel information for next Christmas.

176

Good, thought Dave, he can see the reality. Yeah, give him a cup of tea, Catherine, and some bloody cake, and then he'll choof off. Come on.

But rather than turn towards the kitchen with a conciliatory smile, she stepped across the hall to intercept William, now moving towards the drawing room, her voice defiant, her eyes fixed upon him. 'No, William, we will end this right here, right now. I do want you to be fully aware of the relationship between David and I, and hopefully wish us well, as a true friend might. Yes, I understand you will make judgements of our age disparity, of our different backgrounds, perhaps. But, you see, David brings to me things you never have, and that is honesty and ... sincerity.'

William glanced up at Dave and back at Catherine, as if realising for the first time there was an age difference.

With raised voice, she continued. 'However, what I do abhor is the thought of you meddling into my affairs, the estate affairs. I cannot forgive you for this. And, who? *Who* is giving you this information? This is my home, so unless you are willing to relate everything you know – or think you know ...' She stopped. 'In fact, just leave.' Of similar height to William, she seemed to rise an extra inch with the last short sentence.

Dave watched the continuing interplay, the fear again contorting his stomach, his mind jamming up with worry. Don't challenge him Catherine, don't make him angrier. Does it matter what he knows now? We're over the worst, Mungo is helping us out. Don't spoil it – just give him the bloody cup of tea.

William began laughing, effortlessly, unforced, then he stopped, as quickly as he'd begun. 'Catherine, I know the estate has slipped into deep financial trouble, to the point of bankruptcy. I also know in the past few days £4000 has been paid into your account, no doubt in an attempt to prevent this.'

His voice remained steady, controlled. 'But, a waste of time, aye.' He poked a finger towards her. 'Just see sense, Catherine. Get rid of this lad and agree to my financial ... and emotional help, and your life will turn around. We can then work at our relationship – give it time, perhaps.'

The man's simpering smile reminded Dave of an encouraging game show host. 'Your bank manager, the famous Jimmy Barr, is my cousin. Aye, and my friend, indeed everyone's friend, as you may know.' A benevolent smile now. 'I can convince him to postpone bank action until we sort out all your problems.'

Catherine remained in front of the drawing room door, still glowering at the man. 'William, please leave. You've said enough – too much in fact. Please just leave. Now.' Speaking as if to an unworldly child, she pointed to the still-opened front door and the sunshine outside.

William looked to the door, and then back to Catherine, the head again angled. He suddenly snapped at her, voice high, face contorted. 'Catherine, you're shunning me! I won't be shunned! James did it in Singapore. Always the fucking MacAdams.' William then indicated Dave. 'Does he know how to do it, Catherine? Can't imagine a young boyo like him even getting it up.' He leered at Dave. 'Can you get it up yet, Laddie? Is she a good fuck then, Miss Hoity Toity here?'

The grinning Scotsman advanced upon him. Cold, abject fear gripped the young Australian.

'Stop it, William. I said, *get out!*' Her voice shrill, Catherine again began to cross the hall to intercept him. But this time, with indecent ease the Scotsman grabbed her high up on one arm, pulled her towards him, and slapped her face hard with his free hand. Then, with a casual shove, he sent her plunging off balance like a suddenly unwanted rag doll towards the parlour. The momentum carried Catherine through the doorway into the room, but not before her forehead cracked against the door frame. One desperate hand momentarily was seen to grope for purchase on the ornate edging before disappearing completely from view.

Dave heard Catherine collapse onto the morning room floor, out of sight. Yet, it was the sharp resonating thwack of her head on the solid framing that filled his head, that fired him, that launched him clumsily forward. 'You bastard, you fucking bastard.' How many times he screamed this, he wasn't sure, his mind busy selecting and processing objective and intention.

Reaching the Scotsman, Dave's hands and arms began to flail at the man's head, unsure of how else to attack. But his intention was now clear, and as unambiguous as that of a sniper clinically selecting the target booked for elimination. Controlling the anger, the sudden, deep overwhelming rage at such physical treatment of Catherine, he groped for the other man's throat.

His arms, longer than Boyle's, soon found their quarry, and both hands began to squeeze, almost happily squeeze the man's neck. Now, his arms could feel the frantic pulling of his adversary's hands, but he knew he could resist it. Anyway, he wouldn't need long – the Scotsman's strength was flagging.

The reverie, however, was short lived. Sudden pain, sudden searing pain that tore at his very breathing forced Dave's hands from Boyle's neck. He groped instead for his own crutch where the man's knee somehow had made crushing contact. All other senses dulled with the terrible throbbing, his long body automatically bent over double, lost balance, and fell sideways onto the hall floor. Almost before his internal system could begin to cope with this new agonizing circumstance, an unexpected jolt of pain came to his ribcage, again, again, and then again. Curling reactively into a protective foetal position, he tensed for more kicking.

But none came, yet through the intense throbbing of his balls and ribs he sensed the man's continued presence – his bellowing, and movement on the wooden floor, perhaps a dance of triumph. Taut in readiness for the next kicking, and still fighting for breath, Dave glanced up towards his assailant.

Boyle now was near the front door and indeed performing a sort of jig, jumping about, kicking forward, back, sideways, all the while yelling, sometimes shrieking. But equally involved was a small brownish dog, skilfully dodging the kicking, cavorting legs, yet biting when it could. Blood was on William's trouser legs.

'Wee Kenzie,' Dave murmured, and he might have smiled, had his own pain allowed it. Once or twice, the Scotsman was able to kick or push the dog away, but almost immediately it would throw itself again at the legs, growling and yapping and snapping.

With Boyle so absorbed, Dave lifted his head for any sign of Catherine, but nothing. God, he remembered it all now – the fucking bastard whacking her like that, and the kicking he'd got too. A shame old Kenzie wasn't any fucking bigger.

He could hear the Scotsman yell in snatches. 'Get to fuck away! Owww … yer little shite. Fuck off from me. Oh, shit. Owwwww!'

With Boyle preoccupied with the dog, Dave attempted to rise, piercing pain in his abdomen and ribs restricting each effort. But anxiety for Catherine and the desire to finish this with Boyle forced him up onto one knee, then the other – now unsteadily onto his feet, all the while dragging in great draughts of air.

The Scotsman, still cursing and yelling had moved into the front door space, bracing himself against the polished frame for better defence against Kenzie. The dog held back inside the doorway, just out of range of Boyle's feet, but attacked and snapped at opportune times. The man turned towards Dave, now staggering, bent over, towards him.

'I haven't … ouch. Oww!' He kicked out again at the dog. 'I … I haven't finished with you, yer young tosser.' A hand was up rubbing his neck. 'No one backdoors me … Get off, fuck yer. Fucking dog! No one, not even pre … precious James.' It was difficult to hear him over Kenzie's snarling and yapping.

'Aye, Laddie. If … if I find you here again, I'll kill you.' He let go of the door frame and pointed with emphasis at Dave. 'Catherine and the house belong to me.' As if to disagree, Kenzie dashed forward and bit hard into one of his legs. 'Aaowww! Christ. Call this fucking dog off. Oww.' With the animal now limpet-like on his leg, Boyle staggered backwards through the door onto the front landing, reeling like a drunk reluctant to leave a pub. Dave, desperate to finish this, lurched to the front doorway after him.

'William!'

Glancing up, the Scotsman seemed at first surprised to see Dave in the doorway, but quickly recovered. 'Want some more, Laddie? Aye? I'll show –'

Dave's right fist landed hard on Boyle's jaw, and the man crashed down the front steps, arms flailing like someone trying to attract attention. He landed on his behind in the gravel, a zephyr of dust rising about him. Feeling for his chin, he looked bewildered, eyes searching down and around, as if he should be somewhere else. Blood was coming from his mouth.

Feet apart, Dave stood at the top of the steps, waiting for the figure at the bottom to rise. The young Australian tried not to sway, tried not to look vulnerable, despite the persistent pain in his ribs and crutch, and now fist. Beside him, Kenzie continued to bark and growl at the intruder, the small body shaking with nervous energy.

Despite the many aches, Dave felt terrific, ready to face anyone – anything. He had proved himself – to himself.

Dave waited for Boyle to charge back up the house steps, swinging and swearing. Thus, he was surprised to see the Scotsman drag himself up against the Zodiac and open the driver's door. Propping himself there, Boyle glared up the stairs.

'As I said, Laddie, I'll kill you if I find you here again.' Slowly, he began to climb into the car, but stopped. 'And don't think I won't – I've crossed the line before. As Elaine … as James found out.'

'And I'll call the police if you ever so much as drive near Glendaruel!' It was Catherine, voicing venom, as she leant on Dave for support. She had the maharajah's shotgun pointed at Boyle.

The Scotsman stiffened. 'I … I've warned you, Catherine. You're mine. No one else's.'

'Just fuck off, William.' Dave wanted it finished.

Boyle's head lifted. 'You can't tell me to fu–'

'But *I* can. Now fuck off.' Catherine leant further into Dave. *Fook orf*, mimicked Dave's brain.

The Scotsman stood a moment longer before getting into the car, his movements uncoordinated.

Then, with a deafening roar, the Zodiac backed away from the house, narrowly missing the Morris. With equal clamour, it tore off along the drive, and could be heard for at least another minute impatiently making its way down along Burnhead Lane to the Dumfries Road.

23.

'Next please!' The Sister in Charge hardly looked up as she called out across the white-tiled accident emergency room of the infirmary. It was already half full of the human detritus of a Dumfries Friday night. Relief from the stifling mix of body odour and cigarette smoke only came when the large glass doors to the outside world swung opened to admit more damaged people.

A dishevelled, middle-aged woman with a badly swollen eye and blood seeping from behind one ear arose from a chair with a clatter. 'It's me, Sister. Joyce Reid. I've had an accident.'

The Sister watched the ragged figure approach. 'Aye, it is you, Mrs Reid. And that's a nasty eye you have this time. Scrappin' again?'

'Och, well. I'll tell you, my Jock, he –'

'Now, you pop along to the nurses in the treatment bay and tell them what it is that's happened. They're sure to fix you up – you may need a wee stitch or two. There's a dear.' She began writing in the registry. 'Next!'

Catherine rose and assisted Dave, wincing with pain as he straightened up after ninety minutes of waiting in a hard plastic chair. Few of those sprawled around the room bothered to look up as she helped him move towards the Sister's desk.

'Name!'

'I am Catherine MacAdam, Sister.' The woman's head jerked up, as if having heard a fire alarm. She looked further at the damage to Catherine's forehead, and then across to Dave, clearly favouring his left side.

'Oh? And … and your son? Ribs?'

'Yes, ribs, but he is not my son – or my nephew, for that matter. He's David Lawson, my friend … my lover.'

The Sister sat gazing up at them, her puzzlement clear. 'Um … um.' She stopped.

She seemed to begin again. 'Um … problem?

Catherine smiled into Dave's face. 'Scrappin' again.'

***

A sleepy Catherine had just put the kettle on the stove when Kenzie began her barking. Boyle again? Then she heard a vehicle, and walking over to the kitchen window, saw, with some relief, it was a police car. She was halfway to the front door when the bell began its encouragement and waiting on the front steps was Sergeant Mackay.

'Och, Sergeant, what a surprise!' She hadn't seen him for quite some time.

'Um … morning, Mrs MacAdam, sorry to disturb you so early on a Saturday.' He had a semi-formal face. 'I … I'm following up an incident report issued by the Royal Infirmary casualty department last night and was in the area.' He indicated with a hand. 'And you do seem to have a wee patch on your forehead there. But I … I could come back later if you'd want.'

She hesitated. Then made a decision. 'Och, no. Come on in. I've the kettle on.'

Once inside, she ushered the policeman into the parlour, where he removed his helmet and relaxed into an expansive lounge chair. Sunlight was slanting across the room.

She put a hand up to her unkempt hair. 'Perhaps I should get properly dressed if I'm to be interrogated.' She quickly left.

Fifteen minutes later, Catherine was back, changed, hair brushed, and with some tea. She had woken David and he joined them as the sergeant was selecting a piece of Dundee cake.

Rather than surprised, the policeman seemed pleased to find David still living in the house. 'Morning, Laddie. Haven't seen you since your recovery. Nice to find that wee accident hasn't scared you away from us.'

Catherine interpreted that as the man's approval of their obvious relationship. She had known the sergeant since her first years at Glendaruel, and together on Coronation Day, 1953, they had solved a

183

minor crime here in the house. *The Case of the Careless Chambermaid*, they'd jokingly dubbed it, having saved the MacAdam family considerable embarrassment. Not that either of them had received much thanks, she remembered.

After further pleasantries, Catherine described the previous evening's altercation with William Boyle. David confirmed it all – the fighting, the serious threats, hints about the death of her husband, and admissions of interference in banking procedure.

He didn't know of a William Boyle, the sergeant explained, and it was an awkward situation because the police couldn't act on here-say or threats alone. Later, the man may simply deny them, or claim heat of the moment. 'Mrs MacAdam,' he concluded, 'I don't take your story lightly. I'll contact the Galashiels police, and they'll speak to Boyle, watch his movements, and find out if he has any weapons on his premises. That way, he'll know the police have been alerted to his behaviour here. Now, for peace of mind at least for this week, I suggest you don't stay at home alone. That wee yapping dog is really no protection.'

He looked at David. 'She's your responsibility, Laddie.'

'I know.'

***

With the rock festival only weeks away, Alex lead the Pollcrayvie gang on a tour of the vast open area outside the castle wall. There, Catherine could see fences, kiosks, shops, toilet blocks, lighting and other temporary equipment that had begun to appear, and recent visits by health inspectors, police, publicity agents, a film crew, plus a pegged-out helipad near the castle jetty, did begin to make it a reality.

Alex explained the importance of keeping festival goers away from key areas, and the thick stone wall across the spit would be an ideal defensive barrier, as in earlier times, to protect the castle and guests from long-haired hordes.

Catherine was pleased to be engaged to photo capture all the preparations but was less keen about Alex's request when visiting the near-completed festival stage for she and Dave to help behind the scenes, if necessary, over that weekend. Her hesitant *aye* couldn't match Dave's *bloody oath!*

Mackay rang Catherine at Pollcrayvie to inform her the Galashiels police had interviewed a subdued Boyle at the Island Hotel, and had surreptitiously removed an old, but serviceable shotgun from the premises. With his car 'accidentally neutralised' during a search, the man had since moved little from his pub.

Mungo also had good news. While Glendaruel Estate still had an unhealthy overdraft, there had never been official bankruptcy plans at her bank. Mr Barr had been relocated to head office, and embarrassed senior staff were happy to agree to a suitable repayment scheme for a much-reduced debt.

Buoyed by this news, Catherine suggested Dave should now get a work vehicle, and the following Monday he test drove a used Ford Transit van, recommended by Tom King, to Pollcrayvie. Like Lake Deugh around mid-morning, their mist was clearing.

24.

Parked late-morning in an unused gateway further along Burnhead Lane, William Boyle watched the Morris Traveller leave Glendaruel Estate with Catherine and the dippy old biddy from the gatehouse. Off to Dumfries or Thornhill, shopping, he decided. Either way, there was plenty of time.

He waited 15 minutes in case of a sudden return, then left his car and squeezed through the hawthorn hedge into the estate. Within 40 minutes he was back with a swollen sack and a grim grin of achievement. He again waited. He had all day.

It was almost 1.30pm when the Morris returned and stopped again outside the gatehouse. Aye, now give Catherine MacAdam time to unload shopping at the house, make some tea, and relax. Then, he'd go in again, and return the favour that was owed.

Boyle was about to re-enter the Glendaruel grounds, when the small station wagon unexpectedly reappeared, again leaving the estate. This time she was alone. Och, where to now, woman? Better tail her, as she must be collecting that boy, the fucking nephew. Boyle knew he wasn't in the house.

He followed the Morris down the lane towards the A76, and then on to Dumfries. Initially expecting her to park somewhere in the town centre, he was surprised when instead she took the Castle Douglas Road. Settling into a safe distance behind, he pondered Catherine's destination, and was surprised when she turned towards Ayrshire, at Crocketford. Where was she headed?

While unfamiliar with this road, Boyle understood the traffic was heavy and slow for a Friday afternoon. Yet, he again almost missed the Morris turning, this time off to the left towards Loch Doon, under a large flapping canvas poster – *SCOTTISH ROCK FESTIVAL*. What to hell was her connection with the isolated Loch Doon, or a bloody rock festival? Plenty of traffic on this minor road too, and now he was caught five or six vehicles behind her. A helicopter flew overhead: unusual?

He could only follow the slowing stream of traffic and note the polyglot collection of vehicles filled with long haired, bearded, bright coloured layabouts. What did Catherine MacAdam want with this lot?

At more billowing signs, the vehicle stream flowed right onto a gravel road, and soon they were at another loch. Then, after skirting its edge for some minutes, the vehicles in front spread out into a vast, gravelled area, like wee kiddies pouring into a popular playground.

Large hand-painted signs announced *CAR PARK*. On the left was an ancient, high wall of heavy stone, with a pair of equally massive wooden doors just closing. But not before Boyle glimpsed the distinctive rear of the Morris Traveller inside. On the wooden doors was a clear message: *Private Property – No Entry*. As he stopped the stolen Cresta and got out, the helicopter returned, this time quite low.

William Boyle had no idea where he was, but he could feel a certain sense of occasion. At the head of the carpark was a high metal barrier-fence with ticket booths and turnstile entrances, and behind it, a noticeable human hum. Heard above that and demanding attention boomed announcements and loud popular music.

Scores of vehicles were already in the car park, some parked formally, others left as if they'd run out of petrol. Large bold-printed banners on the fortress wall and surrounding fences proclaimed: *ROCK AROUND THE LOCH! Scottish Rock Festival, 4-6 June 1971, Pollcrayvie Castle, Ayrshire – All Your Favourite Rock Artists!*

Others held lists of names, many foreign to him: *Donovan, Lulu, McGuinness Flint, Edison Lighthouse, Marmalade, Writing on the Wall, Tartan Class, Howl, and many, many more of your favourite artists!* He knew some of the names from the music box in the pub. Aye, well, Bonnie Lulu too. But *Howl*? What sort of bloody name was that?

He grinned. Ha, her wee Aussie lad was going to *howl* before long! Like that yappin' dog of hers back at the house did with the pitchfork in its guts!

The huge rectangular car park area was demarcated on both sides by head-high taut wire fences; on the left between Boyle's car and the fortress wall, and up to the right where the grassed land rose considerably. Ahead, these joined at right angles to the higher metal barrier-fence with its signage and ticket booths.

The opposite end of the large, fenced rectangle, where Boyle had driven in, was now guarded. Although temporary, all the fencing looked solid enough, as did the many uniformed security men patrolling it.

As vans and cars continued to arrive, he walked up to the fence on the higher ground, and from this elevated position, could just see over the fortress wall. Behind it among trees he could make out a tall stone building – Pollcrayvie Castle? Darkish water could be seen at each end of the wall, which suggested it protected a spit of land. And behind all of this loomed watchfully the gaunt, glowering Galloway Hills.

Moving forward along the wire fence towards the activity ahead, this elevated position also enabled him to see over part of the high metal barrier into the festival area itself. A large tarpaulin-covered edifice dominated. A stage? Was this the source of the God-awful music? Nearer to him but still behind the barrier were smaller temporary structures and familiar signs: *Coca Cola, McEwans, Bank of Scotland,* a Red Cross symbol, and others.

Quite a crowd in there, already. Also inside, and to the right, an animated stream of young people moved towards a vast, open area, sloping down to the front of the stage. They seemed to congregate there, standing, sitting – must be an audience area. The hazy far side of this vast enclosure was well over 100 yards away, he guessed.

Boyle returned his attention to the castle and its wall. He could only assume the boy was already in there. *We love each other*, she'd simpered – the only reason hoity-toity Catherine MacAdam would bring herself to a rock festival.

But having already noticed the flinty eyed security people patrolling the wall and festival fences, how was he to get in there? Was a night swim the only option? With the shotgun? His fingers played with the loose cartridges in his jacket pocket.

Later, leaning on the Cresta, Boyle idly watched the endless procession of vehicles enter the car park. His was now surrounded. No going back.

Sometime after 5pm, the large doors in the fortress wall again opened, and as he walked across to the wire fence between him and the wall, two white Transit vans, seemingly full, appeared.

Escorted by a handful of guards, they turned left in the quiet area beyond the car park and ambled towards a set of gates some 40 yards away. Other vans had done this and returned while he'd been up at the wire fence. But what focused Boyle's mind now were Catherine and the very tall boy, both unmistakable in the back seat of the second van.

Now alert, Boyle watched the vans disappear through the gates into a festival area which seemed free of the rowdy crowd, no doubt restricted to the coming and going of entertainers and staff. Bloody well planned and put together, he had to admit, but now his task was more difficult. Or was it?

Wild, loud twanging began to saturate the car park. *'Tuning up. Come onn!'* a wee lad rushing past yelled to his spotty chum. Back in the car, Boyle wondered whether simply to wait for his target to return, but no doubt *her* David was here for the music and could easily be missed if later returning in the dark.

Anyway, the guards would eventually spot an older Jock hanging around the fence for hours with an 'effing shot gun! So, wait till this festival business is over? But that's not till Monday, the signs say, and he's only got Glendaruel's whisky for sustenance. Return to the pub and wait for another chance? Except the polis would already have missed him, and likely prevent that other time. He knew they'd been watching – he wasn't saft. Don't often get strangers in a mid-town pub like The Island.

He took a swig of the Chivas. No, it had to be now, get himself into the festival area, and find them. More difficult with the gun he'd hefted from Glendaruel, but, aye, better than the swimming, and he could shoot over a fence or barrier, if necessary. Catherine MacAdam shouldn't have ordered *him* off the estate with that fancy shotgun. Aye, but now, *he* was going to point it at her skinny boyfriend. Or her. Och, there's a barrel for each! Luckily, the polis hadn't found *all* his ammunition.

Taking another swig, he watched an increasing flow of effervescent people continue past him towards the festival. Almost all young, they were dressed as if fashion had gone out of fashion – bell bottom jeans and those lurid shirts, beards, long hair, shaved heads, bare feet – anything goes.

Some even wearing blankets, like those fucking Mexicans. Like the ragged car travel-rug he was sitting on now. He took another swig and smiled. Hey, Laddie, why not? Another swig.

Boyle dragged the grubby plaid rug out from under him. Aye, patchy in places but well large enough to hide the gun! He took it from the bag.

He stood outside the car, loud live music now pounding him, and absorbed the crowd, still moving past. Right, rip that worn hole in the blanket, down over his head, reverse cap, roll up trousers, scuff shoes, dirt on face. Over £40 in his pocket. And the Chivas. Ready to rock n roll!

He'd spotted a largish group threading the cars towards him, singing, laughing, drinking. He'd go with them. Standing partly hidden behind the driver's door, he quickly put his belt through the trigger guard of the brassy shotgun, allowing it to hang vertically, the butt below his chin, the muzzle touching his knees, the shells in his pockets – all out of sight.

The group momentarily enveloped both him and the car, and tagging on the end, he shared his bottle and bravado with the bearded boyos beside him. Here for the fuckin' weekend, driven from Dundee, they explained, as he laughed at their jokes and gestures. At a ticket booth, he gave one of the lads' entrance money (*left me wallet behind!*) and they moved into the festival's public area together. The music was now deafening. 'That's Tartan Class,' his new chums explained, 'Great band – base player's from Dundee,' they crowed. Hendrix heads together, they told William Boyle, sharing their joints and his whisky. 'Anytime you need dope, man, just find us.'

'Right on, man,' replied the 40-year-old publican, remembering the words but not really sure what they meant.

Right on, man: peace, man: acid head: rock on: groovy: hail Atlantis; he absorbed the language of the place as he wandered the public areas for what seemed hours attempting to infiltrate the section behind the stage. He found they were there, for peering over a patrolled barrier, he'd seen the skinny boy moving what looked like sound equipment.

Together, the pounding music, the crowd euphoria, the grating public system announcements and the gregarious, grassy aroma of hash threatened to overwhelm Boyle. Stoics, Air Force, Tear Gas, and other bands ground out their music to the screaming delight of the crowd, but he wasn't part of it: not in their time. A different rhythm.

In the end, it was quite easy. He offered two enterprising young lads £10 each to penetrate under the side of the stage into the restricted area behind, *to catch in person his favourite group of all time, aye, McGuinness Flint*, he told them – a convenient name from a convenient poster.

Under the suspended stage floor, the heavy guitar, drum, and organ chords were more pressing, more pounding, more piercing. But, as light began to fade, in the relative order of the rear stage area he again found his quarry. Her tall boy was operating from a large tent nearby, ushering bands and equipment up onto the rear of the main stage, and returning them and their gear to another tented enclosure. Later, Boyle located Catherine, in a marquee preparing and serving food to smoking, drinking, long-haired gits. Both wore security badges, and so busy, so absorbed, they didn't notice him.

Yet, a security guard almost did, but for a bunch of cables, which the man propitiously tripped upon. Alerted by the guard's curse, Boyle retreated beneath the stage, a lucky escape: a last chance, he understood. He lay there, again waiting, watching, the shotgun now loaded. Get one of them. Both, if you can.

Some minutes later, as if a director had yelled *action!* it all began. For weeks, he'd planned to *shoot* the scene on the Glendaruel set, but cameras here were ready to roll.

Catherine MacAdam had stepped out of the marquee, and stood alone, as if waiting for her cue. Now *her David* emerged from the back of the stage. Seeing each other, they waved and smiled. He came down the steps to join her, both seeming oblivious to the rock concert booming about them.

On cue, Boyle rose out from under the stage rear, stood behind a near-full industrial rubbish bin and pulled the Maharajah's shotgun tight into his shoulder. And, as the two stars of the show embraced, he pulled both triggers.

Dave looked around for the source of the blast – a lone, leaden boom above the already-deafening music. Probably a blown amp. Alex had warned him about overloaded amplifiers. Replace 'em quick if they're fucked, he'd said. Catherine turned as if she'd heard it too. 'Okay?' Dave mouthed.

She reached up and kissed him again. 'Despite the incessant noise, I'm quite enjoying myself,' she shouted into his ear. She looked gorgeous, as always: now in bell bottoms, leathery waistcoat, billowing sleeves, billowing hair, his own Marianne Faithfull. Thank Christ Jagger's not here, he joked in his head, before grinning a goodbye.

He leapt up the stage back steps as The Incredible String Band finished their set. Waiting behind the inner curtain, he watched Alex, again at the stage edge, grab the main microphone, shouting, waving his arms, demanding even more applause from the energetic, ever-moving assemblage that, in the evening light, might have extended out into the Irish Sea.

Now move. Get them off the stage quickly, their gear too. Keep low, don't hurry, unplug instruments, foot pedals, amps. Remember their individual equipment, don't slip on the sweat-covered floor, careful of the strobe lighting.

Good. Done. Enjoy a smoke, boys. Five minutes max between groups, Alex had told him, but be patient. Remember, they're all fucking *prima donnas*. Then, repeat in reverse for the next band – this time, Writing on the Wall. These groups were well known to Dave, yet he had little time to enjoy them, their music, mixing with them. Donovan tomorrow night, though, would be different!

Then, Alex was yelling, pointing! 'Where's the drummer? Find the fucking drummer!' Bending low, Dave headed backstage for the missing musician, but instead was confronted by a lurching figure, a yelling, bloodied-faced monster. Where …? How did he …?

The face was an oozing mess, pieces of flesh missing, an eyeball hanging loose. But, the voice, the screaming voice was William Boyle's.

'I'll … I'll kill her. I … I've done it before … as … as James found …'

In a riveting second of shock, Dave realised Boyle was dragging Catherine behind him, one arm around her neck, a long, metal tent stake in the other hand. And Dave, with the musicians, involuntarily stepped back.

He waited, ready to act, as Boyle, leaking gore and still holding a struggling Catherine, shuffled to the front of the stage, behind an unaware Alex at the mike. Boyle somehow shoved the announcer to the floor and began ranting into the mike about Dave and Catherine.

He'd killed her husband, James, in Singapore, he told the vast sea of feeding faces, and now he would kill her in front of them all. The crowd cheered and whistled, stimulated by what they assumed was added entertainment. With Boyle now distracted, Dave grabbed the neck of a nearby guitar and rushed forward to stop the man.

But not before Alex, rising to his knees, pulled the tent stake from Boyle's hand, and, in among the instruments, wrestled him to the floor. Quickly, Dave freed a frantic Catherine and helped her to the rear of the stage. Boyle remained on the floor, one arm now thrashing, flinging more gore about.

Recovering, Alex turned, waving wildly at the band. 'Sing Bogeyman!'

Bogeyman!' he again roared, and, pacing about the prostrate, dying Boyle, and the widening pool of blood, Writing on the Wall began to strum and sing one of their hits, about the dangerous bogeyman.

25.

(Yeppoon, Queensland – 31st December 1999)

Already apprehensive about her mission in Australia, and now over four hours late, the Scottish lawyer concentrated on gunning the hire car up the steep driveway. Thus, she was unprepared for the clear ocean panorama at the top – the exceptional view you get at a popular lookout, except here there were only two people and a wee dog. She parked under a large red-flowering tree next to a faded VW Beetle.

She got out of the car and paused to absorb the unbroken vista of islands and ocean, before turning to meet her hosts. One, a short, stocky woman stepped forward, her face conflicted. Expecting someone older, the young lawyer decided.

'Miss Fergusson?'

'Aye, that's me. Mrs Lawson?'

'Yep, we spoke on the phone.' She was fiftyish, loose summer clothes, now with a welcoming face and voice. She turned. 'And this is my husband, Dave, who your business is with.'

Aye, the man she'd come to see. She stopped to take him in. Very tall, as expected, light but greying hair, of similar age to his wife, and quiet – preoccupied? He offered a cautious nod. *Oh gosh, the scar!* Such an awful scar on the left side of his face! Oh!

It caught her out. Embarrassed, she shook their proffered hands. 'Um, aye, but it's *Ms* Fergusson. I must say the view you have here is stunning.' She was talking to recover, to settle herself. She was glad to have worn the grey suit, with her mass of blond hair restricted to a tight bun – to remain businesslike and be taken seriously. And keep a distance. But would she be too hot?

'Yep, it's a fine view, very soothing. But first, Ms Fergusson, we should say welcome to Australia; if no one else has.'

194

'Oh. Thank you both. And I must apologise again for being so late. When, in Brisbane, the flight here was delayed, and then further delayed, I was so relieved to have reached you on the phone.'

'It's fine, really it is. You've come such a long way to interview Dave, unusual as that is, and so your business must be concluded today.' Mrs Lawson looked at her watch. 'Also, friends and family will begin arriving in a few hours, a long-planned Millennium bash I'm afraid, so let's get started.'

She turned and led the way along a wide veranda, broad-leafed tropical plants in pots reaching for their ankles, and soon they entered the house through opened glass doors. Following her hosts, the young woman found herself in a bright but understated room with wide, open windows that offered more of that sea view. She stopped to take in the large, slow-revolving fan hanging from the ceiling.

'Did you have any trouble getting here from the airport, Ms Fergusson?'

'Oh, sorry!' The lawyer turned, tapping her briefcase. 'No. I'm armed with my wee map and directions from Mr Denbigh, a local solicitor.'

Mrs Lawson nodded. 'We know Bill Denbigh. Use him for Dave's landscape consulting, other personal matters. Now, a cup of tea, after your flight. Coffee, perhaps?'

'Och, if it's no trouble. Tea – white, thank you.' The young Scotswoman took off her jacket and laid it over the back of the centrally positioned settee. It was steamy. She placed her briefcase on an adjacent coffee table, and sitting down, found herself alone with the man she had come to see. A sad face perhaps, especially with that long scar, which she found was difficult not to look at. He seemed as anxious as she was.

There suddenly were so many questions to ask, but she made herself stick to the script, with a few simple queries about the house and view, until they were interrupted by loud singing nearby.

Then a young woman, a few years her junior, with a multi-coloured T-shirt and darkish frizzed hair, wandered into the room, and stopped when she saw them. 'Oops, sorry!'

The lawyer was completely thrown. A daughter? There was nothing said …

The intruder grinned and offered her hand. 'Don't mind me. I'm Terri.'

Mr Lawson reacted as if he'd been abruptly woken. 'No, no! T T, please. This is personal business, and … and Maggie did ask you to visit Rachel for a few hours this afternoon. To help her sort some music CDs for tonight.'

'Yeah, but that's only an excuse to get me out of the house!'

'Exactly. Now, please *go!*' Was that more anguish than anger in his tone?

'I'm worried you two are getting a divorce – like Mum and Dad. You're my favourite relatives, except–'

'Yeah, we know, *except for all the others!*' Mrs Lawson had returned with a tray of refreshments and the smell of baking. 'Now, please Terri, you are being rude if you don't leave us alone. No divorce – yet.' She glanced at her husband. 'Ms Fergusson here is a lawyer who's come from Scotland to interview Dave on an altogether different matter, and we must conclude it today. So, scat. I've told Rachel you're coming.'

'Okay.' She said it like a reprimanded child, then grinned again at the lawyer. 'Hey, stay for the party, why don't you? Get to be friends!'

Surprised at the comment, the lawyer smiled. 'Thank you, but no. I'm to fly home tomorrow.'

Terri rose and headed for the door. 'That's a shame. Nice to meet a female lawyer.'

Tea was poured and cake offered as the noisy VW was heard to leave. Yet the visitor hesitated, unsure how to begin. Come on, Lass.

'Well, down to business, I guess. First, here is my card.' She gave one to each of them. 'You will see that I work directly for the Kat Cale Foundation. As earlier communication explained, Ms Cale passed away in May this year, but gathering all necessary details has delayed the execution of her will. We call it a beneficiary in Scotland.'

196

Just keep talking. Keep it legal. 'Now, Mr Lawson, Miss Cale chose to list you as one of her beneficiaries, and this, of course, is why I am here.' She glanced up at him. 'However, and I apologise for asking, I will need to see some proof of identity. It's only a formality as Mr Denbigh has already vouched for you on the telephone. A passport perhaps?'

The older couple exchanged looks until Mr Lawson rose. As he left the room, his wife asked a question. 'Was Ms Cale as famous as the Web suggests? Her photographic achievements are impressive!'

'Aye, she was. Especially since the early '80s.' Find answers yourself, Lass. 'Um, Mrs Lawson, may I ask how well your husband knew her? And … when?'

'Maggie, call me Maggie.' She followed with an awkward smile. 'Now, to be honest, I'm really not sure. He's simply refused to discuss Kat Cale herself, or why he might be in her will.' The face was etched with concern. 'I've never seen him like this before. What … what is his connection with Kat Cale? Why would this upset him so much?'

She offered a lawyer's answer. 'Now, I'm not altogether certain.' Ask more yourself. Dig deeper. 'Mrs … Maggie, if it is not too personal a question, how did you meet your husband?' Would the woman answer something so direct?

There was a hesitation. 'Well, it's a long story, really. Darwin, a cyclone, 25 years ago. He's always been there when I've needed him.'

The lawyer absorbed the words, aware she had heard something similar before. The name Darwin – she knew. Ah, he's now back with the passport.

She accepted it from him, absorbed and mentally checked the details page, and returned it. 'Grand. Now we can proceed.'

'Um …' It was him. 'How … how did you know where to contact me?'

How to answer him? Hide the lie? 'Well, your details were on the beneficiary list, Mr Lawson. Perhaps, it was through the um … do-it-yourself landscaping book you produced together. Aye, published two years ago, was it? It was found … Sorry, it can be found on the Internet. Looks jolly useful. Well done, you two.'

She watched them exchange smiles of surprise, as might students with unexpectedly high marks. She put down her tea. 'Mr Lawson, as you understand, it is a condition of the will that your benefit be presented to you in person.' She opened her briefcase, took out a plain, unsealed manila envelope and held it out to him. Now, first is this.'

He sat staring at it, then glanced at his wife, as if for help. 'You see, I … I've decided I don't want anything. Look, it's great to be thought of, um … remembered, but perhaps the other people in the will can have whatever's been left to me.' He hesitated. 'Yeah, give it all to them. I really don't want any money. Don't deserve anything.'

The young lawyer struggled to keep a neutral face. 'Mr Lawson, for one, Ms Cale has left you no money. And two, before you be so definite, I feel you must understand just what has been bequeathed to you. And why.'

26.

The fatal accident inquiry into William Boyle's death at Pollcrayvie Castle tainted that whole summer for Catherine and Dave. Told by the procurator fiscal to be ever available, they remained at Glendaruel, and saw little of their friends. And, because the circumstances of the crime were so unusual – at one sitting, Sergeant Mackay's description of finding pieces of the man's face and head spattered around the back of the stage from the exploding shot gun drew silence for some moments – the subsequent judicial process was long and ponderous.

A police submission that made clear their innocence in the incident and events leading to it was eventually accepted, and William Boyle was given full credit for his own demise. Some of the papers did run with the story; *Jilted Lover Blows Out Own Brains*, and *Maharajah's Curse Kills Galashiels Gent,* were perhaps the most colourful of the coverages, which happily had ceased by autumn.

David and Catherine separately blamed themselves for allowing the other to be so exposed to a rampaging Boyle, yet each somehow failed to articulate this. With false bravado, Dave relegated the attempt on his life to equal footing with having been impaled on a tree the year earlier.

For Catherine, the shocking episode was far more personal. Growing evidence suggested she had been the second female to be groomed in Boyle's financial intrigue with his cousin Jimmy Barr. An investigation into the death years earlier of Boyle's wife, Elaine Murray, was begun, and equally, the British Army saw reason to follow up on Boyle's disclosures about Major James MacAdams' death in Singapore 13 years earlier.

At a time when increased nurturing, understanding and appreciation would have greatly assisted mutual healing, the busy schedule Catherine and Dave individually set themselves during the unusually warm autumn meant instead they were seeing less of each other rather than more.

Through a Mungo recommendation, Dave began another large landscaping job near Peebles, and also found time to travel with Alex to rock festivals in England.

Catherine, now fully ostracised by the St Georges' community in Thornhill, busied herself in the walled garden, and with antique lists and auction houses, staying with Chlodagh Harris when in Edinburgh. She also assembled a portfolio of exhibitable photographs from those of Pollcrayvie Castle and Lake Deugh while designing colourful brochures for Mungo's tourism venture. It was still an uncomfortable joke for her that David's family in Australia had commented on his improved photography, unaware that she now took most of the photos they received.

As if by mutual consent, the members of Mungo's circle, all of whom had been in the cheering, chanting crowd near the stage at the time of Boyle's death, had avoided each other since then. However, they met again at the castle in September to celebrate Pollcrayvie's opening to the public, and it had begun like a reunion of the Titanic survivors. There was initial shuffling of feet, averted eyes, then sudden strong we-are-forever-joined handshakes and hugs. And lots of drink. Alex, who had suffered a heavy financial loss with the forced cancellation of the rest of the rock concert, was unsurprisingly subdued.

For Catherine and David, the industrious autumn flowed into a hectic winter of parties and celebrations. There was Halloween with Tom King and family, a full house at Christmas with guests Mungo, Alex, Jim and Candice, and Ralph from Florida. And more was to come with Hogmanay at home with Cheryl and her new partner.

***

The night wasn't going well. Catherine had come to understand Cheryl's new man was another ex-military type who struggled to find a purpose in civilian life. Forewarned, she had welcomed ex-Major Rory MacRobertson with a tour of Glendaruel's K.O.S.B. memorabilia. However, that she had a young, long-haired, bead-wearing boyfriend seemed to counteract any military advantage, despite introductions to the two resident colonels.

And, in defiance of their combined campaign of Hogmanay cheer, he was already surrendering to the effects of the sumptuous meal and numerous old smoothies as they retreated to the drawing room.

That Rory had fallen into a deep arm-chair sleep wasn't realised until they'd turned off the raucous New Year's television program. Cheryl glanced apologetically at Catherine and Dave on the couch opposite, and then down at her watch. 'God, it's only 10.23. A while yet till midnight!'

Catherine gave a relaxed flourish with her glass. 'Should we prop him up here with us in the hope of a revival, or get him upstairs?' To that, Rory offered a series of satisfied snores.

The three of them, despite their own alcohol consumption, soon had the weighty ex-soldier upstairs and onto the bed in the guest bedroom. Closing the door, Cheryl apologised again, but Catherine, in comparing her youthful, worldly Dave to this limited Rory character, wished to put her friend at ease. '*Dinna fash yousel*, Cheryl.' The colloquialism that only their grandmothers would have used raised a giggle. 'Come on back down. Another drink? A sherry, perhaps. The three of us can have a wee jig before midnight, eh David? And first footing at midnight – we need your dark complexion, Cheryl!'

Dave put a long arm around her shoulders. 'Come on, Cheryl. I'm expecting at least one dance with you, and a sly snog when Catherine's not looking. Like last New Year!'

Catherine pretended not to notice but heard her friend's giggled reply.

'Well, thank you, David. You are a treasure. They should make more like you. And … and I've a mind to try that marijuana you've mentioned.'

Then her face offered apology. 'Look, I understand now it was a mistake to think this would work. Not your fault. My problem, really.' She sighed. 'Rory can be such a disappointment when he puts his mind to it.' She tried to laugh it off. 'No, you two pop along and enjoy the Hogmanay moment together. Three's always a crowd. Perhaps, it's best I'm here when he wakes up. If he wakes up.' She looked to the heavens. 'Where to pee … where to vomit. No *Tunes of Glory* tonight!'

Catherine looked back as, arm-in-arm, she and David descended the staircase. Cheryl was watching them, envy etched into her face.

A slow inhale and Dave passed the joint back to Catherine. She enjoyed the smokes now, and J.J. Cale's latest album, *Naturally*, offered a suitable background.

'Cheryl deserves better,' Dave said.

'Yes, Darling, but perhaps she doesn't think so. I begin to realise many women don't.' She eased back into the soft couch, dragging on the joint, understanding she'd been sooo lucky to escape that. 'Perhaps, it's the mature Lulu look, high boots and short skirts, she always wears when out. Trying so hard to be *with it*, but only attracting men who haven't *got it*. And probably never *had it*.'

Dave grinned. 'Can't help but like her, though. She's out there – a twinkle in her eye.'

'Aye?' Cathy feigned jealousy, then held up the fag. 'This is the right antidote for a night of Major Rory's forthright opinions and general ramblings. God, at times I was both angry and bored within the one sentence!' She grinned. 'Perhaps an old infantry tactic to confuse the enemy. Must ask the colonels.'

She sucked on the joint again, watching Dave get up and change the music. She quite liked it all now – Carole King, John Lennon, even Joe Cocker and his sinuous songs. They'd gone to Edinburgh to watch *Mad Dogs and Englishmen*, and later she'd had to admit she enjoyed it. Perhaps Rory and Joe should have a pint together! Then, she felt that gush of happiness with her man, her modern, mature, David. 'Everything fine, Darling? After all that's happened? I do think we deserve a better year in 1972.'

Dave gave a mischievous scowl as he returned to the couch. 'Um, Cathy, are you suggesting you shouldn't have run me over in 1970?' He held a hurt look. 'All my bones broken, so you could have your wicked way? Um … ride out your passions?'

She stifled a giggle. Once, sexual banter had embarrassed her, but now …! That's why she enjoyed the hash. Sooo relaxing. Even its skunky smell! Alcohol instead often led to arguments.

'Aye, it was that sexy shaved head from the hospital that initially attracted me, you booby.' She sat watching him roll a joint on the J.J. Cale album cover, until Cheryl's words floated through her mind: *They should make more like you.* 'And, if one wants something enough, one *must* then do everything to attain it!'

Then, like the young thing she once had been, she quickly was on his lap, grabbing at his clothes, on their favourite couch, in their favourite room. Already, as she kissed his neck, the idea was clear in her head. 'We should make more like you!' She shouted it. So, unlike her, never a pestering child. Southern Scotland's model of refinement until a most unrefined Australian had entered her life.

'Shhhhh! You'll wake them.'

She only partially heard, pulling his shirt open, undoing his belt, his jeans. Her mind had slowed, everything now so clear, so bright. The colours, a rich timber brown was their shared responsibility, her love for him billowed, a solid maroon cloud. So in her head, so in her body, and her green, lucid green gratitude flowing into this man, her man, while returning to her was the wee spot of baby blue. She pulled off her knickers.

'Cathy? Right here, now?' He pointed above.

'Darling, Darling.' Pamper his thoughts. 'We need more like you! Let's start a baby. Our baby.' Keeeep going. 'Start now.' She prepared her face, expectation, all happiness, yet submission. Fondle his arousal, Cathy girl. Now straddle him and your dream will begin.

But instead, it dissipated. He reacted quickly, releasing her, pulling out from under her. She looked up into a stranger's face. Surprise, shock even. Mouth hanging. 'Cath?' A flicker in the eyes. Disappointment? Anger? 'Catherine?'

'Sorry, so sorry, Darling.' Say more. 'Must … must be the hash. Makes me ramble.' Say anything, recover, recover. Don't force. So wrong to force it. 'Darling, Darling, I'm only joking.' She drew out the words.

Seeking a diversion, she waved towards the Wedgwood clock looming so large, ticking like Big Ben, on the wall opposite the fire. 'Look! It's now after 11. Less than an hour to be organised for New Year!'

A crucial diversion – from her subversion. Her mind was easing through disappointment and guilt. Better planning needed. She knew he'd appreciate it later. But now, she had to satisfy his still-questioning face. 'Photographs, photographs, Darling! My new tripod – let's give it a test run – the best photos taken in Dumfriesshire – now!' Had she really said all that?

Back onto her feet, she straightened her skirt, and another idea pinged. 'Come on, David MacIntosh, let's dress-up for the occasion! What do you think?' Humour him, Lassie.

'But … but the MacAdam clothes are upstairs in the trunk room … next to Cheryl and roaring drunk Rory.' He sang the last words. 'Might disturb 'em, Catty.' Great. He was cheering up.

'We are in a military house, Darling. A recce party needed.' She was rewarded with that boyish grin she so loved.

'*Things are crook in Tallarook, but they're gonna be cool at Glendarool.*' They laughed it out together, again in each other's arms.

***

Giggling and clowning about like the ham actors they were, it was 11.39 on the clock when they returned, much decorated, to the drawing room. Dave organised drinks and rolled another joint, while Catherine mounted the camera on the new tripod and checked the time delay. He grinned at her boa, orange silk top and ankle length skirt, relics of another fashion age. Of many fashion ages, he joked. 'You look great, girl.'

'Quite a rainbow yourself, J.J., in those grey troosers, blue wescot and mustard jacket …' She turned, whisky in hand, her face alight. 'Darling, could you do me up?' And Dave felt her jump as he licked her smooth skin before buttoning the back of her top.

'I'll quickly stoke the fire, Cat.'

She was now talking loudly, ludicrously. 'As I wish to stoke you, Mr J.J. Stevens!'

Unsettled by that earlier talk of babies, Dave now smirked. She'd remembered the nicknames! He'd bought her the camera tripod for Christmas, but she'd outdone him with her gift of the J.J. Cale album.

It included a groovy take of their song, *After Midnight*. And since Christmas, while listening to it and Cat Stevens' latest LP over drinks and smokes, they'd come up with nicknames for each other, J.J. Stevens for him, and Cathy Cale for her – which was soon reduced to Cat. Kat with a *K*, she'd later declared, 'unlike Sergeant Major who is a cat with a *C*!' They'd laughed then, as they were laughing now.

Dave almost fell over his grin as he passed her the joint. 'Photographer Kat Cale letting it all hang out at Hogmanay!'

She cleared her throat as if for effect. 'Ahem, J.J., would you like a glass of … Oh, bloody hell!' He saw Catherine scan the room in horror. 'Champagne! Where's the bloody champagne? The kitchen, David, the refrigerator. Quickly!'

He was back in the drawing room at 11.57 on the Wedgewood clock. Time enough to pop the cork, fill two flutes and … Pose! Then float into 1972.

'Oh, no, Darling J.J., you've moved. I'll take another shot. But more drinks first! Happy, happy Hogmanay!'

27.

His red, red rose had disappeared, and he needed to find her. To make things right. Mungo and the others were still hovering, finishing, or refreshing drinks, and a vague challenge had been offered regarding the snooker. But it could wait. He got up from the massive table, its pre-supper elegance reduced to the unruly residue of another night of celebration. The lines of the poem continued to resonate in his head.

Considering the food and drinks he'd had; Dave didn't feel too bad. Tired, yeah, but it'd been a long day, dawn start, then stuck with that bloody digger in Peebles till early afternoon, which had started the argument. But he'd thoroughly enjoyed his first Burns Supper, appreciating the wit within the speeches, the ceremony, the Scottish outfits, and, of course, the Grand Hall here at Pollcrayvie.

As usual, Catherine was resplendent in her clan rig, and he'd done his bit, wearing the MacIntosh bow tie and cummerbund she'd bought him in Edinburgh ages ago. Mungo and Jim Rollo had made a *turn you into a Scotsman yet* fuss. And, he'd had the poem ready.

It had been Catherine's suggestion he learn a Burns' poem, if only one or two verses, in case someone demanded it. And, of course, Big Jim had, and together they'd enjoyed the surprise on the older man's face as Dave began the first verse. He had chosen *A Red, Red Rose,* struck by the passion within, and its relevance to their relationship. He'd almost laughed out loud with the final line, *thou' it were ten thousand mile*, the approximate distance from Australia he'd travelled to Scotland to be run over by his red, red rose!

Getting home late from the Peebles' project that afternoon had ignited the argument, and as with silly arguments it had so easily accelerated into shouting. So unlike them, but they'd had a few tiffs lately. That barney at home just before Christmas when organising the visitors' accommodation was memorable.

Today, once here, they'd calmed down with a quick joint in the bedroom while dressing and were back to normal when the Burns Supper itself began.

Catherine had clapped and grinned as he'd read the poem, despite, as Alex, had commented, *your flat Ozzy accent, mate.* But now she'd disappeared – unusual.

'Anyone see where Catherine went?' he asked in general.

Chlodagh Harris looked up from her conversation. 'I think she's with the children. In the nursery. Happy noise coming from there a wee while ago.'

Dave knew she and Catherine had become good friends. *In the nursery* conjured up cosy images of warm, cuddly children waiting expectantly for Peter Pan. Or, perhaps, for their Auntie Catherine to read them a story. Requested, of course, by the child with the endearing lisp, whose modern incarnation was three-year-old Jess. And the Pollcrayvie nursery still had its name etched in the 19th century glass.

So, Catherine was with them now, possibly seeking release from the Burns Supper regimentation. Or just tired. Not like her to be so short tempered, or to blame, as she had in the afternoon. But she'd also had a busy time of it, helping Mungo with his castle tourism plans, and travelling to and from auctions and antique stores to reduce that estate debt – so chuffed to find that replacement gravy boat to complete the Royal Albert dinner set she'd decided to sell.

Now, as well she was sewing and hanging curtains for the whole first floor with Mrs Duffy – *Morning, Master James,* every day since New Year! Why she had to begin this at a time when they were already both so busy, he couldn't understand.

'Come on Aussie, we can beat any snooker team they put together. Even if Eddy Charlton were to walk in the door.' He understood Alex was offering a reward for the poem.

'Look, I'd love to, Alex … everyone, but I must find Catherine. Hardly seen her this week. Tomorrow, before we leave, perhaps?' Smiling again, he moved towards the archway into the Victorian wing of the castle and remembered he must get more hash from the man. 'Sorry. See you all at breakfast.'

A light in the hallway cast a soft glow into the nursery. In the bottom bunk, a few golden curls and one small, white arm was all to be seen of Jess behind Catherine's sleeping bulk. Dave hesitated, before gently shaking her shoulder.

'Cathy.'

'Hmm?'

'Cathy, Love. It's Dave. Coming to bed?' He ran fingers through her hair.

She began to move, slowly raising an arm to brush his hand away, and emitted a lazy *dooon't*, as might one of the children. 'Jus … just leave me alone. I want to stay here.' The voice was slurred with sleep.

'But … But you can't.' He waited. 'Come on, come to bed.' He was desperate to explain again about the digger driver at Peebles whose thoughtlessness had threatened to ruin a month's work in 10 minutes, not to mention their Burns Supper. The details weren't important, but that he had had to make the decision to wait on the landscaping site was. Stuff like that.

'Come on Cat, time to leave.'

'Oh, what now, David! Just leave me alone!'

The clean, crisp shout had Dave reeling, as might that of a drill sergeant. Even in her worst Mrs MacAdam moments, oh so long ago, she'd never snapped like that.

Hamish in the top bunk stirred. 'Mummy?'

Dave stepped out into the hallway to allow the boy to return to sleep. And to cleanse the room. A joint would be good, but it was all up in their room. Why was she so angry? No good him just reacting with more anger. Hmm. Well, it'll be him, his fault. He was happy to take the blame, but an inner voice warned against it. A backward step that could see the return to the old Dave, the ways of old Spazzo Lawson who always took a sort of dysfunctional responsibility for everything; his father's death, of course, was the big one. The monstrous acceptance that had pretty much wrecked his boyhood.

Well, he wasn't going back to that, and this is why they needed to talk, clear the air. Then, together they might understand their tiffs now were over little things – because he was unavoidably late today, just once. Well, perhaps more than once. Or, because she's now always engrossed with those bloody downstairs curtains. Neither of them available for that brief chat, a quick kiss and cuddle, a touch, an understanding nod, or smile. Because … because … too busy.

He noticed lights, heard voices in the great hall. Someone still around. Walking back, he found Bryce and Jean McCargo clearing the main table.

'No snooker tonight, Laddie?'

Dave smiled. 'No, too tired. I've had a busy week of it.' It sounded wimpish, but it didn't matter with Bryce.

'Och, you're just allowing others to win!' Dave knew the half scowl was as close to a grin as the ex-soldier gave. Collecting the small vases of heather from the table, the man moved closer. 'Getting over that terrible business here last year, I hope.' Dave nodded, again remembering that Boyle's gruesome death had happened here, just outside the gates.

'We enjoyed your wee poem, and the sentiment behind it, Davie.' Jean McCargo grinned and pointed to part-empty bottles and decanters standing together on the rich oak sideboard, like a grouping of ejected quiz contestants. 'A nightcap? Quite a collection we have.'

'Okay.' As drinks were poured and he and the McCargo's toasted each other, Dave explained the messages in the poem that had drawn him to it.

Bryce McCargo nodded towards Dave. 'It's all there, right enough, and your red, red rose watched you with considerable pleasure.'

So why was she avoiding him now? 'I'd better go up and tuck her into bed.' Dave finished his drink, then gave a relaxed shrug, as might a playboy with three bimbos waiting upstairs. He reached for a half decanter of red wine and two glasses. In the hope she'd return soon. 'Goodnight, and thanks for a great supper.'

'Good night to you,' they answered together.

***

'David?' He wasn't in their room.

209

Concerned, Catherine undressed quickly, seeking refuge from her behaviour in bed. It was embarrassment enough having fallen asleep on wee Jess' bed, but her anger when he'd simply tried to wake her, she now understood, was totally, totally out of turn, as, as … The shame rose up into her face. So, if he isn't here, it's because she had snapped his head off. Likely he's sought solace with the men in the snooker room. He won't be back till the wee hours, and probably the worse for wear. But she couldn't really blame him. Perhaps he won't remember, but she would. Oh, David, I'm so sorry.

She tried to recapture that luxurious sleep of an hour earlier, but remained wide, wide awake, her mind bumping over their fractured afternoon, ending with her overreaction in the nursery. What was happening? How, indeed why, had she become so bitchy? Not her normal choice of word, but one Cheryl would use to describe women who went to bed alone, because their men were away drinking, washing away the bitchiness of their wives. Had it come to that? They had argued a few times recently. But, God, the poem. He had been so earnest when reading it. And she knew the others had picked up his passion, his commitment, his love for his red, red rose.

She was desperate to talk to him. To sort all this out, to allay any fears, to return to the normal, wonderful partnership they had created and enjoyed for 18 months now. But … but, come on, Catherine, some honesty. You wish to discuss children, their own child. Only one. Not too much to ask. A few adjustments, of course, but something their love and strength together could, would, enfold and nurture. Something she'd begun to realise she wanted more than anything. The Boyle episode had underscored just how impermanent their lives were. But was all this an overreaction?

A soft rap on the door killed the thought. So like David to keep the noise down: always thoughtful. As the unmistakable frame of her lover, her wonderful, supportive, understanding lover neared the bed, she stretched up for him with the desperation of a young pop fan at the edge of a lively, noisy, stage.

28.

She parked the Morris in the vehicle shed at the rear of the house. Getting out, she wondered if they would need a larger car soon. They had repaid Mungo's loan, and from David's landscaping projects and her ongoing bloodhound work with the antiques they were meeting bank repayments, and more. A bigger, better vehicle was possible. She felt so normal, yet so ecstatic.

He was home all this week between away jobs, and she must find him and announce her news. A dry afternoon for early spring, he'll be working in the sun garden. She loved the way he had adapted to the European climate, her ever flexible David.

In the two months since the Burns Supper, things had returned to normal. No more snapping and snarling, or those ongoing arguments. Instead, was a return to caring and listening, and caressing and satisfying sex! How, even yesterday, when the rain had stopped his work, they were soon upstairs in bed, for the rest of the afternoon! Just as before, Catherine tittered. But that might have to change soon too! He'll understand.

She found David working on that new pathway for the proposed summer house, Sergeant Major supervising from the old wooden table, as usual. Always together, those two. 'Lovely to have you home, Darling.' They unhesitatingly kissed, and stood back, smiling at each other. Just as before. Him working at home again, just as … well, before!

'Another long day for you, Cathy. Success, I hope.'

'Aye, Darling, success.' She wanted to tell him right there. Couldn't wait to see his reaction. And of the stunning reserve price McTears had suggested. 'A cup of tea in the kitchen? I've bought home a celebratory bun.' He grinned a reply: that boyishness she loved. She gripped his arm. 'Just give me five minutes. I won't bother changing.'

He was soon in the kitchen. With another kiss, he sat down at his usual place at the combustion stove end of the table. Her suggestion during his first winter at Glendaruel. She sat at the other end as usual. So they could admire each other better was always their joke. So two tall people could recklessly fling their arms about for the salt or pepper, was another. Silly, but comfortable familiarity.

Come on, tell him. 'Darling, I've good news and … and some even better news.' Did she give that the correct intonation? Does she look composed?

She watched that boyish grin as he reached for a piece of bun. 'It must be good, Kat. You're spinning it out.'

She appreciated the nickname, further evidence of their return to normal. Odd, needing something different to return to normal! But there we are. 'Och, sorry. Right, well.' Easy path first. 'Well, Mr Roberts at McTears has suggested we set the reserve for the Royal Albert at …' She hesitated for effect. 'At £1,240!'

'Jesus, that's a load of money.' He came around the table to her. 'Cathy, you must be so pleased! I mean, not just the money, but your detective work, your driving to Edinburgh and Glasgow, the catalogues. It's all paid off!' He leant down and kissed her. 'Perhaps we can now think about something to replace the Morris. You're doing a lot of miles in it.'

Just what she'd been thinking! He's so intuitive. Just wait till he sits down.

'Well? What's the other, better news? Come on, what else have you managed to sell?'

Out with it. He'd said in bed at the castle how the worst was over. Boyle was dead, they couldn't change that. Poor Kenzie too. It all had really shaken them, but if Boyle's death had meant anything, it was to underscore how they were meant to be together, stuck together forever like Siamese twins.

Time now to tell his family the truth, bring them over for a visit, show them Scotland, show them Catherine. Face up to his mother. They'd laughed together at being 'Siamese twins', banging hips under the blankets for effect. And quickly he had been upon her, and then inside her, and as one they'd noisily ridden out the passion, as in those first weeks of their autumn of colours.

'Cathy, you're grinning like a Cheshire cat. What do you think, Sergeant Major?' He twisted around towards the big tabby in its basket. 'Come on, Kat. Out with it.'

Give it the correct intonation, the correct tone. Now. 'Darling, I'm nine, perhaps ten, weeks pregnant!' Sing that last significant word. There, done. Now to help him accept. It will be a shock initially, quite a surprise for him. You haven't shared the symptoms; he hasn't been aware.

Silence for a number of seconds, as his impish grin metamorphosed into a face of total surprise. 'Wha'?' More silence. 'Catherine, you what?'

'Yes, Darling. We are to have a baby. Ours!' You are smirking, Cathy. 'We must have begun it during the New Year period, Darling.'

'Ours?' He fell back. 'Wait, wait.' His hands lifted. 'How, how are you so, so sure?' He was moving in jerks. 'How … how do you know?'

'I've had an examination, earlier this afternoon in Edinburgh. With Dr Wallace in India Street. She is a maternity specialist. I was given a test, and she was able to give me the result almost immediately.'

'Oh.' His answer was also jerky. 'W … why?' A sudden hand movement. 'How?' His hands up again. 'How did you … know?'

Brighten up girl. Enliven him. Don't allow him to run with negativity.

'Well, Darling, I'd missed my period in early February, and then when I missed again some weeks ago …' How pleased she'd been at the time. Just as she had hoped, well … planned, having stopped the pill before Christmas. Keep smiling. Show that pleasure, make it contagious. He'll accept this to please you, Cathy. To be responsible for your happiness. 'Also, I've become so tired. Falling asleep with the television, remember? And everything now has become quite a chore. Jessica said that was natural.'

'Jessica?'

'Dr Wallace, Jessica Wallace.'

213

He was still jerky. 'Oh.' She watched him cast around the kitchen, as if the baby was already somewhere here, crying.

He's up there having a shower now. Thinking about her news – their news now. Absorbing it, analysing every aspect, and the expected ramifications, as he had done with the cottages, and ... and each landscaping job he'd begun. Methodical, Mungo had seen it in him. Under the shower, either warming up to the idea, or ... or cooling down. A good joke, Cathy. It's going well, so far. And yes, already she was quite tired again.

She added a touch of old smoothie to the braising lamb shanks, remembering her initial surprise to discover this was his favourite meal. Considered poor Jock's food in Scotland. But she'd accepted it, as she had come to accept and love everything else about him. Mrs Duffy had given her an old highland recipe, a touch of whisky, of course, not wine. He'll be a wonderful father: proud, caring, methodical, true. Well, the worst is over. Who should they tell first?

Catherine drank a little of the whisky herself. To help get through the next stage with David. In truth she really wasn't sure how her monumental news had been accepted, for he had said so little. Of course, it will be a shock for him.

Of course, and Chlodagh had said to be certain first. She had explained her rush to give Paul the wonderful news after missing one period, and the disappointment of the false alarm had set back their 'family plan' many months. Well, perhaps it was preferable for David to have little time for regret. The child was well on its way now: no going back.

29.

The doubt came to him after hours of lying awake. Was he heading in the wrong direction with this? Since the Burns Supper at the castle, he and Catherine had returned to the good old days: no arguments or sullen silences or grudges. They'd had differences in the early days too, of course, misunderstandings, Paris and the Kontiki chicks, for example, but generally they'd been sorted out quickly. He hadn't realised just how much they'd drifted apart since June last – that Boyle crap, of course – until they'd returned to normal after the Burns Supper.

And he understood now, he was really frightened of losing that normality, Catherine, their relationship and ... and his new self, the mature, takes-everything-in-his-stride Dave Lawson. So, he hadn't really wanted to question her bewildering announcement, and she'd had a certain glow, an added attractiveness he hadn't seen before. Sounds corny, but she did, and he'd melted again. So, he'd tried to absorb her news, accept it, and move on, no matter how shocking, or unfortunate it was.

But now, the doubt. It had come from a sentence she'd said during dinner; *I must have known something, Darling, having begun the curtains on the first floor.* It had now shaped into a suspicion, something Dave was relatively inexperienced with – having dealt more with reactions, overreactions, and ultimatums throughout his former life.

Suspicion had been the luxury of others, but now it shared his pillow, like an immense insect that could inflict considerable pain. Yet, he decided to wait till morning to address it, to ask Catherine to help clarify his misgivings, because now she needed to get lots of sleep. Indeed, she'd nodded off early again, after that first joint, and he'd stayed up to have another. Should she be smoking now?

He rose up on his elbows and studied her in the dim light of the bedroom. Immediately, he was reminded of that first time they'd slept together, back in the outside studio. That wonderful long hair out across the pillow, the serene expression, the longish face with high cheekbones that he'd come to see as the most beautiful in the world. The face that viewed him with love, for the resolve, and the happiness he continued to give her, she'd often said. And, of course, he loved her in return for the very same reasons, the completeness. Boyle and his horror-movie death had shaken them, challenged their inner strength, but they were now back to normal.

Weren't they?

Dave poked at his cereal, but he couldn't put it off anymore. 'Catherine, how did you fall pregnant?' Oops, wrong question, Henry. Not because she was now staring at him down the kitchen table like she'd tasted curry in her porridge, but because, if his suspicions were wrong, and he so hoped they were, he didn't want to upset her. Use the nickname too. 'Sorry, Kat, what I meant to say was …' Her expression, her body, was frozen. 'Um … how do you think you became pregnant?'

Now she was moving. 'I … I really don't know, Darling.' The voice was shrill. 'It … it must have been an accident. Um … a problem with the pill, I assume.'

'So, what did the doctor – I've forgotten her name – say about it?'

The eyes blinked. 'Doctor Wallace. Um … she said something similar, the same thing. An … an accident, faulty pills.'

'But isn't the pill supposed to prevent accidents? I can imagine you missing one, perhaps two, but doesn't it take well over a month for the effects to wear off?' The condoms obviously had been his business when they'd initially had to use them – have them handy, put them on, get rid of them later.

But he understood now he knew almost nothing of her taking the pill, except he'd sometimes seen a card of pills in the bathroom cabinet, and had laughed at the simplistic labelling: Monday, Tuesday, Wednesday, etc. Difficult to muck up really, unlike, he'd smirked, those dodgy unlabelled condoms. Warm memories, all that stuff, their life together, really, but the sense of foolishness at not asking these questions yesterday propelled him to persist.

216

'I remember we had to wait for over a month for it to *take* effect. And then we waited longer!' He gave her a genuine smile. 'All those condoms you'd bought, eh.' He still didn't want to upset her, aggravate her. 'So, how could there be an accident, Kat?'

'David, please don't badger me. I … I'm in no condition to be …' Hands up near her face. 'Darling, the doctor couldn't give an answer and … and neither could Chlodagh …' The shrill voice stopped abruptly.

'Chlodagh? Does she already know?'

'No … I mean, um … yes.' That shrill tone again. 'Well, David … Darling, you've been working away from home lately, and … and I've had to discuss my … my condition with someone informed. Someone experienced.'

'But, why not me … your … your … I don't know what I am now.'

'Well, I didn't want to worry you, away from home. It … It may have been a false alarm, after all that.'

'But, Catherine, you still should have told me, rung me. You tell me when you have a cold, get the flu, when … when you thought you'd sprained your wrist chopping wood during the autumn. Those ordinary things. So why haven't you told me about this, something far more important than …?'

'I *am* sorry, Darling, but I really didn't …' Her face held an expression he'd never seen before – the mouth was smiling, but nothing else. Like an unintended face in one of those children's mix-and-match books. 'I'll put more wood in the stove. More … more tea?'

Dave heard noise at the back door, and Mrs Duffy soon appeared in the servant hall, rubbing her hands together. 'A sharp morning outside, Miss Catherine. Morning Master James! Shall we finish the nursery curtains today, Dear?'

Nursery? Fuck! Was he the last to know?

Outside, the morning air was indeed sharp, but the sky was clearing, and he needed something to do, badly. Like, starting on the summerhouse, a project he'd been saving for better weather. The building material was there in the machine shed, and it would allow him to forget about Catherine's *news*. Or stew on it. Or accept it.

Nursery? He remembered the A A Milne atmosphere the word, the room, had conjured up at Pollcrayvie only months earlier. But, *nursery*, here? Now? Early on, she'd shown him a dusty, soulless first floor room that James and John MacAdam had, as babies, supposedly thrived in. Well, it hadn't done 'em much bloody good!

A cruel thought he knew, but he didn't really care. And through the day as he prepared the raised summerhouse floor for concreting, he came to understand there was a trail of Catherine's seemingly innocent asides and remarks to him, or to others, about children that led back to the rock festival. But she'd never openly discussed it with him. That she'd been wanting a family had come to him as a total shock. But should it have?

And so it went all day. By dark, the slab work was ready, and he'd rung to order a lorry load of concrete – in two days' time, they'd said. If only he could simply ring up for a happy solution to the doubts that were solidifying inside him.

He and Catherine eventually met, again in the kitchen, as she was preparing their dinner. They shared a drink, and during the meal as if by mutual agreement, the conversation was limited to the summerhouse work and further items within the house to be auctioned. Later, they tried to watch the television together, as if the previous day and its tectonic news had never happened. But, of course, it had, and Dave found himself waiting for an advertisement break to ask the question that was gnawing his guts. Christ, as if an ad break would make it easier!

He got up and turned the sound down. 'Catherine, I'm sorry, but I do need to ask this.' She stared up at him. Here goes. 'Have you become pregnant on purpose? And … and if so, why?' He continued to look at her. 'Please be as honest with me as I know you always have.' He moved across to stoke the fire so as not to tower over her.

The hands went up to her face as she shouted a reply. 'David, David, does it really matter now? I'm to have our baby in 31 weeks, and we have to make the most of it! I … we have to prepare ourselves!' Hanging her head, she began to cry. 'I … I thought you would be happy! Happy for the baby, and happy for me. I … I'll soon be too old to have … babies, David. And … and, you don't know what it's like to be labelled *barren.*' As she sobbed out the words his reaction was to move to console her.

But he'd been churning over this all day; he understood now it wasn't so much Catherine's pregnancy as the intent behind it that mattered to him. He knelt in front of her and tried to explain this, but she gave no acknowledgement of his words or his presence. She continued to cry, hands over face. He'd never seen her like this, and so wasn't really sure how to respond. Yet, he couldn't afford to lose perspective, for late that afternoon, he'd thought of a solution to the problem. But, how to mention it, how to suggest it to Cathy in her current state?

Old smoothie! A dram would settle her, settle them both. He poured two tumblers on the sideboard and brought one to her. Initially, her hand seemed reluctant to accept anything from him, but he waited until her fingers tightened over the cut crystal and she took a sip. It would be so easy to quietly finish their drinks, climb the staircase with arms entwined, as they had so often done, and fall into bed, consoling each other until sleep or sex overtook them.

Indeed, he was about to suggest this, but realised she hadn't really answered his question, hadn't allayed his suspicions. He would only be postponing it, the doubt, the resentment. And she had to understand there was an alternative. And her approach to his solution may just reflect whether she'd purposely become pregnant.

His own heart pounding, he took the plunge. 'Kat, I don't wish to further upset you, but there is an alternative to this.' He spoke loudly and clearly, both to catch her attention, and to make sure she understood. He just had to say it, and then wear the consequences. 'Cathy, Love.' Her body language suggested she was listening. 'If this really has been an accident, we … you could have an abortion.' Wait now. 'What … what do you think?'

She began screeching, like that neighbour's always-irate cockatoo during his childhood. 'David, David, what are you suggesting? What … what are you saying?' She leapt out of the chair and began hitting his chest with her fists. 'I hate you. I hate you for suggesting such a thing!'

She was shouting through tears, and he grabbed her wrists to try to control her. 'Kill our baby: is that what you're saying? Is that your solution?' A hesitation. 'Or … or are you deliberately pushing me towards another miscarriage. *I hate you!*'

He struggled to get his arms around her as she continued to shout and sob and hit him.

30.

Dave woke, the first time in many days, with a clear, unclouded mind. Yesterday, in the twilight, he and Tom King had completed two of the stone walls for the summerhouse. And after a few beers with the genial Tom, and later a joint on his own, he'd fallen into bed, totally knackered. He'd been back sleeping in the studio for three or four nights now, and apart from a few cobwebs up between the exposed ceiling beams, it was much the same. And this morning, Sergeant Major was cleaning himself on the outside windowsill in the sun, as if, once more, the sad sack inside needed cheering up. Canny cat.

Difficult to follow time when your mind, your thoughts remained in shock. But it must be about two weeks since Cathy revealed she was pregnant. And since then, his normal life had stopped, and had begun to crack and break away into pieces, as if he was part of an eroding cliff face. Initially, he thought to ignore the sudden overwhelming life change that was expected of him, hoping for a false alarm, or that he'd simply got it all wrong, or … or that it'd just somehow go away. But it hadn't worked. Hadn't worked at all.

Equally zany, he expected to find clarity, answers, in the marijuana, for he'd always felt, like The Who, he could see for miles and miles after a few puffs. But, no, wrong again. Only unrelated, uncoordinated adventures in some other bloody dimension, with some coughing thrown in.

But now, this morning, in his old bed, his now open, ordered brain began a methodical sorting process. Like coming up for air after weeks under water. The issue, the problem, the threat to their relationship and to the very existence of Darling Dave Lawson, had been hovering hazily for days like a lazy swarm of hornets. But now it was easier to identify its sharp, definite edges, like those friendly, rounded clouds adults draw in kid's books.

Clearly too, the problem remained unresolved because Catherine couldn't, or wouldn't, see his point of view. She was determined to have a child, *the child*, and was willing to risk everything to have it.

It's your responsibility to fit in with my baby, Darling. He couldn't help but see parallels with his mum's behaviour after his father died: all responsibility hand-passed to him. *You are responsible, David. You told him to dive.* But not accepted this time.

She'd be in the kitchen now, preparing their breakfast, or perusing catalogues for baby wear, as if she'd not deliberately fallen pregnant behind his back. Treacherously. She'll soon look up the television guide in the local paper to offer suggestions for the box tonight. *The nursery curtains are hanging nicely, Darling. Mrs Duffy's sensible choice of fabric*; she'll mention stuff like that as they watch. Nothing much on her once adventurous horizon except giving birth.

Unwittingly, he'd allowed the summerhouse job, an unimportant project really, to absorb him, and the challenge of it had got him this far. But how bloody far was *this far*? Another day, another fucking week? So what? You're coasting, Dave Lawson; working your guts out to blind yourself to the problems facing you is coasting.

So, what's next? More coasting? Similar stuff had been flashing in his head for the last few days, like those bright neon signs on the rides at Luna Park meant to catch your attention. But, this morning, this clear bright morning, the neon questions had become statements, answers perhaps: *make a decision, make a decision, stick up for yourself, act like a man. No, act like the strong person you've become.* Fuck, heady stuff!

But he knew his emotions were raw and ragged, as the news of Catherine's *accidental* pregnancy had grown into a threat and now an ultimatum. A dangerous directive that continued to shake him, deeply disappoint him, frighten him.

Ah, now we have it. It's the ultimatum he dreads; that he hates about the whole bloody thing. She'd given the ultimatum informally, no thought at all, like it or lump it, Darling. I've got important historic issues to resolve, Darling. James schemed me into marriage, and now it's my turn to … well, manipulate you, Darling. The realisation had totally floored him, and he'd tried to shake her, her mindset, by moving from their happy, ideal, satisfying bed to another – move over, Rory – along the hall.

But no response from Cathy, and so nights later he moved out to the outside bedroom here. But again, no response. Had he been

222

replaced by the baby? And had there been a hint of Mrs MacAdam in her dismissal of these feeble demonstrations, with a David-I-know-best tone? Sergeant Major understands. That's why he's out there again on the window ledge.

Of course, she'd asked him many times to explain his resistance to her news, *their* pregnancy as she called it. The brain confusion, reminiscent of his screwed up teenage years, had made it difficult to explain. But now, clarity from one of those little white clouds as he came to understand the wee baby itself wasn't the issue. He knew he wasn't ready for a baby, children, in his life. Christ, coming from his own shitty childhood, it'd taken him 22 years to grow up – to cease being a shamed child himself!

But more, he was frightened, petrified of losing their love, their special love affair, their wonderful friendship. Just the two of them. And it was her like-it-or-lump-it attitude that really pissed him off. He hesitated with the word, but that's what he really couldn't escape. Disloyalty, for all her self-proclaimed high moral code. Worse, betrayal. How dare she treat him like this? He'd once been frightened of Mrs MacAdam, but not anymore.

Dave allowed himself a grin. Here he was, same bed, same bedroom, 20 months later deliberating the same question; should he stay, or leave? He knew, sure as eggs are oval, she was responsible for the well dressed, quietly confident, respected, and popular young man he'd become. But he also understood if he didn't do something, act now, she may yet take all that away, like stripping off a recent coat of paint. Sorry, David, wrong colour, after all. Still just Spazzo Lawson underneath. Didn't really suit you, Darling.

Yeah, you have responsibility to Catherine, and perhaps the baby, but there's an equal accountability to yourself. Something you always ignored in that crappy past. Be true to the new Dave, don't go back to being a walked over wanker, as before. *Remember Dave, you're not a drongo.* So, save yourself, save what you've got, and go. Get out, or at least get out of here for a little while. It just might shake some sense into her.

***

223

It was a freezing night, but clear. Lots of stars. Now past 1.30 am and he was standing on the A76. Opposite that bloody tree. Where it had all started – ironic, really. No traffic about, so he waited, stamping his feet, next to him the old backpack bought by Ric in a second-hand shop in Frankston, before he'd left Australia – over two years ago. Today, he'd quietly packed it, clothes, travel books, maps, passport, bankbook, some weed, money – cash from the Peebles job. Nothing of hers, nothing from the house. The keys for the Transit van were hanging in the kitchen, the estate had paid for it.

They'd talked and eaten together, like two sensible adults, but of course they weren't. Just playing the game he no longer could take part in. In a sense, it had empowered him that she was unaware he was leaving, but he still felt like a bastard. Sergeant Major knew, of course, and had stuck to him like glue all day. He'd really miss that cat. Felt like a bastard about that too. Look after her, he'd told the big tabby, as he'd left it in the dark at the main gate.

Soon a lorry approached and stopped. Heading for Manchester, the driver said, and later, much later Dave Lawson woke up to Lancashire countryside. Catherine, he thought, was gone from his mind.

31.

He knew it was crazy, but immediately after booking into London's Earl's Court youth hostel, Dave checked the notice board for messages. Perhaps a card – *Hi Aussie, having a great time in West Berlin. Visited Checkpoint Charlie, and tomorrow we're ... Ditched Picko back in ... Join us if you can. Love Sue.* But, of course, nothing. Yet, nice to dream up the past. Hey, had the last two years been only a dream?

He slipped back into the hostel groove; a fringe sightseer and listener to the antics and travel plans of others while sharing a joint or a drink. The New Seekers were teaching the world to sing, Americans were still arguing the Vietnam thing, Scandinavian birds remained bra-less and young Germans continued to apologise for the Second World War. That Kombis and other vans were still for sale on the streets of Earle's Court only added to the return of the long-absent travel buzz.

To fill time till the weather warmed, Dave took a job. The pay at Paddy's Pub wasn't great, but board was free, and he came to enjoy the easy interaction it offered with fellow travellers. He rang Glendaruel a few times, but with no answers, assumed Catherine wasn't ready yet to talk.

More young people came into the pub as spring warmed up, and he enjoyed pouring their drinks, sharing their jokes and smokes, and answering their questions. He understood he was seen as an old hand, the beads perhaps, despite being only 22 and having travelled little, and was asked to lots of parties. He also began to attract some female attention, and while agreeable, he was careful to resist – for now.

Eventually, he accepted an offer to share a van with a cheery mid-20s Sydney couple he'd got to know, who had a good friend arriving in London soon. 'She'll love you, Dave. We'll leave around mid-May. Spain and Portugal first. Okay?'

However, one surly spring day, Catherine walked into the pub. He was pouring a pint of Guinness at the time and dropped it in surprise. He rushed out from behind the bar, but she'd gone. Tidying up the mess, he noticed a woman of similar height and hair now standing with a drink at the other bar. Must have been her.

Three days later, something similar happened. This time he actually grabbed the woman involved and spun her around, and later had had to ply she and friends with free drinks in apology. Soon, Cathy appeared in his dreams, and on the last morning of April, after a frightening nightmare in which she was dying in childbirth, he woke in a sweaty heap to find her fully returned to his consciousness.

Catherine's pleading face now was firmly fixed in his mind, and with it the crushing weight of guilt about the manner in which he'd left. Equally strong was the feeling of having betrayed Mungo and his unconventional friends who'd happily accepted him, the Spazzo, into their midst.

He rang Glendaruel numerous times that day, but again there was no answer. Directory service gave him Mungo's number in Edinburgh and at the castle, but no replies there either. He hated himself for leaving the laconic Paddy without notice, but late that night he was on the bus to distant Dumfries.

It was almost dark, and the big house was secured and silent. As if in judgement, telling him nothing. No welcoming Sergeant Major either. Cold and wet and so desperate to find answers, Dave decided to break the ground floor toilet window to get in. Spare glass panes in the machinery shed, he'd repair it in the morning.

With the broken glass cleared from the windowsill, he slowly lowered his gangly body in through the narrow frame. Going well. Until his foot slipped. Oh, shit! As body weight pulled him further in and down, he made a desperate grab for the window frame. Oww, fuck! Glass pieces! And let go. Then, the left side of his face dragged against the frame and sharp shards ripped down through the soft skin. He was still screaming as he crashed onto the stone floor inside. Oh, Christ, the searing, dancing pain of his face!

With difficulty, he struggled to his feet, and tried to rise above the electrified agony. Something badly wrong with his left cheek.

He touched it. God! Oh, fuck. So bloody tender, and … ripped, a big flap of skin hanging off his cheek, like some half-skinned animal. And blood: even the sickly-sweet taste of it. And it was clogging up his left eye. Must be blood everywhere – would she be angry? He felt for the light switch. But nothing. Yeah, often light problems down here. Get cleaned up and he'll fix …

But, had to stop the bleeding first. And the pain. He moved into the servant hall, the left side of his face swaying tortuously, as if somehow attached by sloppy hinges. Get to the kitchen. Tea towels. Fuck, *the painnn!*

No lights working in the kitchen either. A blackout? Wet now inside his shirt; must stop the bleeding. Found the table, chairs now, and … and shuffle across to the sink. Tea towels down … one, two, three drawers. The towels, thank fuck! A chair. Whoops, ah, got it. Sit down.

Bunching a tea towel, he pushed it hard against the left side of his face. *Fuuuck!!* The jolt of pain almost made him drop it. But he had to stop the heavy, continuous bleeding. The agony was so unbearable he shouted out, and his whole body trembled with the effort to overcome the trauma. He forced himself to do it again. '*Aoww!*'

He held himself tight – in control. God, he was a mess. What if she found him like this? Blood on everything. He could even smell it now! So, think, think. What now? Almost dark outside, so need some light. Um … candles always kept in the pantry. Matches too.

He staggered to his feet, still holding the towel against his face, and shuffled into the pantry. Should be left side, middle shelf. But nothing, nothing. Yes! He felt a candle – broken! Doesn't matter, it's still in the old enamel holder, as he remembered it. And matches. A box of matches!

Fighting pain and frustration, he eventually got the candle alight. And the emerging familiarity of the pantry momentarily boosted his spirits. The colourful calendar on the end wall, marooned on March, when he'd left, six-seven weeks earlier. And there's the old smoothie on the highest shelf. Must be the top shelf was their standing joke. Hiding their stash of weed – yep, still there. Also on a shelf was the first aid kit they'd bought for the cottages work, oh, so long ago. Bandages inside.

Later in the drawing room, he collapsed onto the couch. He'd called and called her. But nothing. He'd searched the whole house – all 27 fucking rooms. Even the bloody tower. But nothing. He'd tried again to ring the gatehouse, then Mungo. Twice, three times. But nothing. Disconnected, like the power. Like himself …

He rolled another joint, trying to calm down. Yeah, they'd spent so much happy time here: music, television, making plans, making love, being together. Everything seemed in place. Except … except for the TV programme, the newspapers, the books, the fruit in the bowl, the booze on the sideboard and other missing favourite things. Like Sergeant Major. And, of course, Cath –

Oh shit, blood on the cushions! Jesus, the Baluchi rug too. Sorry Kat, these bloody bandages. Well, you know, Glendaruel – *the valley of blood!* He laughed at that until the pain …

More whisky, but it wasn't enough.

In the wavering candlelight, he took an LP from the shelf beneath the record player, J.J. Cale, of course. She'd bought it for him for Christmas. And J.J. sang *After Midnight* far better than Clapton. That's showbiz, Eric, they'd joked. Hey, let's play it now. Lift the lid, put it on the turntable thing and … and … Nothing?

Well, no fucking power, stupid! How were you gonna play that? Just sing. She had to be here somewhere.

Shouting the words – *After Midnight, we're* … he stepped unsteadily back out into the cavernous hall. There, the multi-coloured glass of the entrance caught the light of his shaking candle, enlivening the chamber with a confusion of ever-moving psychedelic tints. Even the panther's eyes flashed at him! Fuck, it's beautiful. Fuck, it's tragic. Fuck, it's taunting him, as once did bloody Wil … William Boyle, here.

'Catherine!' But now, the echoes teased. *Catherine, Catherine!* He so desperately wanted to find her. 'Catherine!' *Catherine, Catherine! Had* to find her. Fuck, he'd so stupidly, so carelessly lost her. Janice Joplin knew it all; *Somewhere near Glendaruel, I let her slip away.* Same syllables as Salinas. Where the fuck was Salinas, anyway? Had to think, had to … Hey, the half colonel's watching … enjoying this. Face alive – smirking at the contemptible colonial before him. Mocking the young fool, bringing him to heel.

228

Heel, heal yourself, and stop bleeding on our floor, Laddie. Fuck, these puns! You've never been welcome in this house, boy – on this estate. Get out. Panther, Bagheera, after him! *Hahahahahaha.* Get out! *Hahahahahaha!* The resounding laughter chased him up the empty staircase, and as he reeled towards their bedroom, calling, the echo followed him. 'Catherine.' *Catherine! Catherine! Hahahahahaha!*

This time in their bedroom, he immediately was stopped with the shock of himself, a bloodied, dishevelled mess, in the vanity mirror. No wonder the colonel had laughed, derided him. Look at you! Unsteady on your feet, blood-soaked clothes. Hair poking through bandages, like rough baled hay. Like a savaged scarecrow. And again, supernatural shapes were bouncing about the room. *Stand at attention!*

Yet, he tried to absorb the room, make sense of it. So normal, except … nothing here of her. Like in the rest of the sodding house. No make-up on the vanity, no bedside books, alarm clock, slippers. Dust cover on the bed. Gone, she's gone. Go on, admit it. She's gone!

But he was so tired; he hadn't slept since … since … He couldn't remember. He plonked onto the edge of the bed to roll another joint – so tired. Oops, dropped it … Where, where …? Get down and find it, Spazzo.

Hey, what's this? Something, something right under there. If he just reached … A … a handbag! It's … it's hers. Bought in Paris at … at … Colour to match that wonderful hair. She loved the bag – took it everywhere. So … So, why was it here? And, and what's this …? A glass pill bottle. Two pill bottles!

Why … why were these under the bed? What's inside the handbag? Yeah, purse … powder thingo … perfume, hanky, band-aids, ha! Bank book, spare bloody keys, old … Nooo, her *new* glasses. All here, so … so normal. And … and a photograph. Folded. Faded. He knew it! So … so unsettling. More old smoothie.

New Year's Eve. Hogmanay. There they were. So happy – as they always were together – dressed up again. Using the new tripod. Champagne! The blue writing … *After Midnight … letting it all hang out.* Jesus, oh Jesus, such a jolt. So, normal … as it was, until a month or … or two ago. Can't find her, but now this fucking photo. Shit, his blood already on it. And … and why … her handbag under the bed?

It hit him in the pit of his stomach, in the deepening emptiness, as he tried, as rationally as the booze and weed allowed, to take in these rudimentary clues. He held the typed bottle labels nearer the candle – identical except … except the fucking dates. *Sleeping tablets. Use only as prescribed. Take with caution.* Her name – and … and *31 March 1972*. The other, *19 April 1972*, yeah, about two weeks ago. Had … had he missed her by only that much? Fuck, fuck, fuck! The smudges on the photo. Water? Tears? Her crying? The sleeping tablets – loose ones under the bed too. Spilled, as she's tried to …?

Oh no. Oh, shit, no. She hasn't done anything stupid. He stood up, unsteadily, dripping blood again, staring at the items now on the bed, feeling suddenly very sick, very shocked … very late. She hadn't … No, no. He tried to avoid the only conclusion left as to why she wasn't here. Why the house was so bloody closed up. Why silly white pills were rolling about the floor. Drown the idea. Drown it! Swaying wildly, he took a deep swig of the whisky.

But he couldn't shake it – couldn't shake the obvious fucking conclusion.

Say ittt! You walked out on Cathy, and she's killed herself. No, you … you stupid, gutless fuckwit, *you've* killed her … Like … like with your father!! *You told him to dive!*

***

Sergeant Buckle picked up the photograph from the bedroom floor. But he wouldn't have noticed the laughing Hogmanay eyes of the happy couple as he concentrated on sinking his fist hard into the intruder's stomach. The bloodied, bandaged man collapsed onto his knees, gasping for breath, then vomited. Mentally and physically bashed, the victim could only listen.

'Sarge! You can't … He … he's injured.' The young constable was worried.

'Can't I? He's broken into the house, he's in possession of marijuana and has pilfered that handbag. Like those girly beads he's wearing – get 'em off him. Three crimes there, Robbie. And he's resisting arrest.

'But what if he *is* telling the truth?'

'Well, does he *look* like he fuckin' lives here, as he says? Does he *sound* Scottish to you?'

Buckle began to lift the intruder. 'Grab his other arm, and let's get him to his feet. If not, we'll drag the tall fucker down the staircase. Ugh … watch the puke. Always stinks. Don't walk in it!'

***

'Afternoon, Davie. I've come to get you out of here.' Sergeant Mackay stood in the vacuous visitors' room of Dumfries' Teregles Street Prison, smiling down at the prisoner. He moved to sit down opposite, then, with a start, noticed the cowed man's damaged face, a raised, red-angry scar right down between the lad's left cheek and ear.

He waited for a response, trying not to stare, but there was nothing. He knew many remand inmates clammed up as a way to survive the place, the fear, the treatment, the stink emanating from the prison walls. Where was that happy, strapping young man he'd seen with Catherine MacAdam only months earlier?

Mackay had been away on pre-retirement leave when the orders found him. *Foreign national held on remand for two months, of no fixed abode but perhaps known to you, is to be released and sent out of the country. See to it!* A quick read of the case notes had explained the serious charges laid earlier against the prisoner, but he could see they'd been difficult to prove. Little real evidence. Yet, refusing to speak to anyone, police, legal representatives or Australian High Commission staff, the prisoner hadn't helped his own cause.

The police sergeant tried again. 'Now, Davie, I'm here to get you home. Tomorrow.' He noticed a slight movement in the shoulders. 'I'll be here at 5am to collect you. The prison authorities have been informed.' He stopped, but there was no further reaction. 'We'll travel together in an unmarked police car to London, Heathrow. Chauffeur driven all the way, Laddie – no uniforms. Stop for a pint if you want.'

Again, there was no response, so Mackay cut the humour. 'Tomorrow evening I'll put you on a Qantas flight to Melbourne. Aye, back with your family. They've been notified of your flight and arrival time.' With still no reaction. Sergeant Mackay stood up to leave.

'Ca... Catherine?' So deep within himself, the young man could hardly raise a voice.

But Mackay didn't know the answer. He was at a loss to understand any of it.

***

As the last passengers completed boarding procedures for QF1 there was a final flight announcement. Morrison from the High Commission had already left, and only one Qantas flight attendant remained, waiting. Sergeant Mackay helped the young man to his feet, then held out a bulging travel bag. 'Now, Davie, you already have your travel documents, and the money from your bank account in Australian dollars. But you canna turn up to your family empty-handed. They'll think you've gone all Scottish!'

Inside the bag could be seen a number of individually wrapped items. 'Chosen late yesterday by Mrs Mackay, so should suit your family. Magazines as well, for the plane; I remember you liked *New Musical Express*.' He put the bag on the young man's shoulder. 'Now Laddie, remember to hold your head up when you see them.'

It was the kindness, the sincerity, which dragged Dave to the surface. For the first time, he caught the sergeant's eyes, then mouthed a thank you. The policeman held out his arms and he responded. And again, he choked on the question. 'Cath ... Catherine?'

But Mackay still had no idea. 'Davie, I just don't know.'

'Fir ... first my father, n ... now Catherine ...' The words slipped away from Mackay as Dave slipped out of his arms.

It distressed the old sergeant, and when he'd recovered, David Lawson and the attendant had gone. And so it seemed, had Catherine MacAdam.

PART 4

Australia – December 1974

Christmas Eve.

The sudden, heavy rain lashed the windows of the bar facing Darwin Harbour as if someone had thrown heavy gravel at them. Locals in the afternoon crowd had earlier dismissed the cyclone warnings on the bar radio, but as evening closed in, drinkers looked beyond their beers at the bullying black world outside. More than wet season rain squalls now, and some had to get home to the northern suburbs.

Trev the bar manager said it for all of them. 'This is fair dinkum, blokes. It's even got a name: Tracy, Cyclone Tracy. And it's getting closer. Finish your drinks, the pool games. Bottle shop's closing too.'

Soon, only The Viking, Stretch, Ian, and Jimbo were left. Usually there till stumps, they weren't to be hurried, cyclone or not.

Like a praying mantis, Stretch leant well over the pool table, his long arms and body placed him perfectly to sink the purple. Whack! The others nodded, waited, one shot now to finish the game. The Travelodge gardener could be moody and a mumbler, and, of course, there was that long scary scar now shining with facial perspiration. And they remembered the night he'd smashed up the juke box with a pool cue because of some bloody song – *After Midnight*, wasn't it? But drunk or sober they collectively acknowledged he was easily the best pool player at the Koala Hotel. The black ball crunched into the far-left pocket.

'Trev. Last round of beers. Celebration.'

'Sorry, Stretch, too late. Closing the till. And, apart from the bloody cyclone, mate, it's Christmas Eve, and I've got a family to get home to.'

The Viking was suddenly close, intimidating with that heavy accent and those heavy glasses. Compelling. 'The Stretch Man say a dozen Swan for take away! We win the pool game again. And we have to drink for Saint Nicolaus!'

***

After locking the outer doors, the bar manager stopped momentarily to pick out his vehicle in the dull outside lighting, and now near-horizontal rain. Already, tree branches were down in the car park. He instinctively hunched his shoulders to advance into the deluge, but movement off to the left caught his eye. About twenty metres away, in the lee of the motel block, two fuzzy figures holding stubbies had arms over each other, singing and swinging, though unheard in the growing roar of the wind and rain. A golden flash revealed Stretch and the Viking. Shaking his head, Trev ran for his car.

***

'Maggs, Maggs, wake up! The tent's gone!'

Maggie Pearson dragged herself out of hash-induced sleep. 'Wha … what?'

'The bloody tent's gone, I said.' A drenched Wayne bent over her; long strands of hair stuck to his face.

The young woman jerked up into a sitting position. She felt the rain pepper her face and arms, and, yep, her sleeping bag and backpack were already quite wet. 'God, what do we do? Must be that cyclone they were talking about.' Pointing, she tried to shout over the low wind roar. 'Quick, let's get under those trees.'

They grabbed their gear and moved into a nearby clump of rearing casuarina trees. However, these offered little shelter from the now constant rain and gale force wind. Maggie found her torch in a backpack pocket and flashed it around. 'We should find the tent, Wayne. This mightn't last too long.'

'Fuck the tent,' he yelled, as they huddled down behind the thickest of the trunks. However, flying tree foliage had already found them. Some of it stung.

Looking up towards the Esplanade, Maggie realised the earlier reassuring glow from the streetlights was gone. The power must be off somewhere. She glanced at her watch: 11.57 – hours till morning. Things should return to normal then.

But things were far from normal, when sometime later rain, wind and noise levels had intensified noticeably and two sheets of roofing iron, still joined at one corner, lazily pirouetted past, like a direction-less dance couple on a surreal stage of flashing lights. Then, the trees – their security trees – began to lose branches that tumbled away into the dark, as if some God-like gardener had decided to prune the area.

Maggie hung on to a careening trunk. 'Wayne, Wayne, we can't stay here.' She had to shout above the wind even to hear herself. But she couldn't find Wayne; couldn't see him. He was gone. And so was his backpack.

Reactively, Maggy stuck on her sandals, scooped up her belongings and began to run across the open area up towards the Esplanade. She knew it was about 30 meters away. There'll be houses, shelter, there. Keep going! Other objects, more corrugated iron, a ragged canvas tarpaulin, an empty wardrobe, were also on the move, but the ever-flashing lightning gave warning of their proximity. Yet, once on the flooded road, she tripped on a submerged gutter and pitched head-first into a low metal-wire fence.

Maggie Pearson, adventurous schoolteacher from Adelaide, would now have been safely drinking Bintang beer in Bali with the elusive Wayne, if the afternoon Merpati Airlines flight to Kupang and Dempasar had not been cancelled by the severe weather warnings. And, irrationally, all this came to mind as she lay dazed and drenched on Darwin's Esplanade in the expanding force of Cyclone Tracy.

Soon, however, the piercing scrape of iron sheeting on concrete gave subliminal warning to move, to escape a more fatal reality. Was it 10 seconds or 10 minutes she had lain there, it wasn't clear, but hauling herself up on the offending fence, she staggered through swinging metal gates towards the looming shape ahead – a house!

Since arriving in Darwin three days earlier, Maggie had been intrigued by the city's proliferation of houses on stilts. Very sensible she'd decided. And now teetering into the blasting elements, she dodged more airborne objects until thankfully she was under this sensible house, where three cars also sought refuge. Yet, the driving rain and wind were already there, and more sudden, sharp screeching heralded a length of rearing roofing iron angling across an adjacent car bonnet towards her. She had little time to react before a rusty corner ripped into her right arm.

Shiit! That could easily have cut my head off, she gasped, as panic finally began to set in. '*Help, Help!*' She screamed. '*Help me please! Someone!*' There had to be people home – cars still here. It's bloody Christmas, for fuck's sake! She reached a block wall in front of the cars, and in the wild strobing lightning searched for a door, or stairs, all the time screaming, pleading for help.

But nothing; nothing except a set of hip-jarring wash basins, and the crash of objects thwacking the cars, and the house above her. Crying openly and holding her bloodied arm, in desperation she skirted the side of the house to seek a door – any opening, that would offer safety from this hell.

Maggie did find a doorway just a few metres along, and in it stood a very tall man wearing only shorts. She fell against him to escape nature's mayhem and pushed him into the darkness of the ground floor room.

'Um … yes?' The voice was almost inaudible above the noise.

'I … I … The cyclone … Wayne … gone.' She was shouting yet panting with relief.

'Cyclone?' The crane-like figure peered back out through the door, as if the raging, flashing elements outside were only images on a TV screen. 'Oh, yeah.' Again, she could hardly hear him. 'Jus … just woke up.'

'Oh, thank you so much. I … I was *so* … so frightened.' Despite the incessant noise and sharp lightning bursts outside, Maggie was overcome with relief. Here it was still and dry. And safe. 'Thank you, thank you again!'

'Um … power off,' her host noted, unnecessarily. And, as this stranger organised candles, she prattled on uncontrollably, describing in detail the tent, Wayne's disappearance, and her collision with the fence. Then a heavy crash against the house somewhere above made her dive onto the floor. Yet, her host was unmoved. With the candles lit, he watched her from a distance, eventually asking, 'Are you Scandinavian?' Which made Maggie look down and see she was still wearing her sleeping attire – pink knickers and a white t-shirt, now sticking revealingly to her boobs.

She had never struck anyone like him. As the cyclone smashed its way across Darwin, Maggie came to understand her host was bereft of emotion, totally unmoved by the mayhem outside his four walls. That every few minutes, something could be felt or heard to crash into the house failed to agitate him. Nor did he react or reply when she offered her name. He did find her a pair of shorts and a shirt when asked yet gave no apology for their unwashed condition. Being so short, the shirt hung below her knees, but he failed to react to her attempt at humour about this. He did wrap a dirty tea towel around her bleeding arm wound when prompted yet kept the distance his own long arms allowed. Finally, he hinted they should try to grab some sleep, as if there was an early plane to catch in the morning.

Despite the unremitting clamour of the cyclone outside and the stink of beer and sweat in the mattress she now shared, Maggie slipped into an uneasy doze. Until she was jerked back into consciousness by a deeply penetrating ripping noise – as if she had nodded off in a busy sawmill – from the house above.

The whole building shuddered as large objects crashed onto the floor immediately above them, and water trickled through the floorboards at an ever-quickening rate. And the ripping continued, as huge structural parts flopped down from the house above and fell against the breeze-block wall behind her head. Soon, however, the heavy blocks themselves began to collapse onto their bed.

Christmas Day.

Dawn ...

It was not a jolly Christmas morning. The wind maintained its banshee wail and driving rain outside continued to soak and chill them both – jammed, as they were, down on the bathroom floor between the toilet bowl and what remained of the shower screen. They had scrambled into that final desperate refuge, when, after tranquil minutes of the cyclone's eye, a long timber missile smashed through the bathroom's louver window like a shovel-nosed spear, shattering the glass shower screen only inches from them.

Cowering together on the cold, wet concrete floor, they had endured a further interminable period of crashing and flashing, until, as if replete, the house settled down around them, its groaning and cracking finally finished. Now sensing a change, Maggie looked up at the shaggy head beside her. Spotting his long facial scar in a lightning flash, hours earlier had been an initial jolt, but it wasn't abnormal now. Well, no more than sitting for hours in inches of water and broken glass with a total stranger; all part of this ongoing surreal experience she'd somehow signed up for. Perhaps peeing in his shorts was okay too, but she'd decided to hang on. It'd given her something else to think about.

Now clearly lighter and quieter outside, they eased up from their cramped position. The long timber piece was still there across the room at chest height, like some primitive starting barrier. Her watch had given up at 5.24, and surely that was at least an hour ago. She hardly dared hope the cyclone had passed.

He tried to open the bathroom door, but it wouldn't budge. He next attempted to move the intruding timber, but again without success. 'Shake if free,' was his only directive, and, for about 10 minutes, together they twisted, pushed, and cajoled the long timber batten back out the narrow window, until it crashed onto roofing iron outside. Next, he snaked his long, thin body out through the opening.

It was a considerable time of industrial noise and some cursing before she heard him back inside the ground floor flat. Then, levering with a large screwdriver, he had the bathroom door open for her.

Utterly relieved, Maggie fled her prison. Only a few hours earlier, as the cyclone ceaselessly raged and crashed around them, abject fear had convinced her they were going to die on that cold bathroom floor; she couldn't defy death yet again. Now, she hugged and hugged her fellow survivor, sucking in his wetness, his sweat smell, his humanity. 'I … I just want to thank …' She felt his long arms enfold her tightly and his cheek drop onto her head to complete total envelopment, as if his body was answering a long-buried memory. Yet, like a cheap candle, it quickly sputtered out, and he stepped away.

'You … you don't want to get close to me.' He stood there, seemingly devoid of emotion. Was he actually seeing her?

'Why … why not?'

She waited. Most of the noise outside had abated. 'Because … because I get people killed.'

'What do you mean?' Although aghast at the bald statement, her mind latched upon a simple truth. 'But … but, you didn't get me killed. Indeed, you … you've just saved my bloody life! Our lives!'

'Um … yeah.' The eyes were shut, face now straining. 'But … but people who get too close often … often die.' Was he talking to himself? 'I … I shouldn't have survived that.' Speaking almost under his breath, he looked away again. 'Should have been killed – punished.'

'What are you saying?' She couldn't understand any of this. 'Um, … I know we were meant to survive. God, we didn't go through that hell … that shit for nothing. Whether you like it or not, you were meant to survive. As was I. To get on with your life, me with mine and … and start again.' She indicated the bathroom and its wrecked interior. 'We always have to start again, whatever the circumstances. And … and at least think of your family. Those who need you.'

He looked away again. 'No one needs me. Um … keep the clothes.'

In normal circumstances, Maggie would have taken that as a dismissal. But, despite what he'd said, she was still absorbing, celebrating, this return to life. She grinned up at his gaunt unshaven face, his long scar, his dishevelled mop of blond hair with as much gratitude as she could pack into the one big smile. Until she was distracted by the utter mayhem out through the front door, exposed by degrees by the dawn.

Braving the last of the wind and rain, Maggie ventured outside. Death may have been avoided, once, twice, but the gods had saved her for a very different world. Just yesterday afternoon, she and Wayne had wandered from the Darwin Hotel to find a campsite, enjoying the Esplanade's orderly array of quaint older houses and their luxuriant gardens.

Now, the scene that confronted her was as quaint and luxuriant as she envisaged a nuclear winter to be. Not a house was left standing. Crumpled sheets of iron lay everywhere, and at all angles, as might prodigious propaganda leaflets dropped from a plane, fighting with broken building material, broken furniture, and broken tree trunks for ascendancy, like the flotsam of some monstrous shipwreck.

Moreover, each of the houses had lost its independence, with exposed floorboards and walls seemingly linked together by discarded roofing and wall pieces. As she looked all around, the only semblance of familiarity was the Travelodge, standing alone, like a fat, battered lighthouse above an endless sea of destruction.

The upstairs back walls of their house, she now saw, had somersaulted to the ground, collapsing the rear block walls of both the bedroom and kitchen of his flat underneath. Only one corner of his mattress was now visible under the concrete blocks, and with another burst of gratitude she remembered his quick action in dragging her away into that bathroom. And she thought of the upstairs residents of the house she would never meet, also employees of the Travelodge, who, he mentioned had flown south for Christmas. Still waking up down there; still to hear that Darwin had ceased to exist as a city; still to hear how their personal possessions had been scattered across the town like the ashes of some famous former lord mayor.

Maggie eventually remembered her own plans and possessions – passport, air ticket, clothing and about $1500 in traveller's cheques.

And Wayne. Standing outside among the wreckage, she tried to explain these concerns to the tall bloke, but he just nodded. Then, aware she was still only wearing sandals on her feet, Maggie carefully picked her way through the material carnage to the road. There, the creeping iron tide had also claimed the Esplanade road and footpath.

She picked up a damaged pool cue – where had that come from? – to help her through it. She found the front fence – now quite flattened under a wall unit – where an eternity earlier, she had gracelessly fallen. She poked among the assembled rubbish there, searching for her backpack and its contents. But there was nothing familiar.

She could hear voices now above the silence, and, towards the city centre, she saw a few other people also aimlessly fossicking for lost treasures. With difficulty, Maggie navigated through the building debris spread across the former grassy area of the Esplanade. She tried to pinpoint their camping spot, but everything had changed. Where were the trees? Again, she found nothing that was hers.

Trawling the cliff edge, she came across two young couples, dreadlocks and caftans, sitting among the large rocks above the now junk-covered Lamaroo Beach. They had begun to dry out their gear yet seemed desolated. Did she think it was over? Did she think Merpati's postponed flight would leave today? Or tomorrow? they asked.

She shook her head but told them to check at the Merpati office in Cavanagh Street. Walking away, she was reminded of the popular Leslie Gore hit of years back that some wit had adapted to the small Indonesian airline. *It's Merpati and they'll fly when they want to, fly when they want to, fly when they want to!* She tried to fit *except for cyclones* into the words without success.

Reaching the road again after further searching, she came to regret her fatuous answer to those lost souls, *check at the Merpati office*. Could it now be found in this shattered town? And was she already shelving the overland trip to India and Nepal? Had God, whom she didn't believe in, just demonstrated there was no real need to travel to Kathmandu to have her eyes opened?

Yet, as if having ingested some of her own flippant advice, Maggie followed the line of bent and twisted metal street poles, wires dangling like the macrame of a novice giant, along the Esplanade to the corrugated mayhem of Smith and Cavenagh Streets. There, the cyclone debris from collapsed shop fronts, awnings, and roofs, was far more dense, trapped between the buildings and wrecked parked cars.

Yet already there was a propagation of patient people, queueing zombie-like outside the post office; perhaps, she pondered, hoping a reverse charge call home might somehow reverse time.

Maybe it was the delayed shock that other people talk about, that only *other* people experience, but it seemed to be days, weeks later that Maggie Pearson felt the hand on her shoulder. Inexplicably, she was still sitting on the splintered park bench in that wreckage-strewn park in the devastated town centre. Staring at nothing, sightless. How long …?

'Okay?' was all the tall bloke with the scruffy long hair and the seriously long scar said. And with his long, comforting arm around her, they navigated the streets of cyclone detritus back to the only place she knew in this new world, this new life, which, amazingly, had only begun that morning. Yet, it was old, familiar relief and gratitude that now filled her to bursting.

Later, between gulps of his warm Swan beer, she asked why he had come looking for her. In case she'd needed help, was all he would say.

Before dark, he led her to the rear of the Travelodge Hotel, across what she guessed had once been tidy backyards, dodging lost fridges, ceiling fans with up-bent blades like surrendering octopi, and so much other building debris.

Once there, he took her into an area marked *Staff*, sat her at a table with a kerosene lamp, and left, to return after some minutes with a plate of cold meat, cheese and whole tomatoes, and a bottle of warm, white wine. He refused to explain anything. Later, with the lamp, he led her up a dark stairwell, echoing in ignorance of the devastation outside its solid walls, to Room 466. It was the tidiest room she could ever remember.

He indicated the bathroom. 'You first.'

Inside, with two candles, Maggie examined herself in the expansive mirror. As a teen, she had been pleased often to be compared with Little Pattie, the popular singer – long hair, fringe, short solid build, impetuous. Now, she was happy, relieved even, simply to be the filthy, dishevelled survivor who looked back at her from the mirror.

Then slowly, she unburdened herself into a world of clean, warmish water and gleaming white tiles. Only a temporary reality surely. She washed her hair, and while brushing, wondered if it was at all sensible to share a room with a mysterious man whose name she still didn't know. But, in a 24-hour period where nothing at all had been routine or sensible, and nothing could ever be the same again, she came to understand it really didn't matter.

New Year's Eve.

She waited until the rain stopped before claiming one of the tables on the hotel patio, now clear of all debris except for the car still at the bottom of its pool; submerged, she thought, like a giant white clam waiting for unsuspecting swimmers. The Travelodge, for those lucky enough to be connected to it, remained a pond of peacefulness within Darwin's ocean of utter upheaval.

However, Maggie had a distinct reason for using her evening dinner break to catch him. She was leaving. Thousands of residents had been evacuated in the days since the cyclone, and after ringing home just hours earlier she had gone to the government office to claim a seat on one of the last evacuation flights before they ceased tomorrow, New Year's Eve.

That her mother in a buoyant tone had announced Wayne's safe return to Adelaide was only part of her motivation. Maggie had spent considerable time and emotion in the five days since the cyclone searching for him, and now she could stop. Done her duty. But the relief of not having to find his name on a list of those killed, or to recognise a much-damaged dead face in one of the temporary morgues, and then relay that awful news to the Willenski family, had been replaced by considerable anger.

She had always known his bullying and weaknesses, the relationship driven as much by their two families, as her willingness to settle for second best. And, it had been she who'd been desperate to experience Kathmandu. He'd initially thought she meant somewhere in north Queensland.

With the anger had come the need to get Wayne and the rest of her life sorted out. Thus, the decision to leave. She felt no connection to Darwin, having flown in only a few days before Christmas; a necessary stop on the way to Bali and the rest of the world.

And she wasn't really handy or adaptable, despite accepting the request by Peter, the Travelodge manager, on Boxing Day, to work in the bar and dining room as media and government people began to arrive to put their slant on Darwin's tragedy. For clothes, food, and lodgings, he'd said, which she hadn't minded at all, nor being asked to share Room 466 with other female staff members, instead of the man everyone called Stretch.

Girlfriend, was the term he'd used to get them that much needed room on Christmas night; that hot room where the cyclone-resistant mosquitoes had eventually found them through the broken windows, despite being four floors up.

And Maggie *had* enjoyed this unexpected acknowledgement, for with it had come an interesting mix of notoriety and approval. The non-communicative, yet capable person who had helped her survive the cyclone and beyond, she now understood – or tried to understand – was certainly an unfathomable character. Seen by some as a mumbling drunk, a waster, there were others like Peter, who considered Stretch indispensable.

She spotted his tall figure approaching with drinks, already glistening with condensation. It was the alcohol she'd need to tell him of her decision. She was definitely leaving. Tomorrow.

She couldn't say he was handsome; the long scar had seen to that. And he was too tall, scraggy blond hair, and had eyes that could unsettle you. Yet, there was something about him she couldn't quite isolate, a kindness, a thoughtfulness perhaps, towards women. Had he been married?

One of her roommates had unhelpfully described him being violent in the Koala bar months earlier, but Maggie had chosen to ignore that. Not the man who'd saved her in the cyclone, not the man who'd walked with her twice to the hospital to have her arm sewn up, and certainly not the man who'd gone looking for her on Christmas Day. In case she'd needed him.

Maggie smiled a welcome. 'How's your day been, Stretch?'

Settling his long body into a chair, he nodded. 'Steamy. You?'

No mucking about, Maggie. Out with it. 'Well, I've had some success, some news.'

He took a long swig of the beer.

'I've found Wayne. He's already back home. Arrived on Friday, the shitter.'

A hesitation. 'Sorry.'

She hid for another moment behind her drink. Here goes. 'I've decided to leave, Stretch. Tomorrow afternoon's evacuation plane.' His only reaction was the smallest of eye flicker. Another silence she had to fill. 'What … what do you think? Do you mind?'

He took another swig before answering. 'Not up to me.'

Maggie again waited. She had accepted the reticence as part of his mystique, but now she expected, needed, a reaction: anything. 'I … I've nothing to keep me here now.' The roofless, useless block of government flats away behind him came into focus as if to encourage her decision. 'But it's not to catch up with that bloody Wayne, the coward. He's finished.' And, as if talking to herself, she added. 'But I know he's going to be difficult.'

'Understand.' A pause. 'Sorry.' He turned away. She waited. Was that it? Did she mean that little to him?

'Stretch, you could try and talk me out of it. What about us?'

Another wait. 'Us?' His intense eyes turned and held hers. 'I told you – you don't want to get too close to me.'

She hesitated, marshalling her courage. 'And … and I've already said to you, Stretch, to at least think of your family in …'

An eventual answer. 'Melbourne … Look, I … I fit in here. Melbourne people think I'm strange, but in Darwin I'm just *another* strange person. Don't stand out. Most … here … running from something.'

'Stretch, what are *you* running from?'

He answered with a pull of his bottle.

'Is it Catherine?'

He sat bolt upright. 'Wha … what do you know about … about … her?' She could see he was shaken, his serenity gone, his defences breached – for once.

She sought his hand on the table, but it quickly pulled away. 'Oh, Stretch, I've upset you. I *am* sorry. You said … um, called her name when we slept, um … upstairs. Who … who is she?'

Wild-eyed, he glared up and behind her at the Travelodge structure, as if afraid that name may appear large and bright on its

246

damaged side wall to tell the rest of the world. Would he get up and storm off? She could only wait.

Eventually the face calmed, and he looked across at her. 'Another cyclone.' A hand was up at the scar on the side of his face.

Reflexively, she touched the still-bandaged wound on her arm that could have been so much worse. 'God, I hope mine doesn't scar like that.'

He exploded with reaction, blasting a mouthful of beer over himself and their table. Hell, you've really done it this time, Maggs. But, as he recovered, the smallest hint of a grin rode on the corners of his mouth.

It seemed an interminably long time before he spoke again. Slowly at first.

'Something ... something you said. We ... um ... I ... gotta start again.' The hands fidgeted with the bottle. 'I ... I ... can't keep hiding ... Running.' A searching look away. 'You ... you've got Wayne to ... to sort. I ... my mother ... first ...'

***

Once the rain stopped, Maggie and the other unkempt stragglers were ushered out onto the tarmac of Darwin airport towards the large Airforce plane. It was a little after 4pm on New Year's Eve. An Ansett jet waited away to the left like a large queen bee for another group slowly swarming towards it.

An older man nearby in dirty long socks muttered about *our group* missing out on the bar service, but no one laughed. This was serious business for some – leaving your loved ones, your home, your whole life behind. And already the dress she had borrowed from Peter's wife, Gladys, was creased and sweat stained. Perhaps it didn't matter now.

She eventually reached the plane's rear stairs, and at the top, as if to catch one last glimpse of what was left of Darwin, she turned back towards the big hanger where they'd been processed. And then she saw her mystery man, a head above the other forlorn farewellers. *In case you need help.*

As she gave herself into the care of the RAAF woman in the floppy jungle hat with the understanding smile at the plane door, Maggie finally allowed herself to relax. Her eyes truly had been opened, and, yeah, she may just have found nirvana after all.

PART 5

Scotland – March 1975

Ping! The seatbelt sign went off.

The long, overnight flight from Johannesburg was Catherine's first actual opportunity to reflect on her decision to return to Scotland. To sister Vicky and Steven, her announcement only a week ago to leave South Africa must have seemed quite sudden. And once the decision had been made, she immediately booked and paid for a suitable British Airways flight, so she couldn't change her mind. It had been a teary farewell.

Sitting in the semi-dark of the plane cabin, her daughter's sleeping head on her lap, Cathy wasn't ready for sleep herself, so she asked an ever-smiling hostess for a glass of wine. Almost three years in South Africa had convinced her she didn't want wee Rhona to grow up in a racially divided country.

However, she saw clearly now it was her deluded decision to *forgive* David, early the previous year that had begun a chain of realisations that culminated in her now leaving, or should she say, returning. For months, before and after the birth she had raged about him, his "desertion" of both her and their baby.

However, significantly, the decision to *forgive* had formed the idea that she must equally forgive herself, for in her earlier desperation to have a child, she'd reverted to the bullying, scheming Mrs MacAdam of her darkest, pre-David days. And with that revelation had come the embarrassment of her behaviour when telling him of her pregnancy. It no doubt had caused him to leave, indeed flee.

With Rhona starting to walk had come a further understanding that David should be sharing in his daughter's progress. And this, a week or so ago had become the desire, indeed the need to find him, to tell him of his wonderful little girl, and ask for *his* forgiveness.

That this couldn't satisfactorily be achieved from increasingly isolated South Africa had come a desperation to get *home*, home to Glendaruel.

Yet, there was some sadness in leaving. In the time since her arrival, she and Victoria had mended many fences, and come to understand their mutual judgements and assumptions of the past principally had come from their parents.

Catherine had at first wondered if Vicky gained initial pleasure from the sudden appearance of her 'posh' younger sister, pregnant, in a state of suicide and self-neglect, and accompanied by a queer friend, Mungo. However, from the start Vicky had put her full weight behind Catherine's needs, demanding few answers and making even fewer judgements.

Moreover, as Aunt Cathy, she had become a favourite with her teenage niece and nephew who were amazed at her knowledge of pop artists and their songs, thanks, she knew, to David. Then, there was leaving her sister's cheery, helpful house maids, who earlier had given playful baby Rhona the nickname of Loksie, after *Tokoloshe,* the Zulu water sprite. 'Make sure to keep in touch,' were Vicky's final words at the airport.

She managed a desultory sleep until Rhona woke, needing the toilet. Then, breakfast came and soon they were only an hour from Heathrow. Time to consider the challenges ahead. First, both of them were still MacAdams, and she did want to do something about that. Well, Rhona Loksie Fergusson sounded just fine, but if he … Then, there was the thing of being a single mother in huffy, stuffy old Scotland, the pointing, the judgements; even worse for an innocent wee child.

However, Vicky had suggested an inventive solution for that. Now, the burden of a big house like Glendaruel was not a sensible way to begin her new life, Mungo had warned, yet she was pleased now to have hung on to it, selling all the estate cottages being the price.

After all, she, David, and Mungo had saved the house once, and, well, where else could she go? Moreover, with her decision to return home, she was desperate to parade wee Rhona about the place to demonstrate to the old MacAdam ghosts the fertility of hers they'd

250

always doubted. No, they'd said the miscarriages couldn't be James' fault; had to be the outsider!

With the seatbelt announcement, she moved to secure them both. No, it won't be easy. No more sitting around that big old house as in the past, madam, filling time with boring charity work of dubious worth. With Vicky and Steven's professional lives as examples, she was keen to get that tertiary education – Art/photography – denied all those years ago by her father. This, with Rhona to care for, would fill her time, but also, more importantly, eventually create an income. Land rental wouldn't be enough, so she was determined to try professional photography, a big step up she knew from her small volume sale of pics for travel companies and airline magazines of the last two years. Hence, the duty-free Pentax Spotmatic in her hand luggage.

And she must try to find David. Well, at least make contact, and inform him of his darling daughter. And apologise, in person if possible. However, after three years, no one it seemed was sure where he was, but Australia probably. 'If you can, Cathy, coax him back. Coax him back to Glendaruel.' There, she'd said it, although she understood she didn't deserve him back. However, Rhona did.

***

'There they are,' Mungo said to no one in particular, as Catherine and wee Rhona entered Glasgow's arrival hall. Standing back from the eager crowd he gave them a wave. She's put on some weight, he was pleased to see, and glowed like a healthy young mother.

He and Catherine briefly took each other in before hugging, a still sleepy Rhona somewhat crushed in the process. Then, moving with the press of people towards the luggage carousel, he carried the little girl, asking about the newly-introduced shuttle flight from Heathrow to Glasgow, and of Vicky and Steven, whom he'd met only briefly and in those awkward circumstances. Rhona's eyes were fixed to him.

'And the last time we met, wee Rhona, well, you were well hidden inside your mummy's tummy!' He beamed. 'Och, you're a tall, bonny thing. Aren't you just?' The little girl gave a cautious nod.

251

Some minutes later, Mungo viewed the five suitcases, parked alone on the Terminal's shining concrete floor like passengers who'd missed their plane. 'Catherine, I think we may have a logistics problem. I've um ... only brought the Beast.' They both grinned sheepishly until he squatted down and looked at Rhona, who was holding her mother's hand. 'Do you have enough British money, young lady, to catch the bus?'

***

As the overloaded Triumph Stag warbled past the gatehouse into Glendaruel, Catherine found the emotions she had assembled on the flight to deal with this very moment now to be quite inadequate. Yes, it was so wonderful to be home, her home, her waiting friends, the familiar touch of Scottish spring already on the trees, in the air.

But another more vivid aspect of *home* flashed into her head through the prisms of fear, despair, and torpidity of those last weeks in her bedroom upstairs; groping to find the will to wash and feed herself, or the courage to go down to the phone to ring Mungo and plead for help, or ... or to resist the easy option of taking handfuls of those innocuous white tablets and ending the unremitting emptiness.

And now going through the temporal emotions of finding Cheryl, Mrs Duffy, and even an old, limping Sergeant Major waiting to welcome her on the steps of the house, introducing them to Rhona, thanking them simply for being here, and then entering the big house to find it quite unchanged, didn't immediately settle her. As if she had to choose once again.

Despite the obvious hearty spring clean someone had recently given the place, moving about inside in those first hours, Catherine felt an existence, a presence, something there: in the drawing room, about the kitchen table, upstairs in her – their – bedroom. It was silly she knew, but she kept feeling David: not David and Cathy, just David. As if he'd been here since she'd left. And, then there was Sergeant Major's behaviour.

'Maamee!' The ever-listening parental antenna caught the cry. Annoyance, not danger, not desperation, it said. Catherine pulled herself back to the here and now and returned to the central hall to find the usually stand-offish Sergeant Major attempting yet again to make friends with Rhona. As he had done from the start with her father. Had the cat, like her, also detected David, but within Rhona? Uncanny, but also a touch reassuring that her decision to return was correct. Now, time for that very tired girl to have a wee nap.

What happened as the afternoon and evening unfolded was affirmation for Catherine of her intuition about David. Once Alex arrived from the castle, they all sat around Glendaruel's old kitchen table for a late lunch, and with Rhona asleep, Catherine was able to put her mind to her friends gathered about her to celebrate her return.

Were they aware of her selfish ultimatum to David? Did they understand that in essence, he wasn't here because Rhona was? Was David the elephant in the room, as is said? Unsure, she could only thank them again for their ongoing support and welcome, despite the terrible error, or series of errors she'd made in the past.

Keen to hear of Vicky and family, and learn first-hand about the situation in South Africa, they later moved *en masse* to the drawing room, where a brisk fire had already defeated the afternoon chill. There, Mungo, and Cheryl took control, offering coffee or something *more sensible*, as they worded it, and Catherine relaxed into the familiarity of an old smoothie. They had even anticipated Mrs Duffy's choice of sherry with her coffee.

Rhona was soon awake and joined them to play with her stuffed zebras on the hearth rug. But, as Catherine continued to answer questions, the little girl was up, moving about the room, unfamiliar to her, around the furniture, exploring and touching.

Abruptly, the conversation was damped down by loud, resonant music, and all eyes spun away from the fire. A song, immediately and happily recognisable to Catherine – *After Midnight*.

'Christ, what's that?' Mungo was the first to react.

'J.J. Cale, I think.' Alex grinned.

The sonorous song continued as heads looked about. 'The record player, the hifi!' Cheryl pointed towards the sideboard. 'Rhona's touched something.' Then, her voice raised. 'Aye, but look at her now. She's jiggin' with the music!'

Catherine stared at an animated Rhona, eyes closed, rocking, and moving her small arms and legs to the beat, doing an exhibition to one of her father's favourite songs. That their daughter might just be dancing with him, as she herself had often done here, summoned a bout of tears, though she'd promised herself on the plane she wouldn't cry, under any circumstances. But how could she not cry, when thinking how it would have been if the three of them were dancing together, here, in their favourite room to this favourite song.

'But how could the hifi just start like that?' Cheryl's sensible question broke the spell. Yes, indeed, Catherine asked herself, while Alex stopped the player as the next track began.

'There were no records inside the player when we packed up the house. Certain of it.' Alex took out the offending LP. 'But we may have missed some on the rack underneath.' He squatted down. 'Yep, some still here.' He pulled something out. 'Hey, the empty LP cover – J.J. Cale, *Naturally*.' Alex waved it about like a punter with a successful betting slip. 'Now, if someone had tried to play this record with the house power off, it would just sit there on the stacking spindle above the turntable until power was returned and someone came and reset the play button once again.' He looked at Catherine. 'But who would it be, who could it have been with the place locked up?' Alex grinned again, and squatted down beside Rhona, eyebrows raised. 'Perhaps your daddy spirited the record there, waiting for you to be born to press the button.' She nodded solemnly at him. 'Man, the Aussie would have so enjoyed your dance.' The room buzzed with that thought until Mungo suggested more drinks.

'But Master James *did* return.'

Again, the conversation stopped. All eyes turned, this time to Mrs Duffy, deep in her lounge chair. 'Aye, he did.'

Catherine jumped up. 'When … when was that?'

The old lady hesitated. 'Well … quite a while ago now.' She stopped again. 'Hmm, after you went away with Mr Mungo here.' She smiled towards the big man. 'I like that name. My brother was a Mungo.' She shared the smile with everyone, as if humbled by her family's good fortune. 'Aye, perhaps a week, two weeks after you … hmm?'

'But you … you didn't say!'

'I'm sorry, Dear. But you haven't asked. And there was so much blood on his face, on his clothes.' She looked about her as if this was further good news. 'But the policemen who took him away in their car seemed very polite.'

Blood? Police? '*Blood?*' Catherine almost yelled at her old friend.

'Aye, such a mess there was to clean up. Blood even on the photograph.'

'Photograph?'

'Aye, I found it the following morning. Near the front door, it was. Perhaps they had dropped it.' She reached for her bag. 'I popped it in here to give it you at some time.'

They all watched, transfixed, as Mrs Duffy rummaged in her handbag. 'Ah, here it is.' She pulled out a creased, black and white photo. 'A bonny snap of you and Master James, all dressed up for the ball!'

With as much self-control as she could muster, Catherine accepted the photograph from Mrs Duffy. And, yes, with a sudden rush of excitement, she remembered it. Hogmanay, three years ago. Taken on that new tripod. Probably still in the house somewhere. And he'd written on it, *After Midnight*. And along the bottom, *Kat Cale, and J.J. Stevens – letting it all hang out*. Kat with a *K*. And David's blood.

Much later, Catherine found Mungo still in front of the drawing room fire. She'd come to grips with the enormity of Mrs Duffy's revelation, but now needed to talk it out. She joined him on the couch. 'Well, what are we to do now?' She still wasn't sure whether to cheer or cry, but it was time to be practical. And she knew what she really desired, what Loksie needed. Yet, she asked the big man for his opinion.

'Find him, of course. Bring him back, aye. Can't be that difficult, now with direct dial overseas phone calls. Alex does it often.' Mungo reached across and lifted her chin. 'And, I know, if need be, there's enough money in the estate leasing account to pay for his ticket.'

Catherine considered all this. Her old police pal, Sergeant Mackay, would have known, or found the number, having rung the family in Australia when David was first in hospital. And he might have been with them today if not for the bowel cancer. The letter from Mrs Mackay, readdressed twice, had eventually reached her in South Africa, early the previous year. Another missing piece of her old life.

'Um … well, I remember David's family lived in Melbourne, a beach suburb. He often talked about it; the long beach.' Think, Cathy. 'Sea … Sea– something.' She concentrated. 'Seaford, that's it, as in southern England. We always meant to visit it. And, and … the address had a quaint name … Gum Tree Crescent, perhaps?'

Mungo went out to the phone in the cold hall, and soon returned with a number for a Mrs A. Lawson of Ti Tree Crescent, Seaford, Victoria.

'Aye, that's it!' Catherine brightened. 'That will be his mother, Alma. But he mostly talked of his grandfather, Ric.' She looked at the big man, the friend who had helped her so often. 'Um, … Mungo. May I ask one more favour of you?'

'Aye?'

Rugged up, they sat on chairs under the half colonel's portrait. He has to go, she decided. Restrict all MacAdams to the mausoleum. That bloody panther as well, which should please Sergeant Major. She smiled across at Mungo, fidgeting as Rhona might, in the other chair. It was so supportive of him to make this call for her. She doubted her ability to control her emotions if David were to answer.

From the phone on the small table, he dialled the number, and they waited for the signal to reach halfway across the world.

Then Mungo stiffened. *'Hello, um, Mr Lawson?'*

Watching him, Catherine allowed herself a slight smile.

'Oh, my apologies, Mr Monkavich. But it is Ric?'

'Alright then, Eric. Now Eric, my name is Mungo Rollo, and I'm a former friend, well, still good friend, of your grandson, David.'

'Here in Scotland. I'm ringing from Dumfries, Scotland. The Glendaruel Estate, to be ex–'

'Sorry?'

Catherine leant closer.

256

'Oh.'

'Oh, I am sorry to hear that. Wait, wait, I ... You see, we didn't know. We still don –'

She tried to catch Mungo's attention.

'Aye, but please let me finish, Mr, um, Eric. I still don't know how, how David left the UK, or ... or even when. But–'

'Jail, did you say? Two months on remand? I didn't ...' Mungo waited. 'And his face? No, he didn't have any scars when he was – '

'Aye, I agree. Terrible for you all.'

Catherine pulled at Mungo's arm. 'What is it? What's that about his face?'

'Too late? What ... what do you mean?'

'Say again?'

'Missing? Wee Davie's missing? But how, Eric?'

'Wait. Sorry? A cyclone? Darwin?'

Catherine was frantic. 'Mungo, what's he saying?'

'Christmas Eve last?'

'Did you say 19 ... um, still missing?'

She was dragging at his arm, shouting. 'Mungo, tell me!'

'Yes, I ... I agree. It ... it is tragic.'

'Aye, well after 11 weeks, you ... you would assume–'

With his free hand, Mungo tried to hold her back.

'Well, um, thank you, Mr Monkavich. Yes, and pass on my condol –'

'I'm sorry? No, I hadn't meant to drag this all up again. I'm just a good friend of ... of ...'

'Of ... of course. If you don't want me to. Well, I'll say good ... goodbye then.'

Catherine sat slouched in the chair; her eyes fixed on the black telephone. Such a powerful instrument to deliver such crushing news instantly across continents. But she understood. David had perished in

257

a cyclone, only months earlier – just missed him again. Her hopes, her stupid dreams shattered. Again. Oh, when would life be kind? Why always her?

She was about to deliver herself to billowing emotion and tears, as in the past, when a silver sliver of reminiscence, a minute memory, floated across her swelling grief. A freezing morning, she and David standing together on the cold steps just outside the front door there, she close to bankruptcy, and he weighted down with having to leave her alone for that first time to work at Pollcrayvie Castle. *Cheer up, Cathy,* he'd said. *We're* – and then … and then he'd forgotten the rest! God, they'd laughed and cried together at that. Aye, a silly incident, but it had got them over that initial low point. Together. Later, when David explained how he'd meant to say something profound, like we*'re in this together,* or was it, *whatever!* they'd laughed again.

She found herself smiling at the memory, inappropriate as it was now. Yet, it made her understand how she wasn't alone at all. Spiritually, she had felt David still in the house, and physically, his presence was here in his daughter, Rhona. The little girl was her responsibility now, as for a time she, Catherine MacAdam, had somehow become David's. *We're in this together.*

Aye, that brief, wonderful time together, Cathy, cannot be taken away. You'll always have it, and him. And then there's her small, but wonderful bunch of pals, led by Mungo, her other redeemer. Couldn't let them or Rhona down, by falling into a sobbing heap of self-pity and guilt – for someone to pick up the pieces yet again. So, ultimately it was up to her. Up to herself. It wasn't going to be easy; again, she'd need David's quiet courage. Kat with a K. *Whatever!*

That silly ditty of his was out before she could stop. 'Things is crook in Tallarook, but they're gunna be cool at Glendarool.'

Mungo, sitting so stiff like a soldier on duty, no doubt on guard for her to break down, burst into a wide grin of relief. 'Sort of thing young Davie would've said.'

'Aye, it is.'

PART 6

1999

Scotland, 16th March

Cancer

... a withering word that demands attention – disappointment, respect, outrage even, Rhona understood. Yet, it returned in the car with the two women, as would an invisible passenger in the back seat. Once home in the kitchen, they made a pot of tea, organised cutlery, and sat down opposite each other at the table. An electric radiator was at their feet, the combustion stove, forgotten in the initial reluctance to attend that morning's specialist's meeting, remained cold, aloof.

Rhona waited, watching her mother's face relax into that familiar companionable countenance. What was she thinking? She felt the need to say, *oh, Mum, you do look unwell,* but then Kat really didn't look any different from their previous get-together a few weeks earlier. She hadn't really noticed her mother grow old, no one particular point of sudden change. Always those disarming hazel eyes, and that striking head of hair which, over the years had become fully grey without announcement.

Get on with it, Loksi. 'Mummy, there's much to discuss after this morning's news. So much to settle.' She was aware, though, her mother wouldn't be bulldozed.

'I think a good solution would be for me to take up marijuana smoking again. We did here, often.' Kat flourished a teaspoon up towards the rest of the house.

'Mother, that's not at all helpful.'

The older woman replaced the spoon with an expressive ding. 'Darling, having just been informed I've only ten or twelve weeks to live should allow me to say or do whatever I please.'

259

Yes, it was true. She hadn't believed it at first when Kat had rung the week before and mentioned the possibility of cancer. And now with the test results in Dumfries this morning ... advanced pancreatic cancer. And the choice of ... well, no bloody choice really! Too late for surgery, the specialist had said. Must focus now on palliative care; make her as comfortable as possible and begin to sort out her affairs. Morphine further down the track. Well, all very practical, clinical advice. Easily given when it's not your own mother.

And *she* had to sort out her own affairs as well, Rhona realised. God, it was as if her autobiography now had to be rewritten! She got up to re-boil the kettle, but stood there, hands on the back of her chair. 'Suddenly, there is so much more I want to know, Mummy. Even about the pot smoking!'

15th April

'Cup of tea, Mum?'

A cold, miserable morning that held little promise of spring, the two women sat in front of the stuttering fire, waiting for the drawing room to warm. 'Thank you, Darling. I realise now this whole business of dying–'

'Mum!' It made her jump, as sudden thunder sometimes did.

'Now, don't make a fuss.' Kat raised a hand. 'To quote a famous fictional Scot, *why fear death?* Look, I do understand this will be far more traumatic for you. For ... for those who are left behind. My mind will simply turn off in eight weeks, but yours has to go on with the business of living. And, well ... handling the grief.' She offered a cheery face, those calming hazel eyes. 'My Darling, you must understand I'm not at all afraid. Somewhat vexed to miss the end of the millennium everyone is making such a fuss of, but no, not afraid.'

Rhona stood up. Well, *she* was afraid, frightened of the cul-de-sac life had suddenly taken them into. Yet, since the news of the cancer some weeks earlier, they had got to work, and the simple will, and registration of the Kat Cale Trust and other significant issues had been settled. They were both realists, sensible professional women. Yet she could only admire her mother's courage, and the obvious concern for her daughter's position in this. And since the death sentence had been made public, visitors, like Uncle M and Cheryl, and Jerry, Kat's London agent, had begun to come to the house, each awkward in their mission.

She leaned over the coffee table and poured the tea. 'Some of the cake, Mum?'

Her mother lifted a jaundiced hand. 'Sorry, Darling. Not really eating much. Will try harder at lunch.'

'Any pain yet?'

'Aye, a little last night. But took something before it became too serious.'

'Well, we have the morphine tablets. If you like–'

'No, Darling. No. Only as a last resort. When I begin to need morphine, it really is the road to the end. Let's kid ourselves with regular painkillers for as long as we can, shall we?'

She watched her mother get out of the lounge chair with obvious difficulty and place more wood on the fire. She had certainly aged in the previous four weeks – now slower, a little clumsy, pasty-faced. There was more smoke than flame for a moment or two, but she knew not to interfere.

'It's lovely having you here, Loksie. A whole four days together. Generous of Slaughters to give you the time off.' She felt Kat's hand comb through her hair in passing. 'Darling, this was our favourite, the drawing room.' Kat gave a cough, before sitting down again. 'Especially the smoke and smell!'

Rhona grinned. 'You and my father? Now, is my blond hair from him?'

'Aye. He'd lots of it.'

'Oh, I've not seen a photo of him with long hair. Can't imagine it'

'It was the seventies, after all. Must have a few somewhere.'

'I don't really know how I take after him, but of course, I must in many ways.'

'You do, Darling.' That wistful look. 'Now where are those photo albums we spoke of?'

261

They sat together on the couch, photo albums on their knees. 'Was it difficult at first, Mum, settling back into Scotland, Glendaruel? Having to find work, and with me?'

'Aye, it was. Quite a struggle after those friendly, do-everything maids in Johannesburg. But, having honed my basic photographic skills there, I decided to pursue photography. My friends here helped, and I worked hard, anything needing pics I took on, sports, birthdays, posh weddings. Freelancing mostly. Took you along sometimes. That shocked the gentry, of course, many of whom had once been social friends.' She grinned, flicking through more album pages. 'Ah, here we are, Edinburgh! We moved there after I rented Glendaruel estate to that wealthy American – Craiglockhart, do you remember? It was 1976 or '77, me to University, and you in Grade 1 at the primary.'

Loksie smiled at the coloured snaps of herself, a serious wee girl in uniform, blond pigtails, and a school satchel large enough to be a parachute. She couldn't remember the moment – those years, those classrooms merged now like an honest blended whisky, as did her friends and teachers. Ah, more pages of photos – sports days in the spring and summer, school clubs, dressing up at a friend's home.

And so, the reminiscing went on all afternoon, an attempt at late lunch, wine, and more painkillers around 5pm. Her mother would rise, resisting help, to stoke the fire, or find more albums. Now photos of Kat as a mature aged undergraduate – her elegance holding up well amid the far younger fellow students – and marching for the Campaign for Nuclear Disarmament with Mungo, Alex, Jim, Chlodagh, the others. She looked again at Uncle Alex, pulling a face as usual. Sadly, he'd died in 1987, but they hadn't told her until much later it had been from AIDS.

Move on. 'Oh, Mummy, look here! Remember the wee party you held for us graduating together, Uncle Mungo handing out awards. Me with a bursary for secondary at the Steiner school, and you, with a degree, and a chance introduction to the Miner's Strike.'

*　*　*

They prepared the evening meal together, but as was usual now, Kat had no appetite. So, while her daughter ate heartily, she sipped a good Barossa Valley wine, a far more sensible painkiller, she had decided.

Although having enjoyed the afternoon, she was really tired and wanted her bed.

Later, in the darkness, she couldn't find sleep, despite another dose of painkillers. Her conscience, like the cancer, was gnawing away at her. She had always tried to be honest with Rhona, and that's why they were such good pals. But there are unwanted or unsavoury details parents the world over shield their children from, and that's why she had never told Rhona – Loksie – the truth about her father. But now, the parameters of both their lives, having so suddenly and dramatically changed as if the laws of physics had altered overnight and people *could* fall off the edge of the earth, Rhona had to be told! Imagine, if later, she was accidentally confronted with the truth. She must hear it from you, Kat. She must!

13th May:

'Mummy, anything you need?'

'No, I'm fine, Darling, I am. Balmy weather for May.' They were in the sun garden, and Kat smiled up from the cane lounge into Rhona's shining blue eyes. Her father's eyes. Which reminded her that time was short. Pleased to be over the setbacks of the last few weeks, she must tell the girl about her real father, today.

'It's so lovely outside here. This sun garden and I have been great pals over the years – almost a love affair, you might say.'

'Such a shame the summerhouse over there was never finished, Mum. Why was that?' An innocuous, innocent question that nudged raw memories for Kat. That overgrown ruin, was, for many reasons, her *folly,* the symbol of her considerable foolishness. She shook her head with embarrassment.

'Okay, Mummy? Is the morphine helping? Doing its job?'

Doing its job? Now, there's a question, thought Kat. That nurse who had come some days ago at Loksie's request, made clear that taking morphine wasn't an easy way out, not there to finish people off earlier, either by design or accident. 'Well, it's a relief to know that,' Kat had answered. But the thin face of misery hadn't appreciated the joke at all.

'Well, to be honest, Darling, it's all rather pleasant, thus far. Total reduction in pain, and not a care in the world. Also, my breathing is easier.' She wanted to sound encouraging. 'All that from two tablets!'

'Mum, don't be so flippant. This is serious.'

Rhona, Kat knew, was worried about her and any suffering, yet also about her own future. But Kat was more concerned the morphine would begin to shut her down mentally, before … She looked across the field towards those familiar hills. She and he had often shared this view, and finding herself reactively looking around for Sergeant Major, she smiled. 'Now, where's that scrap book, Darling?'

Rhona moved her chair closer and spread the large tatty-edged jotter over her mother's lap. They began an enjoyable few hours amid the book's contents, despite its slight musty odour. How it had begun life as a simple receptacle for photo-worthy stories while Kat was doing the fine arts degree in Edinburgh. And how, somehow it had grown into a ragged record of her chance career as a serious photographer; that series of black and white prints which demonstrated the massive social hardships and dislocation of the Miner's Strike.

It had all begun at Polmaise, just north of Edinburgh, and fired up, Kat had bothered to drive there and talk to the families affected. They had allowed her to take photos, and as the strike spread it became a sort of mission, travelling across Britain to Birmingham, Orgreave and other affected areas, sometimes taking her daughter along, to capture it all. By then, she now explained, she knew how to present herself to both sides – posh or battler.

'A little underhand, Mummy?' Rhona wagged a finger at her mother.

Kat was riding some pain now, but it was important to continue, so at lunch she forced down a sandwich in a show of normality. A cool breeze helped to keep her head clear.

They came to more recent headlines that described Kat as *an observer who understood change*, bracketing her contribution to British photography with that of one her own heroines, Julia Margaret Cameron. Kat explained to Rhona the irony of *change*, having once been a fully paid-up member of the Scottish Establishment. Next was an article with pics, which underscored the influence of her

264

photography on the decision-making process of various government boards, processes that were to affect the lives of millions in disaffected areas in the UK. Then there was the brochure from the British Museum featuring, as a backdrop, her photograph of the old iron bridge at the town of Iron Bridge in Shropshire, capturing a circle in watery reflection, as, research revealed, its creator had intended. Kat again shook her head at the unexpected and quite unnecessary fame her photographs had brought.

The crumpled sheet music of *Sweet Child of Mine* was stapled to a following page, as if representing another proud achievement. Kat struggled to hide the emotions the heavily underscored words in the lyrics always brought out.

'Bloody hell, Mummy, remember this!' Rhona began humming the tune. 'I was the only girl at the Steiner whose mum was a Guns n Roses fan! You were so cool! Still are!' She leapt up and kissed her mother.

Kat shaded her eyes to hide the tears for Rhona's father, as their daughter sang about the bluest eyes, like the sky – words which the girl had always assumed were for her alone. Luckily, in demonstrating how well she remembered the song, poor darling Rhona didn't notice her mother nearly break down and cry, as the song writer had intended.

Around 4.30, with the breeze rising, Rhona suggested they move inside, but Kat refused to leave, understanding she now must stay, must explain, what she'd been putting off all day. Unaware, her daughter stalked off into the house, but soon returned with blankets, biscuits, and Bordeaux. And the morphine, thank goodness, for Kat's pain was now quite serious. That Rhona had elected to remain at Glendaruel till the end filled Kat with considerable guilt. The girl had her own life to lead and career to build after all, but Kat knew she was a solitary soul, with no current romantic interests.

'Mummy, you must have been a confident person to rise from the nappies and prams of a battling single mother to become the famous photographer you are. A model for all women.' She raised her glass with some authority. 'I've–'

'Loksie, stop.' Kat's pain was almost gone. 'I was not always confident, you know. Far from it, if truth be known. It was your father, although not an overconfident person himself, who somehow imbued in me an Australian–'

Kat began to vomit. Then vomit again. Rhona ran to the house and returned with towels, but as Kat continued to dry retch, she rushed inside again to call the family doctor. Kat's only memory was being carried into the house with an overwhelming emotion of disappointment.

26th May

The last episode, I now understand, laid me low for some time, and poor Loksie, old Doctor Black and the thin face of misery assumed I had reached the end. Perhaps I already have – am I speaking from the grave? Yet, Mungo was somewhere there, Cheryl as well. Their voices entered my subconscious, and it quite saddened me. However, the realisation came that it was a little early for last respects – I needed more time for that one final duty, and so I greedily absorbed the intravenous sustenance, watched my breathing, and conserved what little energy I had. And my reward arrived just 10 minutes ago when Loksie's face lit up with pleasure at my wakefulness, as she came to check on me.

Ah, here she returns with some tea, and that grin hasn't moved from her cheery countenance. Must be afternoon, the sun streaming in from the west windows catching her wavy blond hair, as it often did with her father. The smell of fresh flowers, ah yes, there on my dressing table. I wonder who ...

'Mummy, oh Mummy. You've had us so worried.' She puts the tea down, sits on the edge of the bed and places pillows behind my head and shoulders. Then, with utmost care and deliberation she gives me the loveliest, loveliest hug. 'Oh, Mum, I thought I'd lost you. Lost you before ...'

I'm still really not sure if this is <u>before</u> or <u>after</u> ... However, I try my voice. 'I know, I know, Darling.' Somewhat gritty, but it's working at least. She lifts the special plastic beaker, which I've already taken a dislike to, and I suck in the tepid tea, so soothing on the throat.

Hungry, no. More tea, aye. More photographs, as well. We make our plans and after a wash of my drug-swollen body we begin. Well, of course I don't know where best to begin, but it doesn't matter now. I put my hands onto hers and try to squeeze them.

'I've been so lucky, Rhona.' The emotional rush momentarily stops me. 'I ... I am blessed with a wonderful daughter, the product of a most wonderful romance.' I look into the suddenly querying eyes. 'Though ... not really sure I've deserved it all.' My voice is struggling but I must continue.

Her face is a question. 'Take your time, Mum. Here, drink the tea.'

I suck more of the sweet liquid. 'Your father and I were like Romeo and Juliet, you know.'

Her eyes widen. 'Oh? That much in love?'

'Well, yes, Darling. But, more ... more so in the way it all so tragically ended, I'm afraid.'

'Oh, Mum. My father's early death? Having to dredge it all up again?' The eyes drop.

'No, Darling, don't be upset at all. He introduced me to orgasms, he did.' I know I'm only saying this to postpone ...

'Mother!' She glances around as if others are in the room and might hear. 'You mustn't blurt out details like that to your daughter! Bloody hell, you say it like he's introduced you to golf, or fly fishing!' And we both laugh – well, I try to.

She holds up a framed coloured photograph from her bedroom. 'Jacob Swanepoele, my father,' she says with that tone of someone parading a graduation photo. The snap had been taken at an informal party in Jo'burg, and the alleged Jacob Swanepoele has a drinks-fired grin, standing between Vicky and I, and hoping to get lucky. With no idea who he really was, I shake my head at the shame of it.

'My dad's gravestone, Mum.' A loose photo this time, one Vicky had taken in the cemetery in Vereeniging, west of the capital, no doubt relieved to have found that set of convenient dates. 'But,' she continues. 'I've not bothered you for details, for in a sense he was your tragedy. I never actually had him to lose.'

The poor girl, I've filled her with stupid myths. 'Loksie, Darling, that's not—'

But she continues on, producing this time a faded Polaroid snap. 'Here I am with Grandma Swanepoele and her cat. Did she like me?' Another photo-captured lie, but the real subjects, Mrs Duffy and Sergeant Major, do look well, considering their advanced years at the time. Both had loyally waited for us to return from South Africa before passing on, poor souls. 'Mum, I've often wondered why we changed our name from Swanepoele to Fergusson. And if there are other Swanepoeles I may contact in South Africa, um ... Well, later.'

I grasp her hands to stop the talking. Then, it takes a few stops and stutters to get out those few words I've been attempting to articulate since those defining test results, ten-twelve short weeks earlier. 'Jacob ... Swan ... Swanepoele is not ... not your father, Loksie.' Her mouth falls open. 'Only a ... a fic ... fictitious character, deemed necessary at the time. In ...' I have to keep going. 'In ... in a clumsy attempt to provide you with an acceptable background.'

More. 'Your real father was David Lawson, an Australian. But ... but, my ... my darling David, sadly died in 1974, before ... before I could tell him we produced ... shared a ... a healthy, wonderful daughter.' I really want to blub now. 'And ... and before I ... I could apologise for just ... just how badly I had treated him.'

Exhausted, I can only lie there watching Rhona's face jump through a show of intense expressions, as would that clown she had once wanted to be, no doubt struggling to know what to do with this unexpected and overwhelming gobbet of information.

In more normal times, she would be on the phone to me, or arrange a visit or a meeting over coffee somewhere convenient to discuss it ... two tall, sensible women with sensible things to discuss. But here, of course, the poor, poor girl understands she cannot. Now, having done my shamefully delayed duty, my last depressing responsibility, I ... I ...

***

268

The young woman lurched out of the bedroom and flopped down on the top step of the wide staircase. She felt so lied to, so cheated, far too angry to cry. Not only was she to lose her mother, but also it seemed her own history! The stories, the memories that would have consoled her in the coming years were also to be taken. Already taken! She was left with nothing – like Glendaruel's vast central hall below her – empty. Void. The guilt in her mother's normally bright eyes as she also tried to explain why this David Lawson had left so suddenly all those years ago, and why she, Rhona bloody Loksie bloody Fergusson, had been born in South Africa, had left her unconvinced. Why the need for nearly three decades of lies?

At the kitchen table, with an opened bottle of Bordeaux, Rhona continued to rage at herself. How had she swallowed such a pathetic story about her father for all these years? *A lovely South African fellow, Loksie, only married 15 months, so sad he died before you were born.* Bloody hell, it was such a lame tale.

With the second glass came a partial answer – because she had trusted her mother and wanted to believe the story. She was a good mother, thoughtful, flexible, they'd been best friends for years – for ever. Rhona was teary now, and it took more wine to find the phone numbers of Mungo and Cheryl, and of Aunt Victoria in South Africa. She used the phone in the servant hall, questioning, chastising, and pleading with them for nearly two hours. Both her tears and the bottle were well finished when she hung up.

Now further burdened with perturbing information her mother's friends seemed quite comfortable with – how, for example, the relationship had blossomed after Kat had landed this young David feller in intensive care – Rhona really wasn't sure how to react. Equally unsettling were the unfamiliar phrases they easily bandied about, *David and Catherine, wee Davie, the Glendaruel pair, both your parents*; as if discussing another family altogether. It was all so confusing, so disturbing so ... so new. But, bloody hell, 17 years age difference! What on earth had Kat been thinking? *Because he was always there when I needed someone,* had been her only halting explanation.

269

In an attempt to sober up, Rhona washed dishes, stoked the kitchen range, and folded ironing, then went upstairs again to check on her mother. Despite the tight, distended knot in her stomach the young woman was relieved to find Kat now sleeping, her long silver hair like a fine web out across the pillows.

The nurse would return in the morning, and by then her own emotions may have settled. She checked the flow of both intravenous drips as she had been shown, straightened the bedclothes and tidied up. Rhona Fergusson had spent many nights with her mother since the cancer was detected. They could well afford a private nurse to live in, but once the morphine was begun, she became determined to see this out with Kat, sleeping on a fold-up cot near her mother's bed. However, tonight she sat with a woman it seemed she had only ever partly known, and this was as much a curiosity as a shattering disappointment.

***

... must be morning ... house waking ... poor, poor Rhona ...
... nurse's voice somewhere ... she'll know what to do ...
... can leave now to find David ...

***

2nd June

A suitably cool, early summer's day, both the funeral service at the family mausoleum and lunch and drinks in Glendaruel's vast dining room had on the whole gone well. Still angered by her mother's seeming oh-by-the-way admissions, Rhona had retained emotional distance from the formalities as luminaries of the photographic world and even a former MP said agreeable things about Kat, and her *illustrious* career. Indeed, the King's Own Bloody Borderers had allowed themselves to be represented by an octogenarian colonel who somehow made connections of bravery with Singapore and Glendaruel Estate, as if they were both sites of former colonial wars. And, her cousin Brian, a relative stranger, they'd joked, had flown from South Africa to represent Aunt Victoria, devious Vicky, who was too ill to travel.

Of course, on one level Rhona was pleased for the warm words said about her mother, Kat Cale, the nationally famous photographer. However, it was she, the daughter, who was now left to scrape together the pieces of a totally unfamiliar puzzle, to make them fit into something, or someone, she hadn't really known after all.

Attempting to quench her week-long exasperation, Rhona had drunk more than normal. But what was normal anymore? Suddenly, the estate, the will, probate, the Kat Cale Foundation, a just discovered, yet dead father, and of course, the permanent absence of her mother, had all to be absorbed into her usually simple, organised existence. And, now to tackle Cheryl and Mungo before they wore her down with another welter of wonderful words about Kat. She moved out of the dining room as caterers began to clean up, and in the hall found the pair re-entering the front door of the big house.

Cheryl was smiling. 'That's the last of them; your cousin has gone with Chlodagh and Paul to London to catch his plane. Time for a last wee drink together?'

'Right then. In here.' Determined to set the tone, Rhona stomped into the drawing room and sat in her mother's favourite lounge chair.

Her emotions charged, she watched them both. 'Now, a long time ago my famous mother had an affair with a young Aussie kid touring Scotland, 17 years her junior, and she became pregnant. This week you've both told me what a *wonderful* person he was, almost a knight in shining armour, it seems.' Aware of the sarcasm, she was attempting to stir up, draw out, the information she still needed to know.

But how to frame this, so as to ask pertinent questions, so as to make sense? As she, a legal beagle, should. 'It seems all of you contrived to hide from me and ... and the world, the existence of my real father, this David Lawson. But what I must know is *why*. Was it because underneath it all he really was a charming bastard, like one of those handsome colonial bush rangers, and had fled the scene before I was born? Or was it simply to cover up an inconvenient, potentially embarrassing incident in Kat's life, once she'd become famous?'

With a certain pleasure she watched them, sitting apart like unrequired bookends at each end of the long couch, exchange awkward glances.

Finally, Mungo shook his now-balding head. 'To protect you, Loksie. The contrived name-change from MacAdam to Swanepoele to Fergusson, Kat's maiden name, gave you both a back story, as they say, and solid social acceptance that a fatherless *MacAdam* or *Lawson brat* would never have had. And aye, your aunt Vicky did supply the necessary photographs.' Bloody hell, imagine if she'd become known locally as the *MacAdam bastard!*

Mungo raised his arms, as if in surrender. He wasn't well, Rhona knew. So unlike him to decline the opportunity today to make a speech. She rewarded his effort with a small smile.

'Rhona, there are things you must understand, and be willing to accept. Everything your mother did was for you, directly or indirectly – remember that. That's why you are the interesting, professional, yet well-rounded person, you've grown into. In a sense, Kat's accumulated fame was incidental – behind it was the necessity to provide for you. And to prove herself to you.

'Now second. Your parents, despite the age difference, were a happy, loving couple. And looking back, I'm sure it was the murder attempt that threw their relationship off kilter. They didn't cope well with it – didn't know how to.' He hesitated, his eyes asking the question. 'Well, who would?'

What? Murder attempt? Rhona suddenly had a million more questions to ask, but Mungo had begun again. 'Aye, your father, David, did leave Catherine after discovering she'd deliberately fallen pregnant. She'd handled it all rather poorly, a *fete accompli* no less, but he did return here to Glendaruel later to find her. And indirectly, you too, Lass. Sadly, this was only a week or two after I had whisked Catherine off to her sister in South Africa. Think of it; he'd missed her, or we missed him by only 10 or 12 days. So, Romeo and Juliet.'

God, Mummy's words, too.

The big man got up and went over to the sideboard. 'Despite what my doctor has strongly advised, I think I will have a wee nip of old smoothie.' He looked back. 'Anyone else?' Rhona found herself joining Cheryl for another large sherry.

With her glass recharged, Cheryl explained the evidence of David's return; Mrs Duffy's sighting of him, and an eerie incident where the hifi record player had suddenly begun playing *After Midnight*, to which she, a very young Rhona, had danced. 'Do you remember it, Lass?'

No, she couldn't remember the occasion, as much as she now really wanted to. But she did remember the old hifi set in the room here with lots of 60-70s vinyl LPs, and in her head, she could picture herself dancing and swirling. And she certainly remembered J.J. Cale's *After Midnight* because Kat had often played it. Hey, was that the connection: J.J. Cale and Cath, or Kat Cale?

Mungo began again. 'Suddenly, there were many reasons to try to contact David. Directory assistance provided his home number in Australia, and your mother and I used the phone out in the hall there.' He indicated with a hand. 'We'd even organised wee Davie's airfare to return to Scotland.'

'And?' Rhona couldn't help herself.

'His grandfather answered. Very distressed, he informed me your father had died in a cyclone in northern Australia, only three months earlier. Christmas Eve, if I remember correctly, 1974. The old man told me not to ring again.' Mungo finished; his head lowered.

'Bollocks! You've got to be joking!' Rhona was almost shouting. 'What ...?' She petered out, tears welling.

Cheryl moved behind Rhona's lounge chair and wrapped her in sympathetic arms. 'Of course, that news more than doubled poor Kat's burden of guilt about how she had treated young David. Occasionally, she would mention it to one of us, but made sure it never influenced you, or your upbringing.' Cheryl glanced over to Mungo. 'We, Chlodagh, Paul, the others, were all sworn into silence about your real father – Kat promised she'd tell you at the right time. Perhaps she shouldn't have left it to the very end.'

The older woman stopped, as if reluctant to continue. 'Loksie, Darling, the real tragedy is that your father no doubt died completely unaware of your existence.' She cleared her throat. 'Now, would he have been a good father? That we'll never know.'

Rhona wasn't sure how much later she heard the vehicle arrive. Still sitting in her mother's favourite chair, still struggling to absorb all that Mungo and Cheryl had said before they left – more detail of the attempt on her parents' lives, its ultimately fatal effect on their relationship. She took a few moments to empty her head of it all and compose herself. 'I'll get it,' she eventually told the empty, silent house, as she stood up.

At the door was a shortish, older man wearing a jacket and tie with obvious discomfort, and work trousers. 'Afternoon, Miss Rhona.'

Then, she remembered him. 'Ah, Mr King. What a pleasant surprise.' She recalled Tom King was a stonemason, a closed, yet kindly man who'd done work on the estate over the years, but she hadn't seen him for some time. Retired?

He smiled apologetically and looked about, as if having realised he was at the wrong house. 'Seems I've missed the fun, don't it?' He turned and nodded towards the faded-white trade van behind him. 'Thought to do a wee job for a pal down at Kirkbean this morning before the funeral. But broke down, it did, and I couldn't get a tow till afternoon.'

'Oh, I am sorry, Mr King. Hope it wasn't expensive. Um ...' Come on Rhona, you're in charge now. 'But ... but you're not too late to celebrate my mother's passing.' She smiled. 'And I'll tell you how it all went.'

'Well, after the shite day I've had, a wee something would be most welcome. And to salute Mrs Catherine.'

She led him in through the front door. 'Now, with one condition, Mr King. You must drop the *Miss* from Rhona, and the *Mrs* from Catherine!' She wanted to be welcoming, be on equal terms, to begin anew. 'After all, I have known you for quite a while.'

'Aye, all your life. Right then ... Rhona. And I'm Tom.'

Soon, they were in the drawing room, she with a glass of Bordeaux, and Tom with a bottle of Wee Heavy. She described the morning's ceremony, people attending, things said. 'I've also had an

274

education in family history today, Tom, especially about my parents, Catherine and David.' She said it openly to see his reaction.

The old man didn't hesitate. 'Och, knew them both well. Catherine, of course, more than 30 years, and Davie, well, when he was here. A grand young man, indeed. Got my second lad, Fraser, interested in the landscaping, he did. Gonna use that new internet to advertise his business, Fraser is. And your father and I worked on the cottages and that unfinished summerhouse together.'

Rhona stared at him. 'Did you? Err … did he?'

'Aye!' Tom chuckled to himself. 'He tamed her. Tamed Catherine MacAdam, he did.' Again surprised, Rhona watched him drink his beer as if aware he now had her interest. 'Before young Davie arrived, your mother was as remote and as hard as those front steps out there.' He indicated the front door. 'I should know, as I repaired 'em once or twice. But somehow your father softened that hardness, made her into a complete, bonny person, herself. Like you, aye. And even when she became famous with those photographs, I'd get a ring. *Mr King, I have a wee job for you*, and when I'd come, often she'd only want to talk.'

'Talk? About …?'

'Him, your father, mostly, um … Rhona.' He hesitated, studying her. 'Like him you are. Height, hair, eyes, and that relaxed Antipodean lope. Then, your mother'd make me write out a bill for my time.'

'What … what bloody Antipodean lope?' Yet, behind the initial indignation, she experienced a tingle, an unexpected, unfamiliar small thrill.

'Hmm, nice drop of ale, this.' Tom had suddenly taken interest in the label on his beer bottle.

In the sun garden near the old, weathered table, Tom bent down, and with some effort pushed two large geranium pots from a rough-shaped concrete pad. 'Aye, still here, it is.' He then squatted further, wiping dirt from the pad with a large handkerchief. 'This is why I had to come today, Lass. Here, take a look closer.'

Intrigued, Rhona squatted beside him. Initially, like a long-disappointed gold prospector spotting that first glitter, she was caught between disbelief and pleasure as her treasure became clear. It was a crude message from the past; two sets of irregular initials around a heart shape – *DL loves CM, CM loves DL*, no doubt scratched into the concrete as it had dried. Bloody hell, the last thing she'd expected to be shown! Yet, something she might have done herself, if she'd found a local lad interesting, or interested enough. She ran her fingers around the shapes of the rough lettering, around the heart, and over the letters again. Touching the past, touching her parents together, as daughters normally are able to do.

Standing up, Rhona groped for the table for support. She was crying before she realised it, a low steady weeping, she was now unable to stop. And then she was in old Tom's arms, a calloused hand patting her back. She continued to cry; yet came to understand this was not because of her mother's death just days earlier, nor for the tragic story of her father's short life, but because for the first time, yes, the first time, she felt the sensation of having real parents, and the solid proof they had dearly loved each other.

Yeppoon, Queensland, 31st December

International couriered mail, phone calls and now a Scottish lawyer sitting in front of him to probe his past. It was all so bloody sudden, so bloody hard to absorb. But the big question remained – *why?* Why was he, Dave Lawson, after that unsavoury, unfathomable, and yet unexplained episode of his life, a beneficiary of Kat Cale's will?

Well, of course he didn't know, couldn't even begin to think about why. And Terrible Terri nosing about didn't help. On one hand, Dave did want to hug young Ms Fergusson, for she'd unwittingly cleared him of any responsibility of a long-ago death. All of which, it now seemed, like the worst of dreams, had only really happened in his head. She'd got him off the hook, so to speak, as a good lawyer should. Yippee!

Yet, a thick overlay of shame and guilt smothered any real sense of relief. Just couldn't shake it off. His desertion of Kat, as Catherine, all those years ago must have caused her indescribable distress. And now somehow, he was to be rewarded for it? Ultimately, simple curiosity encouraged Dave to accept the lawyer's envelope.

Inside he found a faded black and white, creased photograph. Intrigued, he took in its scratched surface and the brown stain on one edge. Blood? More on the back. Then, as if waking from long hibernation, which in a sense he was, came slow recognition of its content. First, the Glendaruel drawing room, their favourite room – *I'll stoke the fire, Kat.* Next, the setting, testing her new tripod – *Oh, no, Darling, you've moved!* Then finally, the occasion – *Happy, happy Hogmanay!* He sat transfixed as it all flooded back, his emotions struggling to absorb the picture of he and Cathy letting it all hang out at New Year 1972. Twenty-eight years ago, to the day, he realised – a dreadful coincidence.

'Mr Lawson.' The lawyer again. 'There is something else.' She again reached across to him, this time with a small, greyish jewellery bag, similar to those Maggie had. Out of which fell into his hand, to

277

his complete surprise and absolute joy, a set of Guilamine beads – *his* beloved beads! When … where did he last …? No matter, it was them, all right. The same chip in that second bead. Or second last one. And as he hesitantly handled them for the first time in ever so long, the colourful mosaic pieces on their rough leather cord gave a quiet, yet familiar dinging together, as if to say; *Jesus, Dave, where've you been for so bloody long?*

He stared again at the photograph, then back at the beads. He now remembered he'd seen the photo before. Upstairs in … in their desolated bedroom that other Glendaruel night, that awful, awful night, four, five months after it was taken. In her favourite handbag, with those sleeping tablets, which had made him conclude while shit-faced, she'd killed herself.

Both the photo and beads slipped from his grasp onto the floor.

***

Maggie gave her husband a reproachful look. Then, understanding he really *was* distressed, she rose and left the room, returning quickly with a bottle of Chivas Regal. 'Ms Fergusson?' she asked, offering their guest a filled tumbler.

The young lawyer initially hesitated, then smiled, accepting the drink. 'Well, we're in this together.'

Maggie pushed a tumbler of whisky into Dave's hand and suggested he try to drink it.

She then put on her glasses and picked up the faded photo. Along the top was written in blue pen *After Midnight*. Along the bottom was scrawled *Kat Cale and J.J. Stevens – letting it all hang out*. She took in the couple and their formal clothing. Faces alive, champagne flutes and a magnum on the marble mantelpiece behind them. The man was undoubtedly Dave – a young, life-filled Dave. Hey, hang on … he has no scar!

She looked up at her husband, then back at the photo. The woman was tall – lucky woman! – and although older than Dave, was certainly attractive. They looked happy together. So, this was the mysterious Kat Cale?

'Oh.' Unsure how to handle this sudden evidence of another woman with her husband, Maggie offered the photo to the lawyer, who was wiping her eyes. Had she been crying?

Maggie encouraged Dave to finish the whisky, and soon, he lifted his head, searching about as if awakening from a wild dream. Perhaps he was, she pondered.

'I'm sorry,' he said. 'That … the photo … these beads, have really thrown me. So … so many years ago. The last things I expected.'

'Sweetheart.' Maggie put her hand back on his shoulder. 'I think a break is in order. Why don't you pop outside and get some of that sea breeze?' She looked across at the younger woman. 'Ms Fergusson, come and I'll show you the house garden – Dave's pride and joy.' She glanced at her watch. 'We'll just have time. Now, isn't there something less formal I can call you? I'm afraid we Australians are not good at standing on ceremony.'

'Och, yes, I *am* sorry. Please call me Rhona. Or Loksie. And I promise to call you both Maggie and David.' *Dearvid.*

***

Dave gazed out to sea, little Mac up on the patio-table bench beside him. What was it about the ocean that was so energising, yet so soothing – the expanse, the stillness, the emptiness? Today, he needed plenty of soothing. For one, he'd just made a right dill of himself in front of a stranger, a lawyer who'd travelled half the world to find him.

Christ, that photo, and the raw memories of another New Year's Eve captured within it. What about the others Cathy had taken that night? He'd bought her the tripod for Christmas, and it was the first time they'd used it. And he remembered more: another cold Scottish day, and he'd lit the fire early. Cheryl and that military wanker had come for Hogmanay, and despite cooking and preparing all afternoon, Cathy looked stately in those dress-up clothes … *Do me up please, Darling.* He could see her … somewhat pensive, loose strands of auburn hair across her face – those hazel eyes.

Other memories flooded back – the mysterious big house, the panther, the Morris, the colonels and, of course, his old chum Sergeant Major. That cool cat, spelt with a *C*. Could he begin to talk about it all now, about those times? For, despite the long painful period in between – that yawning canyon of sadness and shame – he now allowed himself to admit those few short years at Glendaruel had been great. No, wonderful.

He had learnt so much – about women, love, life itself! He remembered how, initially, he couldn't get enough of Catherine dressing and undressing. *David, you are looking again*, she'd joke. He hadn't been a pervo, a voyeur – well no more than any other unworldly kid – but it had all been new and sudden for him, and she'd offered a period of pleasurable adjustment.

So, if she hadn't died in 1972, had they been living parallel lives for 27 years, assuming the other was dead? Hang on, hang on! Years earlier, out here on the patio, Ric had mentioned a phone call he'd got at Seaford, the year after the cyclone. *From Scotland, a bloke named Mungo. Told him you'd died in that cyclone, Dave – to protect you.* But also, Ric admitted, to appease his own guilt for having sent his grandson off overseas, only to see him return later even more damaged than before. At the time, Dave hadn't really wanted to understand the significance of the phone call, or of Ric's lie, but now …!

So many questions, *what if* questions. Maybe best left unasked. But perhaps Miss Fergusson … Rhona …

He didn't dare hope Kat had forgiven him. However, that she, or someone else, had organised the photo and beads to be in the will did suggest this. Just the thought of it, of absolution, felt so freeing. So bloody liberating! Now, it wasn't going to be easy to explain everything, especially with friends and family arriving any minute. Would Maggie understand? Would she want to? Well, it had happened in a different time, a different place, to a different Dave.

He'd been *Dearvid* then, as … as Rhona had just reminded him. Didn't someone say the past was a foreign country where things were different? Well, like it or not, it was somewhere he now had to revisit, and explain and absorb. Wasn't Cathy, as Kat, effectively giving him permission, encouragement?

Awkward questions, he knew, but in facing them Dave could feel the shame, the old encapsulating layer of shame loosening, clearing, sliding away, like the natural process of thawing once spring weather begins. He no longer needed to hide in the winter of the past. *Remember Dave, you're not a drongo.*

He sat for some moments stroking the dog – it could have been Sergeant Major – reflecting, remembering. Black cockatoos were screeching somewhere up behind the house. Many years ago, Cathy had offered a wonderful alternative to his young, guilt-filled life. After Darwin, Maggie had done it again. He smiled – perhaps an even better life! And she'd dissolved that decades-long dilemma with his mother with one crisp sentence: *Mrs Lawson, if you can't see the goodness in your son, it's because you don't want to – get over it!* Christ, who gets two chances?

Sucking in gratitude, Dave stood up and pulled on the Guilamine beads. With a mixture of hope and happiness, he walked back into the house to reclaim his past. In the kitchen, he found Maggie and Cathy – no, Maggie and Rhona – hugging, crying.

Easy mistake to make, *Dearvid*, once you'd seen that old photo.